ABOUT THE AUTHOR

David Munday was born in Chippenham in 1992, spent most of his life growing up in Reading and now lives in Devon. After time as a freelance reporter, he has worked for the Plymouth Herald as a journalist and as the editor of the world's number one Fantasy Football website Fantasy Football Scout. He also makes regular appearances on Premier League television and YouTube programmes as a pundit.

Follow David on Twitter: @DavidMunday815

SIGN UP FOR THE NEWSLETTER

Receive special offers, giveaways, bonus content, updates from the author and be the first to hear about new releases.

SIGN UP HERE: www.david.munday.uk

ISBN-13: 9798637094721
Imprint: Independently published

Cover design by: Emily Munday
Printed by Amazon

WRITING IN THE SAND

Book One in the Atlas Nations series

DAVID MUNDAY

To Emily, for keeping me motivated

1

"I can't do this," said Harper.

Bile crept up her throat. She swallowed sharply. The acrid stench of burning fuel and charred flesh did not mix well with the salty sea air. Smoke crept behind her eyeballs, squeezing out tears. Harper covered her face to defend the pervasive sensory attack.

Shards of glass pricked at her palms and forearms. Wincing, Harper prised some from the skin and cast them aside, leaving behind scarlet blobs. Each fragment bounced with a clink off the rock's edge, down to the beach.

In just a few minutes, the flames already towered above the shoreline's remaining trees. Beyond the pillars of fire, all Harper could see was water. This once beautiful island had become an unholy sore shrouded in thick, black smoke.

Had all gone according to plan, the crew and passengers would have been basking in the glory of their new colonial home by now. Instead, it looked as if their first day on this planet could well be their last.

Survival was not something Harper Mulgrew had been trained for.

Watching an alien sun begin its descent into the depths of an extra-terrestrial sea for the first time in her life, she ignored bruised muscles and battered bones to focus on her rage.

"I'm not even supposed to *be* here," Harper whispered through gritted teeth and a crisp Scottish accent. Her blood boiled as she considered those who had banished her from Earth. Blonde hairs that had escaped the head-band blew into her face. She swatted them aside.

A voice came from behind, laced with pain.

"What happened?" it asked.

A slender man, a similar age to Harper, had stumbled from the foliage, shaking. The mauve of his overalls indicated a civilian ticket. A name label on the chest read 'J. Brooks'. He was a man with the scrawny build of someone who had been sent on this trip for brains rather than brawn. His pea-like head was adorned with compact brown curls, littered with sand, foliage and grit. The baby-face was a patchwork quilt of bruises and cuts, the worst of which ran across a round nose. His cheeks were illuminated by the inferno, eyes possessed by the depths of Hell.

Paralyzed by fear and anger, Harper realised she did not have an answer for Brooks' question. Floundering for something reassuring, she managed nothing more than a hesitant half-mumble.

A chilling shriek made Harper jump.

She looked down and spotted a teenage girl crouching over an unconscious woman in the sand. All around them, survivors were wandering about in a stupor. They were dangerously close to the fuselage. It was surrounded by blackened corpses. Emblazoned on the hull, the word 'Concord' was melting away.

The scene hit Harper like a bullet in the guts, shaking her body free from the shackles of shock.

"Let's go." Harper shouted over the roar of flames and started moving. "Focus on getting people clear and see what resources you can salvage. I'll get down to what's left of the ship and try to send a distress signal."

The nervous man nodded slightly and followed her down the small sandbank, carefully edging closer to wreckage. Each step increased the sting of heat on their cheeks.

As she approached the girl, Harper directed Brooks over to a short woman, spluttering as she tried to drag a heavy crate through the sand.

"What's your name?" Harper asked the teenager, crouching and placing a hand on her shoulder.

"Shermeen," the girl garbled, brown hair flailing as she took in the surroundings like a rabbit in headlights. "My mum," she cried.

"Everything's going to be okay," Harper shouted, not believing herself. "We need to get your mother away from the wreckage." She put her arms underneath the woman's shoulders, starting to lift.

"What if she's hurt?"

"That won't matter if the ship blows up," Harper retorted. The girl did not respond. "Come on, grab her legs." The two of them carried the woman towards the tree-line. Harper put her in the recovery position. "I've got to go now."

Harper made a beeline for the Concord, or what was left of it. She noticed a large dark-skinned man standing close to a blazing hunk of metal. He was vainly attempting to douse it with a hand-held extinguisher.

"What are you doing?"

He stopped, somewhat confused at first. Noticing the insignia on Harper's chest, he understood.

"The ship is gone. Just grab what supplies you can and get as far away as possible!"

Harper picked up a small bundle of nutrition crates, stifling a yelp as they disturbed her glass-inflicted wounds. She thrust them into the large man's hands and called over two more individuals nearby.

"Start a collection point up there!" Harper pointed at the rock where she had woken up.

"You heard her, let's get started," said the taller man, gesturing to the shorter individual.

"Thanks. If you can get these people away from burning wreckage too then I can worry about what we need from the cockpit."

Harper could see the pilots' section of the ship had broken away from the main fuselage now, smoke billowing through the cracks. She had to find Captain Case, work out why they had crashed and identify where on Proxima B they had crashed. Only portions of the planet had been scouted by satellite, so ending up in the wrong place didn't bear thinking about. Being able to send a distress signal would be a nice bonus.

Contact with rocks had carved a human-sized hole in the side of the cockpit. Harper stared deep into the smoke, knowing that the searing heat was about to get worse. Looking back at the handful of colonists piling up supplies, she made her peace. If she were to perish today there was comfort in not having to face an uncertain future on an uninhabited alien world billions of miles from home. At least it would be over.

Pulling the hood back over her head and holding up a sleeve to her mouth, Harper took a deep breath and dived through the opening.

There was a hot flash.

Tongues of fire.

She was in.

Harper swore as she discovered the captain's fate.

His lifeless body was still strapped to his pilot's chair. The shoulders were drenched in thick red fluid oozing from a fatal wound on the back of the head. An elongated section of the overhead panel had snapped free and was lanced through the captain's skull, the tip visible through his blood-soaked hair.

A communication panel roared into flames. It triggered another. And another. Fire leapt towards Harper from panel to panel, like a glowing serpent riding the waves.

There was no time for a distress call. Firing the beacon would have to do. Harper lifted the plastic casing around a control switch and slammed her fist down on the button. Above the ceiling, she heard the vibration of a small metal container leaving its housing at high velocity.

Harper clambered over hunks of rubble, looking for the navigation terminal.

A jolt of pain scolded her thigh.

She cursed, batting the metal panel away.

Harper pressed on ungracefully, slipping as she arrived at the appropriate station. The screen displayed a map of the local area. It was exactly what she needed. Scrolling through the options, she selected 'EXPORT TO EXTERNAL DEVICE'. That way, she could access this information without the ship. Battery power would probably only last a few days but it would be long enough for her and the survivors to work out a plan of action. It took some encouragement but Harper eventually convinced the power switch into the 'On' position and the portable machine's screen lit up.

She prayed its motherboard wasn't already fried.

"Yes," Harper said fiercely, beads of sweat flying off her forehead. Extracting the back-up server was still a viable option. The terminal's keyboard was missing a few keys but none of them were needed for this command. Steeling herself against the heat once more, Harper bashed through the various stages of the process.

The ship threw her to the floor.

Harper landed with a powerful stomach-lurching thud. The whole world rotated around her. A thunderous roar clawed at her ears. The captain's body was hurled in Harper's direction, spear protruding. She ducked to the left. The corpse hit the surface with a chilling clang. It was inches from her face. Chaotic yet lifeless eyes stared at Harper, bestowing the leader's mantle upon her. She leapt up and stumbled away from Case's body and peered through a hole in the hull. The main bulk of the ship had exploded. In the distance, fragments crashed into the sea like giant hailstones.

Harper was lucky to be alive. Still.

The device. Where had it gone?

She scanned the cockpit, trying to find it.

"Damn!"

The computer station was no longer in front of her. After the explosion, the roll of the ship had swung it several feet above, now acting as the ceiling.

Grabbing a hanging strap, Harper leapt up to what was left of a seating column and hauled herself closer to the prize. Edging over to the operating panel again, she confirmed that the terminal had not only survived but that the exporting had completed. All she had to do was physically remove the device from its slot.

Swinging closer, she detached the first hook. The second was still out of reach. It took another careful dangle on the strap and Harper had her fingers on it. But not enough to break it free.

One... more...

This time, she hung in front of the switch long enough to flick it. The handheld device slipped out of its holding.

It fell.

Harper's heart skipped a beat. *If that smashes, we'll be building this colony blind*, she thought to herself.

She leapt against the momentum of the strap. It landed in her hands.

The steel hull welcomed Harper's body with an offensive jerk. The breath was sucked from her body. She fought against an abdomen of lead to get off the scolding metal beneath her.

Another explosion rocked the cockpit. Sparks flew once more, like rain in a hurricane.

Harper quickly rolled over, using elbows to get into a crouched position. Powerful legs pushed her forwards, slightly off-balance, but it was enough. She wrapped up the portable machine in her overalls and ran at one of the fresh openings.

Harper closed her eyes.

An intense burning sensation roasted her arms

and legs.

Suddenly there was a saline taste in the mouth and a rough scratch on her cheek. She'd landed face first in the waves. She was safe, for now.

Wading back to the beach, Harper kept an eye over her shoulder as the cockpit washed further out to sea.

Arriving on the sand, she knelt. Looking up at the wooded and mountainous island on which they had landed, Harper could not bring herself to move. After a few moments to get some breath back, she turned to the device. Time to find out just how far away the planned landing site was. She didn't need to log-in. The captain's details had already been accepted and the device's small screen showed that it was 'RESUMING SESSION'.

"That can't be right," Harper muttered under the staccato rhythm of her breathing.

'DISTANCE TO LANDING ZONE: 2,479 miles' read the caption on the on-screen map. Below it was the flight-path the ship had followed during entry into Proxima B's orbit and atmosphere. It had been manually laid into the system.

Captain Case had crashed the ship on purpose.

2

Every night it stopped him from sleeping. He remembered the trigger squeezing past the point of no return. Feet were nailed to the ground. He tried to sound a warning but his tongue refused to move. Bones snapped and ligaments stretched to the point of tearing. His wife's breathing proved a gentle tonic to the agitated state.

He felt the elbow in his ribs and was instantly alert.

"Answer your phone, Donald," complained Sally.

He noticed the unpleasant whine coming from his bed-side table, accompanied by the garish flashing red of the handset.

Groaning, Donald Stafford apologised for the disturbance at such an ungodly hour, pressed the transfer button on his phone and heaved himself out of bed. Not before kissing his wife tenderly on the cheek.

He felt his way to the door, wincing quietly at the stiffness in his right leg. It always protested against bearing weight in the small hours. Don waited until he had closed the door to the master bedroom before turning on the landing lights. His eyes hated him for that. He wished Proxima A's time zones corresponded better with Earth's. He'd already regretted staying up late to watch the so-called lunch-time game.

Once in the study, he triggered the handset's transfer button on the corner of the imposing mahogany desk.

"This better be good," Don snapped in his drawn-out southern accent. The permanent secretary to the department of defence had moved to the city of New Boston specifically to avoid this sort of thing. All that dramatic middle-of-the-night emergency stuff was for those who lived near the Arkan/Choctaw Border. Don had come to his senses years ago, or rather, his wife made sure he did when the Choctaw war had been in the history books long enough. Hopefully this was just another simple clash between overly patriotic citizens and separatist sympathisers. As long as it wasn't anything to do with that damned Teslanium Agreement he'd be happy. Relatively speaking.

On the other end of the line, Anderson, his deputy, sounded uncertain how to answer.

"Err... we've had an incident up at Satellite Three," came the nervous response.

"What's happened?"

"It's gone." Despite having lived his whole life in the Proxima system, Anderson bore the strong New York accent of his parents.

"What do you mean, it's gone?"

There was a moment's pause.

"It's been completely destroyed."

"I'll be right there."

★

"You better have a damn good explanation ready for me Anderson. You know I'm never in the best mood when Carolina quarterbacks throw fourth quarter interceptions," Don cracked as he burst into the office, doing his best to hide the limp. Clearly the staff had not expected him so soon. Almost everyone of them flinch upon his arrival.

This particular night, there was a palpable sense of unease mixing with the smell of warm plastic and dusty servers in the air. Given the current situation, that was not surprising. Normally the night shift consisted of relentless rounds of office golf, excessive coffee consumption, frequent toilet trips and a steady stream of hard rock classics to keep the staff awake.

Right now, the room was silent, save for the whirring of computer fans. The golf clubs and balls had been tossed to one side and every technician was either checking print-outs or staring into their screens.

The dark haired Anderson looked up from the map.

"We picked up a signal from an unidentified object approaching our sector of orbit roughly thirty minutes ago at *this* position," he said, presenting the print-out. "It took us a few minutes to plot its course but by the time we had a fix it was too late."

"So... what happened?" Don asked gruffly.

"Well, it was on a collision course with Satellite Three." Anderson pointed to the line he had drawn on the chart in pencil. "There were no survivors on our side." He struggled to get that last line out without a slight quiver of the lips. "It continued on its course."

11

Don pounded the nearest work station with his fist, frightening the living daylights out of the young man working there. Running a hand through greying hair, he stared at the wall bleakly.

"Years without incident here while everyone back on Earth kills each other... and now this," he muttered, half to himself.

He was not looking forward to breaking the news to the families. Forced into those conversations on a regular basis was another reason why Don had come closer to the capital.

"So what the hell was it?" he demanded, already feeling a temper threatening to escape his control. He looked around the room waiting for one of his staff to tell him. To conjure the answer out of nowhere, almost.

"We don't know." Anderson sounded ashamed to admit.

"You don't know?" Don immediately regretted his accusatory tone. His staff had only been dealing with long-range space traffic again for roughly six months now. An eleven year travel ban to and from Earth meant no tracking approaching ships for the same length of time. It had left skills in that department a little rusty.

"There was no transponder information and the pictures from Satellite One don't offer much in the way of identification." Anderson fiddled with a few switches and pulled up the footage on the big screen.

All Don could make out was a shadow. It appeared cylindrical, although at this distance it was hard to tell for sure. Shown in stop motion, the shape rolled towards the vulnerable two-man listening station moments before the images burst with a menacing white flash.

"I see what you mean."

The uncomfortable silence was broken by one of the fresh-faced juniors timidly offering an explanation.

"Do you think it could be one of those British colonial ships? Their government has been talking about coming out here for some time."

Annoyed by the suggestion, Don challenged the young man.

"What's your name, son?"

"Chad, sir."

"Well, Chad, do you think you might reconsider what you just said?"

"I... don't underst--"

"Because if that was a British ship that just smashed this planet's first line of defence out of the sky, do you have any idea what sort of mess we'd be in?"

"That doesn't mean it couldn't be true, sir," said Anderson.

"Don't you think I know that, Bob? I just want these night-shift guys of yours to understand the significance of a suggestion like that. Can you imagine what Alida Harmon or, heaven forbid, Lothar Stangl would do if they heard such a claim? Just be careful what you say without evidence, kid. You know what they're like."

Looking to Anderson for reassurance, Chad had a stab at explaining himself.

"Well, judging by the speed at which it was travelling it had to have been a ship, not a missile," he said.

"Why's that?" Don asked.

"Well, it arrived on our scanners travelling at such

high velocity that it could only have done so after a slingshot manoeuvre around the sun. Admittedly, the speed could indicate a fired weapon of some kind, but the fact that it survived the impact with Satellite Three suggests it was more likely another craft."

Don and Anderson slowly raised their eyebrows at each other. Chad continued, buoyed by their reaction.

"So, to me, the incident looks to have been an accident, a collision between two manned ships. The strange thing is, if it was anything sent by the Atlas Nations, from the US, the Europeans or the Australians to any of their colonial cities, it would have been on the flight register. And there would have been transponder information too."

Chad was right about that. Since the end of the war on Earth and the lifting of the travel ban, everything that arrived in New Boston airspace did so under scrupulous security procedures. If the rules were respected.

"The only other viable faction is the British," Chad concluded. "They're not exactly trying to do colonisation by the book right now and it's all their government has spoken about over the last few years."

"How can an economy as busted as theirs can afford colonisation?" Don asked Anderson. "Everybody knows Whitehall's been talking out its ass for years."

"Well, they *claim* to have made significant cuts in other areas recently," Chad added. "Maybe they were just hiding more than we thought."

This kid's been reading too many left-wing conspiracy theorists, Don suspected. Typical of someone his age.

"You like your British politics."

The underling blushed, nodding in the affirmative.

"I studied British history at university, sir."

"I see... But if this British space ship of yours had a pilot and a cargo of budding colonists, why didn't he change his course? Are they declaring war on us?"

"I guess... I don't know... Unless of course he couldn't change course. If he was incapacitated in some way?"

"Either that, or it was a deliberate act," Anderson suggested. "A direct assault."

Don sighed.

"That's what I'm worried about," he said. "Where this thing is now? We need to know if it's going to hit another Satellite or attempt to land here."

"We're not sure, but we do have a fix on its last known trajectory," Anderson offered. "According to our long range scanners it left on heading 971.345."

"You've got to be kidding me," Don mumbled, placing his forehead between his thumb and forefinger.

"I'm afraid we double checked an--"

"Did you *triple* check?" Don chirped as he massaged his temples.

"Yes, we triple checked too."

"So it's heading for Proxima B, then," Don announced quietly. The room hit a complete stand-still.

"It looks that way, sir," Anderson replied nervously.

"We haven't heard anything from that planet in five years. Not since those failed colonial missions... Just what in the hell is going on here?"

"Should we try to follow the object?" asked Chad, innocently.

"I don't think so," scoffed Anderson. "Proxima B is the last place we want to go right now."

"No, maybe Chad's right," Don interjected. "We need to find out where this thing is."

Anderson froze, jaw practically on the floor.

"Let's not think about an expedition yet," Don reassured. "I can't imagine Stangl would allow us to use up that much Teslanium at a time like this. For now, let's rig-up alternative surveillance and consolidate our borders. You leave the origin of that ship to me. I think I know someone who can help."

Buoyed by a sense of direction, everybody returned to work.

"And Anderson," added Don. "Get everyone out of bed. The whole department. Let's start drawing up a reconnaissance mission to Proxima B. Just in case."

"Yes, sir," his deputy replied, slowly turning pale.

3

James Brooks watched the survivors fighting on the beach, their stand-off set against the backdrop of an obliterated island vista. Tempers ran high and he didn't have the confidence to break up the heated exchange. A handful was all that remained of Britain's first ever colonial expedition and they quarrelled on the large rock overhanging the beach. Beaten, dejected and scared, they stood amid a collection of bashed-up crates.

James scratched the cut across his nose and winced. He had no clue what any of the nearby equipment was supposed to be. The rare bundle that had escaped heavy damage from the crash appeared as alien to him as this planet itself.

He looked out towards the sea. That blonde woman would have taken charge of this by now. She would have known what to do. But she must be gone. Either burned to a cinder in the Concord's carcass or swept out to sea in what was left of it.

There was nothing James could do about the position they were in. He'd joined this expedition to provide administrative support and economic structure. He laughed in his head at that statement and nervously ran a bruised hand through the mess of curly hair. Flecks of grit fell to the ground. Watching the survivors bicker about whose fault the crash was and what to do next, he wondered how any of his skills could ever be relevant in the wild. Knowledge of fiscal management would almost certainly be obsolete now.

"We wait until we can speak to someone from the crew!" That was the voice of Ben, the tall blonde man who had offered to organise the collection of supplies. He'd briefly introduced himself to James when handing him a crate of vitamins earlier. Ben's optimism was admirable but the other man was making a valid point.

"They're all dead, you fool," he said through his mangy beard. "We might as well just take what we can before we all die." Ben looked around at the others for reassurance. Nobody could bring themselves to disagree with the statement.

James looked over at the brown-haired teenage girl who had been helping her mother on the beach, worried at what she was witnessing. Lingering on her innocent eyes, he noticed that each was a different colour. One brown and the other green. Her mother, conscious but dazed from a nasty head wound under dark tangled hair, held her close.

"That's a ridiculous assumption," Ben replied in his well-spoken voice. "We've been here less than an hour and haven't even worked out what supplies we have," he added, gesturing to the boxes around him.

"We're on an uncharted planet, billions of miles from help and you think we stand a chance after what just happened?" There was anger and despair in equal measure in the bearded man's voice. "Most of the people who were supposed to be building this colony are dead anyway. You really think we can *continue the human race* with what we have left? Just let me have some water."

Moving to block access, Ben grabbed him by the sleeve.

"Get *off* me," the man said as he wrestled free. A small tear appeared on the overall and, pulling himself back, a large portion of his sleeve ripped off.

A collective in-take of breath sliced through the air.

Revealed was an arm covered with tattoos. Just below the shoulder, the largest tattoo showed a lion with a Union Jack flag in its mouth.

Now we've got problems, thought James. This was exactly the type of person he had been hoping to leave behind on Earth.

"Oh great. So you're a racist as well as a selfish bastard," said Ben.

"Don't worry Amos," the teenage girl said to the dark-skinned man beside her, placing a hand on his shoulder. "The rest of us aren't like him."

"Thanks Shermeen," replied Amos quietly.

Staring everyone down, the now-outed member of the Crusaders retorted: "And proud of it! You think I give a damn what you think of me?" There was another uncomfortable pause. "So, are you going to let me have some water or not?" This time there was a dare in his eyes, baiting Ben to physical action. The two squared up to each other.

"Stop!" Came the shrill cry from the edge of the rock.

Everybody turned to look.

It was the crew woman. She was alive.

★

Harper could not believe it. The damned idiots. They were the ones that actually want to be on this godforsaken planet and here they were fighting with each other.

The bearded man rounded on her.

"Where the hell have you been?" he asked.

"Trying to save our lives, thank you very much," she snapped in reply, eyebrows curled in angry confusion.

"Are you the one who went back into the ship looking for survivors, then?" he continued.

"Yes," Harper shot back, gulping in anger. As the group's eyes bored into her, she felt like an insect under a microscope.

"Did you find what you were looking for?" asked Brooks, the cut on his nose still bleeding. He must have missed Harper's glare because his timidity disarmed her. She took a second to collect herself.

"Yes and no," she responded, measuring her breathing. "I was able to get hold of the portable harddrive on board the ship, so we know where we are…" Harper shuffled on tired feet and made up her mind. Lying was easier. "It's not far from the planned drop zone. The important thing is we take stock of what we've managed to salvage, who's alive, who isn't, and then go from there."

Most of the group nodded. They had bought it.

The man with the tattoos had further questions.

"What happened to the captain? And the rest of the crew?"

"Captain Case was killed in the crash," Harper said. She wasn't sure if that was a good or bad thing yet, given his decision to crash the ship. "The rest of the crew were positioned in the rear of the craft which broke off and smashed into the sea some miles out. They're gone too."

"Are you the only one left, then?"

"Yes." And you're stuck with me, Harper thought vindictively.

"Great," Zack shouted, arms aloft. "So the only people who survived your captain's stupidity were a handful of women, the fat black guy who's going to eat all our food and those two ugly assholes over there," he finished by pointing at James and another man.

"...And one snivelling little prick..." interjected Ben.

"What did you say?"

Ben bit his lip.

"Hey, I asked you a question."

"I said: don't forget the snivelling. Little. Pr--."

The punch cut off the final word. The bearded man caught Ben on the chin, who rolled with the punch and, grabbing his attacker's shoulder, landed a retaliatory blow right on the upper lip. Harper dashed between them and held each man at arm's length. Sensing an incoming blow, she reached for the hip.

A whelp went up from one of the women.

Harper pointed her pistol at the aggressor's face. She had drawn it quickly, hand down, clip flicked, firm grip, aim. All in one motion. The target did not look as fazed as she had hoped.

"What's your name, scumbag?" She held his gaze.

He spat some blood on her boot and threw a contemptuous look.

"Zack."

"Right then Zack, you're going to step back and do as you're told."

"Who put you in charge? We're not taking the orders from a bloody woman," he replied, smug.

Harper had been sent half-way around the universe and here she was still micro-managing tin-pot wannabe criminals. She was simply bored of people like Zack.

"Speak for yourself, dick-head." Ben chimed in, nursing the scrape on his chin.

"Will somebody stop this bitch pointing a gun at me? Ain't legal."

Harper chuckled rudely.

"Legal?" She paused for breath. "Unfortunately for you, Zack, we're billions miles away from anyone who gives a damn. Yeah, fine, I wasn't the captain of this expedition. But Case and everybody else are dead, so that leaves me in charge whether you like it or not."

Harper did not like it much either.

Zack stared down the barrel of the gun with gritted teeth. Then his eyes flickered from side to side, looking for support. There was none.

"Well, I'm *still* not taking orders from a bloody woman," he muttered, shrugging away from the group.

"Don't worry about him," Harper said, waiting until Zack was out of ear-shot before holstering the weapon. "I know his type. He's a piece of shit." She clocked the teenage girl. "Sorry."

Guilt crept up on her. Harper knew exactly who

was to blame for her banishment but out here on Proxima B there was no way to make them pay. The only people she could take her anger out on were these pathetic colonial hopefuls. But looking them in the eye, she saw their dreams of another life reduced to ash. Harper was the only one with half a chance of keeping them alive... if she could remember the first thing about leadership. It had been too long since Brixton.

"Look, rather than fight with each other, let's get on with sorting this mess out. I think it's late afternoon, nearly evening, right now. According to the satellite surveys this place turns into a damned furnace by the early morning and we've got no shelter or fresh water supply yet. There were some Krichmar Tarps in the ship but their locator beacons put them several miles further inland after the crash."

Exhausted faces grew even longer. Harper's stomach dropped an inch or two in response. Keeping these people in a good shape was going to be difficult.

"I know a lot of you are in pain right now and are probably still in shock, but if we don't act fast we're not going to last long out here. Each Tarp takes two to carry so I need five volunteers to help me bring them back here."

"I'll join you." Ben was the first to stick his arm up.

"I'll come too," mumbled Amos with very little conviction. Harper noticed he had half an eye on Zack and understood instantly.

A lanky red-haired man and a sleek-figured blonde woman, of similar height to Harper, indicated they would join the trip before Brooks did too. Looking him up and down Harper wasn't sure he was right for the job.

"Are you sure you can manage? These things are heavy," she said.

He looked stung by her remark, but quickly shifted his expression into one of determination.

"I'll be fine."

"If you say so," replied Harper, scanning the remaining people on the beach. Drawn to an olive-skinned man she asked his name and what his job was supposed to be on Proxima B.

"I'm Lucas. I was assigned for manual labour and voluntary law enforcement."

"That'll do," she said, giving him the thumbs up. Leaving a plasma-knife in his hands, Harper pointed towards the shoreline and said: "You make sure he stays away from those supplies."

✳

"So, that was awkward," the tall ginger man said with a squeaky chuckle.

The group was fifteen minutes into the jungle, carefully dissecting their way through prickly undergrowth. Harper spearheaded the expedition, leading them in single file. Occasionally she stopped, switching on the portable hard-drive to check they were still going in the right direction. The aroma of fresh vegetation was a welcome one. She was having a hard time shaking the stench of burning flesh. It had lingered in the nose and haunted her since the crash.

Ben trudged his feet at the rear, a little trapped behind the slow-moving bulk of Amos. In the middle was the outspoken red-head, accompanied by the shorter woman who, Harper guessed from her well-toned waist, thighs and forearms, was probably as fit as she was.

"What do you mean, awkward?" she asked.

"Come on, Lisa. You know what I'm talking about! Back there, the fight."

"Oh right, yeah. Whatever." Lisa shrugged.

"The way you sparked that dickhead like he'd barely hurt you at all," he said, turning around. Ben kept quiet, never once looking up. The taller man continued: "I thought he was going to piss himself after you hit him. It's good that lady stopped you."

"My name's Harper," she chimed in, not letting the pace drop. "What's yours, chuckles?"

"Sam."

"I don't think we need to joke about what happened back there, Sam," Harper said, doing her best to put him in his place.

"But he--"

"But, nothing," she insisted. "You're clearly forgetting that we're stuck with each other for the rest of our lives. There's no point in making enemies and picking sides before we've even got started."

"I guess you're right," said Sam, chastised as if he were a child.

The group fell silent again, save for the crackling and snapping of branches and leaves. Sam was only able to last a few minutes before opening his mouth again.

"So what made you guys come on this trip?"

Harper clenched her fist. *He better not ask me. We've got more pressing concerns.*

"I'd rather not talk about it, to be honest," said Ben. "I lost everything back home, let's put it that way."

"Well, what did you do before this?" Sam asked.

"I had a farm on the Dartmoor Islands."

"Ah, so you'll be growing the food eventually, then?" Sam sounded more upbeat.

"That *was* the plan," said Ben. "We'll have to see."

"Yeah... what about you, Lisa?" Sam asked, tapping her on the shoulder.

"It's a long story."

Sam, spread his arms wide, hands outstretched.

"We've got all the time in the world."

Harper could feel her chest tighten. They better not ask me.

"You don't have to answer these questions if you don't want to," she said aloud.

"It's okay," said Lisa. "I don't mind. I came here because my husband died."

"That sucks," Sam replied.

"After going through that I just had to get away. Like... really far away. I had no family left, no job, no nothing. This was basically my only chance to get back on my feet. What about you?"

"Boredom really," Sam explained. "I just wanted to get out of London's global warming sludge and see some cool stuff for a change. You hear all these stories about what the rest of the world has done in the Proxima system. I wanted to get away and see some of the future for myself, now that we've finally caught up with the rest of the world. Anything's better than sitting through five more years of Benjamin Curtis."

"Surely none of that matters anymore?" Lisa said. "We're never going back, are we?"

"I suppose that's true," said Sam, non-committal.

"Well, I'm sure we can all be happy about sleeping in Krichmar Tarps, when we've found them," Ben said, clearly trying to find common ground. "I never thought I'd actually see one for real."

"Me neither," Lisa said. "I saw parts for a Holst Water Purifier among the gear too. It's crazy that we've had to come to another planet just to have a clean drink.

Ben and Sam laughed along with her.

"Harper?" Brooks spoke away from the group's conversation.

"Yes?" she said, hoping he wasn't trying to pry.

"Can I ask a question?"

"If you must." She sighed, looking at the name label on his suit. "Brooks, right? What does the J. stand for?"

"It's James. I was just wondering if you'd been able to send a distress call."

"I managed to send something," Harper said, omitting that it had only been the beacon. "Whether or not somebody listens and is able to do something about it is another matter."

An hour later they found a clearing. The thick jungle receded and the last of the day's light illuminated a circular space in the centre, like some ancient forgotten grove. To the left was a rock face towering far above the surrounding trees, to the right: dense tangled flora, leaves fluttering like a woman's hair in the wind. The ground was much drier here than the sludge they'd been slipping through since the beach. Rocks ranging from the size of household pets to large cars lay scattered about.

"This should be it," Harper said, looking down at the portable device. She had turned it back on just moments before arriving in the clearing.

There was no sight of the Tarps.

A moment of panic ran through her.

"Over here. I've found them."

James had walked round one of the rocks and spotted them. The trio of six-foot long black metal cases were covered in branches and exotic plumage from the trees they had disturbed on high impact arrival. All three were just about attached to each other by cargo webbing and looked in decent shape. Harper took a deep breath, feeling the tension on her diaphragm dissipate.

"Let's work on freeing them and then we'll pair up to get them back to the beach," she announced.

"How do we know they still work?" James asked.

"We don't," Harper crouched over the bundle. "We need to hurry, though. We can't get caught out here in the dark."

"But what would we use for shelter?" That was the first thing Amos had said to anyone since the beach. Harper had almost forgotten he was there. As bashful as he looked, his quivering voice was uncertain of every word.

Harper replied: "Let's just cross that bridge when we get to it, okay?"

A curse word came from near the rock face. Ben hauled himself away from a crouched position.

"What is *that*?" he blurted pointing to something on the ground.

The rest of the group downed tools and edged over, unnerved by the soulless expression on Ben's face.

"What is it?" Harper asked.

"Just come and look."

In dried mud and sand by Ben's feet were grooves roughly three centimetres wide. They formed various shapes and patterns. In the middle was a vaguely humanoid figure, its head severed from the body. Save for a haunting breeze rustling nearby bushes, silence reigned supreme. The seconds marched past for what felt like an age. Harper's gut tightened, her breath held to ransom. She said nothing.

"Is that... writing?" Lisa quivered, almost rhetorically. She had managed to hold her nerve when discussing her late husband but now that tough exterior was weakening.

Feeling something on her shoulder, Harper jumped out of her skin. It was just Sam trying to get her attention. For a moment she had felt as if some mysterious death would leapt out to strike her down. The writing still held her eyes and mind prisoner.

"I thought satellite surveys of this planet showed no signs of life?"

"They didn't show anything," Harper replied lifelessly. "Nothing that could do this. Just crabs and lizards."

"I don't get it," Lisa's voice wavered further still. "Does this mean there are people already here?"

"I don't know." Harper was fed up of not knowing what the hell was going on. First the ship crashes on purpose and now this.

"Maybe it's the tracks of those crabs or lizards?" Sam suggested.

Ben looked at the man as if he was sat in his own faeces.

"You're telling me a crab accidentally drew this? How would it do that? By dragging its claws through the mud?"

"Well, I don't know," replied Sam defensively.

"We need to get out of here," a panicked Lisa said.

"I agree," added Ben.

Harper extracted her mind from the quagmire of self-doubt.

"You're right," she said, standing tall. "Let's get those ropes off and get back to camp. Keep your eyes peeled for anything suspicious. Sam and Lisa, you grab that Tarp. Amos and Ben take the one underneath. James and I will have this one."

Everybody snapped to it, eager to leave this place as soon as possible. All apart from James. He remained on his knees, as if he was worshipping the writing.

"James? Are you helping me with this or not?" Harper asked, as the others got to work.

"Yes..." He was distracted.

She gave him a look of annoyed disbelief.

"Oh, yes," said James finally. "The Tarps."

He scrambled to his feet and grabbed the end of a Tarp.

Very soon they were on their way.

"What was that all about?" Harper asked James quietly.

"What do you mean?"

"Why were you so obsessed with those drawings?"

James waited until he knew none of the others were listening.

"Please don't tell the others this..."

"Fine. What is it?"

"It's just... I know nobody has ever come to this planet before but... I can't help thinking I've seen that writing somewhere before."

4

Don had not slept. Dawn's glow slid through his office's bay windows, illuminating the vast cityscape beneath. Even at times like this, he still enjoyed the view of the shoreline and the ocean horizon beyond it.

In the three decades since its founding, New Boston had become the most prosperous metropolitan hub in the region, just as the Atlas Nations had intended. Littered with imposing glass superstructures glistening in the sunrise, the tips of the skyscrapers could be seen from Chuset City to the south and even as far away as New Plymouth in the north. These indulgent high-rises housed the haulage businesses made rich by transporting raw Teslanium ore to the planet's capital in the early days and the banks they held accounts with. In the distance lay the city docks. They were linked to the small Salem Peninsula by a recently completed titanic bridge, connecting the ports with the Atlas Nations' formidable navy base.

Watching the first ships arrive from other settlements along the western coastline, Don's tired eyes drooped even in the light. He cursed whoever it was who had dealt him such a hand. After years of trying to prevent another war with the Choctaw, Don might end up fighting one against the British.

Anderson opened the door sharply and stepped in.

"Any luck yet?" Don asked, a little startled.

"I'm afraid not," a pacing Anderson said, hands in his pockets. "We've reviewed the footage and satellite data over and over again and found nothing. By the time the object appears on our radar it's too late to get an accurate estimation of its previous trajectory." He opened his arms wide. "It could just as easily have come from Proxima B or outside the system entirely."

Boring fingers into heavy eyes, Don moved from his desk chair to the sofa.

"Okay, thanks for the update." The words waded through a yawn as if it were treacle. "Keep trying."

Anderson nodded and turned to leave.

"Listen, I'm sorry about last night," said Don before a considered pause. "I've just been thinking about… Choctaw a lot recently." He nursed the tender skin at the base of his leg and remembered his disturbed sleep.

"Don't worry, sir. We're all on edge. Did you get anything from your contact back on Earth?" he asked, taking a seat across from Don.

"Not yet. It'll be another couple of hours before he even picks up my message. But if there's any intelligence to be gathered from Earth, he will know."

The two men took a moment to watch the sun continue its ascent. More and more of the city was glinting in its glare.

"This incident is bad news for New Boston and

everyone on this planet," Don said in a brood.

"I can't help but agree, sir."

"And it doesn't help that we have no idea where the ship came from," Don added.

"Surely it must have come from Earth?"

"We can't know that for sure. Not yet anyway," Don countered. "I mean, if it did, it categorically proves the rumours that Britain are planning to colonise this system illegally." Don frowned. "I was too short with that kid of yours, Anderson. His conclusions were remarkably astute for someone so young."

"Yeah Chad is a smart one," said Anderson. "He should go far in this department."

"Hmm," Don said, looking out the window once more. "This will certainly cause a pissing contest back home if he's right. Our relationship with the British is volatile at best anyway. This could easily push things over the edge. They don't exactly do things by the book and they must know it's illegal for them to colonise here. They lost that right when they shut themselves off from everyone else."

"I wouldn't want to be on Earth right now," Anderson mused in reply.

"*If* it came from Earth." Don reminded him of the uncertainty.

"You're not ruling out Proxima B as an origin, then?"

"We can't afford to. Who knows what happened to the people who tried to colonise there?"

"What's the military latest?" Anderson knew exactly what Don was worried about.

"I've already relocated three squads on training missions to the Choctaw border, just in case. I've arranged a meeting to discuss the wider tactical situation later this morning. I'd like you to be there. Bring Chad too."

"Sure thing, boss. Will Alida Harmon be coming?"

"The council leader won't be gracing us with her presence, no. I have told her about the situation, though. Had no choice, really."

"What about Stangl? Have you told him?" Anderson asked the million-dollar question.

"Absolutely not," Don snapped. "The longer we can keep his bony nose out of this one the better. Even *I* agree with Alida on that one. All our political focus should be on the re-negotiation of our Teslanium contributions to Earth, not putting ourselves on the defensive with the Atlas Nations hierarchy again."

"The Teslanium negotiations," Anderson half-scoffed, rolling his eyes.

"I know," Don replied. "Tell me about it."

There was a knock at the door.

"Excuse me, sir," Virginia interjected politely, reticent to cause a disturbance.

"Yes, Ginny?" Don tried to sound polite, mostly in vain. Thankfully, the short-haired long-suffering assistant gave him a sympathetic look to show her understanding.

"I've got vice admiral Tycho on the line. He wanted clearance for the navy's exercise this morning."

"Ah Sean." Don's mood brightened a little. "It's been too long since we've caught up. Give him the green light."

"Will do. Oh and Dashiell Sona in the lobby to discuss the security roster for today's Teslanium negotiations."

Throwing Anderson a mildly amused look, Don

rubbed his eyes and agreed to the meeting with a grunt.

"We'll keep working on your expedition plans, sir," Anderson said as he left. Don was grateful for his company. *Some way for the Bloodaxe of Choctaw to spend his supposed retirement*, he jibed privately.

*

"A good day's work, Captain. Take us home."

Vice admiral Sean Tycho allowed his first officer to return the ship to condition three. Another training exercise executed to perfection. He expected nothing less of the fleet's flagship, the ANS Diamond. The hulking beast sliced through Proxima A's waters at a frightening pace, the remnants of the morning's targets littering the surface like autumn leaves.

"Taking us home, sir." Commander Saldana gave a sharp salute and turned to her bridge officers, with whom she made the necessary arrangements to get them back to base.

Tycho stood on the Diamond's panoramic bridge, hands clasped behind his back, chest out, chin slightly raised. He was grateful that, despite mankind's obsession with space travel, there were still beautiful oceans in this galaxy on which to sail. From the ship's position in Cod Bay, Tycho could see the eastern end of Victory Bridge, sloping into the New Boston naval docks. Enormous pride swelled up within him. Recently completed to celebrate twenty-five years since victory against the Choctcaw, the bridge was dedicated to the sailors who fought in the final capture of Pacheco City in 2054 AD. Tycho and his colleagues had earned the recognition. The vice admiral spent a few more minutes sea-gazing before inspecting the busy deck below through the bridge's glass floor. It was lined with banks of cannons and their crews while the almighty roaring of Teslanium weapons had now died down. As per usual, the Diamond had destroyed the targets in exceptionally quick time. Thanks to the Teslanium components, there was no weapon in the universe that could fire projectiles as rapidly and as accurately as the Atlas Nations' navy could. The shells themselves were inert but the sheer power generated by the electro-magnetic rail guns ensured they caused maximum devastation upon impact. Weapons so powerful they were effectively instant-hit.

Saldana gave the order for cool-down crews to begin their sweep of the deck's cannons and their Teslanium parallel rails. The alien element was the only metal known to man capable of standing up the seismic wattage required to generate the electro-magnetic fields. Despite that, it was best-practice to constantly treat the Teslanium and avoid any long-term warping or melting. The first cool-down team plugged a corrugated tube into the back of the near-est weapon and began flooding it with liquid nitro-gen. Time to stand down.

Tycho was pleased to get back to his quarters after a long day. The running of the Diamond appeared seamless to most, but given that he involved himself in virtually every aspect of the ship, it took a toll. If he could change one thing about this glorious ves-sel it would be the granite colour of his walls. It was a backdrop that, in spite of his plush bed (by Navy standards anyway) and wooden desk, still made him feel like he was living in the engine room.

Throwing a white cap and heavy-set blue blazer

onto the bed, Tycho splashed water over his cheeks and inspected his face in the mirror above the sink. *Another grey one*, he told himself. His well-groomed crop of blond hair had started succumbing to the stress about five years ago. Thankfully it had crept up on him gracefully and was nothing more than a fading on the sides of his head. Intense blue eyes stared back at him, surrounded by well-worn middle-aged skin. Tycho's refined Roman nose and high cheek bones ensured he looked the part of Admiral, or so his father had always said.

Lying down on his cot, the experienced sailor sank his back into computer programmed memory foam, more than his charges could hope for. He let fatigue wash over him, feeling the welcome support of the bed. Not wishing to waste his precious off-duty time, he leaned across to his small bed-table and picked up his frayed copy of Winston Churchill's *'The Great Republic'*.

He read barely a word of *'William Pitt and the first World War'* when Tycho heard a violent clang on the other side of his ceiling. Something had struck the floor on the level above him. It happened twice more.

Quickly putting his blazer back on, Tycho dashed out the door and up the stairs, soon standing in front of the relevant hatchway. The word 'Communications' was emblazoned on the metal. He unwound the locking mechanism and stepped through.

A young dark-haired ensign was being restrained in the middle of the space by two of the communication officers. The small work-space in front of one of the viewing screens had three shallow, fist-sized dents in them. The ensign's left hand had grazes on two knuckles.

"Officer on deck!" The sailor who noticed Tycho's presence had eyes ready to pop. Everybody in the room immediately flinched and stood to attention.

"At ease," Tycho said calmly. "What seems to be the problem here?" Everybody looked at the young ensign. He gulped before speaking.

"I was talking to my partner, sir," he said gingerly, gesturing towards the communication station he had damaged.

"Go on." The young sea-man needed some encouragement.

"She's a lieutenant in the army, sir. Her whole unit has been redeployed."

"Did her orders warrant losing your temper with her and damaging naval property? Ensign...?"

"Ensign Soslan, sir. And, no. Sorry, sir. It's just going on this reinforcement movement... she's taking my daughter with her to the new barracks against court instructions. We've been having some problems and..."

"It's okay, corporal. I understand." *More than you know, son.* "I won't log this incident. But you'll spend the next twenty-four hours cooling off in the brig. Is that understood?"

"Yes, sir. Thank you, sir."

"Will you accompany Ensign Soslan?" Tycho asked the officer who had announced his arrival. Soslan was taken by the arm and led out of the room.

"One last question, Ensign," Tycho quickly interjected. The two men stopped in their tracks and looked back to their superior officer. "Where has your daughter been taken to?" During peacetime, troop manoeuvres at such short notice were peculiar.

"The Arkan/Choctaw border, sir."

Everybody in the room had returned to their jobs, but the ensign's revelation caused them to stop what they were doing. Tycho realised almost immediately the furore those words would cause amongst his crew. He was caught off-guard too. He addressed the room.

"That information does not leave these four walls. Is that clear?" A sea of frantic nods followed. "Good. Ensign Soslan. You keep that to yourself too." The young man indicated his compliance and was led away. "As you were," he said to the room.

Tycho was soon back in his quarters, but this time Churchill's history of America stayed on the cabinet. Several pertinent questions were swimming unanswered in his mind. Why were the army sending reinforcements to the border? There hadn't been any official trouble in years. But, more importantly, why had the navy not been informed of the development? He'd have to chase the details upon his return to the capital. Thankfully, he knew exactly who to ask.

Everybody had arrived at the conference room for Don's strategy meeting with his security team and military aides. Even the defence minister himself, a bald man maybe ten years younger than him, turned up in his full regalia. Judson Trin was a career politician who had no intention of being involved in defence department decisions. He just liked to look important. At first, Trin didn't say a word. He simply grunted in the affirmative and nodded when appropriate until Don revealed plans for greater presence on the Choctaw border.

"The Choctaw are hardly a threat right now, surely?" Trin said. "We have to be careful about what this might look like."

"It's the territory they occupy that causes the biggest concern," Don replied. "If the Brits are likely to land in any region on Proxima A, it would be there. It's the most fertile of the officially unoccupied territories and already has sporadic groups of inhabitants cultivating the land."

"But they're nothing more than glorified farmers mostly picking fights with each other," Trin continued his protest. "Why rile them up with increased military presence? Especially after the Choctaw war."

Prejudice towards the Choctaw was nothing new, so Don did not blame Trin for it. Their decision to break away from Arkan decades ago had them pinned as deserters by many on Proxima A. Selfish folk who had bitten the hand that fed. That's how they'd earned their nickname. For those familiar with American colonial history, it was a pretty inaccurate term, but it had stuck, and the lawless and ungoverned land they occupied had been known as Choctaw Territory ever since.

"It's a chaotic place, yes, but there would likely be no organised resistance from locals to a well-planned arrival from British forces," Don insisted. "What do you think, Chad?"

The younger man looked like a rabbit in headlights. After a short stutter and a nervous look around the room, Chad finally spoke up.

"I think you're right, sir," he said cautiously. "Given the A.N.'s formal decision not to treat the Choctaw as criminals when they left Arkan and were defeat in the war, the Brits may even try to hide behind that logic when attempting to legitimise their claim to the land. I'd say it's certainly an angle we have to be wary of."

Trin grumbled.

"As long as you know what *you're* doing, Stafford... I'll allow it," said the defence minister.

"Thank you, sir."

Don considered Chad's surprisingly helpful contributions as he made the walk home from his office building. Sally often wondered why he'd never used the drones for his commute, especially with the damage to his leg. It was the injury that had spurred him on. Nothing would get between Donald Stafford and his dignity.

Right now, it gave him extra time to think. He hoped that Britain were only trying to colonise Proxima B and not his own world. That would slightly lessen the chances of conflict between them and the Atlas Nations, although not by much. Considering the other planet in the Proxima system, Don wondered if the British were truly aware of the risks involved with travelling there. The stories about Proxima B must have reached the United Kingdom even if it was more insular than the other Earth nations.

Sally gave him a loving smile when he came through the front door of their two-story Pacheco-brick house. They embraced and she offered him a choice of Plymothian steak or Chuset fish for dinner. A startling rasp jarred the conversation. Phil had returned his call, finally.

"Make it quick," Sally said pointedly as she returned to the kitchen. Don made an apologetic gesture as he opened the incoming video file in the corridor.

His long-time friend, Phil Clarke, appeared on the screen looking a little older than the last time they met. His greying hair was combed over what appeared to be a growing bald patch and his neck looked a lot thinner than he remembered. The glasses were surely new too, as he'd never seen Phil sporting rounded frames before. What was even stranger was the increased level of German accentuation. It really had been a long time since they'd served together.

"Hi Don. It's great to hear from you in spite of the circumstances. I've done some digging at my end, but haven't come up with anything yet. Although we shouldn't be all that surprised. This is the British government we're talking about here. Very glad I don't live there anymore. I'll try and speak to Pete at the Daily Citizen, but he'll obviously have hands tied behind his back. Having a contact in the press doesn't hold as much sway in the UK as it used to do. I'll keep on trying to find out what they're up to. We've both got one helluva of a job on our hands now. Give my love to Sally."

The video file automatically closed down and archived itself for future use. Don couldn't help but feel underwhelmed. He would have preferred a more concrete update from Phil.

His watch chimed again. There was another message waiting for him, time-stamped as arriving when he had been watching Phil's. Hopefully a more helpful update from him. It wasn't. The call was from a worried-looking Alida Harmon.

"You're not going to like this Don," the council leader said. "Stangl wants to see us about Satellite Three. Somehow he's found out, and he's pissed. He's ranting and raving about going to war with Britain, with us, with everybody. You better get down here."

✶

"This is completely outrageous," spat an irate German voice from behind his desk in the council building.

Lothar Stangl splattered the surface, and the touch-screen built into it, with spit and soggy sandwich crumbs. Don would have given anything to pinch his nose and guard against the foul stench of egg.

"The Atlas Nations council will blow a fuse when I tell them of this," Stangl continued. "Yet again you have done everything you can to damage relationships with those back on Earth, Ms. Harmon."

New Boston's council leader Alida Harmon was in full swing herself. The woman's stern brown face was intimidating at the best of times, but right now it was flush with indignation as she paced about the room. Fish-like eyes appeared seconds from popping out of her head entirely.

"Give me one good reason why myself, or any of our defence department, should be at your beck and call? What happened to Satellite Three represents a serious security risk and for that reason it was kept compartmentalised. I should not have to explain that to you."

"Have you paid attention to nothing I've said or done in the last six months?" Stangl countered. "New Boston must accept the need for my involvement in every aspect of governance."

Watching the decrepit old relic of the Atlas Nations' so-called halcyon days lose his temper yet again, Don remembered how this planet used to be treated. Before Stangl and his kind had started exploiting it for every last resource. Proxima A was supposed to do nothing more than relieve Earth's overpopulation concerns but the discovery of Teslanium had drastically decreased travel times between the two worlds. This poisoned chalice turned the colonies into money-making machines for the A.N., until the last war on Earth cut them off. Now there was a desperate fight for control of Proxima A's resources.

"The problems you have caused the A.N. by dragging your feet on Teslanium deliveries were bad enough, without this insult to my intelligence," Stangl went on and on. Don found himself drifting in and out. He was sure that the man's motivations were pure, once. Earth was in serious need of unity in the thirties and forties, something Stangl helped achieve. The Atlas Nations had brought it about in the face of worldwide disease, crippling climate change and destructive right-wing extremism. But another few decades later and Stangl appeared concerned about one thing: power. When A.N. ships had arrived in New Boston for the first time in eleven years, he had been at the very front of the disembarking queue. His opening words to the arrivals crew were an order to take him to Alida Harmon's office, where he tried to immediately force himself back into Proxima A's government.

"The colonies have gone unchecked for far too long," Stangl was saying to Don and Alida, even now, in his temporary office. "You have strayed away from your initial purpose. Governing yourselves and making laws with no input from the A.N. headquarters has not been well-received."

WRITING IN THE SAND

"Lothar we've been going round in circles on this for months," Alida argued. "What did you expect us to do? Wait eleven years before making any kind of political decision?"

Don looked to his right, where the entire wall displayed a panoramic view of the council chambers. Empty perimeter seating tiers sprawled out above and below. At the base was the raised speaking platform like the wick in a deep and intricate candle. The three public servants were sat in one of many work spaces with this view, like luxurious hospitality suites at a sports stadium. It was a hugely impressive construction commissioned and built in the A.N.'s eleven-year absence. Alida had made the tactical decision to house Stangl here, as if to say *'this is what we achieved without you.'* Don shared her sentiment. He had fought the Choctaw with no help from the Atlas Nations and it had cost him dearly. He owed them nothing, although he would never admit it to someone as powerful as Lothar Stangl. The last thing Don wanted to do was piss off one of the highest ranking members of Earth's central government. That wasn't what he was paid for. That was Alida's job.

"The New Boston Council and Mr Stafford's team are more than capable of handling security risks in their own way without any interference from you," the politician continued.

"I think you may have forgotten, young lady, where the New Boston Council draws its power from. I could have you removed from your position in a heartbeat. I think you know I'd enjoy that too." The words slithered out of Stangl's wiry mouth like an aged boa constrictor hunting its prey. But Alida was too strong to succumb to the recital of outdated chapter and verse.

"The New Boston Council currently has its best approval ratings in the city's history," she said placing both arms on Stangl's desk and staring him down. "Most of the citizens here cite the way we've handled the last eleven years without any contact from your bureaucracy as the primary reason for that. I feel that's more than enough of a mandate for me to tell you to take your protocols and *colonial control* and shove them up your fossilised asshole."

"Spare me the patriotic scheisse, Alida. That won't help anyone." Removing his thick-rimmed spectacles, Stangl continued in a slightly less agitated manner. "You mistake my anger on this matter for further attempts to undermine the stability here. That couldn't be further from the truth. If the Atlas Nations is to increase pressure on Britain, to either abandon its colonial plans or submit them for a formal application, then we must be in possession of all the facts at the right time. And if we are to go to war with them, the same is even more essential."

Alida sighed and massaged her temples with thumb and forefinger.

"You have to understand that you've gone about this in all the wrong way. It's far too early in our investigation to take this to your level."

"That may be so. But I've got a job to do as much as you have. So, are you going to fill me in on what you know or not? Were the British involved in the incident?"

Reluctantly, Alida gave Don the nod.

"Unfortunately we cannot confirm or deny any British involvement in the crash," Don said flatly, his usual gruff persona a million miles away. "There was no surviving wreckage of Satellite Three and the craft which hit it left the vicinity on a flight path heading for Proxima B."

"And you wonder why we haven't told you anything yet?" Alida chirped sarcastically.

Lothar's deep-set eyes appeared surprised that Don had finished speaking. "I fail to see why you are still in the dark."

Don looked to Alida for reassurance. She appeared just as perplexed.

"I'm sorry, but what do you mean?" Don asked.

"It sounds as if the answer to this conundrum lies on the surface of Proxima B," Stangl said with a piercing stare directed at Don.

"That's true... but there's no way we could ever salvage anything."

"Why not?"

Why do you think?

"It's too risky," Don began diplomatically. "No drone we've sent to that planet has ever lasted longer than a few hours and anyone who set foot there disappeared and never came back."

Lothar shook his head in disapproval and took another bite of his egg sandwich.

"I'm sorry but the future political landscape in Europe and the rest of the galaxy is not going to be dictated by the whim of a ridiculous old wives' tale," he said with a mouthful of food.

"Are you disputing established facts, now?" Alida returned to the debate.

"I want you to send a scouting party to Proxima B to ascertain the origin of that craft or you can kiss this new Teslanium trade deal goodbye." This time the death stare was directed at Alida.

"You don't have the authority to make that threat," Alida sounded less confident now.

"Unfortunately for you, I do."

Don had listened to enough and finally found a remnant of his usual nerve.

"With all due respect, what you're asking here is for me to send good men and women to their deaths."

"What I am asking for, Mr Stafford, is for good men and women to lay down their lives in the name of peace and *the Atlas Nations* – in accordance with the oath they swore upon enrolling."

That left Don with no choice.

"Well in that case, I'll have to go too."

Two simultaneous protests cut across each other like a boxer's combination. For once both Alida and Stangl appeared united.

"I doubt a man in your condition could do such a thing," Stangl said.

"Surely you can't be serious?" Alida chirped.

Don hated it when anyone questioned his limits.

"If I'm being asked to order my people to put their lives at risk with this, I have to be prepared to do the same."

Alida leaned forward, trying to put some privacy between them and Stangl. Don pulled away and sprung to his feet.

"I know what I am capable of. I can still handle myself."

Stangl spoke up again, slipping back into the comfort of his slimy arrogance with a mouthful of food.

"Needless to say, I do not think it would be wise for you to lead this mission yourself. And remember, if your over-confidence causes... problems, it would be a lot easier to make you disappear than Alida. She's a *hero* of the people; the woman that guided New Boston to its golden age. But nobody will miss Donald Stafford. Do what you want but you must produce answers, and quickly."

Alida grunted. She was eager for another bout but was interrupted by a knock at the door.

"Come in," Stangl replied as one of his aides arrived with a few sheets of paper. The old man ushered New Boston's senior figures away for a few moments. "We'll continue our discussion directly," he said.

In the corridor, Alida took the opportunity to pull Don aside.

"We can't give him what he wants," she said. "And you can't be serious about going there? When was the last time you flew a space mission?"

"Stop worrying about me," Don demanded. "Stangl is a prize asshole but he's not wrong. We desperately need a lead on this before it escalates. If that involves me going to Proxima B then so be it." Don shuffled on his feet momentarily. "We've already drafted a mission brief in case of this scenario."

"Does Sally know about that?" Alida asked.

Don avoided the question.

"It's risky, but it might be our only shot at finding out the truth. We're never going to get that directly from the British, are we?"

Alida briefly paced, coming back to Don with one arm pointing at Stangl's door.

"*He* can't make you do this," she insisted. Always so concerned with beating Stangly in the argument. That's what Don found most frustrating about her.

"He's not making me. I think we need to go," he countered. "I'm fed up of having next to no intelligence on this."

"That doesn't justify--"

"Ms. Harmon?" A young Asian man in a grey suit and tie had come around the corner.

"Yes, Daizen?"

"I've got your husband on the phone downstairs."

"I think you two better come back in here," Stangl called through the doorway.

"Tell him not now." Alida rebuked, glaring at her personal assistant.

Once she and Don were back in their seats Stangl began again.

"It would appear this replacement satellite of yours wasn't good enough, Mr Stafford. Something else has slipped through unnoticed." As per usual, Stangl was relentless in his attempts to put them on the defensive. "But you are a lucky man in many ways," he continued. "It would seem the universe has brought proof of British war-mongering much closer to our doorstep."

"What the hell are you talking about, Lothar?" Alida scowled.

"I've just been informed by one of my contacts that a second craft, similar to the one that smashed Satellite Three, was spotted crashing in the Choctaw Mountains less than three hours ago. It's causing some electromagnetic problems so all we have is images of the flight not the landing."

Chad had been right.

"You've got contacts in Choctaw territory?" Alida asked with mild amusement.

"Of course. Why shouldn't I?"

"You've not been on this planet in over decade, you've spent the last half a year rubbing ass-cheeks with our top business owners and you expect me to believe you are in contact with anyone in Choctaw? Didn't you describe it as the Proxima A cesspit? How do we even know you're telling the truth?"

"I think he is," Don interjected, still pensive.

"What?" Alida replied.

"I've got a young man in my department. Very clued up on the British. He seemed to think Choctaw would be their first target on Proxima A."

"See?" Stangl glowed with pride. "You can question my connections all you like, Alida, but I can assure you this intel is genuine." He produced the documents his aide had brought. They showed a cylindrical shape streaking through the Choctaw sky and disappearing in the north-western mountain range.

"As I just said," Stangl added, leaning back in the chair, "I think we can all agree our hand just got stronger with this little break. Believe you me, I'd be more than happy to send you to the depths of hell but it now looks as if I can send you to the next best thing. Opportunity, like it so often does, has struck much closer to home. A place Mr Stafford knows well, too. I think you should start assembling your team."

5

Washington Parker and his father sat in silence, vegetating in front of the television. The screen was small and portable, hanging over the bed on a mechanical arm. The pale-skinned older man was propped up by a bundle of pillows, his head tipped back slightly. Under a thick, unkempt brown moustache the mouth was ajar, receiving little support from the weak neck muscles beneath. His breathing was hoarse, heavy and rapid.

Wash did not particularly enjoy visiting his father at the hospital. He got the impression the feeling was mutual. All they ever did was watch the news together. On the low resolution screen was a long upright cylindrical object, surrounded by a deluge of smoke. Slowly the rocket crept up, followed by an intense burst of heat, a bright crackling trail in its wake.

"Those were images of Britain's first interplanetary colonisation ship, the Concord, taking off from its Cornwall launch site earlier this year," came the voice of a female news reporter.

"Bollocks! All bollocks!" Wash's father snapped, muting the device.

"Dad! Shh!" Wash hissed, close to nudging his father hard on the arm, remembering the protruding cannula just in time. "You can't talk like that," he added with a cursory glance around the room. Thankfully nobody had noticed.

"I can and I will," Mr Parker replied indignantly. "People in this country deserve to know what's going on."

Wash rolled his eyes.

"And how can you possibly know anything about that?" he whispered.

Wash's father stifled a cough, groaning at the resulting pain elsewhere.

"Look around you, son," he said eventually, leaning forward a little. "How many of us are in this ward? Twenty? Twenty-five?" The old man paused for effect, then sat back in his bed. "When was the last time a nurse or a doctor came down here?

Wash looked around him, unsure how to reply.

"What's that got to with--?" he pointed at the television before he was interrupted.

"And then they destroyed the welfare state."

"Dad, I don't get it," Wash said, growing increasingly impatient.

Finally, his father turned to look at him, staring harshly down a hooked nose.

"You're supposed to be the journalist, boy," he said with disdain. "If you can't spot the link then we really are stuffed."

Wash's father had been irritable before the heart attack and had grown worse in ill-heath.

"Thanks Dad," Wash huffed, folding his arms, debating how much more of this to take. The two of them had never been particularly close, but as they were the last surviving members of the Parker family, Wash didn't have a lot of choice but to visit. The worst part was the guilt. Even though his father had done little in his life to deserve sympathy, seeing such a strong-minded individual laying here wasting away, Wash couldn't help but feel sorry for him. To a point.

He stewed in his father's words a while longer.

"You know, this is exactly why I often don't bother coming up here," he said. "You always complain I don't visit enough, well... just try and treat me with some respect when I do."

"There's no-one else," Wash's father replied in an unconcerned huff, shifting to a more comfortable position and picking his nose.

"Yeah I know," Wash said cynically. "You made quite sure of that."

His father ignored that remark. A few moments later he shook his head.

"How do we have enough money to run this vanity project?" He sparked up again, tipping his head at the screen. "They can't even feed half of the people in this country and now they want to go to space." The old man tutted, the noise laced with mild amusement.

"Dad... come on," Wash replied, calmer than before. "The doctors said you have to reduce your stress. What's the point in sitting here getting angry at all this stuff you can't change?"

His father simply laughed.

"What's so funny?" Wash asked.

"With an attitude like that, you're never going to

amount to anything."

Wash raised his eyebrows.

"I'm not sure how landing a job at the Daily Citizen isn't something to be proud of," he insisted.

"Everybody knows all the national newspapers live in the government's back pocket, especially the London ones," his father grumbled. "Your editor is a politician. You're one of *them*," He paused "*Stuff you can't change*," the old man imitated, increasingly irate. "Back in my day, journalists used their position to educate people and make the world a better place."

"Right, that's it," Wash snapped as he launched out of the chair and pulled his jacket back on. "I'm not staying here and listening to anymore of this bullshit."

His father kept his eyes glued to the screen in front of him.

"Calm down, boy. Sometimes the truth hurts," he replied, impatiently. "If you don't like what I've got to say, get your head out of the government's backside."

"You don't know what you're fucking talking about, dad."

Wash trudged through the streets of central London, bubbling with anger. Even looking at the city from the ground level reminded him of his father's cynical view of the world. In his words, the last fifty years had seen the nation's capital transform from a stunning metropolis of industry and progress into a crumpled, soggy husk. Fried like an egg by the searing post-warming heat, the air was thick and offensive to the senses. The river Thames had become a bloated beast, consuming its surroundings as if by osmosis.

The City had supposedly been the last part of the United Kingdom to succumb to the effects of the global catastrophe. Despite some initial success, years of expensive protective measures in the Thames Gateway had eventually given way. The waters continued to rise vast areas of inner London were soon submerged in a tepid mucky sludge. The only thing that differentiated it from the marshy swamplands of East Anglia and the sunken parts of west Devon was the collection of high-rise office buildings. Here the climate changes in Britain's historic capital were mirrored in its financial sector.

The city's skyscrapers were unforgiving pressure cookers where the strains of the country's shrinking economy took its toll on bankers and stock brokers alike. Temperatures soared in buildings traditionally built to retain heat in the tepid British climate of old, as, one by one, important figures cracked under the burden of their work.

Soon enough the banks were poor and the stock brokers even poorer. They had only just recovered from the worldwide virus of the twenties when global warming came for them. The impossible pressure ensured that the suicide rate in those professions sky-rocketed over the last half decade. Not that the government would ever let you know that officially, Wash's father had always reminded him.

The young man had been raised on the idea that his country had stagnated and fallen behind the other nations of the world. Scientific and technical progress had been stifled by such a strict and controlling government. As a result, experiment and invention had virtually ceased to exist.

Wash knew his father's rhetoric by heart but had no way to verify his ramblings. It was all based on a world that he had no experience of. To his father, the United Kingdom was in decline but to Wash this was all he had known.

He knew his father was right about one thing, though. The newspaper.

Passing through the sliding front doors of the Daily Citizen office building, Wash flicked through the morning's edition in his glasses' head-up display. He cursed the failing technology as several pages refused to load on his model.

The young journalist was grateful at least for escaping the warm winter air. He longed to have lived in the time when Indian summers were a once in a lifetime occurrence, not a regular fixture on the calendar.

Casually gesturing a greeting to the reception desk, Wash adjusted his shoulder bag and sidled through the electronic gate-way. With a classy blend of frosted glass panels and well-varnished oak wood it was a far cry from the poverty of the capital. Wash found his way to the appropriate elevator for his floor and opened up today's edition on his glasses.

The crime section that day was interesting. More slave rings had been uncovered in south Wales and another poor soul had fallen victim to the vicious 'Eye Killer' that had been stalking London's streets. However, each flick of the hinge's button brought up another page without any of his work. He sighed.

"What is the point in me filing this stuff if they're not going to use it?" Wash said to himself. It was if everything he wrote was etched in sand, washed away by the ocean of ignorance that surrounded him.

Returning to the front page, he re-read every word of the top story, as he pressed the button for the fifteenth floor. Yesterday had been a gushing propaganda piece about the heroic Captain Case and the country's interplanetary colonisation programme. Today was much worse.

'UK TAKES BACK CONTROL' were the words splashed across a heavily airbrushed picture of Prime Minister Benjamin Curtis. 'Country no longer held to ransom by welfare state' read the sub-heading underneath it.

Another one of Yvette Hamilton's patriotic editorials on the front page for all of London and the rest of the country to see. He pocketed his glasses angrily, hoping he'd broken them so he could request a new pair from the company.

Wash realised again that he resented his father so much because he was right, about the newspaper at least. The country was in a bad way and the media, ideally the first line of defence, had fallen under government control. What he objected to was being lumped in with everyone else and blamed for it. If only Wash's father knew what he'd been working on recently. Trying, largely in vain, to make the world a better, more informed place.

He had been chasing some contacts at the Office for National Statistics to help him evidence a historic link between a reduction in income subsidies and a decrease in the value of the stock market. However, since that organisation had also been absorbed by the government a little under a decade ago, access to factual information was becoming harder and harder to come by, especially older records.

Admittedly, some of those he knew at ONS had been reticent to speak to him. In the current climate, that was understandable. Still, from what Wash had heard, they were an easier nut to crack than the country's extra-terrestrial colonisation department. Those that were able to leak documents to him had provided some great material, but nobody was interested. They lived in an age where 'the truth' was whatever you wanted it to be.

Wash had considered sharing the research with his father but figured it was best keeping him in the dark. It might earn him more respect but giving the man something to latch onto would probably send him over the edge. It was easier to let him just be disappointed and angry with his son. That was something Wash was used to.

Snapped back to his immediate surroundings by the tone of the lift, the young journalist checked in the reflective walls of the cubicle that his short dark fringe was still swept across the top of his head and ran fingers along his jaw line to ensure he'd caught every last protruding hair in the morning's shave.

Wash entered the hustle bustle of the Daily Citizen's newsroom. The only thing which brought him any comfort was the refreshing breeze of the air conditioning unit. Walking through the central aisle, his ears took a battering from the vociferous jabbering of the advertising team. The morning news conference was already underway in the middle of the long room. All the department heads were gathered around one of the many screens being lectured on the stats and figures of the content produced so far that day.

Arriving at his desk, conveniently in the corner of

the newsroom, Wash heard the end of a conversation his veteran colleague Pete Stewart was having. As far as he knew, the old man was the only one who still used the ancient landline phone on the desk. Everybody else had one but it was covered in dust, redundant in the wake of glasses tech and contact lens implants.

"It's just the way it is now, I'm afraid," Pete said poetically. "Yeah. Well, exactly. Great to hear from you again, Phil. Speak soon."

Noticing that Wash had hung his coat over the back of his chair and had started firing up his computer, Pete hung up and gave his usual warm welcome.

"Washington!" He announced with delight. "The man they couldn't tame!"

That forced a cheeky smile out of Wash.

"If it isn't Pete Stewart; the young man in an old man's body."

"You just watch it, you little jackass."

They both smiled at each other.

"So who was on the phone just now?" Wash asked as he continued to unpack the contents of his bag.

Looking over his shoulder, the veteran reporter began speaking in hushed tones.

"It was an old mate of mine who I worked with in Hertfordshire back in the day. He's with the Atlas Nations' foreign affairs department in Germany now."

Wash froze, staggered that his friend would do something as risky as contacting the outside world. He fumbled at some gibberish.

"It's alright," Pete said with a smile and a tap of the nose. "Just don't tell anyone, alright.

"Of course," Wash nodded. He was full of questions. "How did this guy, Phil was it?" Pete nodded. "How did he even manage to get into the A.N.?"

"He was smart enough to get out of this country when that was still possible, you know."

"Wow, Pete. You're older than I thought!"

"Very funny."

"So why did he call?" Wash asked, turning to his desk. "Wait... how did he call? I wouldn't have thought he'd be able to get through."

"Oh, they've been able to get through the communications barrier for years," Pete replied, tapping his desktop landline unit with a finger. "No sweat for their types... Anyway, the rumour going round Berlin is that New Boston has been in emergency lockdown for the last day or so. Lost one of their orbital observation posts, apparently."

"What's that got to do with us?"

"That's the thing. There's a suggestion that the colonisation ship we sent out last month has something to do with it."

Wash stopped hitting his temperamental computer on the monitor, his interest piqued.

"What's made them think that?" he said with bated breath, immediately thinking of his father.

"Apparently, there was no scheduled Atlas Nations voyage for another three weeks and the only other country with a 'known space programme' is us."

There was a brief moment's pause as the two reporters let their minds wander in investigative thought.

"Are you going to dig any deeper?" Wash asked, already regretting showing such disdain at the hospital.

"You know the answer to that question as well as I

do, Wash," Pete said with half a glance in the general direction of the still ongoing news desk meeting.

Pete was one of the best in the business. His investigative skills, ability to make and retain good relationships with contacts and, most importantly, his almost poetic writing style, made him invaluable – in another time perhaps. He was wasted on the current generation of readers. Pete had become nothing more than a glorified PR man for those in power.

"Come on. Anything like this is just not worth troubling ourselves with," Pete reiterated. Wash opened his mouth but his colleague beat him to it. "You don't have a family of your own yet, do you?" he asked, already knowing the answer.

Wash's thoughts moved to Vicky. He quickly buried the speculative thought – and chastised himself for having it in the first place.

"No," he said. "It's just me and my dad right now. And even then, I don't know how much longer he's got left."

"When you start having to support more than just yourself, you'll understand the true meaning of keeping your head down, Wash."

"I suppose you're right," he admitted. Wash hated the way the world was but he knew there was nothing he could do to change it. His father's scathing words pricked at his confidence once more.

His machine finally flickered into life, displaying today's front page, Yvette's opinion piece there in all its glory.

"I didn't think they'd sink as low as this, though," Wash added, showing it to Pete. "You know those figures I got from ONS?"

His colleague nodded.

"I wrote three leads on what they could imply for the economy now that even more people have dropped below the poverty line. Nothing in today's edition; not even a nib."

Pete gave him a telling look.

"The country's sleep-walking into another recession," Wash continued. "And when we get there, Curtis, his cabinet and the bosses here will tell the population all is fine and dandy – and they'll blindly believe it."

Wash stopped himself, recognising his father's sour tone.

"Either that or we'll just blame it on another country again," Pete suggested, with a cursive glance through the window, out onto the roof of the neighbouring building. "That's what they did with the Chinese about the virus and then the Americans with global warming. But, as I said to my pal in Germany, that's just the way it is now. It's always someone else's fault."

Running his eyes over what had been assigned to him by the online diary, Wash rounded off their frank conversation, the interest in his father's rants and ravings increasing already.

"And yet for some reason we're spending billions of pounds on sending people to other planets and messing with established Atlas colonies," he complained. "It just doesn't add up."

"Just be careful, Wash," Pete warned. "You don't want to end up like Turner."

"No, I don't," he replied, thinking about the former political reporter. Nobody had seen or heard since he disappeared over a year ago.

6

The journey back to the beach felt like a twisted funeral march. The six colonists worked as hard as they could to shift the heavy Krichmar Tarp cases like coffins through an overgrown house of the dead. The jungle had taken on a new persona. As if it were the physical embodiment of some mysterious force waiting to reveal itself at any moment and slaughter them all. They were not alone on Proxima B after all.

Every crunched leaf caused heartbeats to skip. Each branch that swayed deceptively in the periphery of their vision shot ice through veins. Harper checked they were all still present, counting five other flustered faces. Like rabbits, they scurried away from an unknown predator for fear of their souls. The containers on their shoulders weighed nothing compared to the burden on their minds. The last twenty minutes were the worst of all as the setting sun stole all visibility. The small group were guided only by the nearby crashing of waves. It felt as if they were marching headlong into the gates of oblivion.

At last, they found themselves on the sand again

and saw the other survivors had managed to get a fire going. But in Harper's cynical mind she realised there was nothing to suggest they were any safer here.

"Don't tell anyone about what we found," she said quietly as they approached the rest of the group. Nobody disagreed. Good. Harper couldn't be bothered to quell mass hysteria again.

Those who had stayed on the beach were glad to have everyone back and even happier that shelter had been found. The Krichmar Tarps were dumped by the other containers and were set for erection in the morning, when the light was on their side. Sleeping bags and blankets had been laid out.

"He give you any trouble?" Harper asked Lucas, pointing to Zack, who was sat by himself smoking a cigarette a few metres away.

"Nope. He's just kept to himself," he replied, handing the plasma knife back to her.

"Keep it," she said, walking past him. She took a step back. "Actually, have this too." Harper handed him her gun. "I'll get another one for myself, don't worry."

"Why?"

"Just... keep them."

Some food from the supplies was being cooked over the open flame. It didn't smell great, but helped Harper continue to rid her nose of the memory of burning flesh from the crash.

Sam was the first one to strike up conversation as they sat in a circle around the flames.

"How do we decide who makes all the big decisions?" he asked to the group. Harper rolled her eyes again.

"Like what?" Lisa asked.

"You know, like who's in charge and stuff. Don't we need to pick a prime minister or something?" A few chuckles rippled around the fire. "What? I'm serious."

"I think we need to get out of this mess before we think about anything like that," said Ben. "Until then, my assumption is we follow protocol and let Harper take charge." He looked to her for reassurance on that matter. She replied with a silent nod. Not that she wanted to lead this band of colonial hopefuls, but she knew she was their best chance of staying alive – and hers too.

"But when we do get to our designated land, we'll have elections right?" Sam continued. "You know, do a democracy like we had back home."

"Actually… it's not a democracy," James tentatively interjected. All eyes turned toward him, confused.

"What?" Sam blurted. "What are you talking about? Of course it is."

"Yeah, even I know that," Shermeen snarked. James stuttered a little before clarifying.

"The British government is both a constitutional monarchy and a representative democracy. The people vote for elected officials who make the decisions, rather than the whole country voting on everything. That would be a true democracy."

There was a long and uncomfortable pause.

"I don't know what that means, mate." Sam said. Harper wasn't surprised.

After they finished their reconstituted beef, she left the main group with a sigh, her mind exhausted by small-talk. Perching on the edge of the rock that overhung the beach, Harper dangled her legs over the rim. She felt an enormous sense of freedom in removing her restrictive jumpsuit, leaving just a uniformed camisole and shorts underneath. Unclipping her bra from below the shirt's material and untying the knot in her hair she felt a little refreshed. From this position, Harper could hear the calm rustle of the waves tickling the sand below her. But all she could see of the ocean was the alien moon's luminous reflection off to her left. This planet's pale satellite hung low in the sky and, in its current cycle, gave off the appearance of a crescent boat, the upper portion obscured by its position in the Proxima solar system. Her mud-stained shoulder-length blonde hair was carried westward by whispers of wind.

Looking back at the group gathered silently around the fire, Harper counted seventeen Concord survivors. Since they got back, nobody had shown any signs of panic. Harper was grateful for that at least. Right now, she didn't have the solution to their dilemma and had no idea which of their many problems was her biggest concern.

Two thousand miles was more than enough distance from the specified drop zone to make the initial surveys completely useless. Using the portable harddrive, Harper had executed another frantic search through the Concord's databanks after they'd got back, but could not find any accurate information on this region of the planet.

It was entirely possible that they would have to scout more of the jungle on foot to find somewhere for them to stay, and simply pray that they could last long enough until another colonial ship arrived. But there were now too many unknowns about what, or who, already lived inland. Even then, there could be no guaranteeing that they could make contact with subsequent ships. That is, if they did not suffer the same fate as the Concord. Harper had no idea what to believe in terms of further colonisation at this point, considering captain Case's kamikaze plan.

Cutting across her thoughts at irregular intervals was the burning anger at the back of Harper's mind. She shouldn't even *be* here. If she had the chance to strand of those responsible on Proxima B, she'd take it in a heartbeat.

"Mind if I sit here too?" James asked, catching Harper off-guard. "I'm not sure the group is interested in anything I've got to say."

"Sure," Harper grunted.

"I guess, you're not one for large groups then?" James added, sitting down. Harper said nothing. "Me neither."

A few painful seconds went by as James fidgeted. Harper found that irritating. Eventually, he spoke again.

"How are you holding up?"

Another gentle breeze blew wisps of blonde hair across her face. She brushed them aside without grace.

"I'm fine." She threw a quick glance at the rest of the group, deflecting the focus away from herself. "Are they okay?"

She didn't really care what the answer was.

"I think most of them are still in shock. Nobody has said very much," James said cautiously, having seen the look on Harper's face. "They're probably just grateful to be alive. Aside from those who lost loved ones, they're feeling pretty lucky to have escaped without any serious injuries. None of them have talked about what to do next, either."

"We'll just have to take each day as it comes." Harper despised platitudes but she knew they were the hallmarks of most leaders. Another awkward silence settled between them. Harper really hated being subjected to small-talk.

"I just wanted to thank you for what you did today," James said artlessly. "I don't know if I would have been brave enough to risk my life like that." He'd tried to stop his eyes drifting towards her cleavage but she noticed him accidentally looking through the thin material. It didn't bother Harper; she was used to being ogled in her line of work. No, Harper was more perturbed about how to take James' compliment – she'd never been very good at that.

"Just doing my job," she said eventually, still not really sure what it was anymore. Nothing she had done on Earth was preparation for this.

Fiddling with a curl on the back of his head, James continued.

"Is it okay if I ask you something?"

"...Sure," Harper said once again.

"When I found you on the rock this afternoon... You looked as if you were in a completely different place. Like you were a million miles away."

"I could have died when I was thrown out of that ship today," Harper cut him off. "What did you think I was going to look like?"

"You've more than proved yourself with what you did with the ship – so I'm not criticising. Far from it. I just thought it was amazing that you were able to get over the initial shock of the crash quickly enough to take charge and get what you needed from the cockpit. As I said, I couldn't imagine being that brave..." James paused and looked at Harper again. "I'm going to have to learn new skills if I'm going to survive on this planet. I guess I just want to know what was going through your head at that point."

Harper sighed again.

"Let's just say... I've not had the best of luck up to this point, pal" she said after a pause. "That's all I was thinking about."

"How do you mean?" James asked, scratching around the cut on his nose.

"I'd rather not talk about it." Harper could tell James was trying to reach out to her. Already she was laying bricks in her mind, resisting him with a mental wall. And yet she knew the uncertainty of what would happen in the coming weeks and months would be easier if she befriended her fellow survivors. That inner-voice was quickly suppressed. The bricks kept piling up. The more she was invested in someone or something, the more she had to lose. Harper had become well-practiced in shutting people out ever since Brixton. It came naturally these days.

"I didn't mean to pry, I'm sorry," James said, appearing ashamed.

"It's okay," Harper lied.

"Do you want me to head back to the--"

"No. Stay." Hushing her tone, she added: "We need to talk about the writing." Harper hesitated at first but eventually unzipped a pocket on the front of her overalls beside her and pulled out a metal flask. Unscrewing the top, she took a swig and, without looking at James, handed it sideways to him.

"Oh," James said as he considered the container. He took it. "Yes... I suppose we do."

Waiting for him to finish his sip, Harper began quizzing him.

"You said you'd seen it before?"

"I can't be completely certain, I'm afraid." He passed the drink back to its owner. "I just recognise it that's all."

"Where do you think you saw it?"

"On Earth, that's for sure. But I've seen my fair share of ancient writing in my time. It's hard to remember them all."

"Ancient?"

"Yes, I used to be an ancient history lecturer. Specialised in economics, but I read around the subject a lot." Harper stopped mid-gulp and raised her eyebrows. "I know it's not what you'd expect from a wannabe colonial but there's plenty an ancient history professor can bring to the table."

"Like how to study us hundreds of years after we've died?" Harper asked partially in jest, half out of cruelty.

"Well, possibly," James took it in his stride. "My teaching days are a few years behind me now, though."

"A few *years* behind you? How old are you?"

"Thirty-five."

"You're looking good for it," Harper said, wiping her mouth and passing the container to James again. "I assumed we were a similar age. Clearly you're a fair bit older."

"I get that a lot. I've got a baby face, apparently."

"So what did you do after lecturing?"

"After the university cut my department I went for a top brass job with Jackson Ball Accounting and got it."

"How did you manage that?"

"Well, transferable skills of studying ancient economics are more useful than you'd believe. I worked for JBA for about two years and it just drove home to me how much of our country's wealth and power is in the hands of the billionaires. They don't care about anyone other than themselves and just let the country go down the pan. But they've got most of the population brainwashed into thinking that we're thriving on our own because we shut ourselves off from the outside world." James took a breath to calm himself down. Harper was confused.

"Why did you sign up to the colonial programme, then? This venture has turned that one percent of yours into public heroes."

"In the end, I just saw this programme as the closest thing to a way out as I was going to get. They don't let you emigrate abroad anymore, do they? I'm well aware I'm helping glorify them and I know it won't stop them exploiting people, either. But at least if I'm here, I won't have to see it for myself and I thought maybe I could help create a better world. So I signed up to provide administrative and fiscal support," he added with rehearsed irony. "Not too sure how useful that will be since the crash..."

"If you figure out what that writing in the jungle means you'll have been more useful than anyone else so far."

"I'd need to go back there," James said timidly.

"Are you sure that's a good idea?"

"The way I see it, there are a few possibilities," he explained. "Either that message is a friendly communication between indigenous groups or perhaps has some religious or ritualistic significance. Or, it could act as a warning to stay away from that region of the jungle. If that's the case then it would be good to know more details. Alternatively, the markings are territorial; put there by an aggressive faction, eager to protect its borders. Again, we need to know more about them if that's the case. If you want me to translate it, I need to see it again."

"I guess you're right," Harper realised. "We should get everything set up first thing tomorrow before we think about heading out again, though."

James nodded as the two of them noticed Zack skimming stones on the water below. After a short pause, he spoke up.

"You never said why you signed up for this trip," he said.

Harper's chest tightened.

"I wasn't given a great deal of choice in the matter," she snapped, staring out to sea. "It was my job."

"Surely this sort of thing was done on a voluntary basis?"

"That was true in the most part. But not for me."

"Why not?"

"Look, I really don't want to talk about it."

Harper realised this exchange of personal information had been one-side so far. James had told her all about himself and was probably their only hope for this writing. That made her feel guilty.

"I used to be part of SO19 – the police's specialist firearms unit. Until things went a little... pear-shaped. Long story short, the ungraceful manner of my departure landed me with a non-negotiable position on the colonial advanced party."

"That sucks," James said, having a drink. He looked up for a second, pensive. "Are there many overlaps between special ops and running a colony?"

"Not really," Harper moaned, sensing James had

73

accidentally stumbled across the same realisation she had. She was not ready for this. Not at all.

After a few poignant moments, James produced a half-smile.

"At least you've got a chance to start a new life out here. If what happened on Earth was as... pear-shaped... as you say."

Harper leaned her head towards James, eyes rolling.

"It's nice of you to try and cheer me up, really it is," she said, forcing the words out. "But if you don't mind, I'd like to continue being a melancholy little bitch about the whole thing. If that's okay?"

James smiled as he handed the whisky flask back to its owner.

"As long as you keep the rest of us alive, you can be as pissed off as you like."

*

By the end of their first full day, Harper and her fellow survivors had fashioned a rudimentary base of operations further along the beach from the crash site. Thankfully, the three Krichmar Tarps were in working condition. It had allowed them to create living quarters for the men and women, and one to store food, water and medicine. Enough for several months at least. Once they experienced how debilitating the heat was in the fierce midday sun, they were even more grateful for shelter.

The short-term plan had always been to begin colonial life living out of these 'Tarps' – effectively temporary plastic huts – while more permanent structures were slowly, but surely, constructed. Nobody had yet been brave enough to breach the subject of their long-term presence on this planet. The functionality of the Tarps had allowed the survivors to distract themselves with the menial task of making themselves at home, for now.

With help from the diminutive yet surprisingly resourceful Zoey, erecting the tents had proved a helpful team-building exercise. She was much shorter than the rest of the group and her short brown pigtails added to a deceptive image of naivety.

"The hardening process of the canvas material is powered by the solar cells on the spines." Zoey had addressed everyone as they stood around what, at first, looked more like a giant parachute. A Welsh accent ensured her vowels continued to get a disproportionately large share of tongue-time. "So, we need to lay them all out in a way which allows for maximum coverage. Make sure none of the material is covering a solar cell. After several hours charging in this sunlight they should be ready to harden."

"How the hell do you know all of this?" Zack asked as they began pulling the spines up on the first structure. "You're just a kid."

"I'm twenty-four actually, but nice try," she retorted calmly. Zoey had not even lifted her eyes from the now-charged spines. "And as for the Krichmars, I studied them for my engineering dissertation and I worked with them on planning expeditions with Hammond Mechanical Engineering. Thankfully, this model is both more robust and in better shape than the crap I had to work with. Either way, I know more about these things than you do."

Zack had no answer. This Zoey girl had spunk; Harper liked that. She was more than happy to follow her direction on the Krichmars too. They might as well be magic tents, as far as she was concerned.

"If you worked for HME, why pack all that in and come out here?" Ben had sounded very interested.

"They made the choice for me. The company was merged with the government's existing top engineering firm and my department was disbanded. Someone with my skills was wasted on a country that doesn't believe in investing in its infrastructure."

Once all the supporting spines had been attached to the central beam and the resident engineer had adjusted some controls on the internal panel, the group stood back and watched the wonder of Krichmar science.

Slowly but surely, the canvas, which had been rippling in the wind, began to lose its flimsy appearance and took on a sturdier texture, like moulded slate. At first, the exterior of the Tarp adopted a shiny plastic layer before settling on what looked like a steadfast rock foundation. The whole process was accompanied by a thick and crunching crackle as the canvas turned to hard fibreglass in a matter of seconds.

"Ladies and gentlemen, we have ourselves somewhere to live," Zoey announced. Finally some progress.

"Before we start making our beds," Harper added, "Can we load the medical supplies and food stuffs into the third tent? Let's get a bit of a system going."

Everybody nodded and started gathering the crates.

"Ben, can you help me with the water purifying unit?" Harper asked.

"Certainly," he replied with well-spoken tones.

Once they had completed that task, Ben ushered

her away from the hubbub of the main group and into the first line of densely packed trees. The sun had already begun its descent leaving an intense crimson glare in the sky.

"Can I have a word with you?" Ben asked.

"Sure," Harper replied, a little apprehensive.

Staring sheepishly at his sand-caked boots, he began.

"I just wanted to apologise for my behaviour when we first arrived here yesterday," he said. "I shouldn't have resorted to violence."

"Oh come on," Harper huffed. "You don't have to apologise to me."

"I feel terrible about how I acted towards Zack. It was very out of character for me," Ben shrugged his broad shoulders. "I know he's a self-proclaimed asshole but wasn't the whole point of an expedition like this to give everybody a second chance? I could certainly do with one. So why shouldn't he?"

The ruggedness of Ben's face was much more obvious from this angle. The nose was a little crooked, as if it had once been broken and left to its imperfections. His firm cheeks were flustered from the heavy lifting. A little distracted, Harper realised he had noticed her staring.

"Maybe you should go and tell him that yourself?" she said.

There was a moment of reflection on Ben's face. It quickly turned to one of amusement.

"No, I'm good thanks! I wouldn't want to feed what appears to already be a sizeable ego."

"Good point."

They laughed together. Harper couldn't remember the last time she'd done that.

Another pause.

"What are we going to do about that writing out there?" Ben asked.

"I don't know yet. Let's just get everything set up here first."

"And you still don't think we should tell the others about it?"

"Definitely not."

"What's the plan past that?"

"I haven't figured it out yet."

The pair returned to the beach and saw the large bulk of Amos attempting to drag a metal crate through the sand.

"Let me help you, Amos," Ben said as he rushed over.

"Thanks," the large man said with a cough.

"Everything going okay?" Ben asked as he and Harper walked alongside.

"Yes, I think so," Amos replied with a glance at Zack. He had uttered very little since the crash. He was an unassuming sort of fellow who seemed quietly bent on silently proving himself to as many people as possible.

"Don't worry about Zack," Ben said reassuringly. "We've got our eye on him." Amos simply nodded and kept his head down, keen to get as many of the supplies in some sort of order as possible.

Lynne and her daughter Shermeen had been less helpful. Lynne's husband had perished in the crash and the woman was holding it together as well as she could. No doubt hoping to help her daughter stay strong, she wasn't doing a very good job. She approached Harper following her return to the camp.

"What were you two talking about?" she asked.

Harper made sure she did not hesitate.

"Oh, nothing," she said with a forced smile. "Just discussing our progress."

Lynne did not look convinced.

"There's nothing out there we need to worry about is there?"

"No. Nothing at all," Harper continued, mildly annoyed. If this woman was so concerned about that, why did she bring her bloody daughter to this planet.

"What if there are dangerous animals in the jungle?" she asked with a look towards Shermeen. The young girl rolled her multi-coloured eyes.

"All initial orbital surveys of this planet indicated that any natural life here is docile, and more importantly, edible too." Harper replied.

That was true for the drop zone at least. Harper's lies were adding up fast. There was no way she could be certain about their current location. Captain Case's actions still plagued her mind.

Lynne was convinced enough for now, and went back to her things, Shermeen muttering by her side.

At last, a semi-functional camp was starting to take shape. It hardly had the home comforts of a kitted out colonial village, but it would do for now.

✳

Harper woke up to the sound of shouting the next morning.

"Come quick!" came the worried plea from Lynne at the doorway.

Harper leapt from her bed and jumped through the Tarp's front door. Outside was a collection of shocked faces staring out to sea.

"What is it?" she asked in a panic.

"It's gone," James said pointing towards the water.

Roughly thirty metres out was a patch of darker colour with a sprinkling of black protrusions poking out from it.

"What is?"

"The third Tarp," Ben said.

"How di--". It dawned on her. "The supplies!"

7

A heady burst of brine filled Harper's mouth, water stinging her eyes and the fresh wounds on her palms. She propelled herself through the warm water conscious that the Tarp was already a good hundred metres out to sea. Two fellow survivors had dove in behind her. Harper wasn't sure who. Her focus was entirely on the clinking of metal up ahead, competing with the groaning of the waves. Without the food and medicine inside, they'd be screwed.

Harper generated ten seconds of hard slog under the water, full power to her shoulders and legs as she attempted to ride each wave. They were more powerful than expected, forcing her up earlier than she wanted.

Harper's mind was clear, the goal set in stone. To her, this came more naturally than leading the group. Reintroducing her body to its comfort zone, she clawed further away from the beach like a torpedo.

The Tarp and its unwilling cargo went missing from her immediate horizon.

Harper garbled a curse word through a mouthful of water. She stopped swimming and bobbed along with the undulation. Panic set in. She twisted and turned frantically to get a better view, noticing it was Lisa and Ben who had followed.

The waves were steeper this far out and it was difficult for Harper to see much farther than ten metres in front. She noticed the tip of a rock five metres to her left and made a mad push for it. Her nails and the skin on her fingertips tore against the crusty surface as she fought against the undertow. It tugged on her like a starved animal intent on dragging her down to its lair. All of Harper's remaining energy was required to hoist herself out of the water and onto the protruding outpost.

"Where have you gone?" she begged.

All she could see was an enraged dark grey sea. The Tarp had disappeared.

✻

"They must have been caught in the canvas," said James. "The supplies were probably dragged down with it. There was nothing you could have done."

Harper did not appreciate excuses.

"You got further than I did," James added. "I couldn't make it past the first few metres. I had to turn back."

Harper's fists burned under the strain. She had given the beach a damn good beating when she had got back to dry land. She didn't care that everybody had watched her thrashing about, half-naked. It was too much for her. This had tipped her over the edge. Having to come here, nearly dying in the crash, finding out the planet was inhabited after all and now losing most of their food. Last night that Tarp had supplies in to last them months. What they had left would stretch no more than a few weeks at most. All the while, those pricks who had stitched Harper up would be getting fat from their high-society life back on Earth.

"How could it wash out if it was fully operational?" Sam asked. "I thought the hardening process sent metal spikes into the ground?"

Lisa joined in: "Maybe it *wasn't* working?"

"They were all fine yesterday," Zoey clarified.

Zack sparked up straight away. "Yeah and how do we know that's true?"

"Because I checked all of them."

"So what? Doesn't mean you did it properly."

"What are you accusing me of?" Zoey squared up to him. After a glance at Harper, who sat in a heap at the water's edge, Lisa was ready to intervene instead.

"Not having a clue what you're doing, that's what!" Zack ploughed on.

"Hey!" Zoey shouted. Lisa struggled but managed to haul the short woman away.

"Yeah, back off," Ben said. "Zoey knows what she's doing."

"Thanks Ben," Zoey said, standing down. She stared at him a few seconds longer. Furrowing her brow she continued. "You know what's more likely?"

"What?" Zack asked.

"Somebody switched it off."

Nobody spoke for a moment. Zoey's suggestion turning cogs in Harper's mind.

"Why would somebody do that?" Lynne had grown increasingly panicked throughout the whole conversation, her long brown hair still a mess. As per usual, she was close to Shermeen.

Harper watched Lisa open her mouth and close it again. The two women had come to the same conclusion. She found her feet and joined the rest of the group, red faced.

"What do we do now?" Even Amos was speaking now, coughing, of course.

"Look, we can't panic," Harper said, fully aware of the irony. Only seconds ago she had completely lost her temper.

"You don't think that writing in the jungle had anything to do with this, do you?" asked Sam.

Harper clenched her fists. She could feel her chest tighten. *Sam, you FUCKING idiot.*

Lisa nudged him in the ribs, before Harper could get in his face.

The survivors went up an octave, their panic reaching fever pitch. It was hard to discern who was saying what.

"What writing?"

"What is he talking about?"

"How could there be writing in the jungle?" yelled Zack.

"I thought we were the only ones here."

It was hard to tell who was saying what as all the voices scrambled on top of each other.

Harper had to tell them. It was damage limitation at this point.

"Let me explain," she shrieked, letting anger seep through again. Once everyone was quiet she came down a decibel. "On our first day here, when myself, Ben, James, Amos, Lisa and Sam" – she gave him a pointed stare as she said his name – "retrieved the Tarps from the jungle, we found something. It looked as if something or someone had written in the ground."

Harper was hit by a wall of silence. Feeling stupid for having to explain herself to these people, she kept her eyes focussed on the rock behind them. The group continued to process this new information without a word until Zack spoke up.

"So you think there's some kind of intelligent life here on this planet or something?" he asked.

"It's possible, yes," Harper replied.

"Then why the fuck didn't you tell us all the second you got back from the jungle?" He was angry and it looked as if this time he had people on his side. "Stupid woman," he added.

"I didn't think it would be a good idea to tell everybody," Harper dug in deep.

"Why the hell not?" Zack's eyes began to swell, his scruffy appearance emphasising the whites. Several other survivors joined in his protests. "What else haven't you told us?!"

Harper and James exchanged a nervous look.

Ben's assertive voice took over. The exhaustion of the swim seeped between each sentence, his breathing heavy.

"Can't you see? The way you're all acting right now is exactly why Harper chose to keep it a secret."

"Yeah, I agree," said Lisa. "If you want to know about everything that happens to us you can't panic at the first sign of trouble."

Nobody had a response. Not even Zack.

"Let's get some water for these guys," Zoey said. "They're exhausted from the swim."

James was nearest the crate which contained the group's fresh supply, frantically collected from the assortment of bottles found in the crash. He raced along the sand to find one for Harper, Ben and Lisa. He returned a few seconds later empty-handed.

"It's all gone," he said.

"What?!" shrieked Lynne.

"The bottles, the crate they were in. They're not there anymore."

All eyes honed in on Zack.

"Are you serious?" he protested. "Why would I take all of that water for myself?"

"You seemed pretty keen on it when we first got here," Ben pointed out.

"Was it still here before the Tarp...," Harper pointed in the direction of the sea, deliberately not finishing the question. To say it out loud was to accept the defeat.

"Yes," Amos said. "I was having a drink when I noticed it on the water."

"Yeah and I spent the whole time on the beach with the rest of you looking for any leftover supplies," Zack said indignantly.

"He's telling the truth," Zoey confessed sheepishly. "He was with us the whole time."

"See?"

"Maybe the jungle people took the water?" Sam said twiddling the back of his ginger mop. "Perhaps they de-activated the Tarp closest to the water and dragged it in because they knew we'd be distracted?"

"He could be right," Ben said to Harper.

"We should go out there and get it back from those dickheads," Sam suggested.

"Whoa," Harper cautioned immediately. "Nobody's starting a fight, okay? We have no idea who or what is out there." She paused for a moment. "But, we do need to get better intel on the jungle. If we want to survive long enough to move to our designated land, we will have to travel that way. I'm not giving that the go-ahead until I'm confident we can do it safely." Harper knew there was a lot more ground to scout before they could think about moving. It really was time they went further into the jungle. "When me, Ben, Lisa have got our strength back, we'll head out again."

☆

Harper spent the rest of the morning combing the waterline in the hope that some food or medicine might miraculously crawl out of the depths. The sea was calm now, like a sheet of bubbled glass. That made it even harder to take. If the Tarp had washed out now, Harper would have stood a much better chance of retrieving more supplies. It was almost as if those who sent her here were toying with her from afar, taking pleasure from her struggle. Harper felt her resolve harden, reinforced by steel. She wasn't going to starve here. She had to get off this planet any way she could and make those bastards pay. That all seemed like a pipe-dream at this point though, with a new, more immediate, enemy to concern herself with, armed only with an underfed bunch of hopeless colonists.

Harper thought back to the swim, how it had narrowed her focus. She only had one thing on her mind, not the egos of those around her or their questionable hopes for a new life on this planet. For once, she had managed to keep all that out of her head. Harper realised she had almost enjoyed the freedom of that moment. Maybe a fight was what she needed to feel more at ease here. It had been a while.

She pulled a stone out of the sand and threw it out over the rigid reflection in front of her, hoping it would crack and splinter the sea into a thousand pieces.

An hour later, it was time to head out. Neither Amos nor Sam were prepared to venture back into the unknown but Ben, Lisa and James signed up for a second trip. Surprisingly, Zack volunteered to come along.

"How else will I convince you all I'm not a selfish bastard after all?" he said.

Before they left, Harper handed out some more plasma-knives to those on the beach who felt they could handle them. She had been lucky enough to find some of her combat gear now that the fuselage had cooled. It meant she could leave one of her guns with Lucas and still take two into the jungle. The handful of remaining plasma-knives were packed into her rucksack too.

To Sam and Amos she gave a flare.

"If something happens, set this off and we'll come back to help," were her instructions.

It took less time to find the clearing with the writing on their second visit, although this trip was a lot more cautious than before. Harper, as usual, led the line, this time with one hand on her side-arm the whole way. The other, while primarily pulling foliage out of her face, was more than ready to reach for the plasma-knife on her belt. It would only take one unexpected movement nearby for her to pull it from her waist and activate the heat-setting on the blade. The second gun was strapped to her ankle.

"Can you see any tracks in the dirt?" Ben had asked

Harper when they were half-way there.

"None at all," she said, omitting her complete lack of tracking experience.

James and Zack were the only ones interested in the writing when they arrived at the clearing. The former lecturer spent some more time on his knees examining the curvature of certain shapes.

"You guys weren't kidding then," Zack said through his beard, which dripped with sweat. "I thought Sam was making it up."

"No, he wasn't," said Harper as she scanned the mass of trees ahead of them.

"I can't believe you're wasting your time with it," Zack sniggered. James ignored him.

"Where do we go from here?" Lisa asked.

"I think we can safely assume there's nobody living anywhere near our section of the coast," Harper explained. "We'd have seen or heard something by now. They must be on the other side of the mountains if they are anywhere nearby." Harper pointed in front of her, in line with the route they had taken from the beach, and to the right with her other hand.

"We could always split up," Ben suggested.

"You sure that's safe?" Harper asked.

"We'll cover more ground that way," he countered.

"We might be outnumbering ourselves, though," Lisa pointed out.

"We've got enough weapons to stay safe, I think," Zack said.

"He's right," Ben said. "If you give me your second gun we've got one for each group."

Harper wasn't completely confident but felt she was already out-voted if Ben and Zack were agreeing on a course of action. That was one less thing to concern herself with. The pair were right too, they could get the job done quicker in two teams. They needed more information to work with, and fast. Hesitantly, Harper unclipped the pistol from her ankle and handed it over.

"I'll take Zack and go this way," Ben said, pointing away from the rock-face.

"Will you two be okay?" Harper was struck by how much she cared about the answer.

"We'll be fine," Ben replied.

Harper felt herself appreciating his confidence. Maybe this group wasn't as useless as she had thought.

"If you say so," she said. "Keep going that way for an hour and if you don't find anything we'll meet back here, okay? If you do, gather what information you can but return here anyway. We want to retain strength in numbers before trying anything risky."

"Understood."

"Lisa, you come with me. James who are you going with?"

"I think I'll stay here," he said, eyes locked on the writing, scratching the cut on the bridge of his nose. His four companions exchanged a confused look. None of them said anything. He spoke again. "I know you're going to protest but if we want to understand what we're up against here, I need all the time I can get with this writing. If I can work out what sort of tool is responsible for the engraving and what sort of strokes have been used, I might get a better idea of what level of civilisation put it here. Better still, I might even find a way of communicating with them if we do make contact."

"How are you going to work all that out from a picture?" Zack asked, scoffing again. "Come on mate, pull your weight."

"Just trust him. He knows his stuff," Harper said coolly. "We should get moving. See you back here in two hours."

*

"I'm glad the man with the beard went into the jungle with everybody else," Shermeen said.

Amos was sat by himself amongst the array of containers, holding another bag. He still hadn't found what he was looking for. Not much had been retrieved from the missing Tarp and his cough was getting worse.

"Why's that?" He asked, quietly, after catching his breath. Amos looked around for the girl's mother and saw her hanging clothes out to dry on a makeshift washing line further down the beach.

"Well, he's not very nice," she said as she sat down next to him.

"I guess," Amos said as he continued to rummage through another bag.

"You guess? He's horrible," the girl said angrily. "And he hates people like you, Amos."

"Yeah," he said, for lack of a better response. He was much more focussed on the search. Shermeen noticed the crumpled expression on his face.

"What's wrong?" she asked.

"Nothing."

She didn't buy it.

"Are you sure?"

"Yep." He coughed again.

"What are you looking for?"

Amos put the bag down and sighed.

"Medicine... But... please don't tell anyone."

"Why? Are you ill?"

"I have asthma," he explained, quietly.

"Why don't you want everybody else to know that?"

"I just don't want them to know, okay? I don't want to be a... burden. I had too much of that back on Earth."

"They're going to find out soon enough with that cough of yours."

Amos didn't know what to say. He spluttered again, feeling his throat constrict.

"See?" Shermeen said, triumphantly.

"Okay. Maybe you're right," Amos put another bag down.

"You're after an inhaler right?"

"Yeah," Amos' eyes lit up. He hadn't expected anyone to know what he needed.

"I think I have some spares in my stuff."

"Do you have asthma too?"

"No. My dad did," said Shermeen. "He died in the crash."

"Oh," Amos' face dropped. "I'm sorry..." He noticed the fairly unmoved look on Shermeen's face. "Are you okay? You don't seem that upset?"

"Yeah," the girl said matter-of-factly. "I didn't really know him that well, I guess."

Amos didn't want to pry any further.

"Are you sure your mum is happy for you to give the inhalers to me?" he asked, pointing in Lynne's direction.

"I don't care what she thinks," Shermeen scowled. "They belonged to my dad and he doesn't need them anymore." She stood up and trudged over to her belongings.

"Well… thank you," Amos called timidly after her.

✭

The jungle had become thicker after the clearing, more claustrophobic, damper. Warm and moist greenery slopped against Harper and Lisa's shoulders. The air was humid like a spongy mass around them. It was infested with a wonderful assortment of insects whizzing past or crawling on branches. Some looked similar to ones they knew; ants, caterpillars, flies and the like. Others still were completely unrecognisable. Thankfully none of them wanted to bite.

The two women were much quicker now that they didn't have to worry about the others. They were much lighter on their feet and soon realised each one was capable of looking after themselves. They'd been on the move for twenty minutes before they spoke.

"I wanted to ask you, Lisa," said Harper, surprising even herself that she was breaking the ice. "Were you in the army back on Earth?"

"I was. But not for very long," Lisa replied with amusement.

"What happened?"

"I got through basic training alright, became a corporal but I got out as soon as I passed phase two. It was a toxic environment there. How could you tell?"

"You can always spot someone who's had the training. I noticed you trying to track these jungle dwellers earlier. You're up before the crack of dawn, one of the last to turn in at night. Whenever you find yourself in new surroundings you check for possible blind-spots. All adds up... Plus, you've got a great figure." Lisa smiled.

"Thanks. Where did you train then?"

"Oh I wasn't in the army," Harper corrected her. "Police for me. Special forces yes, but not a full blown soldier like you."

"Well you could have fooled me," Lisa joked.

"It's a good thing you're here," Harper said. This was the real reason she had asked about Lisa's background. Mulling over tactics, she could feel the buzz coursing through her veins for the first time since Brixton. "We might need combat experience like yours," she continued. "Ben would be pretty good in a one-on-one fight but he won't understand field tactics the way we will."

"Are we building an army already?" Lisa sounded surprised, but wasn't against the idea. She made another precautionary visual sweep of the space behind her.

"Army is the wrong word," Harper clarified. "We've got a kid back there and a bunch of civilians. It's just fighting is something we're might have to consider... eventually," Harper said, still somewhat excitable, finding comfort in the familiarity of the situation. "If we do find hostile life out here, life which has already attacked us, we'll have to defend ourselves."

"I suppose you're right."

"Let's hope I'm not. Nobody back home thought about defence personnel when recruiting for this expedition. Just a handful of weapons, nothing more. We got lucky with you."

"As long as my being here counts for something, I'm all for it," Lisa said.

A branch snapped thirty yards to their left. The opposite direction to the path Ben and Zack had taken. The pair froze, their feet held firm by more than just mud.

"What was that?" Lisa whispered.

"It came from that way," Harper said pointing off into the mire. "Sounds like it can't be any more than one person. I'll continue forward ten paces and loop round to the left. You head that way and do the same when you've gone far enough. We'll pincer them."

"You got it."

Harper pushed on a few yards further into the overgrowth.

She'd been apart from Lisa barely thirty seconds when she heard the scream.

Her plan went out the window. She dashed back through the hanging branches, gun raised, plasma-knife activated, ready to strike.

Harper stopped in her tracks.

All she found was Lisa's boot.

"LISA!" Harper yelled.

Nothing. The jungle had gone quiet ominously quickly.

"LISA!"

8

"You've got to be kidding me!"

"For goodness' sake!"

"Piss off!"

It was stuffier than usual at St. Paul's station. With no trains running, the tight space lacked the breeze typically propelled by the carriages. Wash added a few expletives to the crowd's uproar. The sound they made carried along the underground platform with a menacing echo. A bearded brown man in a pink hi-visibility jacket and blue overalls stood on a box near a small windowed office, noticeably unperturbed by the pandemonium he had caused. He spoke into his megaphone a second time.

"I repeat. The line is flooded and is closed until further notice."

Wash sighed. He could not return to his flat in West Acton now and certainly wouldn't get to see Vicky tomorrow morning either. Those around him continued to quarrel among themselves, stranded again by the London Underground's latest leak. Years without renovation was taking its toll on the tracks, the tunnels and the trains themselves. Several questions ticked over in Wash's mind.

Anger polluted the air only a few moments longer before the mass of commuters began to trudge out of the station. Wash was the only one who stayed, pushing and squeezing past bodies like a fish swimming upstream. He had a moment of envy when he spotted a well-dressed businessman with electric blue irises. The upgraded version of his smartglasses.

"Excuse me," he said as he approached the station worker, whose name badge read 'Sanjay'. "Why is the line closed?"

"You heard what I said before," the man scowled. "It's flooded, mate."

"How long will it be closed for?"

"I don't know," he replied, his face like a smacked arse.

"Is there anyone who does know?"

"What's it to you?"

"Well, I travel on this line to and from work every day, so..."

"So do the rest of these people, man," Sanjay said with a gesture towards what remained of the horde. "You don't see any of them bothering me with questions. What's your problem?"

"I'm a journalist for the Daily Citizen."

"A what?"

"A journalist..." Still nothing. He tried a simpler approach. "I work for a newspaper."

Looking Wash up and down one more time, the man finally snapped. "I ain't talking to *you*. Get fucked, mate." With that he retreated to his little booth on the platform.

"And the same to you," Wash replied to the slammed door.

At street level, Wash nearly lost his balance leaving the station building, planting his foot on a loose paving slab. Recovering, he took in the surroundings of St. Paul's, illuminated by dim streetlights. Abandoned office buildings crowded the street on both sides, as empty now as they had been for years. Their broken glass was more intimidating at night than when he'd disembarked that morning. Across the road, a gruff-looking man was laying down his sleeping bag on a wilting flower-bed, built into the island of a pedestrian crossing.

Wash thought about turning down Cheapside to Holborn Station and the Piccadilly Line. Pete lived a short distance from Russell Square, just a minute train ride from Holborn. He often allowed Wash to crash on the Stewart family couch whenever the Central Line went down. It had happened a lot lately. Not wanting to overstay his welcome there, Wash had somewhere else in mind.

Getting into the hospital at this late hour was easier than expected. There was nobody at reception and the only member of staff Wash encountered was a janitor in the corridor outside his father's ward.

The journalist crept past the regular host of patients. Many of them had been there as long as Wash could remember. Right now, most were asleep. There was a handful who tossed and turned in pain, not paying the late visitor much attention.

Wash found his usual spot and sat down. He'd always been pleasantly surprised with the plushness of the leather-clad chair. The sponge practically provided a massage as he sank back. It was welcome after a long and tiring day. He looked down at his father, snoring unceremoniously. It was much easier to feel sympathy for the man when he was unconscious. Not having to fend off the customary bitterness, he had time to study the pale skin. The bones and veins were cast in sharper relief than was natural. Viewing the man in such a light, Wash softened a little. He dwelt once more on what Pete had relayed about the colonial programme. Clearly, it had run into some problems. Maybe it was right thing to be suspicious after all. The journalist contemplated telling his father. It was one of the reasons he had come here, as well as the relative comfort of the chair. But there was still the old man's health to consider. He was supposed to be reducing stress levels so discovering his scepticism might have grounds surely wouldn't help.

Were Wash to draw his father into the loop, it would consume him, drawing on every bit of energy left within his body. He'd be a mad wreck, stopping at nothing to find out the latest development. There was no way, Wash wanted that on his conscience.

He leaned back and closed his eyes.

"What are you doing here?"

Wash was startled into consciousness by the sound of someone's voice, already debating where he'd try to sleep next. His father stared with dreary eyes.

"I got stranded in the city," Wash explained quietly. "Tube is down. Thought I'd--"

"Shouldn't you be at work?"

Wash looked out the window. It was pitch black outside. The room was poorly lit by the glow of sporadic television screens.

"Why would I be at work right now?" Wash muttered under his breath.

"No wonder you're such a bad journalist if you're skiving off here," his father continued, unabated. Wash tried his best to zone out but the words cut like daggers. The concern he'd felt earlier bled away.

The young man rolled over uncomfortably and held a coat over his eyes. Even through the muffling he could still make out what his father was saying.

"You're just one of their spin doctors. You'll never make a difference."

☆

Wash felt like crap the next morning. He'd barely slept a wink. Once again, he was arriving at the office with harsh words ringing in his ears. His father was slowly losing his mind to illness but it what came out of his mouth was still hurtful. Even now, it was no different to the what Wash had been listening to his whole life.

Determined, he downed two cups of coffee before placing a call to London Transport to find out more about the line closure.

"Let's see who can't make a fucking difference," Wash murmured while waiting for the connection.

He got through to a rather arrogant press officer, who was twice as difficult as Sanjay had been the night before.

"There was a leakage on the Central Line and we were forced to close it off to the public," came the clearly rehearsed answer.

"Yes, I know that. I was there." Wash was doing his best not to sound impatient. "Can you tell me where the leak was and how likely it is to be a problem again?"

"No comment."

"What about how long until the line reopens?"

"I think you should already know that one. It's already back up and running."

How should I know? There had been no public announcement.

"The line's open again? Since when?"

"First thing this morning."

"The flooding just cleared up over night?"

"No comment."

"Thank you for your time, Mr Loughlin." Wash hung up and swore under his breath. He didn't have much to go on. After a few minutes of comparing notes from the conversations he'd had with London Transport staff, he figured there was probably a story there in the fact that there was no solid dialogue for the public. An hour later his story was filed. After that, Wash dived straight into the newsroom diary. The discouraging monotony took its rhythm from the humming of next door's air conditioning unit, chugging away on the roof that ran level with Wash's window.

Finally, it was broken by Steven Woods, the Citizen's head of news content, coming over to his part of the office to make eye contact with Wash.

"Wash, if you've got time, can we catch up before lunch?" he asked in an affable tone. Both Wash and Pete knew not to be fooled by him.

Deliberately taking his time to look up from what he was doing, Wash finally answered.

"Yeah I can chat in just a few minutes. Just need to send off some picture bookings and I'll come over."

"I'll be in meeting room three."

"He's probably sat there all morning either on the phone or checking his shares," Pete muttered under his breath, forcing a tactically timed snigger from Wash.

Huffing a little, he got to his feet.

Steve was already waiting for Wash in meeting room three, which was more of a glass booth in the corner. Sat at the small table inside he was scrolling through what looked suspiciously like stocks and shares information on his portable computer. Looking up from the device, Steve greeted Wash in the overly familiar way that he always found uncomfortable.

"Hello mate. How are you?"

"Not bad, thanks. Do you want me to close the door?" Wash asked.

"No, you're okay," Steve replied. "I just wanted to have a chat with you about a couple of stories you've written this week."

"I see."

"Did you enjoy writing the ONS stuff?" Wash hated it when Steve did this. We both know you're going to tell me off for these stories. Why not just come out with it, instead of pretending to be nice?

"Yes, it was good to re-connect with some of my old friends who work there now."

"That's nice." There was an awkward pause. The elephant in the room was running wild. "I just wanted to take this chance to give you some advice for the future." Steven raised his eyebrows and smiled, poorly veiling his slippery nature. "I'm sorry that none of them went in yesterday's edition, but sadly they just weren't what we were looking for."

Wash thought of his father's diatribe again, insisting he was *one of them*. Maybe he was right. Too many times Wash had sat back and accepted Steve's judgement on this sort of thing. Now that he was beginning to realise just how much his boss relied on people taking his word at face value. He probed a bit more.

"Can you tell me what was wrong with them?" Wash asked, already suspecting the answer, especially with the MP for Chippenham making the final decisions for them. He just wanted Steve to admit to it, or at least feel suitably guilty.

"Yvette just thought they fell wide of the mark," he said. "I think from now on your stories will have to steer away from this sort of thing."

"I'm happy to talk to Yvette about it, if she's unhappy with them."

"I think you need to be smart about this," Steve said squinting his eyes slightly, clearly believing his words were those of a wise prophet. Something in the man's face triggered thoughts of Turner in Wash's mind again. "I'm not sure what escalating this to the next level will accomplish."

"I don't want to escalate it, or formalise it at all," Wash explained. "But you're telling me she didn't like the stories I wrote... perhaps it would be better for me to speak to her in person–"

"Arguing with me is not going to do you any favours, Wash," Steve interrupted.

Wash worried that the balance of this conversation was slipping away from him. He thought of Turner once again, with that, the threat of vanishing completely.

"I'm not arguing with you," he said softly. "I

haven't disagreed with anything you've said. I'm just saying I'd like to speak to Yvette about it, that's all." He was beginning to suspect that the editor hadn't even laid an eye on his stories.

"I think you're just going to have to swallow this one," Steve instructed sharply. "And that's before we even get started on your attempts to do a smear job on London Transport."

"A smear job? Look, I told you I didn't want to argue with you, Steve," Wash cringed as his tone melted into one of pleading.

"If that was your thinking you wouldn't have filed those stories and then written that ridiculous piece on the trains. Both of those were pretty stupid things to do, if you ask me."

Hurt, Wash chose his words carefully and countered.

"I don't think that's fair," he said, coolly.

"There's no need to take that tone with me," Steve replied angrily, "I'm your boss. You'd do well to remember that."

Wash bit his tongue. Thinking again of Turner, he pursed his lips and tried to wrap things up as soon as possible.

"Was there anything else you wanted to talk about?" he asked.

Calming himself down with a swipe of his fringe and a scratch of his nose, Steve relented and allowed Wash to leave.

★

"Well that was a great big waste of my time," Wash said to Pete as he returned to his desk.

"What did he want?"

"Just thought he'd tear into me for those ONS stories, and this flooded line thing I wrote this morning." Wash fiddled with a few pens and notepads. "Honestly, I might as well write my stories in the sand or something. That way it'll be easier for them to just blow them away without a second thought. I suppose I should have seen it coming. There's only so much truth this madhouse can handle in one day."

"You're right there, mate."

"My dad is always banging on about this place. Says I'm letting him down by working here," Wash added.

"I'm sorry to hear that, Wash," Pete replied.

"Maybe I should just get back to some of the humdrum stuff for a few days."

After all, if there was nothing he could do to make a difference, he might as well just try and earn a living instead.

Wash returned to the news desk diary and scrolled back to the leads he'd been asked to chase. There were at least a dozen jobs in there before his meeting with Steve, including a request for an opinion piece on 'Why we should be so excited by the UK colonising other planets'. There had also been a note from Callum, the chief crime reporter, asking for help digging up info on the latest brutalised 'Eye Killer' victim. They had all disappeared from Wash's list.

"Oh for goodness sake... Don't they trust me with anything anymore?" he muttered under his breath.

"What's wrong?" Pete asked.

"They've cleared my list and sent me a bunch of fecking re-writes," he said. Waiting for Pete to lean across to have a look, he pointed them out. "Look at this B.S."

Two of the entries were requests to alter previously reported quotes from the prime minister in old articles, both on matters of foreign policy. The other job was to arbitrarily replace figures from last year's budget, reducing what had originally been reported.

"Goodness me," Pete said. If even he was taken aback, this was bad. "We've had an upturn in these recently, you know," supplemented the old man quietly. "It's quite concerning, even for me, when you think how much things have changed in my lifetime. They've spent years driving out our desire for the truth... and this must be their final solution."

Wash could only shake his head. The longer he spent at the Citizen, the easier it was to get sucked into the rabbit hole. There was no hope of any investigative work seeing the light of day and if he pushed it any further, he might end up like Turner.

"It's like, what's that book? 1984... but worse," Wash offered up. "Big Brother had to go out of his way to collect all the old newspaper copies after changes were made in the archives... but now that everything's digitised, we can just change it for absolutely everyone at the flick of a switch." He clicked his finger and flopped into the back of his chair with a sigh.

It was getting to the point where Wash was rapidly running out of options. Sooner or later, he'd be exactly what his father had accused him of: nothing more than a government spin doctor. The idea of proving him right only made Wash more frustrated.

His computer chimed.

Wash leaned forward, hoping for something that might cheer him up. It didn't.

"What is it?" Pete asked.

"Well, they've sent me a story, at least," Wash pointed out. "But look at it."

'Female vicar in suspected illegal lesbian relationship' was the subject line. Below the title were a few numbers he could ring, including one for the parishioner who had reported the rumour, as well as some stock copy detailing the recently passed Homosexual Offences Act. Pete put a hand on his young colleague's shoulder.

"I'm afraid you've drawn the short straw there, Wash."

Wash put his head in his hands and considered the consequences of taking on the story for a few moments.

"I could end up landing her in one of those correctional facilities, you know... where they chemically castrate you. I don't want the guilt of that," he said. "What's worse? The fact this country is trying to kill these people off or that they are re-writing history now?"

"I'm not sure," Pete replied.

It had been a long time since Wash had been to Newham. Not since his university days, he realised. His friends had an obsession with classic football grounds and had devised a pub crawl route past locations of old stadia. What was left of Upton Park in Newham had been one of them. Not as novel as a visit to Craven Cottage, which was now submerged below the swollen Thames river, but memorable enough. It was still difficult to imagine that the quiet neighbourhood he ambled through had been home to one of the capital's biggest football clubs merely seventy-five years ago. Most of the houses nearby had ugly wooden boarding over their windows and doors, as did a previously bustling market precinct, old storage crates and marquee hoardings were scattered in the forecourt. This district was slowly dying like many others in the capital, its saving grace merely that it was drier here away from the river.

"Any change?" a weak voice surprised Wash as he prepared to cross the road. Underneath a collection of flimsy sheets of cardboard was a weary man crouched against the wall of a vacated building. His clothes were ragged and his dark shoes were peppered with holes. Hair poked messily out from under the rim of a brown beanie hat like dark stalks of straw. Wash could barely guess his age through his scraggly beard and dirty skin, eyes drooping from extreme exhaustion. The young journalist dug into his pockets and mustered up a few coins.

"Here you go," Wash offered, dropping the money into the man's outstretched hand.

"Thank you," he replied, practically to the sky, before closing his eyes.

"If you want, I can get you some food from the shop?"

"That's too kind," the man stiffened up and began to try and get to his feet.

Wash crouched and placed a hand on his shoulder.

"It's no trouble, okay," Wash said softly. "I've got to speak to someone for about twenty minutes but when I come back I'll bring you a sandwich."

"Thank you."

"What's your name?"

"Noah."

"I'll be right back, Noah."

✳

"Honestly, it makes me feel sick," Mrs Richards cawed from the comfort of her brown sitting chair.

Wash took another sip of tea to avoid eye-contact. The old crow had been baiting him to agree with her slurs the whole time. He felt very out of place in this woman's house, almost like he was on trial. Virtually every surface of her small lounge was covered in Christian paraphernalia and it stank of fruity scented candles. Crosses of different shapes and sizes, some of paper and others metal, hung on the walls. Picture frames with fancy writing strewn across vistas of nature cluttered the mantelpiece and wooden coffee table. Wash had no idea where he could place his dainty cup and saucer without causing a tumble of religious dominoes.

"And you can quote me on that," Mrs Richards added, removing her thick-lensed glasses and attempting to clear them with the sleeve of her mauve knitted jumper. Her jaw-length greying bob of hair and saggy cheeks shook as her adorned wrinkly hands jingled back and forth. Realising she had covered the lenses in fluff, she tried again on her long grey pleated skirt.

"That won't be necessary, Mrs Richards," Wash said, shifting on the middle seat of a blue flowery sofa. "All I really need from you is a point in the right direction."

"I see," she said. "But if you ever need some words from the community, how the parishioners feel about Mrs Faversham, I'll be ready."

Wash didn't say anything, looking at his notepad.

He'd only jotted down a few words, one of which was 'BIGOT' in big capital letters.

"Okay, so you've told me Mrs Faversham has been seen at a suspected establishment for homosexual activity drinking with friends," he said, attempting to recap.

"It's more than just suspected, young man. That place is full of those sinners. Everybody knows about the Carnival. An evil place." Wash stifled a sigh, catching a glance of a framed cross-stitch on the wall. It read: *Therefore, as God's chosen people, holy and dearly loved, clothe yourselves with compassion, kindness, humility, gentleness and patience.* The journalist looked back to a frothing Mrs. Richards, fully aware of the irony.

"Is there anything else you can tell me?" he asked.

"Well, I just think it's such a shame for her husband," she replied.

"Why's that?"

"The poor chap works for the government. It's not fair on someone in his position to have such a sexually immoral woman for a wife. No wonder his name has been bandied about as well."

"How do you mean?"

"The Bakers around the corner have started saying Mr Faversham has been attending the same sinful places too. But I don't believe that for a moment. How could he be like her? He's a government official, for crying out loud. He's clearly suffering for the sins of his wife. Such a shame."

Wash found a small space between a glass cross and a statuette of an eagle straddling a Bible to place his drink. He got to his feet as he spoke.

"Okay, thank you, Mrs Richards," he said. "You've

been really helpful," he lied.

"Are you really sure there's nothing else I can help you with?"

"Very," Wash answered as he put his coat back on and returned to the front door. "Thank you for the tea, I'll see myself out."

Reaching for the handle, he was startled by a muffled cry of pain coming from the street. He and Mrs. Richards exchanged a look before Wash snatched at the door and walked down the first few steps.

Over the road he could see a yellow and blue van pulled up on the curb with its back doors open, 'PO-LICE' emblazoned on the side. Two angry officers were standing over something on the pavement. One of them swung a boot.

"Move, you sack of shite," came a rasping voice. His colleague reached down and recoiled.

"Bloody hell, he stinks."

Noah did his best to resist but could not over-power the two policemen. Wash burned with anger and raced down two more of Mrs. Richards' steps, ready to call out. He stopped short, realising there was nothing to be done without getting himself arrested. Wash clenched his fists, remembering his father's scathing words. *You're supposed to make the world a better place.* Then he imagined Turner being bundled into the back of a van, never to be seen again.

Mrs Richards appeared her door, which Wash had left open.

"Ah good," she said smugly. Wash turned back to face her, shocked. "I've been asking them to take him away for weeks. Makes it look like we live in a third-world country, or something."

He remembered the Bible verse she had cross-stitched by hand.

"So much for God's compassion," Wash muttered under his breath as he reached the pavement again. By now it was far too late to help Noah. The police officers had thrown him inside their vehicle and sped off. He looked back at Mrs Richards and was overcome with desperation.

After the woman shut her front door, Wash cursed the warm October damp and huffed back to the underground station. Anyone listening in would think he was crazy, muttering angry complaints aloud. That had been one of the most pointless interviews of his career. The old lady hadn't given him anything strong enough to prove the homosexuality of her vicar. And now, rather than being able to concentrate on her spurious claims, all he could think of was how she'd condemned a poor homeless man to life in prison.

Wash kept on remembering his father, almost ashamed. For so long he had doubted the old man, largely on account of his irascible nature, but maybe he had a point about a lot of things. There was something suspicious going on with the colonisation programme and the country's inability to look after the most vulnerable people was becoming a serious problem. The young journalist was deeply conflicted. Already he could feel an increasing desire to do more, to earn his father's respect the hard way. But that morning's conversation with Steve kept niggling at the back of his mind too, tempting him to simply conform, to avoid ending up like Turner.

But Wash was done toeing the line.

Mrs Richards had said the vicar's husband had

something to do with the government. He'd start there.

As Wash returned to the turnstiles at Upton Park station, he pulled out his phone and composed a short message to a contact named 'Declan Fitzhugh.'

'You free for dinner at 7.30pm?' he tapped out quickly.

By the time he'd reached the platform below, there was a reply.

'I'm just at golf with the chief whip, let's make it eight o'clock. I thought you'd never ask x'.

✳

Wash was uncomfortable these self-indulgent restaurants. But if Declan was paying, and he'd have been rude not to given his wages, regardless of journalistic etiquette, there was no way he was going to turn down a lavish meal at the Roux in Parliament Square. The room was a perfect oval, topped by a pristine white ceiling with empire pattern stucco edging and three elaborate silver chandeliers. One wall was a set of arched windows through which they could see the busy London night-life. The other was donned with simple but beautifully varnished wood-panelling. Classical art hung at regular intervals throughout the room. The restaurant had done well to preserve the feel of the original building when it was rebuilt at a higher level above the Thames.

Wash sat opposite Declan in the corner and, as the waiter brought over the wine that had been chosen, he admired his former class-mate's immaculate appearance. Despite a long day at the Parliamentary offices, Declan's bleach blond wavy locks were flawlessly positioned, cascading from a perfect parting down the middle. Neither was there a crease on the man's navy suit, a blue tie clipped smartly at the opening of the blazer and a handkerchief of the same colour protruding from his top pocket. Declan's wrist was home to a gold-plated smart-watch and his irises glowed an unnatural electric blue, housing extravagant technology. All in all, it was a brave outfit to wear in the humidity of mid-Autumn, but he always pulled it off. Come to think of it, Wash struggled to remember the last time he saw Declan failing to keep up such high sartorial standards. He wasn't the type to stumble drunkenly around the streets of London in search of old football stadia; that was for sure. Declan was too 'haut monde' for that, or so he'd phrased it once. No, he was more the type to march blind drunk into a gentleman's club, spend the night smoking cigars and dipping his cock and balls into silver-plated tankards of port. It had been a long time since they were at school together and, despite mixing it with entirely different social circles, they had remained in touch.

"So how's life working for Big Brother?" Wash asked as he tested the wine. It was a bit oaky for his taste but he could cope. Declan chuckled to himself before answering, almost purring like a cat.

"You know Wash, no matter how many times you call him that, I'm never going to play along."

"It must be going well, though. Last time it was that Indian place the other side of St James's Park. Now we're in Parliament Square."

There was a moment of indecision on Declan's face. It didn't take long for him to make up his mind.

"Funny you should mention that actually." He took another sip of wine. "The PM thinks I could run for Parliament in the next election."

"Did he tell you that over a round of golf?" Wash asked with a grin.

"No, of course not," Declan chuckled. "The chief whip did."

"That's impressive progress," he said. "You've only been a researcher for what, two years?"

"Yes, it's a little sooner than I'd expected, but no earlier than I'd hoped, of course."

"Where are they looking at putting you up?"

"Hopefully it will be one of the Kent constituencies but I'd be happy anywhere in the south east really. There are a few party members down here considering their future. Anything west of Swindon would be too country-bumpkin for me."

"Why doesn't that surprise me?" Wash joked.

"What about yourself? How's life at the Daily Citizen?"

Like writing in sand, he thought to himself.

"Where do I start?" said Wash, letting out a wry smile and sipping some water. "We've had a lot of changes at the top level in the last six months, as you know. The effect that's had on us has been more drastic than we'd expected."

Declan read the situation astutely.

"Why don't you come work in our press department? They'd love to have someone with your skills." He stared off into the distance a moment as he quickly ran a search for Wash's salary in his AxPrint contact lenses. "You'd earn a lot more too, by the looks of it."

"Something tells me that wouldn't quite be my scene, Dec."

Declan didn't have too long to take any offence as

a waitress arrived at their table with plates of food. As they began to eat, it was Declan that reignited the conversation, with a smirk and a scratch of the ear-lobe.

"So why did you want to see me, Wash? Social calls are hardly the hallmark of a journalist. Not in this day and age."

"Yeah, I know it's a little out of the blue. I think you'll like this one," Wash said after a mouthful of steak. "It's right up your street."

"How can I help?" asked Declan, suspicious.

"I've got a female vicar in Newham who sup-posedly... bats for the other team. Know anything about that?"

Declan quickly did a precautionary sweep of the restaurant with his eyes, visibly flustered to have been questioned on the subject in public. In more hush tones than before he whispered harshly.

"You think we all know each other, or something? Like some kind of big gay following?"

Part of Wash wondered if Declan would be unwill-ing to give this woman up if they knew each other well. He was also aware that his friend might not like being exploited for information. But the two of them had always had a good understanding. If Dec was particularly fond of the vicar he'd say nothing. If not, then he'd be more forthcoming. Ultimately, the man opposite him 'the game', as he'd once called it. Maintaining a good relationship with the press was important, even if they were becoming more like publicists.

"Do you know who I'm talking about or not?" Wash pressed him.

Leaning, back and checking once again for any

wandering ears, Declan asked for her name.

"She's called Julie Faversham."

Declan hesitated a moment before admitting defeat.

"Yes... I know her," he said, taking a bite of meat.

Wash rolled his eyes.

"So these rumours are true, then? Declan nodded, still chewing the fat.

"How do you know?"

"I can't tell you how I know. I just know."

That was all Wash really needed. With confirmation from someone as well connected, you might say, as Dec, he could be certain of running something on it. He wasn't happy about it, but he had a job to do. All that remained was to ask about her husband. After all, in the last four years he'd heard plenty of whispers concerning supposedly prominent gay individuals pairing up with a member of the opposite sex and getting married as a deflection. Who was to say that wasn't what had happened with the Favershams? If he was going to be forced into running a story outing a vicar as a homosexual, turning it into an indirect attack on the government would help him sleep a little better at night.

"I'm hearing that her husband is a shady government official of some kind. Do you know anything about him?"

Again, Declan took some time to formulate his answer and checked the coast was clear before letting on.

"Well... since you asked," he said coyly. "His name is Miles, and I know him for the same reason that I know his *beloved* wife. The reason he's prone to a lot of cloak-and-dagger activity is, firstly, on account of his private life, of course, but mainly it's because of his role with the interplanetary colonisation programme."

"Really?" Wash was surprised. "I knew they were pretty nonchalant about the Proxima Accords but I wouldn't have thought they'd see the need to be secretive about it on home soil. The patriotism generated by that publicity stunt is what keeps a regime like yours going."

"You don't know the half of it, Wash."

Wash felt a sudden thrill of excitement. A dozen dubious possibilities raced through his head.

"The truth is," Declan continued, "there are a few high ranking individuals who are not so happy with how out of control our colonisation programme is getting. It's become a bit of a dog's dinner, actually."

"How do you mean?"

"I can't say any more than that, I'm afraid. But I can point you in the right direction," Declan said as he fiddled with the napkin in front of him. He scribbled a short message down in pen and pushed it slowly towards Wash until he'd tucked it under his plate. Taking a moment to look down, the young journalist could make out an address in Wapping. This conversation seemed to have become very sobering, very quickly.

"Why are you giving me this, Dec?" Wash asked, his breath short.

"Look, this stays between you and me, okay?"

Wash nodded.

"Well, the word going round the chambers right now is that Curtis and the cabinet are not too happy with your editor."

"Yvette? How come?"

"It's her position at the paper that's causing the biggest grief, unsurprisingly."

"But virtually every front page is her gushing about what you lot are up to."

"Yes, that's all dandy. In fact, Curtis writes most of those editorials himself under her name. But she's spending too much time in London working at the Citizen and not enough in her constituency. Her approval ratings there are through the floor."

"I thought approval ratings hadn't meant anything to you in decades."

"Look, we might seem rather faceless to someone as nosey as you, Wash, but we're not stupid. We can tell her constituents whatever we want in pressers and PMQs but that won't stop them from disliking the fact Yvette's never around anymore. She's on thin ice right now."

"And let me guess, if she gets pulled from there you'll be up for the by-election?" Dec gave a devilish smile when he realised he'd been rumbled.

"There's a good chance of that, yes."

"I don't get it, though. How does sending me to the London docks help Yvette lose her job? She's got a pretty good grip on our sub-editors right now. Anything even remotely critical about the government doesn't even get a look-in."

You go ahead and ask Steven Woods about that, he thought.

"Just dig deeper," Declan insisted, pointing at the napkin. "You'll see what I mean. And when you find out what I expect you to, run as much as you can. But be discrete. You'll understand when you get there. If you can undermine Yvette's position in a way that allows Curtis to pull her either from the paper, her constituency, or both, you'll make a lot of powerful people very happy."

9

"Back to Choctaw? You can't be serious," said Sally, stone-faced. She stood in the Stafford's red-brick and mahogany kitchen. Once Don had told her she looked away, busying herself with fixing the wireless detector on the slow cooker. He sat at the central island, a guilty look on his face, fiddling with the house's AI organiser.

"I can't send people out there without me," he said calmly. Sally didn't reply. "I can't make decisions on the situation or recommendations to the council if I'm not there."

"But why do you *have* to?" She snapped, finally looking him in the eye, cheeks flushed.

"It's my job, Sals."

"It doesn't have to be! You're not even the head of the defence department. Why can't Judson whatever-he's-called go instead?"

"You know as well as I do that he's more interested in politics than operations."

"But you've given decades of your life – our lives – to the Atlas Nations and you don't have to anymore,"

Sally carefully swept up a tear from the corner of her eye. "You could have stepped down last year but you didn't."

"I thought we talked about this," Don said.

"No, *you* talked about this *to* me. Not *with* me. You just want to go back to the way it was. When they worshipped you like a god out there."

"That's not fair."

"Will *he* be there?"

"I should have thought so, yes."

Sally rolled her eyes.

"Then it's not safe," she said.

"I can look after myself," Don replied, not entirely convinced, himself. It was easier to hold his own in front of Alida than it was when faced with the woman who knew him best.

"Will you? Donald, you have a metallic reminder in your leg of why you left that place. You feel it every single day. Why would you go back there when it could be even more dangerous than before?"

"Sally, I'm fed up of feeling like I'm some three-legged dog at a rescue centre. I'm not exactly excited by the prospect of going back there but Choctaw is the only place I can handle this thing without having hands tied behind my back by bureaucracy." Don had stood up now.

"You don't need to handle it." Sally was never going to understand his attitude.

"I'm sorry Sally, but yes I do."

That night, Don had his recurring nightmare on the sofa bed.

★

The following afternoon, Don arrived at the bustling Jamestown Spaceport with Sally's words still ringing in his ears. Chad was waiting in the reception with all his research on the British. He had traded in a shirt and tie for brown combat gear and a grey leather jacket. His well-styled brown hair was now underneath a bobble hat. Anderson had expressed disappointment at losing the young man from the tracking station but understood his importance to the mission. The deputy was grateful Chad was the only one travelling to Choctaw though. In fact, he'd been a little surprised to learn how small the New Boston delegation would be.

"I've got all the team I need waiting for me in Arkan," Don had explained.

"How long does it take to fly to Arkan City, sir?" Chad asked on the runway as the pair prepared to climb up the ramp into the belly of a roaring Lockheed C-235P aircraft. The young man was jittery.

"About three and a half hours, these days," Don answered. "Plenty of time to go over your research one more time. We've got to brief Stangl's marines too."

Don had not been keen on these troops coming on this trip, but neither he nor Alida had been given much choice in that matter. After all, the original intel had come from Stangl himself. The eight-strong squadron were already strapped into the seats along the walls of the aircraft, apart from their leader, who stood between them, ready to greet the defence department duo. Don had heard the stories about these genetically engineered super-soldiers, although hadn't realised just how inhuman they really were until seeing them in the flesh for the first time. If you could call it flesh.

Each soldier was close to seven feet tall with

muscles the size of small tree trunks and shaved heads closer in shape to anvils than human skulls. Their most distinguishing feature was the unnatural colour of their skin, which Don could see on their faces, arms and hands; the rest covered by combat uniforms. Three of the troops sported a dull grey, another three were a leafy tinge of olive. One of them boasted a mahogany red and the leader's skin was a denim blue. The hues were far from flamboyant but not subtle enough to go unnoticed.

"Good morning, sir," he half-shouted over the sound of the engines, giving a handshake that felt like being hugged by a bear. "I'm Commander Jacob Murphy. But you can call me Smurph. I's my call sign," the man said with a smile. He gestured towards his comrades. "This is Blaize, Thrombo, Pathfinder, Flat-top, Scissorhands and Cabbage," each one gave a nod as their name was mentioned. "And this here is Diablo," he said pointing at the red soldier whose intense stare was fixed on the empty space in front of him.

"Thanks for the introductions," Don said formally. "Your squad ready for this mission?"

"You bet," Smurph replied with a friendly grin. "We've been on this planet six months and the only action we've seen is what the ladies of horizontal pleasure can offer." Don simply raised an eyebrow. Smurph swivelled to his smiling comrades and exchanged a smutty cackle. Turning back to Don, he was met with a largely unimpressed glare.

"When you're quite finished Commander, we've got an important job to do. Please try and stay focussed," he said as he walked past him to one of the spare seats.

"You got it, sir," Smurph said after a pause. He glazed over with the obligations of rank. "We're ready for take-off when you are."

✶

Alida Harmon slumped into her office chair with a huff. This was the first time she'd managed to be alone all day and it was already dark outside. Unfortunately, her work was far from over. She glanced at the pile of papers in her in-tray and over to the messy bed in the corner. Another night away from home, then. Her husband wouldn't be happy. But, then again, he never was.

A portion of the desk slid open, revealing a rising screen. Someone was trying to call.

"For goodness sake." Selecting audio only from the options. "Alida Harmon, here."

"Sorry to bother you late, Alida. It's Nikolai."

The bloody reporter.

"That's okay," she lied.

"I don't suppose you've got time to answer a few questions?"

"You know the answer to that. Depends what they are."

"I'm hearing reports that one of our satellites has gone down."

"And?" She liked to make him ask the hard questions himself.

"I was wondering if you knew anything about that."

"Have you heard anything from our press office? There was a long pause.

"Should I have done?"

"You're an awkward hack, did you know that? Any

other questions?"

"Yes. Do you know why the satellite is down?"

She hung up. Seconds later it rang again. Alida swore.

"I already told you, I'm not answering any of your questions," she shot from the hip.

"That's one of way greeting your husband," Sean Tycho jibed sarcastically. *Dammit.*

"Oh, sorry Sean. I thought you were Nikolai Govinda, the reporter." Alida toggled the video call feature and sent the images to the projector. Sean's face and books on the shelves of his home study in the background were displayed on her wall.

"So is he the reason I've not been able to speak to you for the last two days?" he asked.

"Oh don't start up on that again," Alida scoffed as she poured herself some Pacheco coffee. "You know why I'm busy right now."

"Well I know *now*. In fact, I now know more than I'm supposed to in my lowly position as the *vice admiral of the blasted navy.*"

"What on earth are you talking about?"

"I'm talking about your back-door reinforcement exercise on the Choctaw border." Alida was caught off-guard. She couldn't conjure up a diplomatic response in time. He clocked her indecision. "So it's true, then," Sean pressed on. "And when were you planning on telling me about it?"

Alida still had no words. Verbally sparring with Stangl was easy compared to with Sean. Her husband made her feel like a child. This was going to make telling him about the kids even harder. The rant continued.

"Why has the navy been kept out of the loop on

this? How stupid am I going to look if my superiors find out about it before I have a chance to tell them? It wouldn't be so embarrassing for me if I hadn't found out from one of my ensigns, rather than my damn wife."

"How did he find out?" Alida came to life again, the source of the leak her immediate concern. She started scribbling some notes.

"I guess I got lucky. He just happens to be in a relationship with one of your soldiers. Some couples actually talk to each other, you know."

"What are their names?"

"I'm not telling you anything," he said, stubborn as ever. "I'm not going to let anyone get into trouble over this, except you." Alida knew he would not budge.

"Are you going to tell the rear admiral?" she asked.

"I don't know. Depends on why these troops are being moved."

"I can't tell you that," Alida tried desperately to regain the upper-hand.

"You absolutely will tell me. Either that or the New Boston Times are going to hear about the communication problems on Alida Harmon's council. That'll look good when you go public about your independence plans, won't it?"

"Fuck you, Sean." Her resolve over the kids was set in stone now.

"That's the deal, Alida. Take it or leave it." She considered the dilemma for a second or two.

"Ok fine, I'll tell you. But on the condition you sit on this for two days until we have more intel."

"Go on."

Alida explained everything, starting with the destruction of Satellite Three. Sean listened to the story unmoved, like a robot. When she had finished, his rude and sarcastic tone returned.

"So there's potentially a British invasion on the way and you felt the navy didn't need to know about it. That is just typical you."

"What are you going to do?" she asked, ignoring his further attempts to bait her.

"None of your business." The pair were interrupted by a short electronic chirp coming from Sean's office. "I've got to go. The kids' dinner is ready."

"Wait," Alida snapped.

"What is it?"

"I need to talk to you about the kids."

"Like you give a shit about them," Sean snarled as he leaned in to cut the call.

"I'm moving them to my house in the city," she announced. For the first time, Sean didn't open his huge mouth. He appeared to have been stunned into silence. Eventually he spoke.

"I assume I have no say in this."

"None at all," Alida revealed, sticking the knife in. It was about time Sean understood not to get in her way.

He cut the call.

*

Three hours into their flight, Don and the rest of the team could see the Choctaw lands spread out below. He never thought he'd see this place again, grateful to be coming here rather than the haunting unknowns of Proxima B. The imposing Choctaw Mountains lined the western coast of the large peninsula, marching away from the aircraft. Stretching out across the east were the miles of expansive prairie and desert lands. Between them was the forest, nothing more than a spongy green mass from this height. The whole region was fenced off from Arkan territory by a thin black line, the Arkan/Choctaw perimeter fence. At the heart of the lengthy palisade was a chunkier cream-coloured section. That was the Arkan City gateway, its guard towers and artillery platforms, the only way in and out of Choctaw by foot.

"The little gap in the forest over there is Peakwood," Don had to yell for Chad to hear him over the engines. "It's where we're heading tomorrow." He'd half expected the young analyst to be something of annoyance on this journey, but he was grateful for his presence now. Stangl's marines had elaborated on their recent exploits. It had been unpleasant listening.

"Do you know Choctaw well?" Chad asked.

"I was stationed in Arkan for 15 years," Don said with a longing look out the window. "I probably know it better than anyone else in New Boston."

"What did you do there?"

"Well, after the war, I spent most of my time making sure the Arkans and Choctaw didn't kill each other. It didn't always work out, but I did my best."

"From what I've heard, they really don't like each other."

"You're telling me."

"Why did you leave?"

"Mainly because of this," Don said gruffly, pointing to his right foot. "But getting offered the position of permanent secretary to the department of defence in the capital is not something you turn down when you've been out here for years."

"Did you want to leave, then?"

"Did I ever? There's nothing worse than being on the front lines of a war, or what's left of it… It brings out the worst in people," he said with half a nod to the coarse banter of the marines. "Although my time in New Boston has hardly been a picnic. It'll be good to feel young again. You never know you miss something until you don't have it anymore."

"Making our descent now," the pilot announced.

Don took one last look through the glass before strapping himself back in. The guilt in the depths of his stomach continued to rise. Damn. He really did want to be back out here, regardless of what Sally had said. This British incursion had simply provided him with a convenient excuse.

"Look who's back," Gisèle Etienne purred as she watched Don make his way down the ramp and into the busy hangar bay. She strutted over to greet him, her wild mop of corkscrew blonde curls bouncing with every stride. "The hero returns," she announced as she stood opposite Don.

"You've aged well, Gisèle," Don courteously said to the vibrant woman.

"*You* haven't, I'm afraid!" Gisèle joked as the pair embraced.

"Complimentary as ever," Don chuckled.

Up close, he could see how Gisèle's skin had matured, cheeks drier than he remembered them. Without a detailed inspection, it would be easy to think she was still in her mid-thirties. There was no sign of the horrors she had seen serving in Don's unit as a teenage soldier in the last war.

"How's Sally?" Gisèle asked.

"She'll be fine," Don said masking his guilt. "Not too happy that I'm back here, but who can blame her really?"

"You didn't want to come back, did you?" she asked with a sympathetic look.

"Not at first," he admitted.

"I'm hurt Donald, really I am."

"Knowing you'd be here was half the reason I came back," he joked.

"That's better."

"Honestly, it's just good to feel useful again."

Don soon realised that Chad had been awkwardly shuffling his feet next to him.

"Ahem... This is Chad. He's our expert on all things British."

"A pleasure to meet you," Gisèle said with a soft handshake and a polite nod. Chad smiled nervously. "And who are *these* specimens?" she asked, as Smurph and his towering colleagues disembarked. Their leader noticed the interested eyes trained on his person.

"The name's Smurph, ma'am," he said with a salute and a smile.

"You're very... blue." Gisèle looked him up and down.

"It's from the DNA work."

"Incredible," she replied, still staring, drawn away only by Diablo and Cabbage walking past, sporting a garish contrast of differing skin tones. "I'd heard they were trying this sort of stuff on Earth but... I never thought they'd be as... colourful. What exactly did they do to you?"

"Teslanium plating on every bone and an array of weapons in our arms," Smurph said. Gisèle raised her eyebrows.

"And how come some of you are all different colours?"

"The bio-enhancements had various effects on pigmentation... depending on the gene pool," Smurph explained. "Some of us came out patchy so we had the old skin dyed for a finished touch."

"Fascinating," Gisèle said.

"And you are?" Smurph asked.

"I'm sorry," she replied. "Where are my manners? I'm Gisèle Etienne, head of Arkan Command," the pair locked eyes for longer than Don was comfortable with. He'd not seen her for years but she was still like a daughter to him.

"You're a civilian?" Smurph asked, raising his azure eyebrows at her lack of insignia. Or at least Don assumed they were his eyebrows.

"Where have you been for the last few decades?" Gisèle suddenly spoke to the soldier like a child, maintaining her cheeky smile. "Ever since the legendary Don Stafford here taught the Choctaw a lesson, this role has been a strictly non-military one."

"My apologies, I'd never been to Proxima A until a few months ago. I don't know a thing about this planet, really."

"Well, you've got plenty of time to learn, Smurph."

"So if you're a civvy, I assume you're not coming with us on the mission to Peakwood then?" Smurph was more interested than Don would have liked.

"Oh no, I'm coming," Gisèle confirmed. "I wouldn't miss this for the world."

"Why don't you get your gear in order, Smurph?"

Don was keen to draw Gisèle away from him.

"Yes, sir." Smurph quickly returned to his comrades. Chad got the idea too, he began unloading his bags.

"They should come in handy." Gisèle pointed out. Don couldn't disagree.

"I assume either Stangl or Alida filled you in?" he asked.

"They both did, actually. I could tell they weren't massively thrilled about the situation. Do I need to be worried, Donald?"

"That's what I'm here to find out," he said. "The real question is," he checked that nobody else was listening and took a deep breath, "is he here yet?"

"Yes, he arrived about an hour ago," Gisèle looked at the ground.

"Thanks for arranging the meeting for me. Where is he?"

"Where do you think?"

★

Don stepped onto the Arkan Wall just as the sun was setting over the Choctaw Mountains. The titanic concrete structure was bathed in dark apricot tones. Arriving from the eastern entrance, Don could see to his right where the wall dropped down to a fence. Over the ledge was the road that led straight into the heart of breakaway territory, heading off into the edge of the forest.

"Arkan Commander Donald Stafford. I thought I'd never see you again," the Scandinavian voice came from behind him. Don's blood ran cold. He turned to see the long-haired Orvan Eld leaning against the back wall, arms crossed. He was smiling malevolently, just like he did in Don's dreams.

Don fought hard to control his breathing. He wasn't as well prepared for this as he thought.

"Not with two legs, that's for sure," Orvan added.

"You know I wouldn't have asked for you if it wasn't absolutely necessary," Don countered, trying to keep up a steely façade. His heart raced.

"Now *that* I believe," Orvan said smugly as he leaned forward and began to pace along the superstructure. "The famed Donald Stafford, asking the Choctaw for help. Now I really have seen everything."

"I don't like you Orvan," Don thought of the metal which supported his left leg. "But I'd never wish a full-scale war on your people. That's why we need to work together."

"Very noble, Donald. It's just a shame you didn't feel that way before I had to cripple you."

"Things were different then, you know that," Don insisted. He couldn't afford to give any ground, no matter how many buttons Orvan fiendishly pressed. "Pacheco and Etterslep had no right to invade the Floriana lands."

"You tell that to the hundreds of *thousands* of our people who were screwed by your glorious leaders."

"No, Orvan," Don snapped. "*You* tell it to the hundreds of thousands of people obliterated by nuclear fallout in the Anguerra Zone."

"I don't know what you're complaining about, Stafford," Orvan purred, characteristically smug in his conviction. "That war made New Boston richer than it could have dared dream. You were the only place with the raw materials for rebuilding... and the money lenders to help everyone pay for it."

Don sighed.

"What is the point in going around in the same old circles, Orvan?" he asked.

Orvan leaned to his right to get a better look at Don's leg, he closed one eye.

"You know I'm still pretty impressed with my aim," he said, pointing a finger at Don's leg and firing it like a pretend pistol. "I'm very proud to have ended Donald Stafford's career. You look like shit."

"Screw you, Orvan." Don had to turn his back to hide the vulnerable expression on his face. All the Choctaw man did was howl with laughter.

"Just do the right thing for once," said Don. "You know pooling resources on this is the best thing for both our people."

Orvan swung his head to look at Arkan City and the rest of the A.N. territory behind it. His hair was still tied back in the same style as always, the ends fraying now. He turned back to Don, paused for a moment, then lurched at him. Don flinched, falling back him into the wall behind. Orvan laughed again.

"Why should I trust you? Any of you?" A treaty with the Atlas Nations may as well be written in dirt or sand, ready for you to wash it away at your next convenience." Orvan looked skyward. "Hey, maybe the Choctaw should pair up with the British and invade you lot through your back door instead?" he added, bearing his teeth.

"Surely... you know that won't end well for you?" Don did his best to dust himself down.

"Do I? Can you honestly tell me exactly what the British have been up to during their years of secrecy? How do I know they haven't amassed the biggest army since man took to the stars and are about to kick the Atlas Nations right where it fucking hurts?"

"I think if you were really considering that, you wouldn't be here now," Don said shrewdly. "Just tell us what you kn--."

"How do you know I haven't come here to finish the job?" Orvan asked as he maintained an intimidating close-proximity. "To finally kill Donald Stafford after all these years."

Don's watch beeped.

"Don? Don, are you there?" Gisèle sounded panicked as her voice came through the receiver. Orvan took half a step back, indecision written on his face, enough for Don to push past and get some distance.

"What is it Gisèle?" Don asked.

"I'd look up, right about now, if I were y--."

The last of Gisèle's words were cut off by a deafening roar above them. Both Don and Orvan put their hands to their ears and looked up.

It streaked through the air, leaving a trail of vapour in its wake. Another British ship. The missile-shaped craft hurtled thunderously above them. The Arkan Wall shook fiercely as the object inexorably towards the Choctaw Mountains.

It disappeared over the peaks and landed with a distant crash.

"Still want to kill me?" Don asked. Orvan's face was devoid of colour.

The two men held each other's gaze for what felt like centuries. It was Orvan who looked away first.

"I'll tell you what I know... on one condition," he said with a glance over the wall.

"What's that?"

"You let me and two of my best men come on this expedition of yours."

10

It had been several days since Lisa disappeared and the group were no closer to finding her. Every morning, Harper, Ben, Zoey and Zack returned to their jungle search. James had been going with them as far as the clearing so he could continue studying the writing in the sand. He had become interested in nothing else but solving the riddle of the dirt. Any breakthrough in translating the symbols might hold the key to finding Lisa.

James had salvaged some paper from the crash and had clipped a few sheets together to form a notebook. On one side were printed spreadsheets detailing supplies, the other bore his mad scribbles.

"That just looks like gibberish to me," Harper had said when she first spotted his work. She was standing over him while he wrote out as many symbols from as many Earth cultures as he could remember. Sat cross-legged, he had donned his brown circle-framed reading glasses. One of the lenses was cracked but the other had gone largely unscathed, barring a few scratches. The cut on his nose had started to scab over now and the weight of his spectacles emphasised the tender feeling.

"Well, I wouldn't have the first clue how to track down missing people in uncharted territory, so I guess we're even," he replied with a smile.

"Have you got anything for us yet?" Harper asked.

"Well, sort of. Whoever wrote that in the ground did so using hieroglyphs."

"What are they?" James could tell she was only half listening, her focus more on checking her supplies before pushing out further on into the jungle.

"It's the use of pictures to convey words," he said. "The most well-known set of hieroglyphs back on Earth was the one used by the Egyptians. You ever heard of them?"

"I've heard of them." Harper looked up to offer an encouraging smile. "Pyramids and mummies, right?" she asked.

"You think this is the Egyptians?" Zack butted in with a confused look on his face. James just chuckled.

"No, not the Egyptians. Look, there were many forms of hieroglyphs. The ones the Egyptians used are the most widely known, that's all. Lots of popular culture interest in the early twentieth century, I think." He could tell nobody really knew what he was talking about. In fact, Ben and Zoey were speaking in hushed tones to each other by one of the rocks and barely listening. "I think I've narrowed it down, though," James said, pushing the glasses back up his nose and digging through his papers. "I'm close to working out where I've seen this before."

"But why does that matter?" Zack pressed on. "How do we know these aliens have read our hieroglyphics?"

"They don't need to have done. Communication by images is the sign of a certain level of civilisation. Pictures were used long before the written word. Working out what sort of imagery this is, how long ago it was engraved, that sort of thing, will tell me how civilised these people are. That could make a big difference when it comes to finding Lisa and making sure these people, whoever they are, don't take anyone else."

While James was worried about Lisa he had enjoyed walking to and from the clearing with Harper each day. They talked more of what their lives were like before they arrived and had bonded over how terrible it had been living in London. The sticky climate, the exorbitant cost of living, the smell of the river. He hoped their time together would continue.

James and Harper met at the edge of the survivors' rock after another fruitful day, as they had done for the last few nights. It had proved useful for them both to talk over their respective problems. And her alcohol helped.

"I think we'll try going further west, tomorrow," Harper said.

"Are you sure that's sensible?" James asked. "You've gone out pretty far already. You never want to be more than a few hours trek away from here."

"Yes, but we aren't getting anywhere with this search," Harper said as she chucked another stone at the sea. "Tomorrow morning will be our ninth day at this." Another stone. "How are you getting on with the writing?"

"Sounds like I'm having about as much luck as you," James fiddled with his papers. "I can't seem to identify any key features. And with nothing to act as a cipher, there's only so much I can work out. I'd give anything for a Rosetta Stone or an enigma machine to help me out here." Harper laughed. "What?"

"Oh, it's nothing," she teased. "I'm not even going to pretend to know what any of that meant," she said with a playful wrinkle of the nose. James didn't know what to say. "I mean to me it just looks like someone having their head chopped off," she added. Harper's pupils had been dilating for the past hour. Now she was slurring some of her words and giggling more than usual.

"Linguistics was never my speciality anyway," James admitted.

"Well, you know more about it than the rest of us put together, J."

"You know, we shouldn't be sat here talking about all of this," James said, changing the subject.

"How do you mean?" James swung on his hips and crossed his legs so that he faced Harper.

"We should be spending our evenings admiring the corn field we've planted," he said with a far-off look. "You know, relaxing on hand-made rocking chairs in the porches of homes we built with our bare hands... or something like that." Harper laughed again.

"You can laugh, but it's what these people signed up for," he said gesturing towards the main group. "Singing songs around a fire and living the dream. One with nature once again, and all that sentimental stuff. I thought that's what early colonial life was supposed to be all about. Not for us, though. Since the crash, everybody has been so focussed on just not dying that we've all forgotten what we really came here for. A new life. One away from the home we knew before. This isn't a home," he paused for a moment and looked Harper in the eye. "Not yet anyway."

The comment didn't sink in as he had planned.

"You're probably right James," Harper replied, breaking the gaze and stretching her arms out to yawn. She got to her feet. "I better turn in."

✴

"I don't know why you won't tell me where they are," Lynne said for the tenth time that evening.

"How many times do I have to tell you, mum? I have no idea." It was no good. Her mother just wasn't listening and continued her rant as the two of them sat alone by the fire, waiting for their clothes to dry.

"You know those inhalers belonged to your father," she said. "We lost everything else in the crash."

"Yep," Shermeen acknowledged with a petulant nod of the head. She tucked some of her long dark hair behind her ears. "I know."

She could see several metres away that Amos was sat by himself outside the men's Tarp, looking at her, clearly trying to eavesdrop. He seemed quite worried.

"What did you eat today?" Lynne asked.

"What do you mean?"

"Did you eat enough?"

"Oh..." Shermeen momentarily panicked, avoiding eye contact. "Yeah."

"Good. You need to keep yourself fuelled."

Shermeen sighed, fed up of being treated like a child. Silence fell on the pair for several minutes.

"Why don't you talk to me Shermeen?" Her mum

started up again. "We need to stick together now that your father is gone. And with that woman going missing in the jungle, you need to stop going off on your own."

"Yes, mum."

"I'm not sure why you think it's safe to go fishing with that Zoey woman either," Lynne said as she stood up and started taking down some drying clothes from her makeshift line. "You know what happened to that Tarp that got swept out to sea. It could happen to you, if you're not careful."

Shermeen couldn't be bothered to respond any more.

"Shermeen? Shermeen?"

"What?" she snapped.

"Are you in this conversation or not?"

"Yeah, whatever."

"I was just saying you should stop going off with that Zoey woman. You're going to get yourself hurt."

Shermeen let out an exasperated huff.

"Zoey takes an interest in me, mum," she retorted. "Rather than constantly telling me what to do, she lets me have fun." Shermeen did not give her mother a chance to reply. She stood up and stomped off towards the women's Tarp. Her mother didn't attempt to come after her.

Shermeen only made it a few steps before she was interrupted by Zack.

"You should show your mother more respect," he said flatly.

"What?" Shermeen asked.

"You shouldn't talk to her that way," he explained, never once making eye contact. The man was sat slumped against a tree, smoking another cigarette.

"Aren't you the guy who hates black people?" Shermeen eventually countered, inwardly proud at her response.

"Yeah," Zack said eventually, enjoying another drag.

"Well then, I'm not going to take any advice from you then am I?"

"Do whatever you want, kid. Just be grateful you still have at least one parent," Zack pressed. Shermeen stomped off before an abrupt u-turn.

"You know," she said facing Zack and trying to hurt him, "your cigarettes are going to run out eventually."

"Don't you think I know that?" Zack rolled up his sleeve and revealed a nicotine patch attached to the outside of his bicep. "I've got myself a whole stash of these, sister, so I ain't worried."

"Then why are you still--"

"Because I can. You run along little girl and leave me alone."

*

Harper regretted drinking so much. She had hoped to save some and savour the last alcohol on this planet. But it was easy to push that out of her mind, enjoying the warm buzz. *Let's find Ben*, she said to herself, half out-loud. Harper could barely feel her feet, and meandered from the rock to the women's Krichmar Tarp. She could hear hush voices coming from the tree-line.

"Shit. It's them," Harper whispered to herself as she fumbled for a plasma-knife, her gun back with most of the gear. The rest of the group were a few metres away, James was still on the rock. A twig snapped off to the left. Her left leg wobbled as she turned. The hushed voices grew a little louder, and Harper realised she could hear a strange noise. *It must be some kind of weapon.* She crept closer to the tree-line, ready to leap in and catch their enemies by surprise.

"It's okay, Ben." It was the unmistakable Welsh voice of Zoey.

Harper pushed up against the bark of the nearest tree and peeked round to watch the clandestine conversation.

Ben was hunched up in the sand with his arms around his knees, making that noise again. It was sniffing. The man's face was blotched with tears. It was a look that didn't suit him. Zoey crouched over him, rubbing his back.

"I'm sorry," said Ben. "I don't want to embarrass you."

"There's nothing to be embarrassed about," Zoey said as she comforted him.

"Thanks. I came here to forget about it. I don't know what I was thinking."

"Don't be so hard on yourself," said Zoey.

"It was all my fault. I should have abandoned the farm sooner and got them out of there in time. But the floods got them all. My wife, and both the girls."

Zoey said nothing, simply stroking his hair.

"Since then, I've tried to keep busy," Ben continued. "It's why I came to this godforsaken planet in the first place. But so far, all we do is make it from one day to the next."

"Once we get through the valley and into the landing zone, you can get the farm started."

"I hope so," Ben said.

"I think you're going to be hugely important to this colony, Ben," Zoey caressed his face.

"No pressure then," Ben finally smiled.

Zoey kissed him on the lips.

"You're hardly useless yourself," he said. "Not many of us have any idea how to use those magic tents."

Harper pulled herself away from the pair, cheeks flushed and lips pressed.

She sighed, collapsing into a bunk. The alcohol in her system forced tears into a swell. Harper rubbed her eyes aggressively. She still felt so... removed from those around her. They didn't understand what it meant to bury your demons and display a show of strength. Harper kept replaying her first words on this planet in her head. "I can't do this." Not after Brixton... She had felt Ben was the only one who might understand. But now. Well, never mind.

✳

The next morning, Harper was the last up and found the rest of the search team waiting at the tree-line. She was already wiping beads of sweat off her forehead when she noticed Ben and Zoey were still in the same as the night before. They were standing too near each other too. Zack was propped up against a tree smoking another cigarette while James had his head buried in some notes.

"Let's go," she said, walking past everyone and well aware of how late she was and how awful she probably looked too.

Some way into their latest trek, Ben tapped Harper on the shoulder.

"Yeah?"

"I'm worried about Shermeen," he said.

"What's the problem?"

"As far as I'm aware, she's not been eating."

"She's probably just frightened."

"Normally I would agree with you, but Zoey says she's not even speaking to her mother either. That's... the weirdest part."

"I didn't know you knew so much about teenage girls."

"I used to have two daughters," said Ben.

"*Used* to?

"Yeah... They passed away a few years ago."

"That's awful, I'm so sorry. How did it happen?"

"I... don't really like talking about it," Ben replied, wiping his brow.

"Sorry," Harper felt a pang of guilt.

"What are we going to do about Shermeen?" he asked.

"Are you asking me to talk to her?"

"Well, I thought a strong female influence might help right now. Especially if her mum can't reach her either."

"I'm not that good at giving advice."

"I'm sure that's not true," Ben said dismissively. "You helped me out when we first got here. When I was upset about the fight." He said that last part quietly so Zack wouldn't hear his admission.

"I was just... stringing together clichés, you know," Harper replied, brushing a branch out of her way and holding it for Ben to crouch under. He was in front of her now. "Maybe you should ask Zoey to talk to her. You seem to like her. Perhaps Shermeen will too."

"Yeah. Maybe you're right," Ben said. They were

close to the clearing now, and minutes later Ben pulled back the last branch obscuring their view. He stepped out into the open in front of Harper and stopped in his tracks. She bumped into his back.

"Ben," she complained impertinently. "What are you--" She saw it.

Zoey came out of the undergrowth and screamed.

They had found Lisa.

Her bloodied naked body was nailed by the ankles to one of the rocks. It hung down from its hook, an inert hunk of butchered meat. There was a deep red gash where Lisa's neck should be, flayed flaps of flesh spurting out like petals. Her head was deposited two metres in front of the torso, staring at the survivors, mouth open eyes wide. Tiny insects gorged on the bounty. The smell was pungent.

"Who would do that?" Zoey begged. Ben had one arm around her, the other covering his nose. Zack threw up in the dirt. Everybody else was rooted to the spot, too shocked to speak.

"I don't know," Zack eventually groaned as he wiped flecks of vomit out of his beard. "But we need to kill them whoever they are."

"We don't even know what they look like or where they live," said Ben angrily, shielding his eyes.

"Ben's right," Harper added. "The best thing we can do is protect ourselves, not go on the offensive. We still know nothing about these people... right?" She looked to James.

He shuffled nervously on his feet.

"I think I might know something," he offered up.

"What?" Harper asked.

"I think I might know who these people are. Or, at least, who their descendants are."

"What are you talking about James?" Harper was confused.

"Are you serious?" Zack rasped. "Are you actually serious? We're about to get carved up by these aliens and all you've got to show for it is crazy theories about the Egyptians," Zack spat.

James opened his mouth to defend himself.

He was cut short.

A mighty whistle sounded above their heads. Then there was a crackling bang.

The whole group looked up.

"Look," shouted Harper, pointing into the sky above the trees.

Sailing listlessly towards the heavens, leaving a smoky trail in its wake was a brightly coloured flare. It climbed several metres before losing altitude and burning out.

"The beach," Ben said.

They dashed for the tree line.

11

On the tube home from meeting Declan, Wash mulled over what his friend had told him. He scribbled down some ideas in his notepad, crossed them out and rewrote them. He would love nothing more than to help remove the parasite that was Yvette Hamilton and her snivelling political bias from his newspaper. His father might even be proud of that too... But if that involved potentially jumping into bed with a different faction of the same party, Wash wasn't sure how comfortable that would make him. He trusted Declan but he couldn't say the same for his superiors. He could hardly trust his own employers, and they were just a doormat for Declan's.

By the time he'd reached his flat in West Acton, Wash still wasn't sure of what his next move would be and whether he would visit the mysterious address.

That was the least of his problems when he returned home and discovered what Jay had been doing that evening.

"I'm telling you Jay, you're going to get us arrested

one of these days," Wash barked when he saw the images on their television screen. An entire wall of their cramped slipshod living space was taken up by an attractive young woman with jet-black hair on the display. She wore a tight-fitting blue dress and sat at a brightly coloured desk. Behind that was looped footage of an object soaring in the night's sky over a coastal city. Various witnesses were being interviewed, looking stunned. The sterility of the news studio was in stark contrast to the ripe scent of Wash and Jay's apartment. Neither of them were particularly tidy individuals but both of them had to work themselves into the ground just to pay the rent.

"Come on, Wash, the police have got better things to do than clamp down on people watching foreign news broadcasts," came Jay's indifferent reply, from a slouched position on the musty, dog-eared sofa.

"I'd rather come home and find you watching porn, to be honest. You just don't understand how seriously they take this stuff."

"Let me guess. You only know that because it's in your newspaper?" Jay said that last part with a dollop of sarcasm, sweeping his dark swirling mass of hair out of the way. This was the fourth time in as many weeks Wash had caught his small but outspoken friend streaming TVNZ1 News to their apartment.

"You've got to be so careful with this sort of thing," Wash said, as he rummaged through the stark contents of their fridge in the corner. Deciding that Declan's chosen beverage shouldn't stop him from having one more, he pulled out a beer. "Complete control is how a government like ours stays in power. They don't want anyone in this country knowing what the other nations on this planet think of us."

Jay made some room for Wash on the couch.

"I've got this thing routed through about seven different domestic servers," he said. "The police would have to actually be half-decent at their jobs to work out who's watching this right now."

Wash hoped Jay was right.

"So what is going on in New Zealand, then?"

Jay looked over at him surprised, probably assuming he was being sarcastic.

"Well, if I'm going to end up in jail for this I might as well learn something," Wash joked.

"It's quite an interesting one, this," said Jay. "Some unidentified object was spotted over the city of Gisborne and then over the coast. Probably just a meteor, the experts are saying. But obviously it's brought the loonies out of their holes."

"You risked jail-time for a story like that?"

"Come on, Wash. Live a little. You of all people should appreciate our media's lack of imagination these days. When was the last time anyone ran a real story like this? We've had all sorts of weird occurrences in recent years that never get reported on. Every waking second has to be about Benjamin Curtis and his record-breaking streak as prime minister. Either that or stupid cat videos."

Wash knew only too well how true that was.

"How was *your* day at work?" he asked.

"Shit, as per usual. Had to reject an application from a widowed lady today. Left with three young kids but I had to reject the food request because she'd worked seventeen hours in the last four weeks."

"I don't know how you do that job, Jay."

"If I quit, I'd be back at nine o'clock the next morning to apply for a voucher myself. How's your dad?"

"Ah man," he replied with a sigh. "I'd rather not talk about it."

"Is he still lecturing you on how to do your job?"

Wash nodded.

"Yep," he said with a huff and swig of the beer. "Worrying thing is, he might be right."

"Wow, I never thought I'd hear you say that," Jay remarked. "Right about what?"

"Well... just a few things," Wash replied, wondering once again about the colonisation programme. "But he still treats me like a child, so I'm not going to give him the satisfaction, you know?"

"I hear you," Jay said.

"By the way, you'll never guess who I saw today."

"Who?"

"Declan."

"Oh right. Don't think I've seen him since school. How is he?"

"He might be running for Parliament soon."

"Wow. Was that the occasion, then?"

"Yeah, you could say that."

"He's not got you in his back pocket, does he? That boy always had me worried about you," Jay joked as he went to the fridge himself.

"I'll be fine."

"Did you see the hot girl on the train this morning? That's what I really want to know." Wash had been waiting for this question since he'd got back in.

"Not for a few days now. Why?" Wash knew why.

"Have you asked her out yet? You've been going on about her for weeks and weeks." Jay had more of a smile on his face now.

"No. I've not asked her. She's more than just a

pretty face, you know."

"Listen to you. You sound like some sort of psychopath."

Wash thought for a moment.

"How about this? I'll ask her out when you finally start calling her 'Vicky' instead of 'hot train girl'?

"No deal."

"Have it your way, mate. Besides I've got no idea when I'll see her next anyway, what with London Transport messing about with the trains. Definitely something suspicious going on along the Central Line route."

"Oh stop talking about work," Jay jibed. "Don't you want to watch some football?" he asked.

"Yes, please. Anything to get this feed shut down." Wash pointed wildly at the screen.

Within a few seconds, Jay had terminated the footage, turned off his VPN and flicked on the default television setting. It landed on a domestic news channel. Before he could find the sports section, Wash protested, his interest piqued by the on-screen headline: 'EYE KILLER LATEST'.

"Can we watch this quickly?"

"Do we have to?" moaned Jay. "Fine – but be quick. Dumbarton versus Brechin City isn't going to watch itself."

"Like you give a damn about Scottish football," Wash joked. "Anyway, be quiet, I want to listen to this." He adjusted the volume as the programme's anchor was interviewing a psychological expert.

"...that's how this serial killer has earned such a unique name. Everything about him is connected to a fascination with the eyes."

"And how has that manifested itself in his actions?" Came another question from the interviewer.

"It doesn't make for very pleasant listening, I'm afraid. In the days before their deaths, all the victims reported being stalked by a man with glowing orange eyes. Without fail, these individuals have all been found dead, with their own eyes gouged out and massive internal bleeding on the brain."

"Are people who claim to have seen this man being afforded extra protection now that we know what's out there?"

"That's a tricky situation to solve, Natalie—" Wash muted the show.

"Come on, let's watch some Scottish Football League Championship, then."

Jay cheered sarcastically.

Wash overslept the next morning, feeling the after-effects of all those drinks. A brisk pace out of the door ensured he arrived at West Acton station to catch the right train, but only just. With things as they were at the Citizen and his father increasingly becoming a burden, anticipating time with Vicky was all he had to look forward to. For Wash, she was as addictive as any drug.

"Hold the door, please!" That was the voice he'd been hoping to hear. It sent shivers through him. Vicky had stepped onto the train, narrowly avoiding the rapidly closing doors behind her. Thick wavy chestnut locks flowed over her shoulders as she patted herself down and checked nothing had been dropped. Wash enjoyed how her black skirt hugged her waist and pulled her bright blouse tight. The beige leather bag strap across her chest brought it all into relief. Seeing Wash, her intense dark eyes lit up and she scrunched her pert nose playfully. Thin lips, tastefully painted red against golden undertones, parted in a perfect smile. Ushering a passenger standing nearby in the direction of his now vacant seat, Wash made his way to the door where Vicky was standing, holding the rail above her head.

"Not like you to nearly miss the train," he chirped with a smile, fully aware that he had come close to doing the same.

"I know, it was touch and go." As Vicky laughed, she put her hand on Wash's arm to steady herself.

"At least the service is actually running today," Wash said referring to the problems that had plagued the line of late.

"Very true. We've been like passing ships in the night recently. I missed you the other day when there was all that flooding. How did you get home?"

"I didn't. I slept at the hospital next to my father."

"Oh dear, I hope he's doing better."

Wash shrugged, not wanting to put a downer on things.

It's so frustrating how often the Central Line goes down," Vicky pointed out. "Half the time it doesn't make any sense. Like the other night. How could there be severe flooding on the line only for it to re-open in the morning? Don't you think that's a bit suspicious?"

"Thank you," Wash half-shouted to nobody in particular, throwing both arms in the air. The whole carriage momentarily directed their gaze towards him.

"For what?" Vicky was amused more than anything else.

"Both my boss and my flat-mate said I was being paranoid when I said the same thing. Good to know you thought the same as me."

"Sounds like we're the only ones who really know what's going on around here."

"Seems that way." Wash let silence linger for a little while.

"Did you get a chance to publish those stories you were telling me about?" Vicky asked.

"Sadly not. I got in a fair bit of trouble over those actually. To be honest, I was an idiot for thinking they'd get published."

"No," Vicky said with another squeeze of Wash's arm. "You should never feel like that for asking the right questions. The world needs more journalists like you, Washington Parker."

"Thanks," Wash said politely, realising once more why he was so drawn to Vicky. There was certainly no way he could get this level of affirmation from his father. "Believe me, that means a lot. Although I'm not sure what good it would do anyway." He thought of the address Declan had given him and whether it was really worth the grief he'd get by getting to the bottom of it. "People don't want the truth nowadays anyway. This country sleepwalked into the dystopian societies that were predicted by the authors of the twentieth century."

"Doesn't say much for human nature, does it?" Vicky tilted her head to the right, a distant pensive look on her delicate face. "I've been meaning to ask you something for some time," she said eventually. "I mean... Washington? What's up with that? I've honestly never made anyone with a name like it."

Wash laughed, the tension leaving his body in an

instant. He'd heard this question many times before.

"Well, my parents were born in America and grew up in the Washington DC area. That was until they got deported because my grandfather was a Brit. I was born a few weeks after they arrived back in this country."

"The Americans forced your family out of the country while your mum was heavily pregnant? God, that's awful."

"Yeah, well. Be careful what you say."

"You get asked about your name a lot, right?"

"Yeah."

"Sorry."

"It's okay," Wash said with a reassuring smile. "When you get asked something all the time you have your answer all rehearsed. I could probably give it in my sleep. Hey, who knows, I could be asleep right now!"

"Am I really that boring?" she said meeting his gaze.

"Depends on whether or not you're talking about another press release about coating things in plastic."

"You're going to regret bringing my work into this, Mr. Parker."

"Can I regret it over dinner?" Wash even caught himself off-guard with that question. Vicky smiled and touched his hand.

"Of course you can," she said sweetly.

"I can make a reservation at the Roux in Parliament Square for 8.30pm tonight," a giddy Wash suggested. The bill would be much more worth paying if spent on Vicky than Declan.

"That sounds fancy."

They continued their journey along the Central Line speaking about developments at Vicky's company. Like so many times before, Wash made the decision to miss his stop to spend a little more time with her. The walk back along the line, past the cathedral and onto Fleet Street, was a bit of a bother, especially with the stuffy November weather. But it was certainly worth it.

*

Despite another great morning with Vicky, Declan's tip was the only thing Wash could think about in the office. The napkin with the mysterious address on it had stayed tucked away in his trouser pocket all the way into work this morning. Since arriving, Wash had fingered it several times just to check it was still there. He had thought to ask Vicky for advice but had thought better of it. He dare not get her caught up in anything untoward. He felt totally safe in her company simply because there was nothing linking the two of them together. That was why Wash had decided to hold this lead to himself. To keep her safe. At the very least, Vicky had given him a boost, reminding him what journalists were supposed to do. And, boy, did she understand positive reinforcement better than his father.

"How was your interview yesterday?" Pete asked. "The parishioner, right?"

"Yeah," Wash sighed, sinking back into his chair. "Well, it was sort of helpful."

"Sort of?"

"Well, I got something out of it but…" Wash paused, scratching the back of his head. "I don't know… She really upset me."

Pete's opened his mouth briefly and then closed it again, eyes unsure where to look.

"I just found her attitude... disgusting, to be honest," Wash explained. "She was sat there with all this Christian memorabilia, littered with Bible verses about kindness, compassion and all that."

"What's wrong with that?" Pete asked, a little defensive.

"Well, nothing in theory," Wash replied, noticing concern in his colleague's eyes. "I just don't understand how she can have all that crap in her house and not practice a word of it."

"Oh dear," Pete sighed. "What did she do?"

"She called the police on a homeless guy who had been sleeping on her road. He got carted off as I was leaving. She was happy about it." Pete shook his head. Wash continued, feeling the anger bubble back to the surface. "Not to mention the fact that the entire time I was there, she acted as if her vicar's private life was somehow giving her a mental breakdown or something."

"I'm sorry about people like that, Wash," Pete said, rubbing his forehead.

"*You* don't have to apologise," Wash replied.

"Well, for what it's worth, mate, they wind me up as much as they do you."

"I'm not surprised," Wash snapped, fiddling with his pockets another time.

"No, with me, it's... different," Pete leaned across, dropping his pencil. "*You* hate the hypocrisy and, well, I do too, but for me what also bugs me is the fact that people just get the wrong idea of the whole religion when they meet people like her."

"Oh," Wash replied. "I didn't realise."

"It's alright, I don't mention it as often as I should."

Wash wasn't sure what to say. It wasn't often that things were awkward between him and Pete.

"I guess... I honestly think people like that say more about deep-seated right-wing British arrogance than any religion," said Pete. "Just... don't let one hypocrite tar the rest of us with one brush."

"I'll do my best," Wash replied, checking his pocket once more.

"Of course, what I really want to know is how many times you're going to examine your pockets this morning." Pete asked returning his attention to the computer screen.

"What do you mean?" Wash thought he had hidden it better than that.

"I've seen you throw your hands in there at least seven times in the last two hours. Is everything alright?"

"Yeah, I'm fine. Just expecting a phone call, that's all."

"Well, whatever it is, be careful. You don't want to set Steven off again."

"You're telling me," Wash said, as he noticed one of the health reporters come out of the 'fish bowl' office. She carefully wiped at her damp blotched eyes with a tissue, trying to disturb as little of the mascara as possible. The head of news content came out moments after.

"Goodness sake. He's at it again," Pete muttered. "He's on a roll this week."

"He certainly is," Wash said after a long while. His mind was made up. When his shift finished, he would go to Wapping.

*

Coming to the end of the small street, Wash surmised he was now behind the abandoned Bow Arts Rum Factory. Exactly where Declan had sent him. Its distinctive red-brick rear wall ran the length of Pennington Street and climbed five metres high. Taking a left turn, the impressive structure was now on his right with antiquated warehouses lined up on his left. Together their height created the feeling of being inside a tunnel. Further down the cobbled path, Wash could see the water's edge. According to dated maps, this road would once have continued on through the edge of the docks' industrial estate and rejoined the nearby Highway Road. But what remained of the Tobacco Docks was slowly slipping further into the depths of the Thames. The great river lapped at nearby buildings, hoping to claim them too. Between the Rum Factory and the old Tobacco buildings, rusty bins were turned over, floating on the swill made up of their rotten contents. The air was ripe with the smell of putrefaction.

Checking the address, Wash realised with disgust that he'd have to navigate the sloppy dross to get into the right building. The tall reporter wrapped both hands firmly around a pipe attached to the wall and hoisted his feet onto the first small ledge at around knee height. Lifting his arms a little higher to get purchase for the next climb, Wash felt himself lurch backwards. Screws were dragged out of the wall under the stress and the pipe snapped in half. Instinctively, Wash pulled his feet down to catch his fall and watched helplessly as both of them plunged into the scum. His shoes and socks were immediately filled with sludge. It felt slippery between his toes. He immediately regretted coming down here in his smart work clothes. He only had one set. The top half of the pipe joined him in the gunge. Its splash sent some of the foul-smelling muck into his hair.

Wash trudged his way back to dry land, bringing what was left of the pipe. He measured up the length and confirmed it was long enough to reach the lower part of the wall from where he stood. Holding it in front of him like a caber about to be tossed in the Highlands, he measured up his angles and allowed it to fall. Luckily, it landed exactly where it needed to between the top of the lower wall and the summit of the gatepost. *Perfect.* All Wash needed now was good balance for a second or two. The pipe-turned-bridge held his weight well and he was soon able to lean towards the prize with his hands. With purchase on the wall, the journalist leapt onto forearms and heaved himself onto brick. Walking along, Wash found the shallowest point of the factory's quadrangle courtyard and jumped down.

"This had better be worth it, Dec." Wash said out loud.

Breaking into the building itself was easier than getting onto the premises. A quick strike to a long-since-rotten door and Wash was through. The interior was mostly dark, save for beams stealing through cracks in the boarded up windows. It was enough to not need a torch. The floor was covered in piles of dark rubble closely resembling ash, rusty remains of metal equipment and rotting wood, all of it stewing in stagnant puddles. Work benches lined the same wall as the windows, littered with dusty junk. Thinking very little of what he'd found, Wash continued to the left and another room.

Half an hour later, Wash was no closer to understanding why Dec had sent him here. Save for the large central expanse which contained nothing but heavy production machinery, the building was all but completely deserted. It was as if nobody had set foot there in half a century.

"Why the hell have you sent me here?" Wash asked, hearing his voice bounce off the walls. "What can this have to do with colonising other planets?"

He was feeling more and more disgruntled with what was turning into a wasted trip.

"Time to go home."

Wash heard a distant rasping buzz and the rippling of water. The echo of both noises resounded through the building. The sound drew him to a door in the corner, one which had gone unnoticed before. Grabbing hold of the metal staircase Wash ran up the steps, his shoes clanking loudly. Like the entrance to the whole complex, it was locked but it took no effort at all to bash through the sodden corrupted wood.

On the other side was a small rickety boathouse. Down below him, Wash could see a platform several metres wide and roughly three metres long, tapering off to slope into the water. He figured there was probably about a small swimming pool's worth of water under the boathouse roof before it simply became the Thames. Through the entrance, Wash could see more submerged buildings which had been sketched around by a small one-man speedboat. It clearly hadn't come anywhere near his current location but the waves were still shimmering against the decrepit structure.

He saw something in the brown liquid.

The undulating of the water level sporadically revealed various segments of a bulky object.

It had hands.

Wash's veins froze in an instant. His legs weakened.

The next moment he was pounding down the creaky steps for a closer look. Standing on the launching platform, Wash could see the body in more detail. The only movements were caused by the gushing of the river.

It revealed a lifeless husk of a face that stared Wash down with haunting empty eye-sockets.

12

Don's head was split in two by the screams. Like a chorus they worked their way into a morbid crescendo.

Then there was nothing but a gaunt quiet.

Don watched the sweat dripping from Orvan's brow, the tall man's face contorted in a fit of rage and anguish.

He looked down at the weapon, its trigger pulled past the point of no return. Don was powerless to stop what was about to happen. Again.

His leg erupted like a supernova.

Bones vaporised like snow crystals under a blowtorch.

Ligaments snapped under the strain.

Don woke up in a sweat.

He felt across for Sally and remembered where he was. Hundreds of miles away from her. Checking the time he tried to get back to sleep, but did not have much luck.

✳

"Is everybody in the briefing room?" Don asked Gisèle the next morning. The heart of Arkan's barracks was a rabbit warren of sterile white corridors, easy to get lost in.

"They've all reported in. Even Orvan and his men."

"Good. How did the marines take to them joining up?" Don felt he had no choice but to bring them in after the arrival of another British ship.

"Not particularly well," Gisèle said with a worried glance through the doorway. "But I think both sides realise a disagreement is not in our best interests right now. Especially here in Arkan."

"That's promising I suppose."

"Optimism, eh? The big city life has changed you, Donald." He didn't have a chance to joke back as enormous roar of laughter struck up from the marines. They appeared to be treating their surroundings like the mess hall.

"...and how is he going to lead a combat op with a leg like that?" one of them said, Don couldn't work out who. "This isn't his heyday anymore."

Don stepped into the room, making sure his footsteps were loud and ominous as he marched down the aisle. The marines were scattered around the small auditorium with their feet up. Orvan and his men were sat in the corner, not joining in the conversation. There were wolfish smiles on the Choctaw faces as they listened. Chad sat by himself, eyes front, face forward. Don and Gisèle's arrival triggered timorous looks of guilt. The Marines put their feet down. Orvan continued smiling.

"Let's get something clear," Don said gruffly, taking his place underneath the glowing mission screen.

"You might be Stangl's men but you answer to me on this mission and I will have no qualms benching any son of a bitch who doesn't fall in line. Is that clear?" There was no answer. "I thought so," he said snidely as he laid out some papers. "Okay then. According to the intel supplied by Orvan and his people, the two British are likely to be in *this* section of the mountains," Don used his laser pointer to highlight a section on the map. "It's approximately ten miles north-west of Peakwood. In order to get there we will fly to the city, move from there to the lower hills before continuing onto the target area on foot."

"Why can't we just fly to the target area?" Smurph asked, dumbfounded.

"Well, there are several reasons for that. Firstly, the terrain up there is difficult for aircraft and I don't think anyone wants to attempt landing operations when potentially under fire from British artillery."

"Has anyone actually sighted British troops yet?" asked Smurph.

"Orvan? Would you like to field this one?" Don said. Orvan took out his knife and began to fiddle with it, playfully.

"Your scepticism is understandable, marine," he began, focussing solely on the weapon in his hands. "British military forces have not been spotted in the flesh, no. Not yet anyway." He looked up. "But we are hearing unconfirmed chatter from Peakwood and Whitehill of foragers going missing in the mountains. Whatever's going on here is not friendly. I don't think we can rule out artillery at this stage."

"Have any bodies been found, though?" Smurph asked without emotion.

"What's your point, Smurph?" Gisèle chirped in

for the first time. Smurph appeared surprised. He looked between her and Don as he explained himself, gesticulating towards the mission screen.

"My point is that if we have little to no confirmation that this group of Brits is armed or dangerous, why not airlift us straight in."

Don held his hands up.

"Look, just let me explain our second problem," he said quickly, before flicking to the next slide. It revealed an image of the Choctaw Mountains with a large purple patch covering a section of the peaks. "We've tried taking satellite images of the region in which the British ships have crashed. As you can see, the estimated area of impact is affected by a wide-ranging magnetic field. It has messed with the aerial photography and would likely wreak havoc on any aerial attack." Smurph's confusion abated, but Don pressed home the advantage. "You have to remember, large scale military action is not the purpose of this mission. There were already six squads of A.N. troops present on this base before you arrived. It's the lack of complete intel that we are here to solve. I'm not taking any risks with anyone's lives until we have it. If air support is required, that option *is* available to us, but given the uncertainty about what we'll find up there, it has to remain a last resort at this point."

"If you say so, sir," Smurph said as he leant back in his seat with a raise of the eyebrows.

"Any other questions?" Don asked the room.

"What sort of weapon-set are we looking at, boss?" The red marine, Diablo, asked in a sharp deep voice. It was the first time Don had heard him speak. It sounded as if he was asking Smurph the question, rather than him but it was Orvan who interjected.

"Come on red, you should know the answer to that one," he said. Diablo just sat there blankly staring at him. "Wow," Orvan continued. "Do they not teach you anything back on Earth these days? The third amendment to your border sanctions stipulates Teslanium weapons are not to be brought into Choctaw."

"Why not?" Smurph asked angrily.

"There's no centralised government in Choctaw, Smurph," Don explained. Smurph interrupted straight away.

"I don't need a damn history lesson, Stafford."

"You have a real problem interrupting people don't you, blueberry?" Orvan stabbed. "Let the *legend of Arkan* finish," he added with a hint of sarcasm. "Talking is all he has left these days," he said finally. Don rolled his eyes and tried to continue his explanation but Orvan wouldn't let him, taking control of the meeting himself. "You should know that the entire economy and infrastructure in Choctaw is built on what was salvaged from Arkan and the other border cities in the early days," Orvan said. "This place hasn't had anywhere near the same level of development as the rest of Proxima, which includes weapons technology. If any of your Teslanium equipment ends up in the wrong hands out there, any idiots with the wrong ideas would be difficult to stop. Strength is power in Choctaw. Allowing Teslanium into the region would be like dumping fuel on a fire."

"I don't give a shit about that," Smurph barked. "I've been sent here by Lothar Stangl to locate and put an end to aggressive invaders by any means necessary."

"Do you think Stangl is going to be particularly happy if you or one of your men triggers a civil war on the most important battlefield with the British?" Orvan held Smurph's fierce gaze. He was still every bit the hard-ball Don remembered.

"Are *you* seriously suggesting any of us are gonna get fucked over in the arse end of nowhere? It's just a bunch of jumped up farmers out there."

"Keep telling yourself that, blue man," Orvan said calmly. "Then wait and see who fucks who in the arse end of nowhere."

Smurph stood up, fists clenched and eyes staring Orvan down.

This mission is off to a flier already, Don thought to himself.

"Look, Smurph," he finally interjected. "I can't authorise your weapons coming on the mission unless we face a real emergency. Stangl knows that. I'm sure you're more than capable of holding your own with your lower grade weapons. You're all eight foot tall and built like a tanks, for goodness sake. Like the air support, if we need Teslanium on our side, we can call it in."

Smurph sat down and folded his arms in a huff.

"At the first sign of trouble I'm ordering a pallet drop of our proper weapons, you understand?"

"Believe me, Smurph, if we find ourselves in a situation even *you* feel like your team can't handle, I'll make that call myself. Any other questions? No? Grab your gear. We're leaving in fifteen minutes."

★

"Daddy, where are we going?" Corinne asked, her young voice wavering. She was wrapped up in a spotty pink dressing gown and holding a grey fluffy elephant. Tycho kissed the top of her brunette head lovingly and carried the little girl across the lawn in the darkness.

"It's okay, darling. We're going somewhere safe," he said, as he loaded her into her seat in his car.

"I don't understand why we have to go out this late," Tristen grumbled as he plonked himself down in the passenger seat. The boy crossed his arms after plugging in the restraint. He'd refused to put his night clothes on and was still wearing the athletics apparel and trainers he wore for after-school club.

"If Daddy wants us to go out this late at night, that's what we do, Tris," Corinne insisted petulantly, while Tycho adjusted her straps.

"Thank you, Corinne," he said.

"Yeah, whatever," Tristen snivelled with a distant look into his ocular implants. As he climbed into the driver's position, Tycho could see that his son was playing another round of his favourite computer game. Nobody spoke again until they had been on the road for ten minutes.

"Zainab wants to know where we are going, Daddy." Corinne asked innocently.

"Stop pretending your elephant can talk, Corinne," Tristen snapped.

"Come on, son," Tycho chided. "Let her have her fun." He leaned round slightly to address his daughter. "We're going to the navy yard to see some ships. And then we're going to visit your Auntie Kara in Cahors."

"Why?" she asked back.

"Because we've not seen her in a while, that's why."

"Is mummy coming?" Corinne asked.

"No Corinne, mummy isn't coming."

"Why not?"

"She's busy with work."

"I thought we were supposed to be going to mum's in the morning," Tristen interjected, his tone accusatory.

"Well… that's not happening anymore, son," Sean explained. "Your mother made that quite clear."

"I like Auntie Kara, Daddy," Corinne said sweetly, staring out of the window. "And Zainab does, too," she remembered with a smile.

Arriving at the Navy base, Tycho parked up the silver six-seated vehicle in a rush and hurried his children out. Tristen complained again but still carried the bags, like he'd been asked, and Tycho held Corinne in his arms. After a short walk through the expansive docking area, they could see the bright lights, illuminating the collection of ships. They hulked above them like cathedrals, lit up like jewels in a crown, the reflection shimmering in the water.

"Look! It's pretty, daddy," she declared.

Tycho took them through the officers' entrance, which bypassed the many security checks between them and the water's edge. He'd made all the necessary arrangements earlier so didn't have to visit his office. In just a few minutes, the three of them clambered up the metal gang plank to board the ANS Diamond.

"You remember where Daddy's quarters are, right son?" Tycho asked in the foyer.

"Yes, dad."

"You take your sister there please," he said, placing the girl on her feet. Irradiated by the ship's corridor lights, Tycho marvelled at his daughter's beautiful eyes. One was a rich hazel and the other a deep cerulean blue.

"Get off!" Tristen pulled away disgusted as Corinne tried to hold his hand. The two of them stamped off down the metal corridor in protested unison. We're nearly clear, Tycho thought to himself.

"Are you sure this is a good idea, sir?" Captain Saldana asked as Tycho set foot on the bridge. She had been sensible enough to leave the lights setting on stealth mode. Of all the usual light sources, only the expansive dashboard glowed in the darkness. The panoramic glass surrounding the room, which acted as window, ceiling and floor all in one, was covered up by the ship's blast shield. Next to the other vessels this one was barely identifiable.

"We'll be fine. It's a few days from here to Cahors and, once we've dropped off the kids, we can steam on to Choctaw," he replied, inspecting the engines panel.

"What did you tell the Fleet Admiral?" Saldana asked, leaving her station and coming closer to Sean.

"I said this information leak needs investigation. He agreed with me and thinks we should do this as off-the-record as possible. Are we ready for launch?"

"Yes, sir. We'll pick the relief crew up in Teslapolis in two days' time. Are you sure a skeleton crew will be enough?"

"It has to be. We've got to keep this operation under wraps."

"Did you manage to get hold of Stafford?"

"Unfortunately not," Tycho replied. "I certainly trust him a lot more than my wife but from what I can tell, he's not at the ministry right now."

"What did Alida say?" Saldana looked worried.

"Nothing," Tycho replied. "She has no idea the kids

are with me."

Saldana's jaw dropped. She pulled Tycho away from the work station.

"Isn't that going to make things messier?"

"Probably," Tycho said timidly. "But she forced my hand. She's planning on taking them away from me, going for full custody."

Saldana stroked Tycho on the arm.

"I'm sorry, Sean."

He put his hand on her ebony-skinned cheek and kissed her lips.

"That's rich from Alida, though," she said eventually. "You spend a lot more time with the kids than she does."

"Yes, but I find it hard to believe that Proxima A's council leader is going to lose a custody battle, do you? The judiciary won't risk pissing her off."

"She doesn't know about *us*, does she?" Saldana's eyes grew a little wider.

"No, don't worry. I think I'd like to keep it that way for now, if that's okay? Things are *bad* between us, to be honest."

"Of course."

"And it'd be good if we could keep it from the children, too."

"Yes, sir."

"Right," Sean said with an impatient rub of his hands. "Let's get this show on the road."

＊

Don allowed himself to reminisce as he set eyes in Choctaw's wastelands for the first time in years. Tall cactus-like plants cast long shadows on browning desert scrub in the warm afternoon sun. Dust hung in the air, disturbed by the helicopter. The lingering smell of creosote and sage told Don that it must have rained a little in the last week, the grateful pores of the fauna still active. There was nothing but this lonely untilled landscape as far as Don could see to the east, aside from sporadic swollen hills. Winding through the wilderness were a collection of dirt tracks, worn into the terrain by years of human footfall rather than industry. They came from all directions, and joined up as one, like tributaries of a river under Don's feet.

Turning back on himself and stepping around the aircraft that obscured his view, Don remembered the first time he had arrived at Peakwood all those years ago. It had not changed one bit.

If the Choctaw Desert was desolate and uninviting, the woods were exactly the opposite. An outpost at the end of the world. The brush-like trees were hardly healthy but clustered together so closely they gave more indication of life than anything that lay eastward. The forest sat in front of the mountains like a line of soldiers defending city walls. At the heart of the woodland were the large wooden buildings which formed Peakwood's two main streets. The slats used in the structures were either bent or cracked in places. A total repair job was needed out here. But there was nobody with enough resources to help, Don knew that. To the left of the main group of houses was a large field brimming with stalks of a tall green plant. It was fenced off from a herd of cows.

"I knew that Choctaw wasn't a luxurious place, but I didn't think it'd be as backward as this," Chad said after a long stare. "I'm starting to see now why Teslanium weapons out here wouldn't be a good idea," he added.

"Yeah," Don replied. "The wattage of even an assault rifle with Teslanium tech could probably take out that row of houses instantly."

"That's insane."

"Yep," Don said. "Remember Teslanium weapons are effectively instant hit. They're so fast that the friction alone would probably set the whole row on fire."

"Damn," Chad replied, mulling over the thought. "How do they live like this?" he asked eventually.

"This is one of the nicer places in Choctaw," Don revealed. "But to answer your question, I'll be honest with you, Chad. I really don't know. Remember that living like this is a choice."

"You keep telling yourself that, wobbles," Orvan sneered as he walked past the pair, brushing Don's shoulder as he went. He and Chad set off after him, hoping to keep pace. All they got was more obnoxious back-chat, though.

"You telling me that if we turned up on the Arkan doorstep asking for help we'd be welcomed with open arms?" Orvan asked.

"You know it's more complicated than that," Don said. "If you worked with us you could leave this wasteland behind or get our help to live a better life."

"Out here we live off the land," Orvan said with his arms stretched out wide. "And we're proud of it too. We respect it and it respects us in return. We don't rape it, gut it of everything it has to offer and worry about consequences later. No, we're more sensible than the Atlas Colonies."

"Still, I expected more of a so-called city," Chad said.

"Oh, Peakwood is no city," Orvan replied quickly.

"That's even by Choctaw standards. It's just a town with delusions of grandeur. Mind you, as the only Choctaw in this conversation, I'll leave myself to criticise my own kind, thank you very much."

"This place looks like a shit-hole," Smurph grunted having caught up. Gisèle gave him a cautionary stare.

"Don't make this any worse than you already have, you big blue moron."

Orvan probably would have exchanged some unpleasant words were it not for a worried woman pacing out to meet them, a greying mess of flowing behind her.

"Orvan? Orvan Eld? Is that you?" she cried, sporting tattered overalls and a grubby apron.

"Levina... Nyusha, right?" he asked, trying to remember.

"Yes, that's right. Laptev is my husband. He fought for you at Oldshade."

Don and Gisèle exchanged an awkward look, remembering the conflict.

"I think I remember. Is everything alright?"

"He's gone," she said, as her voice broke, face in hands.

"Laptev?"

"Yes."

"What happened?"

"He was out on a hunt with some friends but never came back."

"Hasn't Honit done anything to help? He's still the boss round here, no?"

"Yes he is, but nobody's been able to find him either."

"How long have they both been gone?"

"Ever since the cylinders landed in the mountains."

"How many people have gone missing since it arrived?" Orvan asked.

"At the last count, it was nine. Laptev and his friends make it thirteen," she said through feeble tears.

13

Wash hurled the contents of his stomach into the water beside the dead body. He heaved himself away from the corpse, reeling from the sharp pain in his throat, cursing the gag reflex.

"What the fuck?" He groaned before spitting out the remnants of his vomit. Wash fought for breath and held his head in shaking hands. Bent over the sodden wood flooring, the journalist grimaced at the smell of his sick. Panicking, he fumbled for the glasses to call Declan.

"Answer, you damn prick," he yelled until his friend picked up.

"Hello?"

"Have you gone completely mad?"

"Nice to hear from you, Washington," Declan spoke with rehearsed composure. "Is something wrong?"

"Is something wrong? Of course something's fucking wrong! This is the last time I follow one of your leads."

"What *are* you talking about?"

"I'm talking about–" Wash looked into the holes punched into the lifeless skull and stopped. He calmed down a little, out of necessity. "Don't you think it would have been nice to warn me about what I might find here?"

"You've lost me completely, Wash. This isn't more carrot and feather nonsense is it?"

"What?"

"Look, if things are as bad as you say they are, call the police. Not me. I'm not your mother, Wash."

Declan hung up.

"You posh twat," Wash said, exasperated. *Carrot and feather... Why had Declan mentioned that?* It was a combination of words he'd not heard in years. And then he remembered.

"Oh Declan, is this some kind of sick school prank?" Wash begged aloud. His eyes were drawn again to the remains that haunted him. Grabbing a nearby sheet of plastic, crispy and rough to the touch, Wash crept towards the body with his hands covered. Grabbing hold of what was left of an arm, Wash dragged it slowly up the slope and dumped it down again. Even though the eyeballs were long gone, crushed to jelly and cleared out by the water, Wash still felt as if his every move was being watched by a strange monster. Its mouth hung open in a death-fright, murky sludge stagnating in its throat. The smell was unbearable. Thankfully Wash found what he was looking for quickly.

Around the body's waist was a satchel tied tightly in place. The knots were wound with intention, from naval experience, perhaps. It was something attached to the body after death. Like the unfortunate victim, it was full of water and Wash had to be careful opening it when he realised it was mostly papers. He did not dare try to read a word for fear of destroying them in their soggy state. He wrapped the satchel in a roll of the plastic and placed it carefully in his backpack.

Next, Wash logged into Jay's VPN. He placed a call to the police to inform them of what he'd found, holding a sleeve over his mouth to muffle his voice.

Wash left the warehouse and waited in a nearby street for thirty minutes so that he could confirm the police had actually arrived on the scene. While he waited, he used his glasses to dictate a simple report of what had happened for the crime section, like Declan had told him back at the restaurant. He'd wait a few hours before filing, at least until it was likely to have reached the police's press office. Wash made sure to leave out any details that they might reveal, like the state of the eyes. If this was another 'Eye Killer' murder, he'd rather not draw undue attention to how he found out about it. He was careful to explain that the 'Daily Citizen understands that a body was recovered by police at the Tobacco Docks'. Even in this day and age, the editors still tended to allow reporters to keep their contacts anonymous. Hopefully, nobody would ever find out he was acting as his own.

Wash spent at least an hour perched on a bench in Parliament Square, a hood hiding his face. Only sparingly did he look up from the large wooden decking platform that had been erected around the central lake. The creaking stage was a never-ending conveyor belt of life, sight-seers and professionals clunking along above the great river. The quadrangle of exposed water was what separated Wash's seated position from the crumbling House of Commons, supported by scaffolding. The river lapped at the archways on the building's base and the tips of dead trees submerged in the old courtyard. Beyond the iconic clock tower he could see the dripping paddles of the London Waterwheel. Once a gleaming tourist attraction, now it was a rust-covered hydro-electric power station plugging away in a vain attempt to sustain Westminster.

It had been light when Wash arrived but the sky had hardened to the colour of lead and the streetlamps had ignited. He spotted Declan marching in the artificial light, emerging from one of the doors on the Chancellor's Tower at the south of the complex. The young researcher was sporting a tight-fitting charcoal grey suit with matching waistcoat and a blue tie. He held a brown leather brief-case.

Wash bore down on Declan hoping to surprise him. He bumped into his friend, grabbed the lapels of his suit and pushed the man into a red-brick alcove between two buttresses.

"What is going on?" Wash asked threateningly.

"Hey, what are you playing at?" Declan's eyes flickered, shock quickly evolving into annoyance. He glanced down at the damage done to his attire and made the appropriate adjustments.

"You got lucky that I remembered that stupid game," Wash insisted, "the one where we tied things to each other. Else I'd have left that warehouse with nothing."

"You know I can't talk here," Declan hissed.

Wash looked right towards the endless stream of

bodies.

"Well where can you talk then? I don't think anyone's going to notice us here."

"They will if they see a government official talking to a man in a hood. Take that damn thing off," Declan said as he dragged the fabric off the journalist's head, exposing his wet hair. "God, you stink."

Wash sighed.

"Look, if you won't talk to me over the phone, then talk to me now, when nobody can record us. What the hell is going on?"

"Did you run the story?" Declan deflected.

"Why does that matter?" Wash kept half an eye on the crowd to check they weren't being watched.

"Just tell me," Declan said hurriedly. "Did you run it?"

"I've filed a few hundred words on it, yes. But I don't understand how this is going to expose the IPCP. Hell, I don't even know what I'm supposed to be uncovering at this point."

"Just be patient, okay? Running that story is how it starts. We need Yvette to publish more pertinent details than she realises."

"What does that even mean?"

"You'll find out. Trust me. You found the carrot then?" Wash sighed again. He was already starting to regret playing Hansel and Gretel with Declan.

"Yes, there was a bag with some papers in it. That's what I was supposed to find, right? They were ruined by the river."

"That's fine. Dry them out. When you do, you won't be able to thank me enough."

"Is that all you've got?"

Declan looked from side-to-side, planning his escape.

"Look, I've got two committee meetings and a scrutiny panel to attend, Wash. I *have* to go. Please try not to accost me in public again."

Declan pushed past and rejoined into the multitudes. Wash did not want to follow him for fear of drawing more attention.

He looked at his watch.

SHIT!

8.57pm. *Vicky.*

★

Wash burst through the restaurant's sturdy oak door and instantly drew a look of derision from the maître d'hôtel.

"Can I help you, sir?" he asked, almost sarcastically.

"I have a reservation for half-eight," Wash said, out of breath, wiping sweat from his palms onto his scruffy jumper. Looking in a nearby mirror, he looked a mess, hair stuck up in a cow's lick.

"That was thirty-nine minutes ago."

"Yes I know. I'm sorry. I err... got caught up."

"Of course you did, sir," the head waiter said before staring into the air above Wash's head.

His irises pulsated and a garish graphic could be seen glazing across the eyeballs.

"Lucky for you, your lady friend was a bit more punctual." He looked Wash up and down, scrunching his nose. "If you'll step this way, sir," he pointed to the table in the corner that Wash had shared with Declan.

He saw Vicky. She was not happy but, boy, did she look good.

Most of her hair was pulled back in a tight pony-tail with loose curls left to hang just behind each temple. They sat on the shoulders of a red dress with a plunging neckline.

"What time do you call this?" Vicky didn't look up from the wine list.

"I'm so sorry," Wash said pathetically as he pulled out his chair and sat down.

"I'll arrange for the menus to be sent over," the waiter left with an amused look on his face.

Vicky peered over the leather-bound booklet in her hands and rolled her eyes.

"You looked suitably dressed for the occasion too," she whispered angrily. "My god, how are you so wet? It hasn't rained today."

"I'm so, so sorry. And you look so, *so* good too. I've screwed this up."

"You can say that again," Vicky huffed. An awkward silence hung between them while the clink of crockery and glasses tickled away in the background.

"I don't know what to-" Wash tried to explain himself but was cut off.

"You know, I thought someone like you would be here an hour early not late," Vicky began. "You've clearly wanted this for weeks and yet you can't even turn up on time. Do you have any idea how embarrassing it is to sit alone in a restaurant like this all dressed up?"

Wash muttered another apology.

"What was so damned important that you couldn't bother to make an effort tonight?" she questioned, arms folded.

Wash didn't know how much to say. *Maybe I should just say nothing and write this off? There's no point putting her in danger. I always said I'd keep her safe from this stuff.*

"I don't think this is a safe place to say," he whispered, against his better judgement.

"What?"

"I'd rather tell you somewhere else…"

"Are you kidding me? You're seriously trying that old trick after being here just five minutes?" Vicky looked up and rubbed carefully underneath her eyeliner.

Wash had a moment of selfish weakness.

"I found a body," he said.

Vicky froze.

"What did you say?"

"I found a body."

"Are you taking the piss?"

"Believe me, I wish I was."

"Seems pretty convenient to me," she said, gathering her things.

"Please, don't go," Wash leaned forward and put his hand on top of hers.

"Wash, what is wrong with you?" she recoiled.

"I promise you I'm telling you the truth," he said, staring into her eyes. Vicky quietly looked him up and down, her mind whirring. Then she let out a short sigh.

"Oh, god. You're telling the truth, aren't you?" she said, incredulous.

Wash nodded.

"I assume it was—"

"Dead. Yes." Wash said with another nervous look around the room. "I'd really rather not talk about it here."

"Are… you okay?" Vicky's anger had slowly turned to concern.

"Just about. If you want to know what's going on, we'll have to leave, I'm sorry."

Vicky packed her things into a velvet clutch bag and started fiddling with her coat.

"Come on, let's go."

☆

"So what happened?" Vicky asked once they were several streets away from the restaurant. She had her hands wrapped tight in her fur coat and placed each foot in front of the other carefully, high heels clacking against the crumbled pavement.

"I did what you said, I carried on pressing for answers," Wash said. "I ended up finding one I didn't even know I was looking for. I got a tip off about the colonial programme and ended up finding a dead body at a warehouse in Wapping."

"Did you say the interplanetary colonisation programme?"

"Yeah."

"Did they kill someone?"

"I don't know. Have you heard about this Eye Killer?"

"Yeah, of course. Everybody has."

"I think it might have been him. The body I found had no eyes."

"So what's that got to do with the IPCP?"

"I don't know. I've got a thousand more questions than I did before. I managed to get my hands on some paperwork but it's too wet to read right now," he said with a chatter of the teeth. He'd been running on adrenaline for so long and felt weary now. His wet clothes gave him a chill.

"We need to get you indoors," Vicky said, rubbing

Wash's back. "God, you really smell."

"Sorry."

"It's okay, let's get you somewhere warm. My place is closer than yours."

A rickety train ride later, Wash and Vicky were walking up the echoing staircase of her building. She opened the large oak door and revealed a quaint lounge-kitchen set-up. Harsh lights built into the ceiling illuminated a beige laminate flooring. An old leather sofa sat opposite a small television to the left with a kitchen bar, sink and cupboard space to the right. There was a door next to the television which he assumed led to the bedroom and bathroom. The whole apartment smelt positively feminine, like berries. It filled Wash's nose and forced his heart-rate up a little.

"Nice place," he said politely.

"Thanks. Only been here a few months," Vicky said as she kicked off her shoes, coming down a few inches from the high heels. "I think you should have a shower," she suggested as she threw her keys onto the bar and removed her coat. Wash allowed himself a long stare as Vicky bent over to retrieve some post.

"I don't have any spare clothes," Wash said, at a loss.

"It's okay. I've got some leftovers from some old boyfriends." Wash chose not to ask for any more details.

"If you say so. Have you got a radiator?"

"Yeah, over here," Vicky pointed to it below the window which overlooked the couch as she removed the tie from her hair and swished it from side to side.

"Before I get in, I should start drying these papers," Wash fumbled with his bag.

"Definitely," Vicky said. Wash handed over the bag carefully.

"Listen, Vicky… I'm really sorry about tonight. I had such a perfect idea about how it was going to go and I messed it up." Vicky came up close to Wash and put her arms round his waist, her eyes fixed on him. She said nothing. Then she leaned in and kissed him on the lips.

"Lucky for you, I fancy the pants off of you, Washington Parker," she said playfully. "Go have your shower," she added as she caressed his chest.

★

Wash threw himself down on the plush bed sheets, welcoming the velvet touch on his naked skin. Vicky ruffled her hair and let out a long gasp as she rolled over to face him. Wash put his arm underneath her head and held her close, enjoying her soft warmth.

"That was long overdue, don't you think?" Vicky purred as she stroked Wash chest. He laughed.

"I didn't realise you wanted this as badly as I did. Especially after earlier," he replied.

"You're a handsome boy, Wash." She let her hands roam free. Wash breathed in as she squeezed him. "As for earlier, I hadn't realised how much trouble you were in. I'm the one who should be sorry."

"You don't have to be sorry. I embarrassed you. I should have remembered."

"I wouldn't change a thing about tonight," Vicky said.

"Neither would I." Wash leaned in and kissed Vicky's red mouth, drinking in each undulation of her lips. Vicky pulled away.

"Do you think those papers will be dry by now?"

"I don't know... reckon they could do with another 10 minutes."

"And what can we do in that time?" Vicky said suggestively, a devilish smile blossoming on her face. She kissed Wash on the neck and climbed on top of him.

*

Vicky found a blue woolly jumper and a pair of grey tracksuit bottoms for Wash to wear when they returned to the living room. She had put on a translucent black chemise with slits on the hips. Wash could still see every detail of her figure through the mesh.

"The documents are ready now," Wash said as he tentatively tested the crusty wad of papers. He sat down on the settee just as Vicky brought him a drink and planted herself on his lap.

"Let's have a look, then."

"I don't think that's a good idea," Wash said carefully.

"What do you mean?"

"I don't want you to get in trouble for looking at this."

"With who?"

"You know who."

"Look, it's not your decision, okay. Just because you've slept with me doesn't give you the right to start protecting me. I'm not your property."

"Sheesh, sorry. I had just always told myself I'd keep you out of this sort of stuff."

"It's okay," Vicky turned her scowl into a smile and

kissed Wash again. "Come on let's have a look at these things." He couldn't say no any longer.

They split the pile in half and flicked through them, failing to see anything noteworthy. Most of the papers contained spreadsheet print-outs with random numbers in each cell.

"What does any of this mean?" Vicky asked.

"I don't know..." Wash said in passing as he studied the gibberish in front of him. "Does Declan think I'm some kind of mathematics expert?" he said under his breath.

"This looks more interesting," Vicky said, producing a collection of papers firmer than the rest, clipped together with a metallic tie. "It's got pictures."

"Show me?" Wash asked. Vicky produced several pages of passport-like photographs with occupation details, weight, height and other various pieces of information underneath.

"Amos Yega, Israel Barrett, Zoey Smith..." Vicky listed off the names she saw. "Who are these people?"

"I guess they must be the colonists."

"That one looks different," Wash pointed out as Vicky pulled out a file with a bright red topper which read **RISK CANDIDATE**.

Underneath the caption read the words *'Lisa Houghton'* next to a small photo of an attractive-looking blonde female. Scribbled in notes at the foot of the page were the words: *'Possible flight risk. Consider termination. Preferably after crash, if possible.'*

"Here's another one," Vicky said, producing a second red-topped form. This one featured the name *'Harper Mulgrew'*. This woman looked considerably fiercer. It had notes on it too: *'Serious flight risk. Termination a priority.'*

"Are these recommendations to kill colonists?" Wash asked aloud. "What is going on?"

14

"They're here! Run!" someone yelled from outside the tent.

The voice was exceptionally hoarse and came from just a few metres away.

Shermeen was on her own inside the Tarp. She froze, breath turned to glass. It threatened to shatter in her throat.

"Help me!" the voice cried again.

"I don't--" Shermeen whelped. She paced a few steps before cowering in the corner. She scrunched her eyes and covered both ears. Her glass breath sublimated into a short sharp rhythm.

"Help!" The voice still pricked at her conscience. "Somebody please... help!"

There was an acute whip at the doorway.

Shermeen's opened her eyes. She screamed.

Instinctively, she was on her feet, pushing her shoulders into the Tarp's soft inner wall.

Standing upright in the sand was an arrow, immersed in a flame. The tongues of fire danced in the breeze and flashed as they ignited the nearest bed.

The neighbouring one tickled alight. Each in turn, another object succumbed to the blaze. It was getting closer.

Shermeen was edged closer to the doorway. She hesitated at the threshold then leapt through the opening.

She whelped when she saw the beach.

There were at least five bodies strewn across the sand between her and the treeline. Fizzing noises continued overhead as more arrows pierced the ground, some lit, others not.

Like a rabbit caught in headlights, Shermeen's eyes flickered desperately, trying to work out where they were coming from.

The trees.

Where was her mum?

Shermeen felt the vicious heat on the back of her neck. The fire in the Krichmar Tarp was getting bigger. It forced her out into the open.

"Help!" It was Amos.

He was laying on his side, attempting to drag his large body through the sand. There was a thick dark trail between him and the men's Tarp a few metres away. It was now engulfed in flames and black smoke. Amos looked right at her.

"Shermeen! Please help!"

There was nowhere for her to hide. She ran over, crumpling at his side in a stream of tears.

"What's going on?" she asked through sprawling hair, shaken by more cries yelling out from the beach.

"I don't know but--." Amos recoiled in pain. Shermeen looked up and saw a dark patch around his left hip. "They got me," he said, rolling up his shirt revealing a short piece of wood embedded in the side of his waist. There were raw burn marks around the puncture. "You have to help me, please. I can't walk."

"What?" Shermeen leaned back. "I'm not strong enough."

Amos looked away in sheepish resignation.

"I'm sorry...," she added. "I didn't mean to say... It's just. I'm not that strong."

There was an awkward moment between the two of them, played across a backdrop of screams of terror. Shermeen felt guilty and searched her mind for anything she could do to help.

"Can you use that leg?" she asked, pointing to the side of his body that wasn't wounded. Amos tested it with a wince and a cough.

"Just about, I think."

Shermeen shuffled across on her knees, next to the man's injury and lifted his arm over her shoulders. She exhaled as Amos dropped his weight. He was heavier than expected. Setting herself, Shermeen explained her plan. "Lean on me and kick with your good leg," she said. Amos grunted in agreement as they began edging forward.

"It's working," he said.

"Where should we go?" Shermeen asked.

"I don't know," Amos grunted, unable to lift his head too high from the sand.

Shermeen scanned the beach and spotted a large cluster of rocks roughly ten metres to their right. They were closer to the tree-line but looked large enough to hide behind.

"I've found somewhere. We're going to have to change direction, sorry."

After a few adjustments, the pair were ready to

push on. Amos' wounds had forced her into action, given the girl focus. Shermeen's blood pounded through her veins, ringing like a tribal drumbeat in her ears. It was a hard slog. Every few steps, Amos proved too much for her. Each time, Shermeen tasted a mouthful of sand. Sharp grains scratched at her eyes, undefended with each hand engaged in the rescue operation.

The two colonists got behind the rocks. Shermeen's positioned Amos so he could sit up with his back against them. She generated some saliva, washed her mouth and spat the wet sand out. Clawing at each eye, her gritty hands only made them both sorer.

An arrow sliced the air above their heads.

Another cracked and splintered against the rock.

Shermeen screamed aloud. That frightened little girl bubbled back to the surface.

"They're getting closer," she snapped in panic. "Amos, what do we do now?"

There was no response.

"Amos?"

Still nothing.

"Amos?!"

Shermeen turned to look at the man, his eyes closed. She shook him, jolting him back into consciousness. He said something unintelligible, gurgling blood. Shermeen recoiled.

"Shermeen! Shermeen! Where are you?" Lynne's voice called out from the camp.

"Mum!" Shermeen answered, although she couldn't see her. "Help! It's Amos! He's been hit!"

Lynne arrived at the rocks. She threw both arms at Shermeen wildly, patting her all over. She didn't even look at Amos.

"Come on we have to go," she shouted, cheeks quivering, eyes vacant.

"What about Amos?"

"Come on let's go." Lynne grabbed the girl's arms and pulled.

"Mum, no! We can't leave--" The breath was knocked from her as Lynne started moving off, hands locked around each arm in a vice grip. Shermeen tried to kick back but wasn't strong enough, drained from dragging Amos. She looked back and to see that Amos had drifted off again.

"No! Amos!"

✳

Harper beat the others back to the treeline. The air was thick with the smell of burning and screams rose up from the beach. Harper scrunched her nose. She had only just managed to shake that stench from her brain just a few days ago. Finally, Ben, Zack, Zoey and James arrived, hot and flustered.

"What are you doing?" Zack asked with incredulity. "Let's go," he ordered, lifting an arm to brush the leaves out of his way.

Harper grabbed the man by the shoulder and pushed him against the tree. His scraggly wet beard dribbled on her forearm. Zack's eyes widened.

"If you waltz out there on your own, you'll be dead in seconds," she snapped.

Harper relaxed her grip and started inspecting her weapon.

"We need a plan, okay?" Zack nodded and shook himself down, but was still keen to have the last word.

"I *have* been in a firefight before you know," he insisted.

"That's great, but we still need to co-ordinate. We edge out to get a fix on the situation. Spread out and stay behind until I say so, okay?" They both nodded. "James and Zoey you stay here."

"But--" James tried to protest, even though he had no weapon.

"Don't." He quickly relented. "Come on you two, let's go," she said to Ben and Zack.

Adjusting the branches, Harper shuffled slowly forward, weapon ready to fire. Looking left, she saw that they were about twenty metres from the camp. Both remaining Tarps were on fire, their equipment and belongings strewn across the sand and the survivors left alive were cowering behind whatever cover they could find. Dotted around the scene were a handful of bodies, pricked all over by thin shafts of wood. More arrows fell on the camp.

"Oh god," Harper said to herself. "Let's get closer," she said to the others. "Use the trees as cover." Within a few seconds they were near enough to the water purifier station to see Lucas hiding behind it. His weapon was drawn but he could not find a break in the onslaught to fire. Next to him was Lynne, her arms around a weeping Shermeen.

"Lucas!" Harper called to the man. His eyes lit up.

"Thank god," he said. "We're getting torn to pieces here."

"Where are they firing from?" she asked.

"From that way, I think" he said, with a nod towards Harper's left, further along the beach. "I can't get a shot off. I haven't seen a single one of them."

"Are you hurt?" Harper asked.

"No I'm fine," Lucas replied.

"What about Lynne and Shermeen?"

"They're shaken up but they're okay, I think."

"Anyone else?" she asked.

"I've got no idea," he admitted.

"How many rounds do you have left?"

Lucas turned looked down to check, popped the magazine back in and opened his mouth.

Two thin black sticks hit his face with a thud.

One punctured his cheek. The other lodged itself beneath his left eye. The skin was taut and raw around the wounds. A deluge of blood flowed down his neck as he keeled over.

Lynne saw what had happened to Lucas and grabbed Shermeen by the hand.

"No Lynne! Stay where you are!" Harper cried.

It was too late.

The woman stood up instinctively and began to run away from the jungle. Shermeen was dragged along the beach. She lost her grip and fell ungraciously face-first into the sand. As Lynne reached the large rock, she was crippled by three arrows. One went through the back of her left calf. Two more sliced into her right thigh. She hit the ground with a shriek. Clutching the nearest wound, Lynne wailed like a banshee.

"Mum!" Shermeen cried out, face caked in sand. She began crawling towards Lynne.

"Shermeen, no!" Ben said from their position. "Get back behind the purifier! We'll get her!"

"But she's hurt!" Shermeen was terrified.

"I know! Let us help her, you stay safe," Harper ordered. A few seconds later, Shermeen did as she was told, crawling back to cover. Lynne was still groaning, painting the sand a deep red with every feeble movement.

"I'll lay down covering fire," Harper said to Ben. "Can you get Lynne?"

"Yeah, no problem," he said, a steely determination in his eyes.

Harper leaned out of her cover and fired off five shots in the direction of the enemy. Ben made a dash for Lynne. He crouched over her and lifted the woman up. Harper fired off four more rounds to protect his retreat back to the purifier.

"What now?" Zack asked.

"We've got to fend them off, somehow." Harper said. "You ready for another firefight?"

"Yeah I guess so," he said.

"Okay then, get ready to follow me," she instructed. "Ben! Hold your position here."

"Got it," he replied, looking

"Wait!" It was Shermeen.

"What is it?" Harper asked, frustrated.

"It's Amos," she explained. "He's hurt by one of the rocks over there," she said, pointing in the direction of the enemy fire.

"Oh, forget about him," Zack proclaimed. "We haven't got time to save the fat guy."

"We're not leaving anyone behind," Harper insisted.

"Oh come on. I'm not getting myself killed for that ni--." Harper glared at Zack. "--guy," he finished his sentence. "How are we supposed to get him back here? He weighs a tonne."

"I managed to help him over there from the Tarp, and I'm just a kid," Shermeen shouted petulantly.

"You've got no excuse now, Zack," Harper said with

a wry smile. "Come on, let's go. Ben, give us some cover."

She darted for the next tree, firing off one shot on the way. Crashing her shoulder into the wood, she unclipped the magazine and reloaded. Zack was close behind. The pair continued their staggered advance along the tree line until they were close to their target.

Something cracked Harper over the head.

Next thing she knew, she was on her backside in the sand. The attacker swung an object towards Zack. He shimmied his shoulders, trying to dodge the blow. There was a yowl of pain. Through blurred vision, Harper watched red liquid spurt from underneath the weapon. Zack stumbled backwards and slumped against a tree, helpless. The blade was raised a second time. Harper couldn't stop it, nailed to the floor.

"No," Harper muttered as she tried to haul herself up.

She jumped at the powerful thud.

The weapon fell, dropping softly into the sand, next to a falling stone. Zack was still alive. The attacker's body, humanoid in shape, was not as rigid as before, Something had struck the looming figure.

Another stone flew through the air. It caught the attacker square in the middle of what Harper assumed was a torso. Instantly, it turned to flee, dashing into the jungle. James and Zoey came round the tree line, stones in each hand.

"Are you okay?" James asked as Harper strained into a standing position.

"Zack's hurt," she said. "See what you can do for him. I'm going after it."

Harper motioned away from the beach but was stopped by retreating fire. She dove behind a nearby rock as two arrows fizzed past her and landed in the sand. Putting her back up against it, she looked across and saw that James and Zoey had ducked for cover. Poking her nose over the top, she fired off more shots and received no reply.

Harper saw an opportunity, holstering her weapon.

"No Harper, don't!" he called.

Harper vaulted the rock, hitting the ground running at full pelt.

Shimmying from side to side, she bore down on the target. Catching up with the creature, Harper was able to make out some of its features. It appeared to have a thick coat of fur, rough and straw-like, greyish in colour. She counted two arms and two legs. From this angle, they were about the only elements of the assailant that even remotely resembled human life.

Harper got close enough to grab the fleeing native. She leaned out to grasp at the spines on the creature's back. Its arm swung back, dispatching a sharp blow. It left a deep red puncture. Harper lost ground but was still within touching distance. She stretched forward and stumbled, closing her hand around a hairy leg. The creature hit the ground with a thud too. The limb wrestled free from her grip with ease. It swung to kick her in the face. Harper partially blocked the blow with her right forearm, the back of her head thumping painfully into the soil. She cursed, activating the plasma knife. She slashed. The intensity of the blade's fizz increased as it tore through the fur, coarse strands landing on Harper's face. The creature didn't even flinch. It sprung up, lifted its weapon and caned her on the chin.

She was on the ground once more, watching the figure resume flight. It took a few seconds recover from the latest blow before Harper could see the enemy now several metres away. There was no way she'd catch up now.

She pulled out the pistol. Without the composure to aim properly, Harper lifted the weapon and hoped for the best, firing three rounds. One cannoned off a nearby tree, the other rasping through a collection of leaves, the other sailing through the foliage and into the sky.

"Damn it," Harper said, deflated. She stared at the greenery above, the canopy low and oppressive, mocking her. Those pricks back on Earth were probably laughing too.

Harper had been right all along. Brixton's legacy. She had not been ready for this. Not for another fight. Not for any of this. So many lives had been lost already. Now they had been directly attacked and defeated... badly. Without even so much as a hostage, the odds were overwhelmingly against them. Huffing, Harper snatched at a clutch of the plumage she had severed from the creature and dragged herself back to camp.

15

"What's *he* doing here?" Jokubas asked angrily, blocking their way. Don should have seen this coming.

Orvan, his two men and Levina had led the group through Peakwood's main street to get to the Nyusha farm. The woman had agreed to let them use the family truck for the first leg of their journey, to get to it they had to pass under the piercing eyes of Peakwood's residents. Each of them looked up from their daily routine, startled by the colour and stature of the marines. A few mothers ushered children indoors, concerned at these newcomers. Once the appearance of three well-dressed Atlas Nations employees was made clear their apprehension quickly soured into resentment. Faces grew in length, stretching with silent seething anger.

Don tried to stay under the radar, staying as close as he could to the soldiers around him. They acted as helpful cover. This was one thing he had not considered: how the people of Peakwood would receive them. Don had been so concerned about his own party, particularly Orvan, that he had not considered the danger of showing his face in Choctaw again.

The group walked past a small wooden house, a woman and her son sitting on the porch sewing some clothes. The pair gave into their bubbling emotions.

"Arkan scum!" the mother rasped from the comfort of her chair, spitting in the dirt.

"Yeah, get outta here scum," her son echoed. The boy, no older than ten, picked up a stone and swung his arm. It bounced off Cabbage's back and skittered along the ground. The marine paid no attention.

They kept moving, the sound of muttering voices growing louder as news of their arrival spread through the streets. Only two more individuals were brave enough to say something. Neither was sufficiently brazen to start a fight though. The marines were doing their job nicely, just by existing.

The real trouble started as they approached the Nyusha gate, a wooden frame hanging off a wiry fence that ran round two buildings and some wider open space among the trees. A bearded blonde man and two smaller males stood in their path, each one holding rudimentary weapons. Their clothes were tatty and torn, covered sporadically in a brown material. From this distance, Don could smell the manure. He wasn't sure if it was coming from the farm itself or Jokubas and his men.

"I said, what's *he* doing here," he repeated himself, pointing through the crowd of bodies with the barrel of his weapon.

"Who?" Levina asked, turning around.

"I'm talking about Donald Stafford," he said, eyes fixed on their target. "He may have aged badly, but

DAVID MUNDAY

I'd recognise the Bloodaxe anywhere." The man spoke with a similar accent to Orvan. It was the Choctaw chief who spoke up first, moving away from the group.

"Yes, that's him alright," Orvan said, patting Jokubas on the back.

"Get *off* me." Jokubas contorted away. "This isn't even your territory. You expect me to welcome you when you walk up to our city with a murderer in your ranks?"

Don heard Chad whisper something in Gisèle's ear.

"What is he talking about?" he asked, quiet as a mouse.

"Keep it down," she replied in an angry hush.

"I'd reconsider your tone, Jokubas," Orvan said, hands on hips. "I remember when you were just a little boy, wetting yourself on the field of battle. I don't think you want me to make you feel like that again."

"What do you want?" Jokubas replied, calling Orvan's bluff. It was Smurph who answered.

"We're here to get a lift, so we can complete our mission," he said, stepping forward.

"I don't care about your mission. The Atlas Nations shall have no help from us."

Levina pushed past Smurph.

"Stop it, Jokubas," she said, her voice wavering. "They're here to help."

The man looked them up and down.

"Like fuck, they are! How do we know they haven't come here to finish us off after all these years?"

"Jokubas," Levina was on the verge of tears again. "They've offered to help find Laptev and the others."

"Have they?" Jokubas looked at Orvan, then and Don. "And how do we know the Atlas Nations aren't behind this whole thing to begin with? Who else would benefit from disappearing our hunters and fighters into the woods?"

"It's the British," a small voice from behind. Don turned to see it was Chad.

"Excuse me?"

The young man looked to Don for reassurance.

"He won't listen to anything I've got to say," Don muttered.

Chad pushed to the front.

"I said it was the British. From Earth."

"How do you know it's them?"

"They're running a colonisation programme without authorisation from the Atlas Nations... that's why they've come here, to Choctaw. They've gone to pretty extreme lengths to do so. We have to find out what they're up to and stop them starting a war, either with you, with us, or both."

Jokubas sized Chad up and laughed.

"You expect me to believe the word of this whelp?" he looked either side of him and elicited similarly amused reactions. Chad blushed.

"Please, Jokubas," Levina tried again. "Just let them through. Why would they come peacefully if their intention was to destroy?"

"If you're so worried about your husband, why don't you go looking for him yourself?"

"You know I can't do that," she replied. "I have to think of my daughters. Who will look after them if I get lost in the mountains?"

For the first time, Jokubas did not know what to say.

Levina continued: "Think about it. Ever since the war, the Atlas Nations has had the power to go back on the treaty. If they wanted to raze Peakwood to the ground, would they have not done so already?"

"Maybe you're right," Jokubas said eventually. He grew more confident again. "Way I see it," he started with a sniff, "if some Arkan scum want to risk their lives looking for our men, we should let 'em. Spares us anymore Choctaw blood."

Don breathed a sigh of relief. This had been the last thing they needed.

"Thank you, Jokubas," he said.

"Don't think I've finished with you, Bloodaxe," the man replied, strolling into the heart of the group to stand opposite him. Don felt his nostrils come under attack. The manure was definitely emanating from this man. "My father and brother died at Oldshade," he continued. "That was your doing."

Don stared him down, taking a deep breath.

"I had my orders," he said. "So did you. Both sides lost men that day. But that war is over now. Peace exists between our two nations. We should keep it that way."

"That may be," Jokubas replied, slinging his rifle over his shoulders, sizing up the Marines, who had grown increasingly tense. "But I'm still not taking any chances. You can have the Nyusha transport if you intend to find Laptev, Honit and the others... but the Bloodaxe stays with me, as a hostage."

Orvan approached Jokubas with a smile and a hand outstretched.

"Deal," he said. "That's no problem with me."

"You can't do that," Gisèle finally broke her silence.

"That's not happening," Don insisted, smirking. "I didn't come all this way to get bandied about like some pet. Especially not by you, Orvan."

"You think I care about why you came back here, Donald?" Orvan laughed. "Sometimes you've just got to pay for the sins of your past."

Don rolled his eyes.

"You sanctimonious jackass. You're no saint either."

"Maybe not, but if you want to stop this war of yours, you better do as you're told. Don't make me regret letting you live… multiple times actually."

"What's to stop you killing him once we've left?" Gisèle asked Jokubas.

"Not a lot."

"Nope. This isn't happening," she said, nudging Smurph in the arm.

"You want a hostage?" the soldier asked, eventually.

"What's it to you?" Jokubas retorted.

"It's my job, you hillbilly. I've been sent here to get this man up that mountain. I'm not letting some backwoods simpleton stand in my way."

Jokubas' eyes burned with anger. Smurph responded by punching downwards through the air. His arm clunked and whirred with metallic scraping. In an instant, two gun barrels appeared above the back of his hand. The marine pointed them in the Choctaw man's face.

"Like I said, just let me do my job."

Jokubas lowered his weapon.

"That's better."

"Thank you, Smurph," Don said.

"I didn't do it for you Stafford," he replied, coldly. "Hey, Joku-whatever your name was. You still want a hostage?" The man dared not answer. "You can have one of my men. A gesture of goodwill," Smurph added with a smile. "I'd like to see you try and snuff one of *us*." Jokubas was still lost for words. "Pathfinder, give us your food pack," the soldier called. "You're staying here."

"But, boss," the soldier protested.

"Don't even think about it," Smurph shot him down. "Just think of the mission," he said with a wink.

"Yes, sir," Pathfinder replied.

"If you're leaving one of these beasts in Peakwood, my men remain here too," Orvan quickly interjected. "Just to be safe," he added with a smile.

Don knew exactly what the Choctaw chief meant. There wasn't a great deal of trust going around right now. Smurph simply nodded his head.

"Where am I going?" Patherfinder asked.

"You can start on the farm," his superior officer replied. "See if this lady needs some help," he added, pointing at Levina.

"Thank you," she said, gratefully. "The truck is this way, I'll show you how to operate it."

*

Sean had put Alida's whole day out of order. When the children didn't show up at her office, she assumed at first, that they had simply been caught in traffic. After an hour, she was worried. Sean wasn't answering her calls and any attempt to contact Tristen's implants had also failed.

Alida held her key up to the receiver and burst through the front door of the family home.

"Corinne! Tristen! Are you here?" She cried out, flapping her way through the hallway. She checked every room on the ground floor. "Kids! It's your mother, where are you?"

Alida flew up the stairs, desperately hoping they were still in bed. It wouldn't be the first time Sean had let them oversleep during the holidays. Whipping each quilt cover away she found nobody in either bedroom.

Running out of breath, Alida pattered down the stairs at pace and checked the kitchen again. Eyeballing every detail she eventually spotted a piece of paper attached to the shiny grey fridge by a magnet.

'You can't have them'.

Alida growled and punched the appliance. She recoiled in pain, cradling her fist in the other hand. There was a massive dent in the metal.

The children were gone and so was Sean. She should have seen this coming. It was exactly the sort of rash move a man like him would make. Clearly it had been so long without a war to fight in that he needed to make one at home just to satisfy a sick need for victory.

"Where the hell are you?" Alida asked out loud, marching back to Sean's study. It still reeked of old books. She sat at his desk and turned the computer on, hoping for a way to log in. While it was booting up, Alida fiddled through the papers in front of her. Nothing gave her any indication of where they had gone.

The machine lit up. The council leader typed in a few passwords, none of them letting her in. She punched the desk, aggravating the already forming bruise from the fridge.

"Damn it," she spat, launching herself to her feet.

Her iris rang. It was Daizen. She answered in a flash.

"What? Have you found them?" Alida shouted impatiently.

"I'm sorry... Ms. Harmon," he replied gingerly. "I know now is hardly the best time... but we've got a problem."

"What is it now?" she asked, pacing around the study.

"We've got a massive gathering of reporters outside your office," Daizen explained. "At least twenty of them. All of the mainstream services, by the looks of it."

"Why? What's happened?" Alida snapped back.

"I... can't say for sure," Daizen hesitated. "Do you think news has got out about the children?"

"It better not have. Have you spoken to them?"

"Well, that's probably the strangest thing," he began. "When I went out and asked why they were here they said, and I've got no idea why, that *you* called a press conference."

"What? That's bull. Did you tell them that?"

"No, I didn't think that would be a good idea."

"What? Why not?"

"I didn't want to risk us looking disorganised," Daizen explained. Alida allowed him to continue. "I know that we're not, but someone has stitched us up here. Obviously, you're under a lot of scrutiny right now with the Teslanium negotiations, Stangl and the A.N. breathing down your neck on every decision. We already know some of the press have caught wind of the British situation."

Alida thought to herself for a second.

"You're right," she said eventually, before thinking aloud. "Factor in our plans for pushing independence once these negotiations are concluded, we need the press on our side."

"Absolutely," Daizen replied. "So what's our move?"

Alida made for the hallway.

"Tell them I've been held up on a matter of Atlas Nations liaison duties and that I'll be there as soon as I can," she said.

"You're going to turn up?"

"Yes, it's time to roll with the punches," Alida declared, picking up her keys to lock the house. She had a pretty good idea where this play had come from.

"And what are you going to tell them?"

"I'll think about that on my way over. I'll be half an hour."

＊

Tycho and the children stepped onto the bridge following a hearty breakfast. The Diamond had made good progress overnight. Saldana guided the ship along the continent's western coast at excellent speed. The room was uncharacteristically quiet, but a skeleton crew allowed the children some freedom, even on the bridge. Corinne was busy clacking toy cars along the floor. The vice admiral checked the maps. They were a little under half-way to Cahors and would pick up relief personnel soon.

"Come and look at this, Corinne," Tycho beckoned with a smile. She looked up at her father's voice, each eye aglow with green and blue excitement. Tristen remained up against one of the panels at the back, lost in his virtual reality.

"What is it, daddy?" she asked, grasping Zainab the elephant in a firm cuddle and scampering over. Reaching the front of the room, she craned her neck. "I can't see."

"Oh sorry, sweetheart," Tycho replied, remembering that stealth mode was blocking all views apart from the traditional window displays. He flicked a few switches. "I'll put surround-view back on."

Once the ship had received its command from the control panel, the room emanated with a soft and satisfying hum, like someone delicately sliding through silk with a pair of scissors. The metallic appearance of the walls and floor slowly faded away, replaced by a beautiful panoramic view of the ocean. Immediately below them was the deck of the Diamond, coated in a thin layer of apricot light, peeking out from the horizon.

"How does it work?" Corinne asked, hugging her father's knee.

"Well, those viewports at the front aren't actually windows," he explained. "They're just very high quality images fed to us by cameras on the outside. That way we have better protection in here. There are cameras all around the vessel so that we can customise how much we can see."

The young girl just nodded her head.

Off in the distance the sun discharged a brilliant blaze and illuminated the rippling water as it climbed higher.

"Let me just..." Tycho muttered to himself, fiddling with more switches. The clear glass gradually changed in hue, soaking itself in a deep purple. "Now you can look at it without hurting your eyes," he explained.

"It's pretty," Corinne said, beaming like the sun she was watching. "I think mummy would enjoy this," she added as Tycho ran his hands over her soft brown hair.

"Yes… she probably would."

"Wow, what's that over there?" Corinne asked, pointing to the right.

The morning light had brought the city into view, hidden away in the bay. It had been several years since Tycho had been here but he'd never forget the striking view from the water. Huddled into the massive alcove was a metallic jungle of steel structures, not unlike New Boston. Embedded into the hill at the southern point was a giant metal structure. Right now the gateway was closed, but Tycho had seen it open many times. Beyond the doorway was a tunnel five-miles long that led to the caves. Coming over the crest of the hill, running into the frame of the structure, were five metal tubes which, along with the tunnel led to Proxima A's largest Teslanium mine. The city was sitting on top of a rich deposit of the element and had expanded in concentric circles around the entry point ever since its discovery. This was where the ore was collected and transported to the docks, before being shipped to New Plymouth for processing.

"What is it, daddy?" Corinne asked again, transfixed by the impressive sprawl of buildings.

"That, Corinne, is Teslapolis."

"Tes-a-plis," she repeated back to him.

Tycho laughed and noticed Saldana, who was steering the ship, gently crack a smile too.

"That's good. You nearly had it there," he said, encouragingly.

The young girl nodded without looking away from the sprawling coastal city.

"Yeah," she added, for good measure.

"It's Tes*LA*-polis, dumbo," Tristen interjected.

Tycho shot him a glare.

"What?" The boy replied, pleading innocence.

"Come on, son," Tycho said. "You're not going to have many chances to see something like this up close and for real. It'll make your computer games look like cartoons."

"Fine," he huffed, deactivating the iris display and dragging his heels over to the front of the bridge. "What's that?"

Tristen pointing to a long, thin concrete construction running along the bay between the apex of each headland. In the middle was a big round tower, approximately ten metres in height.

"Oh, now you're interested," Tycho joked, raising his eyebrows playfully.

Tristen mumbled an unintelligible reply.

"That is the Teslapolis Breakwater," the vice admiral explained. Both his children stared back at him with vacant expressions. "It's a massive wall in the sea," he clarified.

"Why would somebody build one out there?" Tristen asked.

"It's to protect ships inside the bay from really big waves and bad weather. Back in the beginning, the trawlers and transporters coming in and out for the Teslanium would often get wrecked by the storms. Now they don't have to worry so much. Saves a lot of money."

"Oh right... cool."

"Are we going into the bay, daddy?" Corinne asked.

"No, we'll be heading around the sea wall so we can get to where our crew is based. We can't have people seeing our ship at the public port."

"Why not?" Tristen inquired.

"Those are my orders," Tycho replied breathing in. "In fact, it's time we put stealth mode back on." He flicked some switches and returned the bridge to its previous incarnation, a claustrophobic metal box with thin window slits. Both children were disappointed.

Tycho chose to stay silent, smiled and ruffled them by the hair.

"Is the relief crew ready?" he asked Saldana, leaning toward her and taking his voice out of parent-mode.

"Yes, sir," she replied. "Message just came through."

Twenty minutes later, the Diamond had sailed past the breakwater and beyond Teslapolis bay. Sheltered by a conglomerate of bright red rocks was a small fort. There was no way the Diamond could slot in alongside it, the ship was far too large.

"Here they come now," Saldana announced. "Over there," she added.

Streaking away from the circular structure was a small boat, heading for the Diamond.

"Great," Tycho replied. "I'll meet them on deck." He turned back to his children and lightened the tone of his voice once more, clapping his hands together. "Right, guys, I'm afraid it's time to go back to daddy's quarters."

Both of them let out a long sigh of desperation.

"But I want to stay here," Corinne begged.

"I know, I'm sorry, but we're going to have a crew again very soon. I wouldn't want them to get in your way," he explained.

"Okay..." the young girl replied, her face dropping. With both children dropped off in his room,

Tycho made for the deck. The hairs on the back of his neck stood on end as he drank in the sea air and enjoyed the soft breeze. To his right was the ship's crane, which was half way through lifting the speedboat into a storage platform.

"Permission to come aboard, sir," Ricketts barked as he stepped down. He raised his hand in a salute, the tips of his fingers touching the side of a bald head. The middle-aged man was a little shorter than Tycho but was exceptionally well-built.

"Permission granted, Ricketts," the vice admiral replied calmly, eager to keep things as informal as possible. "Thanks for signing up for this mission. You're exactly who I need for this. I trust my usual crew, of course, but this operation calls for more experience in covert operations."

"What's this all about, Sean?" Ricketts asked. "We haven't had an assignment in quite some time," he said with half a gesture towards the twenty or so other men and women who were unloading their belongings.

"As I said, we're off the books on this one," Tycho explained. "Nobody needs to know we're out here. Nobody needs to know about this mission afterwards either."

"You got it, sir. What are we doing this time?"

"Well, strictly speaking, we're spying on the government and the army," Tycho announced with half a laugh. Ricketts smiled back to him.

"Fine by me," he said cheerfully. "What do we know so far?"

"Troops are moving north towards the Choctaw border and Donald Stafford himself is heading up a scouting mission. It's response to a suspected British invasion in the region. Full-scale war with either the British, the Choctaw or both, could be on the horizon but the Navy has been kept in the dark. It's our job to find out what's going on up there and, if I deem it necessary, to provide support for our armed forces."

"Roger that," Ricketts replied. "Donald Stafford eh? This must be serious."

"You got that right," Tycho said.

"What's our next destination?" Ricketts asked.

"We're making a stop in Cahors and then we'll move on from there to the Choctaw Sea. We can use the cover of the western mountains to get there undetected and make port on the northern coastline."

✳

Looking into the mirror, Alida pressed the blue blazer against her body and winced at the weight she had put on recently. It wasn't much, but enough to make inspecting her figure an unpleasant experience.

"Ready when you are, Alida," Daizen whispered into the small room. She gave him the thumbs up.

Seconds later, the council leader emerged onto the stage and was instantly hit with a wall of noise and squirming journalists, climbing on top of each other to batter her with questions. Alida continued her defiant march to the wooden podium, adjusting the microphone once she had arrived.

"You can ask your questions later," she said calmly, her voice booming through the announcer. With an eye on Nikolai Govinda, the tubby brown man as animated as the rest of his colleagues in the front row, she added: "I'm sure you've got plenty to ask about."

Eventually, they took their seats. Alida waited for a

moment, to collect her thoughts.

"Thank you for meeting me here at such short notice. As you know, the New Boston council has spent the last nine weeks negotiating with the Atlas Nations on a new trade agreement for the transportation of raw Teslanium from Proxima A back to Earth. This has been a long and arduous process, made harder by the two planets' lack of tangible trade routes for over a decade." She took a deep breath and looked down at the blank sheet of paper below, hoping it would appear she was reading a statement. "In our opinion, this has warped the Atlas Nations' expectations of these negotiations. Naturally, this has led to their representatives taking up an unrealistic position in this process, one which New Boston will no longer accept." Murmuring began to stir through the journalists once again. Alida raised the level of her voice a little and rushed her final words, anticipating the reaction. "Therefore, I am suspending the Teslanium negotiation talks until further notice. I'll take your questions now."

All the reporters leapt to their feet. Daizen chose a tall, older-looking man. He quickly fumbled with his notes waiting for the roving microphone to reach him.

"When were Mr. Stangl's representatives informed of this decision and what was their reaction?"

"I told them this morning," she lied. "That's where I was before meeting with you... and as for Mr. Stangl's reaction, you all have vivid imaginations. I'm sure you already have half an idea," she added with a smile. Some reporters, those loyal to her side of the political spectrum, joined her in a chuckle.

Another journalist attracted Daizen's attention.

She was a young, sharp-nosed blonde woman with a European accent.

"Are you not concerned that angering the Atlas Nations is a risky political move?" she asked.

"We have all the cards here," Alida replied defiantly. "This planet mines and processes the Teslanium and has done so for eleven years without the help of Earth. We have become a self-sustaining colony in the time that they have bickered amongst themselves. It is time the Atlas Nations understood how much it will cost us to accept a depletion in our Teslanium supply."

The journalists competed once again, this time Daizen chose Nikolai.

"Is it true that our first line of defence has been breached by an invading force?"

The room fell silent. All eyes initially fixed on Nikolai, and then shifted to Alida, who had to do everything she could not to explode on the journalist. She held his gaze.

"Firstly, we are only answering questions on the Teslanium negotiations this morning. And secondly, this government is not in the way of speculating on matters of planetary security."

Daizen motioned for Nikolai to relinquish the microphone. He ignored the aide and continued asking away.

"If that's the case, Ms. Harmon, then why have forces been deployed north?"

"And what forces would they be?" Alida replied instantly.

"I'm asking you the question, Ms. Harmon."

"As I've already explained, matters of national security are not up for discussion and any manoeuvre of troops into any region of this continent should not be considered as a response to the actions of another faction."

Daizen interjected: "Defence minister Judson Trin would be better placed to answer such questions," he said. "It is his remit to be informed of any and all military training exercises."

Alida smiled and nodded.

"We'll take one more question, provided it is on topic," Daizen announced. Alida didn't have time to clock this journalist.

"Is it true there is currently a widescale government search underway to find one or more of your children who, at this present point in time, are to be considered missing?"

A harsh and pregnant silence descended over the room.

Alida felt the skin of her face burn with anger. She twitched for a moment, holding in words that would write the news headlines for weeks. Clenching her fists, she walked away from the podium without uttering a word.

The furore returned unabated.

The truck could take Don and the group no further. It had helped speed them along the rudimentary dirt tracks that wound through the outer woods but soon they were surrounded by cedar and sprucelike trees. It felt good to get away from the rickety vehicle as the ride had not been a gentle one. The old machine had burped like an alcoholic and filled Don's nose with the thick aroma of clutch oil. He had perched in the back with Gisèle, Chad and the remainder of the troops. Smurph drove with Diablo in the passenger seat and Orvan standing behind the two soldiers giving them directions. It had been too loud to enjoy casual conversation, so the group had remained silent for their journey.

They had only been walking for an hour or so when the light started to fade.

"Let's make camp," said Orvan, as they approached a formation of rocks. The forest was starting to blend with the foot of the mountains.

"Are we safe here?" Don asked.

"Yes, don't worry old man. Anyone who doesn't know these woods will never find us here."

"What about those who *do* know them?" Gisèle asked, cynically. Orvan didn't answer.

"As long as my unit is here, you're safe," Smurph added.

"Gisèle," said Don. "Can you contact Alida and inform her of our progress?"

"Will do," the woman replied, initiating the video call mode on her iris head-up display.

Once Smurph had made a similar report to Stangl, he squatted down and dragged some rocks apart as if they were feathers, shaping them into a circle. Leaning back and scraping the muck off each hand, he pointed to a nearby tree.

"Hey Scissorhands, hand me that branch," he ordered.

"Yes sir."

He strolled over to the trunk, grabbed hold of a thick branch and tore it off effortlessly. On his way back over, Scissorhands snapped it in half and tossed it into the small pit Smurph had dug. Diablo was now standing over it. He held out his arm and squeezed gently. Flames sprung forth igniting the wood instantly.

"Let's have a few more branches, Scissors," Smurph directed. The soldier went about his work. The commanding officer slung a backpack on the floor, unzipped it and started chucking out tins and forks.

Don caught one, fingers stinging a little at high impact with the metal.

"Thanks," he said.

There wasn't much room to spread out but the group still naturally segregated into its three component parts once the food was ready. Smurph and his soldiers sat huddled close to the fire, hogging all the heat. Orvan was on the edge of the camp, out of earshot. Don leaned against some trees alongside Chad and Gisèle. The woman tied her frizzled hair back ready to eat.

"Well, we've made it this far without any of these bone heads killing each other," she said, staring into her rudimentary dinner. "Bet you didn't think we'd manage that."

Don grunted a faint laugh.

"No, I did not."

"I still can't believe Smurph stood up for you back there," Gisèle continued. "I thought we were going to have real trouble. Especially, when Orvan took their side too."

"Yeah," Don replied, not really listening.

"You're distracted Donald," Gisèle surmised.

"That obvious, huh?"

"To me? ...Always," she replied. Chad chanced a look across at the two of them before his eyes scurried back to the floor.

"What are you thinking about?" Gisèle asked.

"Come on, you should know the answer to that, girl," Don pulled the left knee closer to him with a small groan. "She was like a mother to you."

"Sweet Sally," Gisèle said shaking her head. "What a woman."

Don nodded.

"Indeed." The two of them fell silent listening to the idle chatter of the soldiers. "You know, crouching here, all I can think about is what she's doing right now. How much she's worrying about me."

"I'm not surprised," Gisèle replied. "You're too old for this," she added just before taking a mouthful of beans.

Don chuckled.

"You know, I think you're the only person I let get away with insubordination like that."

Gisèle smiled sweetly in return.

"I regret coming back here, already," Don continued. "The way they looked at me in Peakwood. I'm like the devil to these people. Seeing the anger in their eyes, it makes me feel guilty for having a loving wife." He stared into the fire. "But I was damned if I do, damned if I don't."

"How so?"

"Well, there was no way I could stay at home," Don explained. He looked away from the flames and made eye contact with Gisèle. She smiled. "You know me. I've got trust issues."

"Believe me, I know," Gisèle replied, raising her eyebrows. She cast a glance to Orvan. "Do you trust *him*?" she asked, under her breath.

"Like hell," Don replied with a huff. "You know, I think if that second British ship hadn't turned up when it did, he might have killed me on the Arkan Wall."

"Oh my god," Gisèle said, struggling to contain her outburst. "You never told me that."

"It's alright," Don waved it away.

"Do you think that's why he came along then? Just to kill you? He didn't hesitate to hand you over in Peakwood."

"I don't think that's it. He has always been a man of his people. Orvan lives and breathes Choctaw to the very core. At the very least, coming on this mission helps him protect his territory."

"But why would he agree to our mission? Wouldn't he be better off doing this on his own? That's always been his style."

"Perhaps you're right," Don admitted. "But look around you," he continued. "Choctaw might have numbers but they've never had quality troops like this to count on. Maybe he thinks he stands a better chance with us for a change."

"Excuse me, sir."

Both Don and Gisèle were surprised to hear Chad finally open his mouth.

"What is it, son?"

"I'm not trying to intrude but... if Orvan presents such a danger to you. Why is he here? Why do *we* need *him*?"

"It's a simple question of experience, Chad. He knows these woods and these mountains better than any of us. We'd be a long way behind if it wasn't for that, even if it pains me to admit it."

"But... didn't you used to work out here?"

"Yes, I did. But that was a long time ago. Even the best of us have a fading memory." It fell silent for a moment. "Speaking of experience," Don began again. "Well done for what you did back in Peakwood. That took guts, kid. Keep up the good work."

"Thanks," Chad replied, lips struggling to form more words. "Just... trying to do my bit, sir. I'm a little unsure of how much help I can be on this mission."

"Don't talk like that. Your knowledge is something most of us don't have."

"What do you know about their government?" Gisèle asked, louder than before. Don had forgotten the woman had spent her entire life on this planet so her understanding of Earth countries was not as informed as his. A few of the soldiers overheard the question.

"You know, I've been told the A.N. has spies in Britain," Cabbage interjected, leaning forwards, addressing the whole group. The man continued, proud of his contribution: "Once they announced the borders were going to shut down entirely, they sent loads of them in."

"How do you know that?" Flat-top said through a mouth of beans, scraping at the tin.

"My uncle was screwing one. Left his wife for her but wasn't allowed to go with her."

"What an idiot."

"Yeah I know."

Smurph sat quietly, rolling his eyes. He threw Gisèle an almost apologetic look.

She then turned back to Chad, beckoning him to give his answer.

"It is very right-wing, that's for sure," Chad spoke quietly, with half a glance to the soldiers. "Over the last fifty years there has been a massive swing towards isolationism. The population appears to be along for the ride too. They were distrustful of other nations to begin with but it went into overdrive after the virus. I guess you can't blame them for that. The Curtis administration has been in place for well over four terms now and is exceptionally skilled in populism. They blame the country's problems on external parties, convince the people that they were the answer, even though they were the originators of the problems in the first place. They've been talking a colonisation game for the last few years, probably accelerated by what the Atlas Nations has been doing here."

Gisèle nodded intently.

"When was the last time they went to war with anyone?"

"To be honest, their excursions into the Middle East were the last major conflict they were involved with," Chad answered. "They went in with the U.S. before the A.N existed. That as at the turn of the century. Since then, isolationism in the UK has so extreme that they've largely kept to themselves. Having said that, their culture places a lot of importance on their role in World War Two, Earth's biggest conflict of the twentieth century. Most of their other wars are seen as shameful but their cultural identity was shaped by World War Two for a long time because they were on the defensive, backs against the wall. If Curtis' government is as skilled in populism as I think, then a war which pits them as the underdog would certainly appeal to the British."

"Is that why they've come here?" Don asked. Chad looked into the air for a moment, thinking.

"That would make a lot of sense. If Curtis is telling his people that they are exercising their right to break new ground, advancing British territory into the Proxima system, and then the Atlas Nations comes along to stop them through force, he's on to a winner."

"You mean aggravate the enemy into a war and then blame them for it?" Gisèle asked, unimpressed.

"Pretty much, yeah."

"Wow," she shook her head. "How could that fly with the population?"

"That's the thing, the recurring theme of British history in the last half century is unquestionable nationalism. The people there know very little of what's going on out here, what the rules of colonisation are. They mostly just believe whatever the government tells them."

"That's pretty scary," Gisèle admitted.

"Well, I suppose to some extent, the Atlas Nations organisation is no different," Don countered.

"How do you mean?" she asked, a little defensive.

"Well, Chad's a little too young to remember but you should know by now why the Choctaw hate us so much. The A.N.'s territory allocation policy in the early days was nepotistic mess. Certain groups were favoured, others not so much, left with barren wastelands to live off. That sparked the war we fought in against Orvan and his people. But, you go and talk to anyone on the streets of New Boston and the Choctaw are a filthy disease we should rid from the planet for their invasion of our territory."

"I guess you're right," Gisèle said. "I never thought of it that way before."

Don shook his head.

"If it wasn't for that, then I wouldn't have to

fear for my life in places in like Peakwood and walk around with a nickname like the..." he paused and checked Orvan wasn't listening "...like the Bloodaxe of Choctaw."

"How... *did* you get it?" Chad asked nervously.

"It was at Oldshade," Don explained quietly, staring into the mud. "The war had left many places un-inhabitable so a bulk of the Choctaw population were desperate to cross over into Arkan territory. They chose Oldshade because it was close to the estuary on the east end of the wall. We had no choice but to deny them entry. So Orvan and his people sent in troops to try and force their way through." Don's voice caught in his throat. "Anyway, one of their leaders led a covert mission to break into a fortified section of the wall and I caught them out, snooping around our weapons centre. In the fight, I... ended up killing him with his own axe and," he took a deep breath, "in the confusion our artillery targetting system was damaged. It fired on the refugee train, wiping wiped out half their civilian population. Orvan arrived too late. He was convinced I had killed them on purpose... so he... did this."

Don hoisted up the material of his trouser leg. Chad's face grew flush when saw what lay below.

Where the calf muscles and shin bones met with the ankle was an array of strained white flesh, pulled taut by a ring of screw heads. They plugged the limb into an ankle composed entirely of metal. Don lifted his foot gently to show off the hinge mechanism in action.

"You can't see it because of my socks, but it's still my real foot under there. Just need this damned thing to actually use it."

Silence fell. Gisèle rubbed his shoulder.

"It wasn't your fault, Donald," she said softly.

"Back then I believed in the war. Maybe if I'd spoken out sooner, it would never have got to that."

"Just... don't be so hard on yourself," Gisèle added.

The three Atlas Nations personnel sat quietly for a few minutes. Don looked over at Orvan, still on his own. He still hated the man for what he had done, but maintained respect for the passion he had for his people. Don desperately wished things had gone differently all those years ago.

"Tell me, kid," he broke the silence eventually, nudging Chad's arm. "You ever heard of something called Star Trek?"

"Was it a book or something?"

Don laughed, patting the younger man on the back. He needed that to lighten the mood.

"No, it was an American science fiction show from the twentieth century. My granddad was a big fan. It was very ahead of its time. Perhaps *too* ahead of its time." Don paused for a moment. "It aired during a very divisive time in America's history and was the first show to depict people from all nations on Earth working together to explore the universe. The recurring theme was that mankind could only master interplanetary travel when it had learned to overcome the differences between the nations of the world." Don raised his arms in the air. "Just look where we are now, potentially on the brink of yet *another* war. All we've done is bring our prejudice and hatred of each other with us on this journey across the galaxy. Like I said, ahead of its time. Perhaps the guys who wrote Stark Trek should have known we'd never achieve peace before we found another planetary system. But hey, maybe that's what it means to be human. To strive for better things but fall desperately short."

16

Wash left Vicky sleeping peacefully in her bed to have a morning shower, admiring her shoulders and back on his way out. The last few days had been amazing. The two of them had spent their evenings sifting through the information held in the papers Declan had handed over. The nights had been incredible.

Vicky had been the perfect tonic to the traumatic experience at the docks. That said, neither of them were closer to working out who the murdered man was or what the paperwork meant. The spreadsheets heavily populated with undecipherable data were particularly frustrating. However, at the very least, both Wash and Vicky were convinced there was a plan to assassinate several colonists upon their arrival in the Proxima system.

Wash thought of his father, chained to his bed, full of medication. With each piece of the puzzle, he realised how right the man had been. It was still hard for Wash to forgive the verbal and emotional abuse he'd received most of his life, but at some point, Wash would have to tell him about this investigation. If his father was on death's door, he deserved to know he was right about... something.

Wash had started making some toast when Vicky entered the kitchen, naked. He noticed a missed call on his glasses from Jay but ignored it once she wrapped her arms around his waist and kissed him.

"I need to get ready," he said, pulling away.

"You know, you really don't have to worry about this secret agent stuff," she said, pouting her lips.

"Yes I do," Wash countered. "The contents of those papers could land both of us in jail," he said, pointing with his buttered knife at the documents on the bar. "If I get caught with them, I don't want anyone to tracing them back to you."

"I know," Vicky said. "But think of all the things we could be doing if you didn't have to leave half an hour before me." She place her hands on hips and batted her eyelashes.

"I'd love to," Wash said, hugely conflicted. "But I don't want something to happen to you, okay?"

"Chauvinist pig," Vicky joked, pulling a face.

Five minutes later Wash picked up the packet of papers, placed them in his bag and donned a large hooded coat.

"See you on the train," he said on his way out the door.

*

"Just in time, young man," Pete said cheerfully as Wash arrived at his desk following his walk through St Pauls.

"Hi Pete," he replied. "Just in time for what?"

"The first colonial broadcast."

"What?" Wash felt his breath quicken. "I didn't know about that."

"To be fair, they only put the press release out about it late last night."

"Last night?" Wash considered the suspicious nature of the timing. Even a trainee journalist knew a late press release about an early story the next day was a textbook way of playing down its importance.

"Yeah, I know. It's odd," Pete admitted. "It should make for interesting viewing though."

"You bet," Wash agreed, lunging back into his seat. "I wonder if they'll mention what happened to the New Boston satellite," he whispered. All he got back was an unimpressed stare.

Two minutes later, Steve Woods unmuted the television screen in the centre of the room, ready for the broadcast. It showed a middle-aged grey-haired man sat behind a newsroom desk with a red backdrop. He held a hand up to his earpiece.

"Yes, I'm hearing that we can now bring you the first footage from the forefront of our colonial effort," he announced, as he swivelled in his chair and watched a display behind. He disappeared and static replaced him on the Citizen's screen. The female reporter who had been reduced to tears by Steve a few days ago looked up and frantically burrowed through the belongings on her desk. She grasped her glasses and scurried up to the screen to catch the words on audio.

A man's face appeared, captured in low resolution. He had short brown hair and black stubble lined his chin. Trees and greenery filled the background behind him. The footage was jittery and the audio somewhat crackly but every word was audible.

"Hello Britain," the man said through in a faded northern accent. "This is colonial captain John Case speaking to you from the surface of Proxima B. We've been living on this planet, waving the flag for the United Kingdom, for nearly two weeks now. We entered the atmosphere with no problems and our landing was as smooth as we could have hoped for."

Wash and Pete exchanged a discrete confused look.

"We're making good progress. Everybody has been doing well and our plans to found New London are coming along at good speed. All our efforts so far have gone into putting up our communal building, which is nearly finished. You should be able to see it behind me." Case leaned his left shoulder away from the camera to reveal a sturdy-looking wooden structure, roughly the size of a small house. "We're really happy with how it looks, I hope you are too. Next week we'll start putting up the first of the colonial houses so that we can move out of the Krichmar Tarps. We like the Tarps, but I know we'll prefer our new homes." Case looked off into the distance, closed his eyes and drew in a long breath. "The air is so clear here, guys. It's wonderfully refreshing. Let's just hope the Americans don't join us and pollute it all," he chuckled. "Wow. Recording this short message has used up a bit too much power. We'll need even more to send it back to you. I better sign off. I don't know when you'll hear from me next but keep working hard for Britain. Over and out."

The feed ended and the TV anchor returned to the screen. Steve re-muted the channel and the reporter who had been recording went back to her seat and began typing up the quotes. The prime minister was then shown on the screen, speaking in front of a podium outside Downing Street.

"Well, never mind, then," Pete said to Wash.

"Hmm... yeah," he replied after a pause. "I was hoping for something juicier than that." His heartbeat returned to resting speed, although he realised he should probably call the hospital and check the broadcast hadn't killed his father. "At least I'm not the one who has to write up the propaganda piece on it," Wash added, throwing a glance in the direction of the woman across the office frantically crashing away on her keyboard.

"True," Pete said. "I'd love to read what you would write, though. Would be good entertainment," he joked. Wash found himself laughing too.

His glasses lenses flashed blue. An incoming call. It was Declan. Wash had already missed two from Jay this morning, but this was probably more important.

"I should probably step out to take this," Wash said, climbing out of his chair and racing out of the room. He answered when he had sealed himself in one of the building's lifts.

"Hello," he said.

"Hi Wash," Declan said. "Did you just watch that?"

"Err... yes. Why are you happy to call me all of a sudden?"

"Why can't I call an old friend from time to time to discuss exciting current affairs?"

"What is it you want?" Wash asked.

"I just wondered what you thought of captain Case's message. The chaps at the golf club loved it. A momentous day for our country, right?"

"It was interesting," Wash said cautiously, conscious of who might be listening. "I'm glad every-thing is going so well over there."

"Agreed," Declan said. Wash could tell his friend was putting it on too. "Would you like to meet up later to talk about it some more? Same time and place as before." That presumably meant the Parliament arches again.

"I'd love to," Wash said. "I've got to go but I'll see you later today?"

"Done," Declan finished off.

Wash was so engrossed in adjusting his glasses when he returned to his desk, that he didn't no-tice who was standing behind it, waiting. He nearly jumped back several meters.

"Washington Parker?" The middle-aged woman said, offering an outstretched hand covered in spark-ling coloured rings. She wore a grey blazer, a profes-sional blue dress and a relatively modest golden neck-lace. Her smartly cut pale-blond hair went no further than her jaw-line. Weathered skin dimpled either side of a smile.

"Uh, yes, that's right, Ms. Hamilton," Wash replied, panicked and fearing the worst. Standing next to the editor was Steve.

"Ah good, I'm not sure we've actually been for-mally introduced," Yvette said politely as she shook Wash's hand. To keep up appearances, he smiled back. Pete was trying to keep his head down in the next seat, although Wash knew he'd be all ears.

"I don't believe we have," Wash said.

"You're the reporter who called in the story about the latest Eye Killer victim, aren't you?"

"Yes, that's right," he replied with a small nod.

"Well done on that one," Yvette smiled again, adjusting a rogue strand of hair. "It's not often we're able to beat the police to their own story these days."

"Thanks," Wash replied, shuffling his feet. "Just doing my job."

"Well, I have some good news for you. A reward for your hard work, if you will."

"Oh right."

"I've just been told that the police have finally identified that latest victim." The over-bearing woman left him hanging on her words for a few seconds. "It's Miles Faversham, the husband of that vicar. Julie, was it? And more importantly, he's one of the brains behind our fantastic colonial programme."

"It came from that story I gave you on the gay vicar, didn't it, Wash?" Steve said, attempting to make eye contact with Yvette too. As usual, he was desperately trying to appear relevant. She ignored him and kept all her attention on Wash.

"I assume, you found a link between the two stories?" she asked. Wash was forced to think quickly. He had been hoping nobody would make the connection.

"Yes, that's right..." He took great care with what he said next. "...Although my contacts are keen to be kept anonymous at this point." He was faced with a wall of silence. *Shit*. "I think it would be in your best interests to stay in the dark as much as possible, too. Err... given your role here and with the government." Wash clarified. "I wouldn't want to cause you any unnecessary trouble."

"That's very kind of you Washington," Yvette said eventually, the cogs clearly whirring in her mind. "I'm inclined to agree with you there. The less I know the better at this point." *You don't know the half of it, lady.* "But there's clearly more to this story than meets the eye. No pun intended, of course," she rolled her eyes and chuckled to herself. "I want you to dig up as much as you can on this. If someone is trying to undermine our colonial efforts, they must be stopped."

Wash nodded awkwardly, fully aware of the irony of this development.

"And Steven," Yvette added.

"Yes, Yvette?"

"Don't send this young man any more of those shitty re-write jobs," she said sternly. "Just let him get on with his job."

"Of course," Steve said, producing a wry smile.

"We'll leave you to it, then," Yvette said as she marched off, her minion in tow. Wash finally sat down, eyes wide, unsure of what to do next. Pete waited a few moments before breaking the silence.

"Didn't see that one coming," he said.

"Yeah... me neither..." Wash replied, scratching his scalp. He picked up a pen, removed the lid and put it back in place several times over. Then he took out his glasses to give them a wipe. Wash wasn't used to having to only focus on one story at a time. "I know..." he muttered, as he propelled himself out of his seat.

"Where are you going?" Pete asked.

"Callum," Wash replied over his shoulder, as he strode across the newsroom.

Arriving at the crime desk, he noticed that the erratic reporter was guzzling down another pack of nuts, crunching loudly. The rotund man was leaning back in the chair to suck down the remnants from inside the plastic, shoulder-length grey hair dangling below the back of his head. The desk itself was a miasma of papers, books and food wrappings.

"What do you want?" Callum asked through a mouthful as he straightened in his chair.

Cautiously, Wash leaned against a nearby pillar and explained.

"I was wondering if we could talk about Eye Killer victims."

"I'm not surprised," Callum replied, scrunching his latest packet up and chucking it on his desk. "You're the talk of the office today." Brushing the crumbs off his belly, Callum made eye contact and smiled. "So what do you want to know?"

Wash was a little taken aback by how happy his fellow reporter seemed to be about all this. The man had been in the business as long as Pete and was hugely proud of his work down through the years.

"Wait... it's as easy as that?" he asked. "I thought you'd be annoyed about this."

"Are you kidding?" Callum replied with a chuckle. "You can have the whole thing if you want."

"What? How come?"

"Yeah, I'm sick of it," Callum said, flapping his arms in the air.

"But the readers love this stuff." Wash leaned forward, away from the pillar and perched on the armrest of an empty chair.

"Yeah that's because the readers are a bunch of twisted wankers, that's why." Callum scrambled for another packet of nuts. Parts of the shell tumbled onto his desk. "All I've gotten out of this is more and more abuse for being a so-called 'lazy reporter'."

"But, this has been one of the biggest stories we've had in years, hasn't it?"

DAVID MUNDAY

"Oh yeah. You and I understand what stories like this mean, because we have more than half a brain cell. Here, look at this," Callum said, leaning into his computer monitor. He scrolled for a moment and pointed at the screen: "If you weren't such a lazy journalist, you'd have caught this guy by now. PlumberMan123. A fucking plumber thinks he knows how to do my job better than me."

Wash didn't say anything.

"And he's not the only one. Here's another. KnittingGrandma87 says I should be sacked because this killer got someone else. Bitch. I hope she's the next one and he does it with her knitting needles."

Wash couldn't help but laugh with Callum on that one.

"Oh for god's sake, there's another one. CurtisfanFC says the Daily Citizen shouldn't be spreading so much negativity and we should stick to all the positive news about our 'amazing country'. Give me a break."

Callum shook his head and looked back to Wash.

"So you reckon you can put up with these twats?"

"Yeah I think so," Wash replied, confidently.

"It's your funeral," Callum said. "Well, hopefully not actually... So, yeah what do you want?"

"Do you have names, occupations and backgrounds for previous eye killer victims?"

"Of course." Callum scrambled with the sea of papers and produced a scruffy list. He began reading it out: "Mary Scrivener, fifty-two, librarian from Notting Hill. Jack Stacy, twenty-four, shop assistant from Brixton. Gwen Englehart, forty-three, tourist from Luton. Adam Derricks, thirty-three, web designer from Greenwich. Simon Crabtree, twenty-two from Kensington and now Miles Faversham, a civil servant from Newham."

Wash stroked his chin. Callum was right, there really was no correlating factors up until this point.

"So from the list of people killed, Miles Faversham is the only one who worked for the government?"

"It looks that way, yeah," Callum confirmed.

"Weird."

"Yeah, well it's a dead-end this one mate. Killer never leaves finger-prints and there's no pattern emerging from any of his victims," he said cynically. "As I said, you're welcome to it." Wedging his hand under some more papers, he collected them together and shoved them into Wash's grasp.

"What's this?"

"It's everything I've done on the killer so far. All yours now."

"What does it say?" Wash asked, looking from the bundle and back to Callum.

"It says we know fuck-all, that's what."

"Well, thanks... I think." Callum was an experienced crime writer and if he thought such a story wasn't worth holding on to then he was probably right.

"What have you got there, then?" Pete asked as Wash sat down.

"All of Callum's research on the Eye Killer."

"He just handed it over?"

"Yep. Strange, isn't it?"

Pete nodded, rolling up his sleeves in an attempt to adjust to the warmth.

"I once saw him practically resort to fisticuffs when Will wanted to take a big corporation fraud story off him. Although, it *was* fifteen years ago. A lot's changed since then."

"So you keep reminding me," Wash said with a grin as he sat down in his chair. "Did you want to help me with any of this?" he asked.

"You know the answer to that one Wash."

"Worth a try."

✶

Walking through the humid London streets on his way to see Declan, Wash considered the Eye Killer. In reading over the notes, he had come to the same conclusion as Callum. The only story that could come out of this serial murderer next would be about the next victim. There really was no conceivable pattern in his or her targets at all. Wash was starting to wonder if Miles Faversham had been nothing more than unfortunate. In the wrong place at the wrong time. That couldn't be true, though. Firstly, Declan had obviously known about the body, which meant he was closer to this than he wanted to admit. The fact that Faversham's corpse came with confidential information from the colonisation programme surely indicated that his death had something to do with it.

When Wash arrived in Parliament square, he took a roundabout route through the gardens to get to the small alcove. Declan was indeed present, but did not acknowledge his friend's arrival. Wash put his faith in the decaying wooden floorboards of the scaffolding and positioned himself against the stone wall. Below the thick brown water of the Thames trickled away.

"Why am I here, Declan?" Wash whispered round the corner.

"The video you watched was a fake." Wash nearly jumped across to face the politician.

"What? Are you serious?" He checked the crowds to see if anyone had noticed his animation.

"Dead serious."

"How do you know?"

"Well, we've not heard from the Concord since it left the launch pad last month. There's been no contact whatsoever. No way was that video genuine."

"So that wasn't captain Case?"

"I don't know," Declan said after a pause.

"You don't know? How can *you* not know?"

"It certainly looked a lot like him but given the radio silence we've got from the Concord, I find it hard to believe it's actually him."

"What about the other ships we sent up?"

"Other ships?"

"Yeah, there was more than one right?"

Declan raised an eyebrow and carefully considered Wash's question.

"The Concord was the only one that got any press... but I suppose there could be more than one ship out there somewhere."

"Why are you telling me this anyway?" Wash asked. "How does this fake video fit into the big picture?"

"Consider it a heads-up. You'll find out soon enough."

"Does it have something to do with these rumours about the Concord attacking a New Boston satellite on Proxima A?" Wash asked, desperately.

"I've heard the rumours," Declan acknowledged. "There's no way they can be true."

"How can you be so sure?" asked Wash.

"I just know they can't be true," Declan insisted shortly. "Impossible, actually."

"If you say so."

"How are you coming on with the carrot and feather?"

"I'm getting there. It looks like there's some plot to--"

"The less I know the better, Wash. Make sure you've got the whole story before you break it."

"What's that supposed to mean? You obviously know more about this than me in the first place." Declan didn't reply. "I mean, how I am supposed to know you didn't kill Mr Faversham yourself?"

"You don't."

"Helpful."

"I've been more than accommodating, considering my position," Declan insisted.

"None of it's clear though," Wash said. "Most of what I found at the docks is indecipherable. Where do I go next? I need another lead. Something else to work with."

"Have you done the death knock yet?" Declan asked.

"You mean, Mrs Faversham?"

"Yes."

"I've not spoken to her, no."

"Wow, they really don't make journalists like they used to, then."

"Oh, fuck off, Dec. You sound just like my dad. I simply assumed she wouldn't be willing to speak to the press given her personal situation."

"*I'm* here, aren't I?"

"That's different. *You* hold some sway. And let's not forget we go back several years. You trust me. She's not going to trust a complete stranger is she?"

"You'll have to make her tell you what you need. If you can get access to Faversham's work, you'll make plenty of progress, I assure you." Declan began inspecting the crowds. "I've given you more than enough," he said. "I've got to go."

17

James ran up to Harper when she re-emerged from the jungle.

"Are you okay? What happened?"

"I'm fine," she explained, trying to catch her breath. "But got away."

"What did it look like?"

"Two arms and legs but it was covered in something. I managed to cut some of this off." Harper opened her palm and revealed the feather-like objects. "Fat lot of good this will do."

"You never know," James said as he inspected the talons. "It might help us somehow."

"Can it help us find out how to kill them?" Harper asked. James inspected a few moments longer. During that short time, she looked beyond him at the smoking Krichmar Tarps and bodies strewn across the beach. Quiet had finally fallen, the crashing of the waves the only sound. By now, it had faded into Harper's subconscious, like the ticking of a clock.

"I... guess not," he surrendered.

"Thought so," Harper huffed. "Here, you take

them," she said, stuffing them into his hand. "We've got more important things to worry about. Where is everybody?"

"We've set up by the water purifier," James explained.

"Okay let's go."

When they arrived at the metal structure, Harper saw Ben and Zoey tending to the wounded. Lynne was lying on her back, eyes drooping as Zoey sat underneath one of her legs, supporting it with a shoulder. Her hands were stretched out in front of her tightening a tourniquet from strips of clothing around the top of the woman's thigh, above the arrows.

Next to Lynne, Zack was sat up with his back against the purifier. His face was a complete mess. There was a deep red slash along his right jawline, the top layer of skin and hair now sliced off. The man's beard looked even worse now that it had lost symmetry. The flesh of his right cheek was swollen and taught, putting some pressure on the underside of his eyeball. Ben ripped off the rest of Zack's shirt, revealing a smaller but deeper chunk missing from the top of his shoulder, where the weapon had landed.

Just a few feet away lay Lucas' body. Sam stood above and draped some material over his broken head.

"Where's Shermeen?" Harper asked.

"She's over there," said Zoey, nodding in the direction of the treeline. "She's helping Amos."

"We shouldn't leave her on her own so close to the jungle," Harper insisted. She turned to James: "Here, take this." She handed over her weapon. "Go and stand guard until one of us comes over." His eyes darted from the gun to her eyes and back again. "Look, it's pretty simple, just point and shoot," Harper explained as she forced it into his grip. James began to amble over to the rocks, occasionally looking back towards her.

Opening his eyes, Zack exhaled a little, mostly through his nose. He spoke through gritted teeth.

"Did... you... ge--" He winced in pain.

Harper shook her head silently.

For once, Zack was without a snappy response.

"What do we do now?" asked Ben. Harper ushered him over to her position and waited until he was close enough to speak to quietly.

"How are they doing?" she asked.

"Zack's injuries are mostly superficial, even if he says otherwise. We just need to keep his cuts clean and he should avoid infection. He was lucky. A few inches to the left and that blow would have cut his head in half. Still, it should shut him up for a while."

"What about Lynne?"

Ben took a deep breath.

"She hasn't got long," he said. "I think one of those arrows nicked the femoral artery in her leg. I think. I'm no doctor. But the blood-loss has been pretty devastating and without performing major surgery, which we don't have the expertise or equipment to even attempt, I think she'll bleed out within a few hours."

"Do we have anything that could make her comfortable?"

"No," Ben shook his head. "Most of our medication was in the Tarp we lost. What we had left went up in the fires they started."

"Damn," Harper said, looking over at Shermeen in

the distance. "Does the kid know how bad it is?"

"Not yet," Ben said quietly. "She's distracted at least for now. She's been with Amos since the attack stopped."

"What happened to him?"

"He took an arrow to the hip and has some pretty nasty burns too. He should live, but I don't think he'll be able to walk for a while."

"Do you think we can carry him? He's not exactly a small guy."

"Carry him? Where to?" Ben asked.

"We have to get off the beach," Harper said.

Zoey looked up from what she was doing.

"Sam, can you come and hold Lynne's leg above her head?" she called.

"Yeah sure," the red-haired man said as he took over. The Welsh woman approached Harper and Ben.

"Did I hear you say you want to leave the beach?" she asked, now opposite them.

Instantly on the defensive, Harper replied: "It's our only choice."

"Are you joking?" Zoey rasped in an angry whisper, gesturing to the wounded. "There's no way we can move like *this*."

"I know it's not ideal but we are horrendously exposed here. We need to use the jungle to our advantage."

"If we try to move Lynne, she won't...," Zoey paused, tears forming. "She's losing blood too fast as it is."

"If we stay here she's not any safer," Harper turned her face away from Lynne, Zack and Sam. "They could come back at any moment and with the Tarps gone and most of our equipment roasted, they'll finish us off." Zoey didn't say anything. "Besides, Ben says she may only have a few hours left. By the time we've packed up and got ready to leave she could... she could be gone anyway."

Zoey bit her lip and looked up to the sky. Harper felt guilty.

"Look, I know it sucks but we need to think about the group," she pressed. "Our best chance of making it is to get off this beach. We might just have to accept that not all of us are going to make it." Harper made eye contact with both of them.

"Someone has to tell Shermeen," said Ben.

"I'll do it," Zoey said as she sniffed and wiped her eyes. "I'll go."

*

"You're going to be okay Amos," Shermeen said as she squeezed the last few drops of water from the cloth onto his forehead. The large man was sprawled against the rocks, his head aimed heavenward. He was fully conscious but closed his eyes to protect them from the hot sun. While she kept him cool, Amos held a clutch of sopping material pressed against his wounds. Shermeen tried to speak again but was interrupted as he leaned forward to hack out another cough.

"Did he have medication for that cough?" James asked, a metre or so to the left, inadvertently pointing at Amos with the gun. "Damn, sorry," he said and switched the weapon to his other hand. Even Shermeen, as young as she was, could tell he'd never wielded one before.

"Yes," she said. "I gave him my dad's inhalers but

they're gone now."

"They were in our Tarp," Amos groaned.

"Ah okay," James said as he shifted his feet and looked once again over at the rest of the group.

"Do you think I'll be able to walk again?" Amos asked.

"I don't know..." Shermeen admitted. She fought to fill the awkward silence: "But even if you can't, we can make you some crutches so you can still get about," she said. "Won't we, James?"

"Uh, yeah," he replied. "That sounds like something Ben could do," he said unconvincingly.

"Yeah exactly. We'll make a pair for you and one for my mum. We'll be okay," Shermeen added, half to herself.

"Ah thank goodness," said James. Shermeen looked up and saw him staring in the direction of two approaching figures. They were virtually silhouettes against the sun until they were close enough to be identified as Harper and Zoey. The latter's face was red and blotchy.

"How is he?" Harper asked. Shermeen looked at Zoey a moment longer before answering.

"He's awake and in pain but the bleeding has stopped, I think."

Amos pulled the rags away from his hip and had a look: "Yeah," he confirmed.

"I heard what you did, Shermeen," Harper announced. "That was impressive."

"Thanks," the young girl replied.

"Shermeen, I think you need to come with me," Zoey suddenly spoke.

"What is it?"

"Come on, I'll tell you on the way," the Welsh

woman explained as she leaned in and offered a hand. Shermeen grasped it and hoisted herself up.

"I'll take over here," Harper explained.

Shermeen and Zoey walked several steps before she was brave enough to ask.

"Is this about my mum?"

Zoey eventually replied: "Yes… It's not looking good."

"What is it?" Shermeen questioned. Zoey's eyes said it all. She stopped in her tracks, faced her and grabbed both of her hands. Looking at Shermeen's feet she explained.

"I… I don't think she's going to make it."

"You mean… she's going to die?"

Tears began to build-up along the base of Zoey's eyes and her breathing got heavier.

"Yes," she said, squeezing her hands. "I'm so sorry."

"But they only got her legs," Shermeen felt tears of her own welling up. "She can't--." The girl's words caught in her throat. "Isn't there anything we can do?"

"Not without a hospital," Zoey finally made eye contact and squeezed her hands again.

"How long does she have?" Shermeen asked, her voice breaking on the last word.

"Not long. We're planning on leaving the beach very soon… I don't think your mother is coming with us." Shermeen fought even harder to keep the tears balanced on her eyelashes. With a deep breath she took her hands back from Zoey and wiped them away.

"I should say goodbye," she announced, flatly. "I wasn't able to do that for my dad."

"You're so brave."

The two of them arrived at the purification equipment. Shermeen's mother was lying on the ground, Sam stood above her holding the leg that had two arrows lanced through it. The bandages were thick and heavy, blood dripping from them as if falling from a leaking tap.

"I don't think you need to do that anymore, Sam." Zoey said.

"Oh, ok," the tall man said hesitantly. "I'll just... go and round up some more supplies." He placed the leg in the sand and left the purifier station.

Zoey and Shermeen crouched over Lynne and together lifted her to a sitting position with her back against the water tank. The woman's skin was incredibly pale, the last of her life ebbing away. Already the version of her that Shermeen knew was gone. All that was left was a feeble figure, whispering unintelligible noises with her remaining breath.

"Mum," Shermeen said, grasping her mother's limp hand. "Can you hear me?" She got nothing back except more murmurings. She would never hear her voice again. Shermeen's eyes suddenly became full. "Mum, it's me. Shermeen."

Still nothing.

A single tear escaped its confines and the others followed in a deluge. Shermeen's face crumpled as she held onto her mother's hand with increased tightness. Zack was close by and turned away, closing his eyes.

"Mum, I'm sorry," she said, taking in a deep breath before continuing her lamentations. "I'm sorry I was so awful to you. Since dad died in the crash you've been so alone and I didn't help you through it at all.

I was only thinking about myself." Shermeen paused as she searched her mind for something else to say. Something meaningful.

Lynne's head flopped forward.

"Mum?" Shermeen dropped the hand to lean in. It fell in the sand lifeless. "Mum?"

Zoey crouched down and picked up the arm, feeling for a pulse. She shook her head.

Shermeen buried her head in her mother's chest, muffling her cries.

★

"Okay, I've got you," Harper said as she took the weight of Amos' right arm on top of her shoulder. He certainly was heavy. "James, you get underneath the other side and we'll see how many steps we can go."

Amos put his good leg out in front and leaned into Harper. She exhaled as he pushed down onto her shoulders.

"It really hurts," Amos yelped.

"I know," Harper huffed under the weight. "But we've got to get you off the beach."

Ben noticed their struggle and had brought Sam over to help. The four of them completed the journey and placed Amos in the shade. Shermeen, Zoey and Lynne were gone now. The young girl was sat by herself under the shade of a tree while Zoey was a few metres off digging a hole in the sand. Lynne's body lay under a cloth next to her while she worked.

"If you want to get off the beach," Amos cleared his throat again. "Just leave me here if you need to."

"We're not doing that," Harper chimed in. She noticed Zack silently rolling his eyes. "We're going to have to find some sort of stretcher," she continued. "Sam, you've been looking at what we have left. Anything flat enough to do the job?"

"Some of the plating from the ship might have survived the attack," he said. "I'll do what I can."

"Thank you," Harper said. "Ben, are you alright looking after these two?"

"Yeah, no problem."

"James," she announced as she turned to him. "Let's take a walk."

A few moments later, the pair had arrived at their rock. Harper sat down, aware that this would probably be the last time she'd be able to. As the sun was still high in the sky, she could see the rest of the camp in case of another attack. James landed next to her.

"Look, before we make a move, you need to tell me what you know," said Harper.

"What about?"

"Just before we saw that flare in the sky, you said you thought you knew who those... things were. Something about their descendants?"

"Yeah," James replied, scratching the back of his head. "I did say that. I'm not so sure after your close encounter in the jungle."

"Just tell me what you know," Harper said, with as much encouragement as she could muster. "I'm sure you have a good idea what you're talking about."

"Well, for a start, I'm pretty sure I know what the writing is."

James pulled out the notebook from his pocket. The annotations were extensive. Pages and pages of scribbles.

"You've been pretty thorough."

"Yeah, well you have to be when you're trying to

pluck something from your brain that's been under the surface for years," James replied. "Do you want me to go through all of this?"

Harper raised an eyebrow.

"I guess not," James said as he tucked his papers back into the small book. "So the writing itself, I am confident it closely resembles a glyph system called Rongorongo."

"What's that?"

"It was discovered on Easter Island about three hundred years ago. It took a long time for me to notice the similarities. I've never formally studied Polynesian cultures but a friend of mine once did her dissertation on the Aruku Kurenga." None of this was making any sense to Harper. James continued: "But it came to me when we saw... when they killed Lisa." He stopped for a moment to consider his next words. "I think she was sacrificed," he said.

"What?"

"I think whoever these people are killed Lisa as part of some ritual. Human sacrifice was common in the Pacific," James explained.

"Wait, in the Pacific? You mean, back on Earth?"

"Yes, that's right. Easter Island is a body of land about two thousand miles off the coast of South America."

"So how did the writing get here? On Proxima B?"

"I know it's confusing. I was stumped at first but then I came up with a theory. What if the people on this planet are ancestors of the Polynesians?"

Harper was puzzled. Working it out aloud she said: "You... think life on Earth started here? On Proxima B?"

"Maybe," James said.

"But..." Harper's thoughts were all over the place. "The creatures that attacked are definitely dangerous but they don't strike me as a particularly advanced," Harper said. "How could they have built space ships?"

"You're right, the ones that we've encountered almost certainly aren't capable of that level of technology. But it means that maybe somewhere else on this planet is intelligent life we never knew about. It's fascinating."

Harper frowned.

"I don't want to burst your bubble but does any of this help us know where to go next?" she asked.

"What do you mean?"

"Well, were you able to translate any more of the writing? Can you tell us anything else?"

"Oh," James chuckled to himself again. "No, that would be impossible."

"Huh?"

"Nobody has ever translated Rongorongo."

"I thought you said your friend did her dissertation on it?"

"Yeah, that's right. But she wasn't able to translate it. It's been studied for hundreds of years and the best anyone's ever come up with is a guess at some kind of lunar calendar."

Harper sighed as her head dropped.

"I'm sorry," he said softly. "I guess you wanted more from me than that."

"Don't apologise," she replied.

The two of them sat in silence for several minutes, stumped.

"Unless..." James muttered.

"What is it?" Harper asked.

"Well, it's just if there are still civilised people

on this planet. Maybe we could try and track them down?"

"Civilised life? What are you talking about?"

"I can't see any other reason why there's Rongorongo on this planet," James began, shaking his head. "If these people are ancestors of those on Earth, it means that space technology was developed at some point. For all we know, those people are still here."

"That's one hell of a leap, James," Harper chided.

Breath caught in James' mouth, gesticulating hands returning to either side of his hips. A few seconds passed.

"Just think, if you were stuck on an island in the Pacific with no knowledge of the Earth," he said. "You'd have no way of knowing that the rest of the planet is inhabited by a technologically advanced race. It could be the same on Proxima B. Who's to say there isn't someone out there who can help us? They might have even picked up your distress beacon."

"It sounds like a wild goose chase to me," she said, sighing.

"What else are we going to do, though?" James asked. "You think we should move position anyway. I think you're right about that but where were you planning on taking us?"

Harper stuttered for a second.

"You've got a point," she admitted.

Harper mulled the matter over in her mind. At this stage, they virtually had nothing to lose.

She jumped to her feet.

"We better get going," Harper announced.

"Where?" asked James.

"We'll have to find that intelligent life of yours."

But she had to do something else first.

*

Harper stood before what remained of the group, ready to explain her plan. Amos and Zack were still sat against the water purifier, groggy. Despite their wildly different personalities and prejudices, the two of them were equals in pain. A huffing and puffing Amos had just tested getting on and off the makeshift stretcher. Ben and Sam stood beside the wounded while Shermeen leaned into Zoey, who had an arm around the girl. James was next to Harper, ready to back up her plan. They had packed remaining supplies into some rucksacks, ready to leave. All they needed now was a destination.

"So as most of you know, we're leaving the beach," she announced. "As for where we're going next, that's sort of complicated. I'll let James explain," she continued, "as simply as possible," she said, looking him in the eye. He took a deep breath before addressing everyone.

"I finally figured out what the writing in the jungle is," James began, staring at a sea of blank and weary faces. "Um... it's from a system of language used by inhabitants of Easter Island over three hundred years ago on Earth. That means the people who attacked us are likely ancestors of humans on our planet. Obviously, these creatures are very primitive, but I think there could be intelligent life somewhere on Proxima B. A civilisation that could have developed space technology capable of travelling to Earth." Silence reigned, although Harper imagined Zack would have said something if he could. She took over again.

"Our plan is to try and find this intelligent life and

hope they can help us."

"How are we going to find this civilisation?" Ben asked, mildly concerned. "Surely if they were near enough for us to reach they would have noticed us by now. Didn't you send out a distress beacon?"

"Look, it's a long-shot, I know," Harper admitted. "But if we have a chance of finding them, we have to try. Plus, we don't have many other places to go."

"I mean you're right, we *do* need to move," Zoey began, "but... I thought this planet was supposed to be uninhabited?"

"Yeah, exactly," Ben spoke again. "And how are you going to locate these people? We don't even know if they exist."

"I'm going to use the portable device I salvaged from the Concord," Harper explained. "It's not got a great deal of battery left but it should have just enough for what I need to do with it. Currently the only thing installed on its hardware is information about our allocated colonisation zone. Since we can't trust that anymore, I'm going to perform a new search, this time scanning for any form of advanced communication. It will probably take at least a day or two to perform that function, so until then we are going to move inland, away from where we've been attacked and make a temporary camp in the jungle."

"Just out of interest," Sam said, raising his hand. "Why didn't you do that new search before?"

"When I was removing the device from the main databanks all I needed at the time was data on our landing zone," Harper explained. "I didn't think to request any information from the computer outside of that. I just didn't have time."

"How do you know anything will come up?" Ben

asked.

"I don't," Harper admitted. "But it's worth a shot. We have to get help somehow."

Ben replied: "But surely if there was intelligent life on this planet, something we could pick up on the scanners, we would have been told about it before we landed. That would mean the government would have known about it but didn't tell us."

"Would that really surprise you?" Harper said.

An awkward silence fell across the group.

"Why would they want to keep us in the dark?" Sam asked. Harper took a moment to consider her next action and made up her mind. Time to let the lies end. If their plan was going to work, everybody needed to be on the same page.

"There's something I need to tell you all," she said. "I think this colonial mission was doomed from the start." Colour drained from a handful of faces. Ben, in particular, left his mouth hanging open. A wave crashed on the nearby shore, the only sound. "Captain Case crashed the ship on purpose."

"On purpose?" shrieked Zoey. "Why?"

Zack had been quietly stewing in his pain but the commotion had stirred his face into a more familiar one, full of anger and outrage. Harper thought she heard him swear.

"Does that mean we're in the wrong place?" asked Sam.

"We're around two thousand miles away from the official drop zone," Harper replied with difficulty.

"How long have you known?" Ben asked. He was cut off by Zack, forcing his words through closed teeth.

"First the writing, now this," he said.

"I promise you I didn't know until after we landed here. The information was on the portable hard-drive when I extracted it." Harper could feel her voice ramping up on the defensive. "I've known since our first day here."

"Why didn't you tell us straight away?" Sam asked.

Harper turned to James for reassurance. He remained conspicuous by his absence in the protests. Much to her surprise, he stayed that way, avoiding her glance. The look away cut Harper deeper than she expected it would. She sighed.

"I was trying to keep you safe," Harper said gently. "I thought, by compartmentalising the information I'd—" she was interrupted.

"Did you know about this?" Sam asked James.

He shook his head and found comfort in examining the sand. Zack chuckled to himself.

"How can we trust you with that thing now?" Zack accused, pointing at the device.

Harper fumbled for a response. The clear lack of support of her closest ally was permeating through the group.

Ben turned to James, ignoring her: "Is the writing stuff a lie too?"

"No," he murmured, blushing.

"This all sounds like a load of bollocks to me," Zack cried. "I'm not leaving the beach to chase a liar's hunch."

There were no disagreements.

James stared into the dirt a little longer, but then his face flushed fiercely, eyes taking on newfound determination.

"You know, I'm sick of you lot treating me like some kind of second class citizen, just because I'm cleverer than you."

Harper raised her eyebrows.

"Excuse me?" Zoey chided. James ignored her, arms flapping with increased frustration.

"Outdoor survival might not be my strong suit but when it comes to ancient history and anthropology, I know my stuff, alright. Much better than any of you. The hunch about the writing is mine, not Harper's." James risked a momentary glance in her direction. "To be honest, she was like you guys when I first suggested it. She's not exactly sold on it. But what choice do we have?" James threw each arm out either side of him, nostrils flaring. Without waiting for a response, he swivelled and walked a few metres away and started to pace in the sand, trying to cool off.

"Bloody hell," Sam muttered.

Harper still wasn't sure if anyone wanted to hear from her.

"Shit, here we go again," Zack grumbled as James strode back into the circle.

"You know what, doubt Harper all you want," he shouted. "Who knows what she's not told us, but why don't you start thinking like intelligent people for a change." James pointed at Harper. "She's trained for these sorts of situations, she knows how to act under pressure. That's her job. Harper's got us through this far because she's only told us what we need to know, when we needed to hear it. So let's just grow up, shall we? There's nowhere else to go, so let's just do what we can to survive."

Harper had expected such an outburst to act as a catalyst but a pregnant silence reigned. The fact it came from James, a previously mild-mannered man, was probably what set everyone at unease.

"Look, I'm sorry I didn't tell you all as soon as I knew," Harper said. "I've been trying to wrack my brains for why the captain would try and kill us all but I couldn't come up with anything. Since the crash, my sole focus has been to keep as many of us alive as possible. I understand that some of you might be angry about this but I chose to reveal the information now because I need you to trust me--"

"Funny way of showing it," Zack said.

"Have I kept you safe up until now?" Harper asked, without considering their present situation.

"Are you taking the piss?" Half of us are dead!"

Harper sighed.

"Look, I know we're in a bad place right now. But that's why we have to move. James is right, this idea is his not mine. Trust him, not me. We just have to get moving as soon as possible. Those... things... will be back soon."

"We don't disagree on that," Ben said, with a more measured look on his face. "We *do* need to get going."

"Honestly, does anyone have a better plan?" Harper asked the group.

Nobody offered a word.

"Let's get moving, then" Ben announced, although he still looked far from happy. He helped the wounded to their feet and began leading the line.

Harper waited for everyone to pass her so she could check in with James. He had calmed down, eyes soft again, although cheeks were still rosy.

"James," she said, softly. "I'm sorry I didn't tell you sooner."

"It's alright," he replied, brushing past without meeting her eyes. "Let's see if this hunch turns anything up."

18

"It was a fake?" Vicky was gobsmacked when Wash told her over a cheap dinner. The two of them were sat at the bar in her kitchen.

"Yeah, that's what I was told," he replied.

"And this Declan guy... he's fairly important?" she asked, scooping the remains of a chocolate pudding out of its container.

"Well, not officially no. He only graduated three years ago, so he's just a researcher at this point. But he's come up with so much information so far that I find it hard to believe he's not up to his neck in this."

"You suspect him then?"

"I don't know... maybe?" Wash shifted uncomfortably on his seat, squinting one of his eyes. "He could be behind the whole thing for all I know. He always *was* ambitious."

"It does sounds as if he's trying to help you," she replied standing over the bin, disposing of the rubbish.

"Yeah, I suppose."

"I mean, the guy going to the press with the inside

story is normally trying to expose something unto-ward behind the scenes." Vicky rolled up her sleeves as she climbed back onto the stool.

"Yeah, that's normally how it goes."

"Did he tell you anything else?"

"He said I should interview the widow. That vicar," Wash curled his lips.

"Don't you want to?"

"I'm just not sure what I'll get from her."

"She's the wife of the dead guy."

"Well, not the usual kind of wife. And besides, what's in it for her? Why would she talk to the press?"

"You never know," Vicky suggested warmly. "Maybe she could expose the whole thing."

"Perhaps but..." Wash was afraid to admit it. "I've not done one of these before."

"One of what?"

"A death knock."

"Oh... right," Vicky said, scratching her head.

"I wouldn't even know where to begin."

The journalist was fully aware of the irony. He had already come face-to-face with a dead body but was scared of sitting opposite a grieving woman.

"Don't they train for you for this kind of stuff?" Vicky asked.

"Not... really, no," Wash replied awkwardly.

"Bloody hell," Vicky sighed. "You weren't kidding when you said the standards had dropped."

Wash looked at the floor.

"You'll be fine," she said with a gentle punch on the arm. "I think you should do it."

"Maybe you're right. If she's the key to this thing, I should just throw myself in."

Vicky opened her mouth, but cut herself short with a short breath, changing her mind.

"I guess you'll still have the same problem as before, though? Getting your story through that god-awful editor."

Wash sipped his drink before carefully returning the mug to the table so he could gesticulate.

"That's the other crazy thing," he explained, a smile returning to his face. "Yvette Hamilton herself came down to the newsroom to speak to me." Vicky raised her eyebrows, impressed. "Yeah, I know, right? She told me that the police had confirmed the body was Miles Faversham and putting two and two together she worked out I must have known that too, although, of course I didn't."

Vicky laughed again.

"Yeah… it's all a bit confusing."

"So what happened next?" Vicky's smile tempered. "Thinking about it, do you think she suspects you were the one who found the body?"

"No I don't think so. I can't imagine I'd still be breathing if anyone knew I had been there. At the very least, there's no way she would have given me free reign over the story if she was worried about me."

"You're right. That's good." Vicky leaned on both elbows and supported her head. "The longer they don't see you as a threat, the better."

Wash wasn't sure whether approval from the Daily Citizen was worth much anymore. He suddenly grew conscious of the fact that he hadn't asked Vicky about her day.

"That's enough conspiracy theories for one day," he said. "What happened with you?"

"Oh, you don't want to hear about that, Wash," Vicky chuckled slightly, pulling away from the table. "You said it yourself, how interesting can it be writing press releases about plastic?"

Wash put his hand across the table and caressed hers gently. She came back towards him.

"Oh come on," he said with a smile. "You know I was joking."

"I know, don't worry." Vicky's eyes drifted to the paperwork sprawled among the dinner plates. "Besides, all I've been thinking about all day is this anyway."

"Really?"

"Yeah," she said with a broad smile. "Is that so surprising?

"I guess not."

"I mean you tell a girl you're involved in a story like this, she can't stay away for too long, you know."

"I'll have to keep telling you about it then, won't I?"

They shared a lingering kiss.

"So what else did you learn today?" Vicky whispered, still close to Wash's face.

"Not much more," he said. "I don't really want to bore you with the details of my conversation with Callum."

"Who's he?"

"The crime reporter. Weird guy, to be honest. Loves his food. Can't we get back to--" Wash cut himself off as leaned in for another kiss. Vicky turned her face to present a cheek instead.

"What if something he said was important?"

"It wasn't, I'm sure," Wash replied, leaning in closer still.

"How do you know?" Vicky asked, playfully.

"Believe me, I read his work and there's nothing there. Dead end."

"What if you're just saying that because you're thinking about something else?" she asked, her breath hot on his lips.

"I'm not," Wash replied as he leaned in and pressed his mouth against hers. This time she reciprocated.

A metallic rattle shook the table.

It was an incoming call on Wash's glasses.

"Oh go away," he said.

"Who is it?" Vicky asked. "Anyone important?"

"No," Wash sighed. "It's just Jay. Probably got his hair caught in the toaster again." He rejected it, and leaned back into Vicky. "Now, where were we?"

★

"Thanks for meeting with me at such a difficult time, Mrs Faversham."

Wash hid his displeasure at the cup of tea. The vicar had been too upset to remember the milk. The modest front room was in stark contrast to that of her parishioner Mrs Richards. In this small wooden clad room, there was no religious paraphernalia, no Bible verses anywhere. In fact, there weren't any pictures on the walls either.

The middle-aged vicar was dressed in a tatty beige jumper and torn jeans, hunched in an arm-chair opposite Wash. The woman's face was pale and her ratty hair appeared as if it hadn't been washed in days. She had not made eye contact since he had arrived and even now was staring into space, frantically nibbling at one of her finger nails.

"I was wondering if we could talk about your husband," said Wash. "I believe he was popular around here?"

"Yes... he was," came the empty response.

"That's great to hear. I'm sure there will be great interest in his obituary."

"Yes."

Wash found it hard to get his words out. He felt completely out of his depth conducting this interview and was a ball of nerves. Then he looked at Mrs Faversham's vacant expression and felt guilty. Yes, this was a difficult challenge for him, but at least he wasn't going through what she was.

"Can you tell me about what people liked about him?" Wash tried hard to put on a smile and prepared to start writing in his notepad.

"He was..." Mrs Faversham sniffed. "He used to do the soup run in the evenings, and helped with the seniors' lunches at the weekends. They lov--" She buried her head in shaking hands, sobbing quietly. "I'm sorry," she said with a weak squeak, eyes squinting hard. "It's just..."

"It's okay," Wash said softly. "I know it's been a rough time. I can't begin to imagine what you're going through." Pretty soon he was going to run out of platitudes. "You just take your time," he added, plunging into an empty notebook, pretending to read what was on the paper. As the seconds went by, the young journalist cast fleeting glances in Mrs Faversham's direction as he continued his little charade. She was wiping both eyes, constantly clearing hair away from her face and taking deep breaths. Wash became acutely aware that this woman was more than just grieving her husband. She was having serious trouble holding it together at all. The fact that her husband was dead and people were now asking questions, Wash wondered if Mrs Faversham was now in fear of her life. Remembering the guilt when first handed the story, he switched off his professional voice.

"Listen," he said tentatively. "I know about... you and Miles."

Mrs Faversham made eye contact for the first time.

"I won't report it, don't worry."

The woman's face retained its pallor.

"Believe me, I'd rather be using my position to help others than to put innocent people in jail."

Still nothing.

"I don't think your husband's death had anything to do with your situation. My suspicion is that his murder was motivated by his position within the government."

"Really?" Mrs Faversham asked, mouse-like.

"I'm fairly confident," Wash said. The woman shifted in the chair, sitting up a little. "The only thing is, reverend, I don't know much about what he did. Unless I learn some more, it will be hard to work out what the perpetrator was hoping to achieve."

"She began biting her nails again.

"It's just... there's not much I was allowed to disclose about Miles' work."

Wash remained silent, hoping it would encourage to carry on.

"If you know about... my situation... then, you can understand why it wouldn't be in my best interests to violate the official secrets act." The woman was beginning to find colour in her face once again.

"I get that. I really do," Wash replied, trying to be as diplomatic as possible. "But I'm worried that without your help, I may not be able to get to the bottom of this. There's definitely something not right about the colonisation programme. They are definitely hiding something."

"The only thing is... what was your name again?"

"Wash."

"The thing is, Wash, I'm not sure conspiracy theories are worth losing my life over."

"You think you could be the next victim?"

"It's possible," Mrs Faversham said through a nervous mouthful of finger nails. "And even if they don't send that thing after me, I'll probably end up in one of their hormone prisons... and that's as good as being dead anyway."

"You think the Eye Killer is working for the government?"

"I do," Mrs Faversham said confidently. "I just never thought it would be to do with Miles' work. I figured they were hunting down... people like us..."

Wash was desperate for more information but didn't know how he could get it. This conversation was awkward enough already. The vicar's last line gave him an idea though.

"Okay, Mrs Faversham, I understand your position. I'll try and chase some other leads," Wash said, standing up and heading for the hallway. She shot up, chased him to the door and grabbed his arm.

"You really won't tell anyone... about me?"

Wash lifted his hand towards hers, placing it gently over the tense knuckles. Gently, he loosened her grip.

"Your secret is safe with me."

★

275

Wash went straight to Callum instead of his own desk. As per usual, the large man was snacking on rubbish, tipping a packet of pungent BBQ flavoured peanuts down his throat. Two missed the mouth and landed on his collar, where they remained.

"Morning Callum," Wash said, hands in pockets.

The senior reporter swivelled in his chair and smiled, peanuts caught in his teeth.

"Morning kid," he replied. "How's the story coming along? Any luck?"

"Not many any real progress so far. Just spoken to the widow so I've got myself a nice colour piece on the latest victim but there's still no link from what I can tell."

"Not surprised."

"I was wondering if there was anything else you could tell me about the previous victims."

"Everything I could tell you is in that file, I'm afraid," Callum said.

"What about their social media profiles?"

"Their social media profiles? A little bit archaic don't you think?"

"Yeah I know that, but surely the data exists out there somewhere? People spent years building those things before they got shut down. Surely there's a way to access it."

The larger man scratched his nose, suddenly in deep thought.

"You might be right," he said eventually. "I used to know a guy a few years back who might be able to get me some additional information on the victims. What are you after?"

"Any group pictures on their profiles, their location history and any time the two of those over-

WRITING IN THE SAND

lapped with each other."

"Okay, I'll see what I can do," Callum nodded, casting another packet into the bin and springing into action. "Worth saying that there's probably nothing on Simon Crabtree. He would've been too young to have had a profile when these websites went down."

"Fair enough," Wash said. "Not necessarily the end of the world. What about Jack Stacy? He was only two years older."

By now, Callum was surfing his keyboard with newfound purpose.

"He might just slip into our net. I'll see what I can find."

"Amazing, thanks Callum," Wash said as he strode over to his own desk.

He noticed Pete had been craning in his direction as he arrived.

"What's Callum up to, then?" he asked.

"Wouldn't you like to know," Wash replied with a wink. He lifted the bag strap over his shoulder and placed it on the floor next to the chair. "I thought you didn't want to be involved," he joked, sitting down.

"I don't…" he said, hesitantly. "But you two working together on this… that's really something. You're both excellent investigators."

"Thanks, Pete. That means a lot," Wash smiled. "We could do with a mind like yours too."

The older man's eyes sank. He leaned in closer.

"Look, I'd love to help," Pete said quietly. "Nothing would excite me more than getting back to the way things were, you know that."

"I know, I'm sorry," Wash replied.

"But right now, the political climate just doesn't lend itself to this sort of investigation. Even if Ms.

Hamilton is happy for you to dig, she's hardly top brass."

"Do you think I should stop?"

Pete carefully considered his response.

"I know what you're like Wash. You remind me of myself in the old days. Dogged, determined... a relentless git." The two of them smirked. "I know that you're the type of person who won't stop until they find the truth. I think you've got to follow this through, more for yourself than anything else. Just... be careful, alright? And I don't just mean what questions you ask and to who. Be mindful of those around you. As I'm always telling you, Abbey and the kids are the reason I stay out of this sort of thing."

Wash put his arm on Pete's shoulder and smiled. His colleague responded with a friendly nod.

The young journalist got to work on Miles Faversham's obituary. He didn't have a great deal to offer on the subject, but had managed to get enough quotes from his wife to paint a nice picture. Wash was starting to realise it would serve him well to cover his tracks with innocent-looking pieces.

The exposé would come later, he hoped.

It took an hour to finish the story and Wash submitted it directly to Yvette Hamilton. Within a few minutes, the editor clocked her way along the newsroom floor in a pair of ungainly high-heeled wedges and arrived at Wash's desk.

"Very good Washington," she said, looking down her nose. "I felt a keen sense of loss reading about what Miles Faversham meant to the community."

"Thank you, Yvette."

"I think it's important to put a human angle on these sorts of stories, don't you think?"

"I couldn't agree more," he said with a smile.

"I noticed you didn't mention Mr Faversham's involvement in the colonial programme though," Yvette left the sentence hanging in the air, hands on hips. Wash inwardly panicked and stammered slightly as he answered.

"There's still a few things I need to iron out before I'm comfortable reporting that."

"Oh really," Yvette put a hand on her cheek. "That's a shame."

The woman had clearly been hoping to splash this all over the front page and was frustrated that Wash was trying to stop her.

"Yeah, I just want to be sure of a few more things before we break that element of it. We don't want to panic people unnecessarily... Just in case his death was as random as the others, you know?"

Yvette thought to herself for a few moments.

"I don't think we need to worry about that," she said, eventually.

"Oh really?"

"Yeah I don't think so. What's the worst that could happen? If anything, we'd be doing the colonial programme a favour by making this public."

Wash wasn't sure that was such a good idea as far as his own investigation was concerned. The colonial department had long-since held a reputation for being hard to penetrate. Running this story now could make it harder to get answers later. Yvette was waiting for his response.

"Maybe," was all he could muster.

"I tell you what," Yvette said with a wide-eyed look and point towards Wash. "We'll run the obit now, garner some attention that way. That should give you the time to firm up your story on his job and the threat this poses to the colonial programme."

"Well, I'll do my best," he said, with half an eye on Callum. "But I can't promise anything."

"Hmm, I see," Yvette said, her smile disappearing. "Is there really nothing you can do for the rush hour time slot?"

Wash checked the time. Still early in the afternoon. Searching his mind for anything he could offer up, he seriously doubted it. Wash had forgotten how exhausting it was being at the forefront of something the editor actually cared about.

"I might be able to cobble something together, yes," he said vaguely in an attempt to stave Yvette off.

Without even questioning him, she smiled again. "Ah good. I look forward to reading it," she replied as she waddled off.

Wash stared at the blank screen, wondering what drivel he could spin in a few short hours. He started writing down everything he knew so far.

First, an Atlas Nations satellite had been reportedly damaged by a British colonial ship. Then Miles Faversham had been murdered, it seemed, because of his involvement in the programme. However, at this point, the only reason Wash knew that was because of Declan, whose motivations were currently unknown. The information that he had received on Faversham's body indicated that there was a plot to kill colonists upon their arrival on Proxima B, although revealing the specifics could jeopardise both his safety and Declan's. Meanwhile, the colonial video that the country had seen was a fake. It was all pretty jumbled stuff and of course the big question in his mind was: *Why?*

Wash leaned back in his chair and sighed. Rubbing his forehead, he stared into the empty space above his screen. Then it hit him. The perfect way to run the story.

He'd have to be careful about the specifics of the assassination plot but with Faversham dead, it seemed pretty obvious that someone was attempting to sabotage the colonial programme. Wash wrote the first paragraph and smiled:

'The latest Eye Killer murder has been linked with a plot to sabotage the British colonial programme, the Daily Citizen understands.'

Perhaps Yvette was right. Regardless of what was going on behind the scenes, maybe running the story would get them on-side with the Citizen. That way getting to the bottom of this could get easier and easier. Declan did mention that a lot of what Wash uncovered would be easy to push through his editor.

Wash was sending the finished piece to Yvette when Pete's landline phone rang. The two men jumped. It was not a regular occurrence.

"Could it be your friend... from?" Wash asked hurriedly, hoping for something else he could write up before the end of the day.

"I really hope not," Pete replied as he picked up. "Hello?" he said. "Ah yes, he's right here." The older man covered the receiver and whispered to Wash. "It's for you."

"Who is it?"

"He says his name is Jay," he replied, handing over the receiver.

"Oh right, okay," Wash said, holding it up to his ear; a surreal experience.

"Hey Jay, what's up?" Wash asked.

"Where the hell have you been?" came an angry shrill voice through the handset.

"I'm at work," Wash replied.

"I've been trying to call you for days."

"Yeah, sorry, I've been… busy."

"Look, just get here right away. Something's wrong."

"What is it?"

"I'm not saying over the phone."

19

Stangl was waiting for Alida in her office. The council leader cursed when she saw him. The old man did not say a word. He simply sat in her desk chair staring. She wasn't used to him being this quiet. It was unnerving. He was obviously here to read her the riot act for announcing the suspension of Teslanium negotiations.

She cracked.

"You left me no choice, you filthy rat," Alida said, opening a small cupboard in the corner and pulling out a bottle of whiskey.

"Did I now?"

"Oh come on, Lothar," Alida replied as she started pouring into a glass. "You've been undermining me since the moment you got here and now you're interfering with the running of my own office."

"How did I do that?"

"Oh, I don't know, shall we start with the fake press conference, the leak about the British or the fact that the press somehow caught wind of my children?"

"You think that was me?" Stangl protested innocently.

"Of course I do," Alida turned away from the old man. It took everything within her not to punch him in the wrinkled face.

Stangl leaned into his walking stick and got to his feet.

"I just wanted to come by and see how our teams were getting on in Choctaw... Oh and, while I'm at it, to hear from you face-to-face whether the Teslanium negotiations have really been suspended."

"Of course they fucking are," Alida snapped. "Did you think I was just going to cave and send those reporters away? No, you've been sticking your nose in too much these last few months and it ends now." She slammed down her glass on the desk and walked towards Stangl, facing him. "You want your share of the Teslanium you are going to have to pay up, you understand?"

Stangl simply laughed.

"This doesn't exactly bode well for our joint-operation in Choctaw does it? I do wonder what the A.N. council will make of that back on Earth," he said smugly.

Alida had put up with this long enough.

"You know what? I don't give a shit what a bunch of old men on a planet I've not been to since I was child have to say on this subject. I think you seriously underestimate the balance of power here, Lothar. Gone are the days when the Proxima colonies relied on regular reinforcements and cash injections to make ends meet. The whole western seaboard is a self-sustaining network of bustling super-cities. Proxima doesn't need the Atlas Nations any more.

If anything, it's the other way around. You need us more than we need you."

Stangl held his stance, arms firmly resting on the walking stick, now leaned out in front of him at an angle.

"You obviously want something, Alida. Speak your mind." Stangl sounded as if he was almost baiting her.

"I want three things," she said. "First, I want your best men looking for my children. Second, a promise of no more leaks to the press."

"Done," Stangl said instantly. "What's your other request?"

Alida steeled herself. This wasn't quite how she imagined asking this, but that's just how politics goes, she told herself.

"I want Proxima A to have formal independence from the Atlas Nations," she declared, spreading her shoulders and lifting her head high.

"I've never heard anything so preposterous in all my life," Stangl said, turning to leave the room.

"You're not getting any of our Teslanium until you give it to me, Stangl," Alida called after him.

Don held an arm aloft to guard his eyes against the bright morning sun, watching Orvan lead the group away from camp. Very soon they approached the boundary between woodland and rocky mountain passes. The last few metres of the forest had been at an increased incline, pulled at the tight ligaments in Don's leg.

Emerging from the tree-line, they found themselves half-way up the first mountain. Looking down, they could see the vegetation through which they had climbed. Peakwood was just a speck in the distance. The outstretched prairie lands of central Choctaw dominated the horizon, encircled by mountains to the left. It was too far away to see, but Don knew that following the hilly terrain led to the northern coastline.

"What a view," Chad said quietly.

"It's beautiful," Don confirmed. The soldiers kept their professional silence but Orvan jumped in.

"Oh, you think so?" he said. "It's looking a lot better since you left, you know." Don said nothing and walked past the man, who continued undeterred. "The grass grows, the people eat the food of the land, the only corpses left to rot are the ones who deserve it. Not the innocent victims of your war."

"It was *our* war," Don said calmly. "We both played our part. Stop trying to re-write history." He made apologetic eye contact with Chad, referencing the previous night's conversation.

Orvan huffed.

"Me? Re-writing history? Like hell," he muttered.

Gisèle and Smurph had moved to the front of the group as they turned away from the cliff edge and into the pass. It wound up through two smaller peaks and further into the heart of the mountains. They had only been on the path a few minutes when smoke was spotted round the corner. Smurph, his troops and Gisèle broke into a jog and laid eyes on it before Don and the others.

"Orvan?" Gisèle asked.

"Yes, what is it?" He replied.

"What were you saying about corpses?"

Don and Orvan shared a confused glance and did

their best to catch up. When they came around the bend, the Choctaw leader simply raised his eyebrows. Don wanted to be sick. It had been some time since he'd seen this sort of thing.

The group had stumbled upon a campsite, not unlike the one they had made for themselves the night before. The fire was smouldering now, giving off wisps of black smoke, untended. Spread out around it was an array of tattered cloth bags, wooden sticks, and various farming tools, all of them glistening with blood. Each of the five bodies was headless, a mess of skin flaps and bodily fluid spewing forth from the necks.

The smell was foul and dragged up Don's memories of the Choctaw War. He was out of practice but managed to hold it in. It was too much for Chad though, who hid away to empty his stomach.

Orvan moved in closer, inspecting the bodies, with particular attention on each of their hands.

"Yeah, here he is," he said, sadly.

"Who is it?" Don asked.

"Laptev," Orvan replied, dropping the hand he had been holding.

"The head's gone," Gisèle countered. "How can you tell?"

"He was missing these two fingers," Orvan explained, pointing to his own ring finger and pinky. "It's an old injury. You bastards blew it off at Oldshade. Remember that?"

Don and Gisèle had nothing to say.

"I didn't think so," Orvan said, raising his eyebrows.

"You know, I'm fed up of you two banging on about the way things used to be here," Smurph interjected. "All that matters is the here and now, so can you too just focus?" Neither of them had a chance to defend themselves as Smurph continued: "We've got five dead bodies within spitting distance of the target area. I'm no expert on the British, but surely it's very likely they did this. Looks like they're openly hostile to me."

"We don't know if this was the British," Orvan said. "It's not like we saw who did this."

"No," Smurph replied. "But at the very least, there's a good chance it was. We should be even more alert." Everyone nodded.

"What does our esteemed expert on these people have to say?" Orvan asked, somewhat sarcastically, nodding his head towards Chad, who was still bent over a few feet away, breathing heavily. Don called him over.

"You okay, son?"

"Yeah," said Chad hoarsely with some enthusiastic nodding. "I'm sorry, I've just not seen—"

"We get it," Orvan interrupted him impatiently. "What can you tell us about the British? Do these deaths match up with what you know of their methods?"

"It's hard to say—"

Chad was cut off again.

A sting of bullets fizzed past him.

They thudded into one of the corpses.

Don turned to see three dirty-looking men and a woman, dressed in brown overalls, firing off automatic weapons in their direction. They stood guarding the trench-like passageway leading deeper into the mountains. The bullets continued to fly. Don, Chad, Gisèle and Orvan scattered.

Smurph's men slipped into combat mode. The big blue soldier punched down through the air and released two shiny metal cylinders on the outside of his arms. The tubes returned fire in crisp staccato.

He caught the woman in the shoulder first. Her firing arm was flung off by the impact. Flat-top and Cabbage were the next to launch their attack, sweeping aside two more assailants with their in-built weapons. Scissorhands activated his implants and produced a long shiny blade from just above his wrist. It sliced out of its sheath with a grating clang. Swinging his arm back, he lurched his arm forward and the blade flew out of its trap. It painted the sand a deep red as both hands of the final gun-man were sliced from their arms.

Don allowed himself to breathe. Stangl's men had been brutal in their attack. He'd never seen anything like it.

"Let's find out who he is," Smurph said, strolling up to the sole survivor.

The man's eyes burned with fear as he struggled to hold up the two stumps, dripping with blood. Then he dropped to the ground with a snap, lifeless. A bullet had finished him off from the trench.

"They shot their own man," cried Gisèle. "Who the hell are these people?"

"We'll find out later," Smurph bawled as more fire whizzed out of the trench.

"Contact, seven o'clock," shouted Cabbage.

Smurph responded quickly.

"Team Tauron, take up central positions and lay down covering fire. Sagittarius Team, on my six. We're going up there."

Flat-top and Scissorhands prepared to make the

ascent as Blaize, Thrombo and Diablo crouched onto one-knee and released heavy duty weaponry from their arms. The barrels looked similar to those of a minigun and the three soldiers rattled off rapid fire. In turn, each soldier complained as they had to strap ammunition blocks onto their forearms. Don could see they were missing their Teslanium weapons.

"What do you want us to do?" he asked, shouting over the gunfire.

"Just stay back and let us handle this," Smurph said in passing as he dashed for a more advanced position, joining up with the rest of Team Sagittarius. The three troops began climbing up the trench, either side of Tauron's blanket fire.

Suddenly, a grenade flew through the blockade, landing near the decimated campsite.

Gisèle pulled Don and Chad behind some cover. Orvan crouched next to them. The explosive went off, wreaking havoc with Don's hearing. Scraps of cloth, wood and flesh rained down on them.

"I'm not going to sit here and let those toy soldiers get us out of this fight," Orvan shouted indignantly, brushing some debris out of his long blonde hair. The Choctaw chief broke ranks and pulled off in the opposite direction to Sagittarius Team, pistol primed. Don and Gisèle rolled their eyes at each other, like new parents with a young child.

"Smurph will be pissed if he gets in the way," she said.

"Guess we better go after him."

He watched on as Orvan bypassed the trench and started climbing the rocks either side of it.

"You can't get up there, Donald," Gisèle shouted.

Don ignored her and started following Orvan anyway.

Another grenade propelled itself down the trench. It exploded above Gisèle and Chad.

Rocks slid down the ledge.

Chunky fragments landed all around, knocking both of them over.

"Just go," Gisèle called out, wincing as she shifted the debris. "We'll be fine." She certainly hadn't lost her edge since the war.

The adrenaline was running now. Don could barely feel his ankle, eyes set on the target. He bent over to start the climb over the rocks, like steps up to the level above the trench. Orvan was still only a few metres ahead. The noise was deafening, heavy fire coming from both sides. Don crouched as he moved along to avoid detection. He couldn't see what was happening down below. Orvan had laid down between two boulders, using them to spy on the conflict. He looked back, saw Don creeping up to the same position and frowned. The two men were crouched next to each other, backs leaning into the nearby rocks.

"What are you doing, old man?" Orvan rasped.

"Saving our asses."

"How exactly?" Orvan asked, nose wrinkled in annoyance.

"By stopping you from getting in the way," Don insisted, unclipping his gun and aiming it at Orvan's face.

"Is that what this whole thing was about?" The Choctaw chief asked, unimpressed but calm. "Getting me to some remote location and getting your revenge for what I did to your leg? I'm disappointed, Donald. I thought you weren't as petty as that."

"For goodness sake, Orvan," Don said with a shake of the head.

A bullet clipped against a nearby rock, flicking dusty residue into the air.

The two men launched themselves into the hard surface below. Peeking his eyes over the edge, Don could see that Smurph and the rest of Sagittarius Team had emerged from the other end of the trench and made it to some open ground further along. They had engaged the attackers partially from their flanks. It had probably been one of their own weapons which had nearly hit the two older men up above.

"You're gonna get us shot to pieces by our own troops up, here, Orvan," Don whispered harshly, desperate not to give their position away.

"Looks like these giants of yours might not have time for that..." Orvan muttered with a glance to the higher ground on the other side of the trench below, opposite where the two older men were based.

"What do you mean?" Don asked.

"They've been outflanked, themselves."

Don followed Orvan's calloused finger pointing over to the raised trench directly opposite them. Four men creeping up on them, automatic weapons at the ready.

The timing of the enemy was impeccable. The foremost gunman took something from his pocket and threw it towards Smurph and his troops. It exploded with an engulfing dull pop. As the smoke took over, the grenadier's colleagues turned their attention to Team Tauron, who had been slowly pressing forward into the trench themselves, opening fire.

Thrombo took two shots in the forearm with a

deep thud. The bullets appeared to bounce off his grey skin like rubber. He, Diablo and Blaize adjusted accordingly. Two of them kept their focus on those engaged with Sagittarius. Blaize returned fire on the surprise group, taking one of them out. The repetitive barrage of bullets took its toll on the hairless soldier. His muscular forearm exploded into a mess of red pulp. The weaponry inside clattered into the rocks below. The three remaining three aggressors shifted their focus onto Blaize and Diablo, one of them using their concern for their comrade to jump into the trench and get close enough for a better aim.

"It's a good job I took the initiative," Orvan said with a cheeky smile, drawing a long knife. "We better help them out, I suppose. I'll draw the fire in the trench. You take out the two guys still up there," he said, readying himself.

"How are you going--?" Don didn't have a chance to get further clarification. Orvan vaulted the rock in front of them and landed on one of the gun-men with a sickening slice and thud.

Don jumped above the cover and hit one of the attackers square in the neck. The man went down clutching a fountain of red below his jaw. The other one didn't have a chance to react. Thrombo used Don's distraction to sink two blasts into his chest.

Finally, it went quiet.

"Well, it's not the British," came Orvan's smug voice from the trench. Don looked down and saw the trail of bodies, a dusty crimson post-modern painting. Orvan stood among them with the final attacker in a headlock, knife trained on a fresh abdominal wound. "You can come out you pussies! It's just one of Peakwood's weakest fuck-boys, Honit the Hinawa."

"Screw you, Orvan," Honit said. He was a relatively short but stocky individual with dark hair and oriental ancestry.

"You're supposed to be missing," Orvan reminded him. "Your people down in Peakwood are getting worried about you. They think you're dead... which we can arrange." He pushed the knife into the shallow opening on Honit's belly, forcing a whelp and a growl.

"You think I'm up here for my health?"

"I think you're up here to kill people."

"That's rich coming from you, Orvan. Thanks to you, I'm the only one left from Peakwood's military."

"*You* attacked *us*, dipshit," Orvan replied.

"I had good reason," Honit insisted. "You and those multi-coloured aliens were the ones who killed my people. We've been up here for days looking for them."

"They're not aliens, you fool. They're human enough, just a little bit doped. And what are you talking about?" Orvan asked. "We didn't kill anyone until you turned up, all guns blazing," he added.

"Back there," he shouted, pointing at the destroyed camp. "We saw what you did."

"That wasn't us," Orvan insisted, breathing into Honit's ears, pulling away a little as he noticed an angry Smurph stomping over. Peakwood's leader shrunk a little, concerned the giant was coming to finish him off. As the soldier moved closer, Honit shifted further backwards, Orvan's feet shuffling with him.

"Seriously, what in god's name is that thi--" Honit rasped with an inhalation, instantly cut off.

"What the hell do you call that?" Smurph yelled at

Orvan.

"That's a fine way of saying thank you," he retorted, wincing to hold onto Honit, who breathed a sigh of relief.

"Next time we end up in a firefight, you do as I fucking say, you understand?" Smurph barked.

"If it wasn't for me, these so-called farmers of yours would have torn you apart. Fucked you over in the arse end of nowhere."

"Cut the insults, you inbred," Smurph continued, returning his weapons to their hidden position. "What do you expect from us to do without our proper Teslanium guns?"

"Excuses, excuses, eh?"

By now, Gisèle, with Chad in tow, had caught up with the group put her arms around the soldier. Smurph grunted in Orvan's direction.

"Go and help Thrombo," Gisèle said. "He's been hurt."

"Fine," Smurph huffed as he turned away to help his man. The wounded soldier was already receiving treatment from Scissorhands. He was preparing to cauterize the wound, while Diablo salvaged what remained of the weaponry.

"If *you* didn't kill my people, then who did?" Honit asked his captor, poorly disguising his unease.

"It must have been the British," Don said from above.

"What the hell?" Honit called out. "You're working with the Bloodaxe?" He tried to break free but Orvan held him tight.

"Can someone help me down?" Don asked.

Smurph directed Cabbage who held out two long arms above his head. All Don had to do was sit on the edge and slide down a few feet before the solider caught him and placed him on the ground. He thanked Cabbage and turned to Gisèle.

"Can you report this to Alida?" Don asked.

"Will do."

"Hey, Diablo, pass the same message on to Stangl for me," Smurph ordered.

Don then moved over to Honit.

"Yes, it's me," Don said. "I'm back. You're not happy about it. Join the damn queue."

"What are you doing here? What have the British got to do with it?" Honit asked, eyes flitting from side to side.

"They're the ones who have invaded this territory," Don explained.

Honit stared at him for a second, breathing heavily. Then he just leaned back a little and produced a shrill unbalanced laugh.

"Oh come on," he began. "You expect me to believe that? We know the Atlas Nations sent those ships. What else do you want us to think?"

"I can assure you we've done nothing of the sort," insisted Don.

"And you believe him, Orvan?" Honit asked, tilting his head. "I thought you were better than this."

Orvan made eye contact with Don.

"Well if the Atlas Nations *are* behind it all, they're doing a very good job of pretending to be shit-scared. Even the Bloodaxe is rattled."

"How do I know you haven't sold your balls to the A.N., Orvan?" Honit asked. "Stabbing a few old friends in the back is your regular gig."

"Believe me, Honit. I would never team up with these war criminals unless it was the only way to stop another load of them from messing with my territory."

"And that just happens to involve you snooping around in mine, does it?"

"Yes, it does. And there's nothing you can do about it. Especially not since you led your boys and girls into a firefight you couldn't win," he said as he kicked one of the dead, just below them. "A great shame."

"Look, what do you want from me?" Honit demanded, eyes flickering.

Don stepped in.

"We want to know what you know," he said.

"What do you mean?"

"You've been up here searching for several days, right? You're convinced these British ships are ours. Have you seen them?"

Honit looked up and down, cogs whirring in his brain.

"Yes, I've seen them."

"Where are they?" Orvan asked.

"They both landed on the other side of Torsevain Rise. We've kept away from their base during our search."

"Their base?" Gisèle jumped into the conversation. "They've set something up?"

"Yeah, both ships have embedded themselves in the terrain up there. They've formed a crater into the side of the mountain. We weren't completely sure but we think they could be doing something under the surface."

"Have you seen any of the people from the ships?" Don asked.

"No, not yet. But we didn't stick around long enough to find out. We just wanted to find our missing people. I guess they got to them first."

Don took a moment to consider the new information.

"What now?" Honit asked. "You're not going to..." his voice trailed off with a glance at a fallen comrade.

"No," Orvan said, finally releasing him. "You've got a job to do. Head back to Peakwood and you tell them the British killed those people and your men. Get them ready for a fight. Just in case."

"Why would I tell them the British killed my men? You did."

"Because, we haven't got time to piss around with Choctaw politics anymore alright?" Orvan replied. "Every man for himself works fine when the borders are secure. But right now, we've got bigger things to worry about okay?"

Don was impressed to hear such maturity from Orvan.

"Do you know where Torsevain Rise is?" he asked the Choctaw chief.

Orvan nodded.

"Let's go get the British then," said Don.

20

Harper's back was in agony. She had been carrying one end of Amos' stretcher for several hours and it was beginning to take its toll. The ground was uneven and dry. Navigating protruding roots and rocks increased the strain on her back muscles, inside her legs and up her arms. The top of Harper's head was producing streams of sweat, which stung her eyes with no way to wipe it away. By now, she had begun to notice the smell of body odour over the stench of the jungle. Still, it had given something for her to focus on after the debacle back on the beach.

James had clumsily asked her and Ben if they needed breaks but neither of them had been keen to stop. Every minute they stood still would make it easier for the creatures to find them. Zoey led the way with Shermeen and Zack was just behind, smoking another cigarette. Harper and Ben kept up the rear, partially to protect the group but also because they didn't want to hold them up. The distance they had covered was much less than Harper wanted but it was important they took care of Amos.

"How is the search coming along?" she called forward to James, who had been entrusted with the portable device. Before handing it to him, Harper had turned off the head-up display so it could run its program without wasting battery on the screen. James twisted the wheel on the side of the machine, gradually pulling the brightness up.

"It's only on eighteen per cent," he said, still being short with Harper. She heard the click of the brightness wheel back to zero.

"I guess that means camping for the night," Ben said over his shoulder.

"Afraid so," Harper said with a wince. "We'll need to find somewhere with natural cover. Somewhere that minimises their angles for approach."

Sam and Zoey looked to Ben for confirmation, who gently nodded.

"What are we looking out for?" Sam asked.

"Anywhere with rocks or caves will do."

"We'll see what we can find," Zoey announced.

Two hours later, they still hadn't found somewhere ideal to camp but Harper was ready to collapse. Every muscle in her body had been beaten into submission by lactic acid and it had grown too dark to continue. At least the thick tree trunks were no more than a metre or two apart, the sprawling maze of timber around them offering some protection.

"I think this will have to do," Harper explained when they came to a stop. "Find yourself a tree and get as comfortable as possible."

"Are you sure this is going to work?" Sam asked.

Harper let out stifled a grumble.

"This will be fine," Ben said. "When are we moving again?" he added, turning to Harper.

"At first light," she said. James came over and handed the hard-drive to Harper, without a word. She flicked the screen on temporarily. "Twenty-five per cent scan completion."

Sam crouched down and pulled out a lighter, flicking it on and pointing at the jungle floor.

"No, Sam," Harper instructed. "No fire. Not tonight."

*

Harper woke with a fright, startled by the sun in her eyes. She had wanted to get up at dawn. Panic set in upon realising she had failed. Her eyes flitted about checking her companions. All still asleep. Her breathing calmed. Everything was fine. There was a groan and a shuffle to her left, coming from where they had laid Amos against a tree.

"You're awake," he slurred. Even by his usual languid standards, Amos was far from a lucid state.

"Yeah," Harper said, forcing a smile. "How are you doing?"

Amos didn't answer, instead his eyes slid up into his head. A moment later they returned, with a wince and a cough. It was obvious he'd not slept much the night before, the pain clearly too much to allow any solace.

"Amos, are you okay?"

"Yeah," he said, short of breath. "I s--" his words sank into inarticulate garble.

"What?"

"--something."

Harper got to her feet and went over to the man, grabbing a bottle of water along the way. She held it to his lips and he drank.

"Try again," Harper said. Once he had taken a few sips, Amos spoke more clearly. He looked her in the eye.

"I saw something."

"What did you see?"

"In the sky." He pointed upwards.

"What did you see up there?"

"A plane."

Harper was stunned into silence. Maybe James was right all along.

"What did it look like?" she finally asked.

"I don't know," Amos replied, all of a sudden short of breath again. Steeling himself he continued: "All I saw was wings either side and a--there it is!"

Harper looked up. All she could see was blue sky and clouds. In the background was the gentle buzz of the jungle's wildlife and a breeze through the leaves.

"Where?"

"Can't you see it? It's right there," Amos insisted, louder than before, stirring the others. "It's leaving a cloud behind it. There!" This time he raised his hand to a portion of the heavens. There was a streak of clouds alright, but Harper couldn't see a plane, or anything that even closely resembled it. She felt Amos' forehead and her heart sank upon realising how hot it was. His condition had clearly worsened overnight.

"That's good!" Harper said reassuringly, touching Amos on the shoulder. "It could mean there's some-one out there we can contact."

"Yeah, or it could mean he's just hallucinating and all he saw was a cloud," Zack chimed in. It appeared his pain had subsided enough to open that foul mouth once again. Thankfully, Amos was in too much of a trance to have heard the taunt.

"Come on, Zack," Harper said, half begging. "He's not doing well."

"I can see that," came the reply. "I can also see how exhausted you and Ben have gotten just carrying him around. I see how much water you're giving him when you know he doesn't stand a chance."

"I wouldn't have thought you'd care about how exhausted I got," Harper countered, busying herself with Amos' fever.

"I don't bloody trust you, Harper, but any idiot can see you're useful. You're better off saving your strength to protect us rather than drag that fat lump of flesh around."

"Leave him alone," said Shermeen. She was stood behind Zack, arms by her side, fists clenched, nostrils flaring. "You just can't help yourself can you?" She pointed at his tattoo. "After all we've all gone through, you're still no different than when you were back home."

"Step off, little girl," Zack said, taking a step towards her. "You don't know what you're talking about."

Zoey quickly dived between the two of them.

"Yes she does," the Welsh woman said firmly. "You back away. You started this."

"I'd be saying the same damn thing even if he was the bloated *white* guy." Zack threw his arms in the air. "We should leave him here. He's not going to make it."

"And what would have happened if we had said that about you on the beach?" Ben asked. "I could have easily left you underneath that tree, but I didn't."

"Difference is, mate, I can still move my damn

legs. And if you had to carry me on a stretcher, you wouldn't end up with a hernia."

"We're not leaving Amos behind," Harper said authoritatively. "We have to keep moving and give him the best chance he's got," she explained.

"How long has that search got left?" James asked, rubbing his eyes and yawning. Harper noticed he was looking her in the eye for the first time since they left the beach. She pulled away sharply, still carrying yesterday's guilt. She returned to her makeshift bed and turned the head-up display back on.

"It's on forty-seven per cent," she said. A collective groan went up from the group.

"Another day of trekking," Sam said with a sigh.

"We better get moving," said Harper.

★

"--rper!"

Someone was calling her name with a muffled voice. She dozed for a second longer before they tried again.

"Harper!"

It was Ben, crouching over her.

Harper snapped her head up.

She was on the floor

There was a heavy weight pressing down on her left leg.

Looking down she saw it was underneath Amos and the stretcher.

"What happened?" Harper asked.

"You must have passed out," Ben explained. "You need a break."

"No, I'm okay," Harper insisted, hoisting herself up. James put a hand on her shoulder.

"No, Harper," he said, with some of that newfound strength he'd discovered on the beach. "Let someone else have a turn."

Sam came over and lifted the corner of the stretcher off Harper's leg while Ben and James dragged her clear. The two of them helped her up slowly and Zoey handed her a bottle of water.

"No, thanks," Harper said. Zoey gave her a scolding look until she gave in and took a sip. "We haven't got time to keep worrying about me," she added as she handed the bottle back. "Come on, let's go."

Sam picked up the back of Amos' stretcher immediately, groaning as he did so.

"I think I'm going to have to swap with someone soon," he announced as the group began moving again.

"I'll go next," James said.

"Are you sure you can manage that?" Harper asked quietly, not wanting to embarrass him in front of the group but immediately regretting the question. For a brief moment she had forgotten yesterday's outburst and had slipped back into taking comfort in James' presence.

"Do you remember when we first arrived here and you needed volunteers to get the Tarps?" he replied.

"Of course."

"When I said I'd come, you weren't sure if I was up to the work, right?"

"Sorry," she said sheepishly.

"It's alright," James replied. "I know I'm not much to look at," he said with a shrug.

"Come on, that's not true."

"Hey, you don't have to worry about my self-esteem. All I'm trying to say is that I'm stronger than you think. I carried that Tarp all the way back to camp so I can definitely help carry Amos some of the way."

"Listen," Harper interjected. "I'm sorry I didn't tell you about the captain." James didn't saying a thing, sucking more clumsy words out of Harper's mouth. "I just didn't want you to be scared. There was plenty of horrible things to worry about already." Still nothing. "Do you understand why I didn't say anything?"

"Yeah," James said, eyes-front, face-forward.

"Please talk to me, James," Harper begged, sounding more desperate than she liked. Ever since the beach, she had become overcome with guilt. During their time on Proxima B, Harper had looked down on the colonists for wanting to come here, bitter at those who sent her here. She had let her insecurities about Brixton poison her judgement. Now they had sustained heavy losses and were on the run. That was her fault. It was time to start treating these people with more respect, especially James.

James looked over his shoulder.

"I get it, really, I do," he said sincerely. "I just wish you'd told me before we spoke to the group. It would have been easier to handle. I felt embarrassed standing there next to you."

"I know, and that was my fault," Harper said. "You know, we're lucky to have you," she added.

James looked at the floor,

"You don't have to—"

"I can't imagine what we would have done without your knowledge," Harper pressed. "I certainly wouldn't have thought to run another scan. This planet was supposed to be uninhabited."

"Well, I guess the people back home knew what they were doing after all, letting me come," James joked eventually.

"I *do* think they did know what they were doing. But whether it was in our best interests is another thing."

"I've been thinking the same," said James, lowering his voice. "If we manage to find a way home, we might have to decide whether we want to take it or not."

"I think you're right," Harper replied in kind. "The captain of this mission crashed the ship on purpose and there was no mention of life on this planet in any of the briefings. Something doesn't add up. Either they sent us to Proxima B knowing what would happen, or they screwed up big-time and sent us in completely blind. Whichever way you look at it, they won't be very happy about us coming back and telling our story."

"Exactly. Well, most of us chose to leave home behind anyway.

"Speak for yourself," Harper said, tapping the insignia on her overalls.

"Oh yeah... I forgot."

The group continued on for a few more minutes, navigating Amos' stretcher over a shelf of rocks. Sam and Ben supported him underneath, Harper and Zoey pulled him up and over the ledge while James made sure the large man stayed on the sheet of metal. Once they resumed their journey, Harper took up the rear, just behind James.

"Hey, how about...," he muttered

"What is it?" Harper asked.

"Well, let's say we do have the chance to leave this planet, who says we have to go back home." He waited for his point to sink in and then clarified. "We could go somewhere else. Somewhere in the Atlas Nations. They'd probably be a lot more receptive to fugitives from the British government. You never know, maybe Proxima A is the place we should head for. Would save us a lot of time."

"That's not a bad idea," Harper replied, tilting her head pensively. "Let's not get too ahead of ourselves though." She pulled the portable device out of her pocket and inspected the search. "We're still only on sixty-eight per cent on the search."

★

The group found a rock formation as the light was fading. It was at the base of a minor cliff within the jungle, caked in tangled vines and feelers. The rocks themselves went back into the wall of sediment far enough to allow a few survivors the chance to sleep with something resembling a roof over their heads. Harper was a lot happier with this location than the night before.

"We'll let Amos, Shermeen and Zoey sleep in there," she said as they settled down. "The rest of us can stay out here."

Harper found herself a big tree-trunk about two metres away from the small cave and leaned into it, welcoming the back support. After her incident in the jungle, she had contributed two more shifts to carrying Amos, insisting that Ben take some breaks too. He was a physical specimen but even someone in his shape needed rest from time to time.

Harper still had their primitive enemy at the back of her mind, motivating every step, but she was grateful to stop for the evening again. Not only were her joints on fire, it felt as if her brain had turned to

WRITING IN THE SAND

mush as well. For two days straight they had trudged through the jungle living the same monotonous march over and over again.

She heard a wince to her right and leaned around her tree to investigate. Zack was sat by himself, head tipped back and both hands hovering over his wound.

"Ah shit," he said, impatiently.

"Are you okay back there?"

"What's it to you?"

"Well, we can't have you giving away our position because you can't cope with the pain," Harper snapped in a half whisper.

"Fine," Zack said, dropping both hands to his sides. "Have you got a knife?"

"Yes, why?"

"I... need to get this hair out of my cut. What's left of my beard keeps getting in and itching it."

"You know without any foam or soap that's going to hurt right?"

"I doubt it'll hurt more than this," Zack replied, pointing at the hunk of skin missing from his jaw.

"I guess you're right." Harper unclipped the pocket on her belt, took out the knife and chucked it over to him.

"Thank you," he said, ignited it. A small flash of light went up with a fizz, not enough to alert anyone to their position.

Harper leaned back onto her tree and tried to get comfortable again. Seconds later, she heard another complaint from behind her.

"Argh," Zack cried. "Stupid fecking thing."

"Will you be quiet?" Harper walked over in a subdued huff.

"It's not like I have a mirror is it?" Zack replied.

Harper sighed to herself and snatched the knife back.

"Give it here," she said, reaching for the bottle of water in her belt's side-pocket. "I'll bloody do it."

Harper unscrewed the top and tipped some liquid into her other hand. She sat opposite Zack and tipped the water on his right cheek. Some of it dribbled into the wound.

"Ouch. Watch it will you?"

"Do you want my help or not?" She said as she applied the searing blade to the hairs, carefully singing them off the skin. At this distance, she could smell his foul breath and his body stunk of sweat and cigarettes. Harper couldn't believe he still had some left over after all this time on Proxima B.

"Well, I feel like I'm owed," Zack said when she had finished the first sweep.

"How do you figure that?" Harper asked as she went in for a second run.

"Because you've spent the last two days hauling that sack of shit around the jungle."

"And your point is?"

"He's not the only walking wounded is he?" Zack laughed as Harper pulled the blade away again. "Although it's not like he can stand on his own two legs is it?"

Harper couldn't be bothered to listen to his drivel any longer so chose to ignore it. The sooner she'd finished here, the sooner he'd stop complaining and go to sleep.

"You know I can see right through you," said Zack snidely. Harper continued to ignore him. "Sometimes I look at the way you conduct yourself around here and I can tell why you do it."

"Can you?" Harper said, her words laced in sarcasm. By now, she had nearly cleared the wounded side of Zack's face.

"Oh yeah," Zack said, eyes widening momentarily. "You don't do it out of the goodness of your heart. If you did, you'd have told us about the captain on day one. You're not some heroic saviour, you know."

"I certainly feel like one when I'm raking this gunk off your face."

A devilish smile crept across Zack's face.

"No, you're not a knight in shining armour," he continued. "You think you're in hell."

Harper stopped and looked him in the eye.

"What on earth are you talking about?"

"You think you're being punished for something," he explained, believing every word. "Each time you do something noble around here I can see the begrudging look on your face. It's as if you're sick of cleaning up after other people but you know you have no choice."

"And you know about cleaning up after other people do you?"

"More than you know, sister."

Harper leaned back, eager to change the subject. Holding the blade up to his face to act as a torch.

"Look, I need a serious opinion from you now, alright," she said. "I've taken all the hair off this side of your face. Only thing is you've still got a load on this side, it might look a bit silly. Shall I take that off too?"

"Yeah, go on then. You might as well."

"Right then, please try and stay quieter this time."

Cutting the other side was a much easier task without having to worry about a gaping wound beneath it. The hair came away in under a minute.

"All done," Harper announced as she flicked off the knife.

At the back of her mind she noticed something familiar but could not quite put her finger on it.

"Wait."

She reignited the blade and held it to Zack's face. It looked completely different with the hair removed. He was ten years younger.

Harper stared a moment longer, mouth agape. Mind blown.

"Err... what are you looking at?" Zack asked.

Harper looked down at the tattoo on his arm, saw it in a new light and realised she'd been an idiot from the start.

"It's... you..."

"What?"

"You're Israel Barrett."

21

Harper Mulgrew did not like to be kept waiting. The Special Forces sergeant had assembled her team of four officers in the briefing room and eagerly anticipated the police's contact from the government to show up. The small space was a dingy sterile environment, poorly lit by two window slits near the ceiling and it stank of shit coffee. Harper's department was situated in the basement of the building, away from prying eyes and all the front of house staff.

She was sat at the head of the table, opposite the door. Immediately on her left was Seth Jackson, a tall, rugged man sporting curly blonde hair and a tight beard covering his neck. Opposite him was Kaz Oaks, a small demure woman with shoulder-length brown locks and a pointy nose. At the other end of the table were Adam Buscema and Jon Byrne, older than the other three and less prone to asking questions. By contrast to the two buzz-cut individuals, Harper, Jackson and Oaks were fidgeting incessantly.

She checked the time again and was startled when the creaking door was firmly pushed open. All five officers stood up to greet their guest.

Declan Fitzhugh strode into the room as if he owned the place. Harper was immediately struck by his youth. He could not have been any older than twenty-five and yet here he was about to brief a Special Ops mission without a single grey hair. He was young, fresh and attractive. Everything about him was precise and sharp, his pressed grey suit, even his glowing skin.

"Good afternoon, ladies and gentlemen," Fitzhugh said, moving to the table and inspecting the notes he laid out. "Thank you for meeting me at such short notice. Please have a seat," he continued, his silvery voice purring.

Harper and her colleagues sat down and waited for the man to continue. He remained standing and placed a small device in front of him. A speck of light flickered in the man's iris, sending a command to project a virtual bust. It was a hard face with thick eyebrows and angry eyes. The visualisation also portrayed his shoulders and the top of the forearms, one of which featured a tattoo of a lion with a Christian cross in its mouth.

"This man is Israel Barrett," Fitzhugh announced. "I need you to intercept him at his Brixton safe house and bring him to justice. I've included a map and directions to his current location in your briefing documents. I want you in and out in flash. The less noise the better." He looked around the room, making eye contact with everyone in turn. "Is that clear?" Each officer nodded their head and made a noise to the same effect, apart from Harper. Her silence was conspicuous. "Sergeant Mulgrew, is there a problem?" Fitzhugh snapped like a parody of an impatient school headmaster.

"I don't know how often you've led one of these briefings," Harper began, aware that her salty Scottish accent probably didn't sit well with such a man. "But we usually need a little more to go on than that."

Fitzhugh didn't even bat an eyelid.

"I've got my orders, and now you have yours," he said. "You will follow them to the letter."

"You haven't exactly given us many letters," Harper pushed back again, aware that her colleagues were getting a little uncomfortable. "What has this guy done to piss off Curtis?"

"That's on a need to know basis, I'm afraid."

"Come on, how often does a government official lead these missions? Normally we are deployed on internal matters, you know, related to the police. We're the best the Met has to offer but you want us to go in without knowing anything about this man?" Fitzhugh remained silent this time. "I don't think your superiors are going to be very happy if this all goes wrong because you didn't tell us enough information." Harper leaned back in her chair and placed both hands on the back of a shaking head.

From a standing position, Fitzhugh eased his palm into the table surface and looked around the room again.

"I think your team has heard all it needs to," he said. "Sergeant Mulgrew you stay behind and we can discuss the finer points of this mission." Oaks looked to Harper for reassurance, which she gave with a nod. There was a hurried scuffle of chairs against the floor, as the officers departed.

Once the door had slammed, Fitzhugh huffed and continued speaking.

"I suppose a little bit of colour around the edges can help entertain the weak-minded," he said, face like a smacked arse. "If you really must know, Barrett is currently wanted for racial hate crimes."

"I thought racial hatred wasn't indictable anymore."

Fitzhugh ignored her query and flicked another button on his remote. The image on the table changed, showing Barrett among a group of similarly shabby-looking individuals, all sporting the same tattoo.

"As far as we can tell, Barrett is the head of a racial persecution ring called Supremacy. He preys on black communities and is connected with fourteen deaths in the London area."

"Are those deaths currently being investigated by the Met?" Harper asked.

"No," Fitzhugh said, clinical and cold.

"Then it still doesn't follow," Harper insisted. "Why do you need us? If this man is persecuting these people, he's more likely to get a medal from Downing Street than a bullet."

"I understand it's a difficult idea to process," Fitzhugh admitted. Finally sitting down, he continued: "The truth is, Westminster is starting to understand the need to keep these groups under control. I assume you understand the concept of radicalisation, Sergeant Mulgrew?" Harper nodded. "The longer a group is marginalised by society, and the longer they are victimised by vigilantes such as Mr Barrett here, the more radicalised they become. The more radicalised they are, the more likely they are to strike back in some public way."

"You know what," Harper replied after a pause,

leaning back into her seat again. "I'm actually impressed. Well, sort of. So where exactly can we find Mr Barrett?"

"His last known whereabouts were at a known Supremacy stronghold in the centre of Brixton. As far as we know, their group is roughly four or five strong. We think they will be moving some weapons at twenty-one hundred hours."

"You want us to bag him tonight?" Harper asked. Fitzhugh nodded. "What about his men?"

"Inconsequential," Fitzhugh decreed. "We have no interest in speaking to them. If they get in the way, use whatever means necessary to complete the assignment."

"If they're as bad as you say they are, I won't have a problem with that."

✳

"Route is secured," Jackson reported. His voice crackled through Harper's ear-piece.

"Acknowledged," she replied, releasing her finger from the switch to end her brief transmission. The Special Forces sergeant held her rifle tightly and began to move along the dark tunnel. The curved redbrick ceiling had once been painted white here, but the colour had long since flaked away. Only one of the four lighting strips was active, merely flickering in the gloom. Each wall of the tunnel housed old shops, their rickety metal shutters pulled down for good and smeared with graffiti. The whole thing smelt of garbage.

Harper sidled out onto the pavement, covered by a wooden awning. Above her she heard the last few carriages of an underground train departing Brixton station. Thankfully, nobody had alighted there; if they had, she would have waited a few seconds longer for them to clear the narrow staircase descending to street level on her left.

She powered past more dilapidated shops before turning left into an alleyway. It took her under an imposing red-brick railway bridge, the tunnel much higher than the pedestrian one she had just emerged from. On the other side, Harper ran past metal cages on wheels and a burned out car before she arrived at a cosy high-street. Dimly lit by street lamps, only a corner shop five metres to her right showed any sign of life. A red and blue sign shone brightly in the window, bathing the pavement in colourful tones. In just a few seconds, Harper had passed over the circular brick layout below her and had arrived in another alleyway at crossroads with the high street. She left the claustrophobic confines of the back road and was struck by the wide open space. Harper had arrived at the Brixton Hill crossroads.

Directly in front, at the opposite end of the busy highway was the Lambeth Town Hall's clock tower. Climbing up into an ornate marble structure, the hands on its face displayed the incorrect time of eighteen minutes to one, the word 'RAILWAY' written around the circumference instead of the usual digits. Below the tower the building formed the corner of two converging roads, marble columns lining each side of the structure. To her left was a wide open courtyard space, paved with beige concrete slabs. At its heart was a large tree, its leaves gone and sturdy branches sprawling out from the thick trunk, covering a distance of probably five metres in each direction.

Gathered around was a throng of people, producing incredibly colourful noise. Driving through the hubbub of the crowd was relaxing music, played on an acoustic guitar and steel drums.

"In position," came the feminine tones of Oaks in Harper's ear. She could make out her colleague's location ten metres to her right. "The government guy didn't say there'd be this many people around," she continued, her voice wavering a little. "What do we do Sarg?"

"We stay sharp," Harper said, leaning into the dark red walls of the abandoned theatre building on her left. The intel Fitzhugh had provided said Barrett and his men would be inside. With all the merriment going on a few metres in front of her, she felt like a sore thumb donned in combat gear and wearing a helmet. "Are you in position yet, Jackson?"

The sniper took a few moments to announce his reply. I'm nearly at the top now. Harper could hear the muffled slam of a door creep through her communicator.

"In position," he replied. Shortly after, Harper spotted a brief glint of light flash just below the clock. Jackson had found his perch.

"Run heat signature search on the theatre building." Harper requested her eye in the sky. "I want to know exactly where they are before we go in."

"Affirmative," he replied.

Harper looked along the row of structures adjacent to the theatre and opposite the courtyard. An intermittent flashing red light at the other end indicated that Buscema and Byrne were in position too. All they needed was a signal from Jackson.

"Negative," he announced over the radio.

"What?"

"It's a negative on the heat signatures," Jackson explained.

"But why?"

"I don't know Harper, they're not in there," he said.

"Did we miss them?" Oaks asked.

The rattle of gunfire went up, accompanied with a flash of light. The screams alerted Harper to the weapon's location. Above the gathered crowd was the barrel of a rifle, repelling people like leaves from a blower. The gun dropped below head height and fired again, intensifying the cries and causing a loud yowl of pain.

"I think we've found Barrett's next target."

"We have to engage!" Oaks yelled.

"No, not until we have clear shot," Harper replied defiantly. "Jackson?"

"Negative," he replied.

Harper cursed to herself.

"Sergeant, we've got a real problem," Jackson snapped.

"What is it?"

"Look at the branches."

Harper saw a line of rope looped over one of the boughs, landing the other side, presumably caught by one of Barrett's men. Unthinkable screams pierced the night sky. She looked on in horror as the cable went taut and started to drag something into the tree. It was a short dark male, clutching at his neck, legs writhing. There was a dark red patch on one of his limbs, presumably where he had been shot.

Harper swore.

Her radio crackled. It was Oaks again: "We *have* to engage."

"No wait," the sergeant replied.

Both Jackson and Oaks protested in unison: "What?"

"We have to do this just right."

"Harper, he's going to die," Oaks complained.

"If we are sloppy, more people are going to die in the confusion," she pushed back. "Jackson, wait until that rope is stationary."

"Stationary? By then he'll be dead," Jackson cried. "I can hit it now."

"Right now it's swinging all over the place and lighting is poor. I can't take a risk on your arrogance," Harper insisted.

A tense few seconds followed. They passed slowly. The man's struggle against his fate grew weaker, body stiffening, rope slowing until...

"Fire," Harper snapped, immediately racing into a sprint.

The booming shot rang out around Brixton Hill, louder than anything Barrett's weapons had produced. More screams came up from the group. The rope snapped in an instant and the man fell to the ground. Through the collection of bodies, Harper could not see where he landed.

Five metres to go.

"Harper, I've got eyes on one of the targets," Jackson announced.

"Take the shot."

Another discharge crackled in the air, smashing one of the armed men into the pavement. Harper caught the end of his fall as the large group began to disperse entirely. Another of Barrett's goons spotted her running towards him and raised his weapon.

BANG.

Jackson's next round hit him square in the chest, driving him into the ground.

Harper looked up and noticed Barrett jogging backwards, trying to blend into the escaping masses.

"Oh no you don't," Harper whispered to herself, raising her rifle. She squeezed the trigger and prepared to fire. At the last moment, Barrett lifted his left arm to dodge a young boy who had tripped over, revealing he was holding the hand of a blonde woman next to him. Another of Jackson's shots ripped through the air, felling the final Supremacy man. Barrett and the woman turned in their tracks.

BANG.

Another weapon fired.

Harper's hip roared into a flame.

She pulled her trigger.

Red liquid splattered over Barrett's face.

Falling, Harper saw the blonde woman dropping in unison with her.

The floor slammed into her face.

Everything went dark.

The wailing of the crowd became muffled, seeping into the background.

Her senses roared back into focus as an authoritative voice verbally assaulted her from the right.

"Stand down," it screamed.

"What the fu--" Harper moaned as she curled on the floor, nursing the wound on her waist. She looked up. Standing over her was a short-haired middle-aged woman with a disgusted look on her face. Paterson.

"Order you men to stand down Sergeant," she snapped. "And get your arse off the ground. You're in for some real shit now."

★

"I'm not going to ask you again, Mulgrew," Paterson shouted as she slammed her fists down. "Who authorised this mission?"

"I already told you," Harper rasped, not looking her in the eye. "Declan Fitzhugh did."

It was several hours later and she was still handcuffed to a metallic table in an interrogation room. After Paterson had shot her, Harper's helmet had been removed and replaced with a small cloth bag. Then they had bundled her into a van and sedated her. She had woken up in this small space, accusing lights bearing down on her brain as a nasty headache shook her skull. Her side was sore, the wound now dressed in bandages. Harper surmised the bullet had merely grazed her, although the real pain might have been temporarily stifled by whatever they injected her with.

"You're telling me that a crack Metropolitan Police Special Forces unit was deployed by a Parliamentary researcher?" Paterson continued, her words dripping with derision.

"For the hundredth time, yes," Harper yelled. "Why won't you tell me what the hell is going on here?"

"You want to know what's going on here?" Paterson asked, standing up and hurling her chair at the wall. "It's the end of your career. You're finished." The woman stopped short of throwing her fist into the wall. "You've ruined nearly a year of undercover work to bring Barrett in."

"Undercover work?" Harper asked quietly, shrinking back into her sitting position. Thinking of the woman who had been with Barrett. "Who was that woman?"

"One of my officers," Paterson said softly. In a second, her rage returned. "You killed her because you didn't do your job properly."

Harper's blood boiled and nearly burst out of her veins.

"*I* killed her? Are you for real, lady? There's no way I would have hit her if you hadn't shot me in the first place you stupid bitch."

A slap rattled Harper's face and rang a whine through her head. She spat on the floor.

"Fuck you," she said, undeterred. "That woman's death was y--."

Paterson hit her again.

"Things will go much better for you if you start co-operating."

"How many times do I have to tell you I was sent on that mission by Declan Fitzhugh? He said the government wanted Barrett and his men taken out before they radicalised minority groups beyond repair."

Paterson straightened herself out, picked up her chair and returned to her sitting position. She opened a folder on the table and flicked through the plastic wallets.

"And I don't know how many times I have to tell *you*, sergeant Mulgrew, that there is absolutely nothing on record to say this mission was authorised."

"That can't be true. It came from Whitehall. That's what he said..." Harper began to realise how hopeless her situation was. "What's going to happen to my team?"

"I don't know," she replied. "I'd be more concerned about yourself right now, if I was you."

Harper's headache was pierced uncomfortably by a strident ringing. Paterson's eyes lit up and she rolled them impatiently.

"You see what you've done? This is the press." Answering, the woman stormed out of the room. "I don't have time for this Pete."

She slammed the door and locked it from the outside.

☆

Harper was woken by a knock on the cell door. She raised her head from the pillow and sat up as far as the handcuffs would allow. Dazed and confused, she looked at the oppressive slab of metal that detained her.

"It's me," a voice said on the other side, accompanied by the jangling of keys. "Get away from the door."

Harper rattled the restrains around her hands and half-chuckled.

After a moment of heavy clunking inside, the door swung open, quickly shut again by a smart man with wavy blond hair and a pristine suit. He locked it.

"You son of a bitch," Harper yelled at Fitzhugh, attempting to take a swing, held back by her handcuffs like a dog on a leash. The young man took a collected step back.

"Look, just give me five minutes to explain this."

"Are you taking the piss?" Harper replied, her fringe scratching at tired eyes. She tried to flick it aside with a jerk of the neck. "I've been stuck here for two days and that's all you've got." Fitzhugh shuffled for a few seconds, adjusting his collars, not saying anything. "Are you going to tell me why they can't find any record of this mission? It's like you never even came to us."

"I know," Fitzhugh admitted. "That's why I've come. I need you to retract your statement. That I was the one who authorised the mission."

"What? You want me to do you a favour now? Surely you coming here isn't going to look very good."

"It's the middle of the night Harper, and I know enough people behind the scenes to make sure nobody knows this meeting happened."

"Well, good for you."

Fitzhugh put hands in his pockets and started pacing around the doorway.

"Look, if you're not going to do this for me, then do it for your team," he said coolly. "If you persist down this route and try to pin this operation on me, I won't be around to make sure they don't get caught up in this." A horrible falling sensation punched down through Harper's gut. She knew where his was going.

"Why do you think I tried my best to compartmentalise the intelligence?" he added.

She sighed.

"Fine. You've got yourself a deal."

"Thank you. You're going to have to say you acted alone on this one. That you were on a vendetta against Barrett's group."

"What happens after that?"

"Well, I'm not sure, to be honest," Fitzhugh said. Harper looked back to him with a frown. "They got Barrett," he said.

"Who's *they*?" Harper asked. "Is that supposed to mean something?"

"All I can say is the wrong people got him. He'll

serve a life sentence."

"Isn't that a good thing?" Harper asked.

"It means we failed. I wanted to get to him first, that's why I brought you in." he explained. "I guess it didn't work."

"You're damn right," Harper replied, plonking herself back on the bed. She couldn't bring herself to look at the slime ball any longer. Staring at the floor, she spoke again: "What I meant was... what happens to my team? And what happens to me? Come on, pretty boy, tell me."

"Your team will be fine. As they were operating under your orders I can get them off with minor disciplinaries."

"*My* orders? That's fucking rich," Harper replied. At least her colleagues would be alright though. Declan ploughed on, not listening.

"Your situation looks worse. Jail-time is likely. Lots of it."

"What's the charge?"

"I don't think there's going to be one," Fitzhugh said.

"They can't blame me for what happened," Harper protested.

"I'm afraid they can," Fitzhugh replied softly. "To the outside world this looks like a rogue government copper went mad and shot vigilantes and ethnic minorities alike. That won't reflect well on Curtis or his administration. The story is going to break any time soon and they're going to need someone to take the fall."

Harper swore, sinking back. "I can't go to prison," she lamented, leaning her back against the tiles. "You know what they do to people like me in prison."

"There's nothing I can do. My hands are tied."

Harper clutched hands to her face as tears began to well up.

"Just... go," she sniffed.

The politician dawdled a few seconds longer before turning round and fiddling for the keys. Then he stopped.

"Unless..." he said to himself.

"What is it?" Harper asked, wiping her cheek as Fitzhugh swung back round to face her.

"I can't promise anything," he said. "But there's a chance I can spare you jail-time on this."

"How?"

"The government is planning a colonial pro-gramme."

"What use will they have for a disgraced Special Forces sergeant?"

"They'll need someone with military experience. Mostly for co-ordination purposes."

Harper was still sceptical.

"Where are they going?"

"Proxima B."

"Proxima B? That planet out in the Atlas Nations' solar system?"

"That's right."

"Your alternative to being dumped in prison is a one-way trip to space?"

"It's all I can do. At least out there you'd have some freedom. A chance at a new life. That's more than you'll get here."

Harper looked down at the handcuffs, shaking them against the cold metal of the bed-frame. This job had been everything to her. She'd been the best for years and now it was all gone. There was no way she was going to end up in a prison. Sighing, she gave her answer.

"Looks like I have no choice."

✳

"How do you know my real name?" Zack asked, half-whispering, eyebrows curling. For the first time since the two of them had arrived on Proxima B, Harper noticed a vulnerability in the man's face. Silence fell between the two survivors, the chirping of bugs and swaying of the leaves taking over. She could barely breathe in her agitated state.

"I don't get it. They told me you were going to be serving a life sentence." She backed away from Zack, her head in a spin, endless possibilities running through it.

"What don't you get?" his confusion was turning into anger. "How do you know my name?"

"Brixton. Two years ago. The Supremacy attack. I was in charge of the unit that was supposed to apprehend you."

"Wait, does that mean you--"

"I'm the one who shot that woman, yes." Harper could not bring herself to look at him.

"That was you?"

"Yes," Harper confirmed. She finally made eye contact with Zack. With Israel Barrett.

"You fucking bitch," Zack snapped, leaning forward and crashing his clenched fist into Harper's chin. She fell backwards, dazed by contact with the floor. He pinned her down with his legs and struck again, this time on the cheek. Then on the forehead. "You're going to pay for that," he roared.

Harper sharply raised a knee, catching Zack between his legs. He recoiled with a yelp, allowing her to push him off.

"Did you love her?"

"What do you think?" Zack replied indignantly.

"Well, she didn't love you," Harper replied, half enjoying pressing her information home. "She set you up."

"What are you talking about?"

"She was a plant. Working you. Undercover."

"You're lying."

"Believe me, I wish I was. She took the bullet meant for you and then my life went to shit."

"You think mine didn't?"

"You deserved it," Harper rasped. "The reason I had to take you out was to stop you killing innocents, just because they were different to you. You deserved to die and yet here you are still living, still tormenting me half-way across the galaxy." Harper turned away to check the rest of the group. Amazingly, they were still sleeping. "It's not fair," she added, sitting down.

Then it hit her.

"Oh shit."

"What is it?"

"*This* is the life sentence," Harper realised, hands on her forehead. Wide-eyed she stared at the ground below her. "How could I have been so stupid? Why the hell else would they have sent me on this mission?"

"What do you mean?"

"Don't you get it? They didn't send us here to be the forefront of their new empire. We've been banished here to die. All of us. Not just me. Not just you. All of us. That's why Case crashed the ship." She paced between two trees. "But... why go to all that trouble?

Why not just take out and shoot us? It doesn't make sense."

Harper's entire time on Proxima B had been about one thing: survival. As much as she didn't want to be here, she had resigned herself to her fate. But now it was different. The anger and hatred for those responsible for her banishment bubbled to the top. She simply had to get back home and find out what the hell was going on.

Zack had been silent for a conspicuous length of time. Then he drew breath, as if uncertain how to begin.

"You know, I've changed since Supremacy," he said. "I'm not that man anymore."

"Yeah you're a real saint, Zack. Barrett. Whatever you're called, I don't care."

"I mean it," Zack said, sitting up. "I don't kill them anymore. Not for fun anyway. Life in prison with their kind changes you."

Harper had no such congratulatory words.

"Just shut up Zack," she roared as she grabbed him by the shoulders. "You're the reason I'm on this god forsaken rock a million miles from home. You, Paterson, Declan Fitzhugh." She let go of the man, discarding him against a tree.

Her pocket vibrated. Then it beeped. She looked down. Zack used that opportunity to catch Harper on the chin with his elbow. She fell back into the dirt, feeling for the device. It illuminated the nearby trees as she restored the brightness.

Four words: "Search complete. No results."

22

Wash rushed out of the office after Jay had called, hoping a rapid exit had not drawn undue attention. After the publishing the article on a potential link between the Eye Killer and the IPCP, news was fast spreading about his increased involvement in the year's top story. The journalist spent the entire train ride back down the Central Line tapping feet and biting his nails. By the time he was back at West Acton, he was damp with sweat in the November heat, his shirt now uncomfortably wet.

Wash fumbled with his keys at the door. He could smell the musty state of the flat from the corridor already. The familiar aroma filled his nose and reminded him how long it had been since he was last here.

Before he could start unlocking the door, Jay opened it and dragged him in.

"What are you doing?" Wash asked as his friend slammed the door shut. In the thick and stuffy environment, he was a sweaty mess, Jay a nervous wreck. "Come on, Jay, you better tell me what this is about.

I've come all the way back here from the office when I'm supposed to be in the middle of an important story."

"Where the hell have you been?" Jay asked, long hair swaying with the gesticulations.

"I've just been away for a few days."

"I worked that out already, dick head. I've not seen you in bloody ages."

"I've been staying at Vicky's." Wash spread his arms in annoyance. "What on earth is wrong with that?"

For a moment, Jay's anger evaporated, a slight grin creeping across his face.

"You finally asked out hot train girl, then?"

"Yeah I did."

Jay shook his head and waved both hands, remembering his frustration.

"That's not important right now," he said. "I think we're being followed."

"What?" Wash's stomach hit the floor. He felt weak in the knees. "What the hell?"

"Exactly."

Wash cast his bag aside and strode into the lounge. The blinds were only half open so it was dingy.

"What happened?" he asked, still pacing.

"So, three days ago I noticed two big looking dudes and a woman in the lobby downstairs. I thought nothing of it at the time. I guessed they were just here to help someone move in or something. But then the next day they were here again and yesterday I'm pretty sure one of them followed me all the way to work and all the way back."

"That could be anything," Wash shrugged, daring himself, hoping, to relax again.

"That's not all," Jay continued, panic rising in his voice. "This morning, I bumped into the woman on my way out of the building and they asked me if I knew where Washington Parker was."

Wash's bladder felt loose. He sat down and held his head.

"What did she look like?"

"Late thirties I reckon, maybe early forties. Short brown hair and a mean ugly face. Pointy nose."

"What did you say to her?"

"What do you think I told her?" Jay asked, arms out wide. "The truth. I've had not seen you for days, man."

Wash recollected the last week or so in his mind, searching his memories for anyone who looked particularly suspicious. He breathed in sharply, realising his friend's error.

"You idiot, Jay," Wash shouted aloud, launching himself off the sofa. He huffed over to the window to peer between the blinds and through the black metal bars of the fire escape. His hot breath misted up the glass.

"What?"

"You've got mysterious people asking after me, stalking where we live... and you thought the best thing to do was to get me to come home?"

Jay didn't say anything at first.

"Ah shit... I'm sorry man. Is this about us watching New Zealand news?"

"Don't forget that was *you*, not me," Wash snapped, as he pulled away from the blinds. "Doesn't look like there's anyone out there. Not yet anyway."

"I'll have a look," Jay said. "See if I recognise anyone."

Wash crashed back onto the sofa and exhaled, realising he should probably clear things up.

Jay came back from the window and sat in his chair again, appearing confident nobody was down below.

"I think I know why people want to find me," Wash revealed, short of breath. "It's about a story I'm doing for work."

"Damn."

"Yeah I know. I think my curiosity may have got the better of me and my dad inadvertently pushed all the right buttons. I figured this might cause some problems but I've really not thought about my own safety as much as I should have. If people are after me now then it's not so exciting anymore."

"Do you know why they are after you?"

Wash had a pretty good idea, but didn't want to panic Jay.

"It's probably best if I don't tell you anything. It doesn't make any sense, though," he said. "They must know where I work. Why not ask to speak to me there?"

"Maybe they don't want too many people knowing they're looking for you?"

"Yeah... which probably isn't a good thing."

Silence hung in the air for a few moments longer. Wash considered his options. If there were people stalking him now, he couldn't stay at home anymore. Where else could he go? Surely they'd have the address of his father's home and Pete was out of the question so he could only think of...

He blurted out a foul word.

"What is it?"

"Vicky," Wash said, getting to his feet. He started to

pace.

"Who?"

"Come on, you know who I'm talking about."

Wash gathered his things. He turned to say good-bye.

"I'll try not to come back for a while," Wash said, standing in the doorway. "I don't want you caught up in this... I'm sorry I've been so distant. Things have just got... really carried away with Vicky."

"That's cool mate, really it is," Jay said, joining him in the corridor. "It just would have been nice if you'd told me, that's all. I kinda rely on you for a lot of stuff around here, not least topping up the air conditioner allowance."

Wash noticed again how warm it was and apologised.

"Is everything okay here?"

"I guess. I'm starving and smell like crap but apart from that I'm doing alright. I'm more concerned about you."

Wash fished in his pocket and pulled out a ten pound note.

"Here, this should be enough for another week."

There was a knock at the door. Wash's heart skipped a beat.

"Expecting anyone?" he whispered to Jay.

"No."

"It'll be them."

"You better go."

"How?"

"The fire escape. Through the lounge window."

"Got it."

Wash grabbed his bag, sprinted through the corridor and into the lounge. He pushed the button down on the handle and angled it up. Swinging the window open he leapt with a cling onto the fire escape. Pushing the window in as much as possible, he began his descent. Wash got just above the alleyway and poised himself for the final jump. It was probably two metres. Leaping down, he squatted close to the pavement, protecting his ankles and knees. Looking from side-to-side, Wash confirmed he was alone and started running to the street. He had grown used to the wetness of his clothes now. They were stuck to him in the heat.

Wash initiated a call on his glasses. He couldn't contact Vicky directly so he tried a different tactic.

The call connected.

"Hi Pete," Wash said, huffing and puffing.

"God, Wash. Are you okay?"

"Yeah. I'm fine."

"Look, I haven't got too long. I need you to make a phone call for me. The old fashioned way."

"Are you in trouble?" Pete asked.

"I don't think so," Wash lied.

"You don't sound so sure to me."

"Please Pete. I only need one thing from you, I promise."

The older man sighed through the phone, making it crackle a little.

"Fine," he said eventually. "What is it?"

"Can you ring Dickinson Plastics' press officer and tell her our interview will have to wait, please?"

"Sounds innocent enough to me," Pete surmised. "Yeah I guess I can do that."

"Thank you, Pete," Wash said as he hung up. By now he had made it to West Acton station, climbed the steps to the platform and jumped onto an approaching eastbound Central Line train. As the doors slid shut, he looked up and down the concourse. Nobody else was boarding.

Wash collapsed into the nearest seat with a sigh of relief. He desperately hoped that Jay was safe. Sticking it to the government was a lot more fun when it didn't involve being on the run. He checked the time, conscious that it took twenty-five minutes to get from here to Chancery Lane and Yvette wanted more. As long as he could stay undiscovered, that might give him enough time to work on the train. Declan had said it was imperative he get as much in the paper as possible. As the Central Line stops went by, Wash thought of Vicky too. He hoped that his message would get to her and that she'd understand. Considering those who were following him, Wash wondered if he should change his pattern. He had set his mind on the office but was beginning to have some doubts. Maybe those after him weren't as worried about apprehending him in front of a crowd as he'd like to think. He quickly decided it wasn't worth the risk. Not yet. He might be able to return later.

Wash wracked his brain for somewhere else to go. Most of his options off the table. Then it came to him.

Mrs Faversham.

She wouldn't like it, but Wash desperately needed more information. If people were watching him based on what he'd published so far, there had to be more to this investigation that he first thought. The vicar was the key to this, the back-door into Mr Faversham's working environment. It wouldn't require too much of a diversion either. He'd simply stay on the Central Line past Chancery Lane and change to the Hammersmith and City at Mile End. Getting there would be easy. Convincing Mrs Faversham to talk would be anything but.

＊

Wash rattled on Mrs Faversham's door repeatedly. He daren't let up, desperate for her to open up and let him in. There was nobody on the street but the incident in Newham with Noah had very much put the journalist on edge.

The woman appeared at the threshold, a distressed look on her face. It abated slightly until she noticed Wash's own expression.

"You..."

He didn't give her a chance to say no, pushing past her into the hallway.

"What do you want?" she asked, irritation in her voice.

"I need your help."

"I already told you. I can't," the vicar insisted, still holding the front door open.

"Can you please close that?"

"Why?"

"I think I'm being followed."

"And you came here?" Mrs Faversham rasped, peering out of the doorway into the street. Wash realised he'd done to her what Jay had to him and was hit with a pang of guilt.

"I'm sorry, but--"

"I'm afraid I'm going to have to ask you to leave," said Mrs Faversham.

"No, this is serious," Wash said, putting his arms up in protest.

"I know," the vicar replied, shaking a little but

maintaining her cool better than the last time Wash was here. "That's why I need you to leave."

Something snapped inside the young man. He wasn't sure if it was self-preservation or his steely determination to get to the bottom of the story.

"What happens when they kill again, huh?" he asked angrily. "What will you tell yourself if you could have made a difference?"

"Excuse me?"

"I thought someone in your position, a religious woman such as yourself, might want to do more to protect people."

Mrs Faversham took a step towards Wash. He was conscious that the door was still wide open.

"Who are you to question my faith?" she growled.

"I don't believe in a God, lady, but last time I checked, that book of yours is filled with people who lay down their lives for other people. You should be prepared to do the same."

Silence fell briefly. Wash prepared himself, attempting to show as much confidence as possible.

"I don't want to be the guy that threatens people. I've fought for the last few years to stay above board with the way I deal with my contacts." He paused. "But, if you don't give me a lead on Miles' work, I'll be forced to report your arrangement with him in the Citizen."

Mrs Faversham turned white as a sheet, clasping a hand to her mouth.

"You wouldn't," she muffled, slowly losing strength. Carefully, she moved backwards into the door closing it, back up against the plastic.

"I would," Wash held firm, shouting at himself inside. He was hugely conflicted about this tactic but could not show any sign of weakness. She had to believe he would follow through.

"But you said--"

"I know what I said." Wash stared her down. "But this has got to the point where it's bigger than you and me. All I had reported on this before today was an obituary of your husband and people started following me. In the last few hours, the Citizen has published my piece revealing a potential plot to sabotage the colonial programme--."

"I know, I've just read it," Mrs Faversham admitted, tucking some hair behind her ear.

"Then you know things are only going to escalate. I've got to get this right or we're both toast." He paused for a moment. "You have to help me do that. It's either that or I'll report the one thing I know for sure about Mr and Mrs Faversham to cover my tracks."

The woman sighed.

"You better get this right," she said bitterly, walking past Wash and up the stairs. He wasn't sure if he was supposed to follow or not. When the woman was half-way up, she turned round. "You coming or not?"

Feeling the boards creak under the pressure, Wash went up after the vicar, arriving on a tight landing area. The woman pulled out a metal stick from behind the radiator and held it up to the ceiling. She hooked it into a latch and opened the loft, unfolding a wooden ladder.

"Come up here." Wash arrived in the attic space and was blown away by the volume of dusty papers. They spawned from a central point, like rubble from a bomb crater. The ones around the edges were atop piles nearly two metres tall. The whole thing looked incredibly precarious. Wash trod carefully to reach the clear space, roughly two metres wide.

Mrs Faversham was bent over a box and he realised there wasn't enough room for the two of them.

"You can perch on that one," she said, not looking up from her task. The vicar was pointing to a wooden crate to her right. "Just tip out the contents and use it as a seat," she explained. Wash did exactly that.

"Aren't the papers important?"

"No," Mrs Faversham said, head still buried in the same box. "Miles figured that the best way to hide important information that he needed hard copies of was to stick it in an explosion of paperwork. That way it'd be harder to find for those who didn't understand his system."

"That's very clever."

"Yeah... he'd have probably made a better reporter than most of you lot."

A few days ago hearing those words would have wound Wash up, especially after years of his father's complaints. Now that he was at the centre of something serious, his skin was growing thicker.

"Here you go," Mrs Faversham announced, leaning round. In her hand was a dusty cardboard envelope which she held out to Wash.

"What's is it?"

"That...," she began, handing it over to him, "...is most likely the thing that got him killed."

Wash pulled out a small stack of papers stapled together. On the top sheet was a marking in ball-point ink that read: '*The Bible.*'

"Are you sure this isn't one of your sermon notes or something?" Wash asked, glancing from his hands to Mrs Faversham and back.

"Open it."

Underneath was a table of contents with three sections. The first read 'recruitment', the second 'operations' and the third 'purpose'.

"What did your husband do for the IPCP again?"

"He was in the administration department. That gave him access to almost every aspect of the programme."

"What does all this mean?" Wash asked, gesticulating towards the contents page.

"Miles got the idea that something was up around six months ago. He wouldn't tell me why, but he started making that document of information that was relevant to his theory. In case he ever needed it."

Wash flicked all the way to the opening page of the 'purpose' section and started to read aloud from the introductory paragraph.

"While none of this information should be considered conclusive evidence, I am fairly confident that the colonial programme is not serving the purpose declared by our government."

Wash's eyes grew wide and he looked up at Mrs Faversham, hoping she'd share his excitement. His gaze was met with one of disdain.

"Are you finished yet?"

Wash did not answer, but continued reading Miles' thoughts aloud.

"Rumours that the UK is trying to spark a war with the Atlas Nations are rife within the ministry of defence and IPCP. While I cannot comment on the veracity of these stories, I must say that if Benjamin Curtis hopes to claim territory on either Proxima A or B, I do not believe he has the infrastructure to last very long against the

Atlas Nations."

"That can't be right," Wash muttered. He thought about the purported attack on a New Boston satellite and frowned. Why would the British start a war in the Proxima system if they knew they couldn't win? Wash went back to Miles' opening page. *"Based on my findings from research into the recruitment and operational staff, I do not believe Curtis wants to commit sufficient spending or resources to the colonial programme in order to make it a true success."*

Wash flicked back to the other two sections and noted three things.

Head of recruitment was listed as a Mia Paterson, a high-ranking police officer. That seemed an odd combination to Wash. He glanced over at the image and recalled Jay's description. The woman was middle aged, had short brown hair and a pointy nose. This was certainly a person he couldn't speak to.

Several pages later, there was a picture of an elderly gentleman named Logan Taylor, a scientist responsible for operational requirements on the project. Reading down the list of his information, Wash's jaw dropped.

"What the?" he whispered.

The doctor's place of work was listed as St. Paul's with a hand-written annotation in brackets that read 'roughly 200 metres from the westbound Central Line platform'. That was where flooding had supposedly shut that section of track down. Wash felt that was too much of a coincidence to ignore, especially the response when he covered that story.

"Can I take this with me?" he asked Mrs Faversham.

"Yes."

"Thank you. You got anything else?"

"Nope, that's it. The culmination of Miles' work at the IPCP."

Wash folded everything back up and stuffed it away in his bag. Back in the hallway he turned back to the vicar.

"Listen... about earlier... I'm sorry--"

"Just take that with you and get out of my house."

23

Wash was on the underground, returning to the office, flustered and struggling to breathe evenly. He scolded himself for threatening the vicar. It went against everything he stood for, but he had to get to the bottom of this. The air felt close and the undercurrent of body odour continued to rise. The journalist inhaled deeply as cool blast permeated through the carriages. It gave him a brief moment of calm as he continued working on an additional story for Yvette, focussing on aspects of Miles' findings. Wash's fingers shook as they tapped the keys on his portable machine. Imprecise, he kept having to delete sentences and start them again.

'A scathing criticism of the Interplanetary Colonial Programme (IPCP) has been discovered at the home of the latest Eye Killer victim. Miles Faversham, who was recently murdered by the serial killer, was an employee of the IPCP and appears to have been on the brink of becoming a whistleblower. The Daily Citizen recently reported a potential plot to sabotage the programme, but Faversham's findings go some way to suggesting such *threats were internal, and potentially run all the way to the top of government.'*

Once he had roughly six hundred words, Wash emailed the copy to Yvette, hoping that she'd receive it in time. Making the journey back to the office was a risk but after what he'd discovered at the Faversham's house, Wash still needed to speak to her in person. He was a little worried that she might try to bury the story but Declan had been right about her so far. The woman was insatiable when it came to exclusive breaking news, and appeared desperate to use the editor position at the paper to increase her usefulness to the government somehow.

There was a loud bang to Wash's left.

His heart skipped a beat, eyes drawn to the noise.

They've found me.

A fellow passenger had dropped their bag and grumbled as they picked it up.

Despite the false alarm, Wash kept on scanning the crowds at each station. There was something going on here and the IPCP were doing everything in their power to cover things up. Once again, Wash considered heading for his father's hospital. He had more than enough to prove the old man was right all along. But surely the IPCP would be watching the building. That would have to wait.

Hopefully, the police would stay clear of apprehending him at the office though. For fear of causing a scene. Wash told himself that as long as he stayed in daylight or busy public places he'd be fine. Maybe.

Disembarking at Chancery Lane, he realised he also needed to speak to Callum. The outstanding angle in this whole situation was that of the Eye Killer. Yes, it appeared as if Miles Faversham had lost his life as a result of his findings about the IPCP, but that still didn't explain the other victims. Hopefully, Callum had uncovered information about their personal lives from the social media archives.

Arriving in the marble lobby, Wash noticed there was nobody on reception. That wasn't uncommon, so he took out his pass and held it up against the scanner. It flashed red and made a chirping noise, his access denied.

"For fu--," Wash muttered. "Now is not the time."

He swiped again. Still nothing.

Checking there was no-one watching, Wash vaulted the glass barrier and adjusted his bag upon landing. That had been easier than expected. He power-walked over to the wooden doors of the elevator. Two minutes later Wash had made it to the office. Now he was safe. Assaulted by the din of the advertising team, he was reminded of how easy it was to keep conversations under wraps in such a noisy environment.

First, he went to his own desk, casting the bag down but staying on his feet.

"Did you get through to the plastics company, Pete?" he asked.

Pete turned round.

"Wash, you're okay," Pete spoke with some relief.

"Yeah I'm all good, don't worry," he lied. "So did you get through?"

"Yes, I reached their press officer. She understood the message."

"Did she mention anything else?"

"She suggested an alternative venue for the interview."

"Where was that?"

"She said somewhere memorable by the river."

She must mean the warehouse in Wapping.

"Ok thanks, Pete," he said as he began moving in Callum's direction. Pete leaned round and grasped him by the arm. "Hey, wha--"

"Just be careful, Wash. This girl sounds like she really cares about you. Don't do anything to put her in harm's way, alright?"

"I appreciate the concern, mate, but I've got a plan okay?"

"If you say so," Pete replied, relaxing his grip.

Wash made a beeline for Callum. The large man noticed him coming and pulled something from a draw.

"Ah, Wash. You're back."

"Yeah, what have you got for me?" Wash wheeled over a vacant chair and sat.

"I got the social media profiles."

"Brilliant. Any correlations?"

Callum pulled out a stack of printed images, all of them featuring group shots.

"Well, I wasn't really sure what I was looking for, so I just pulled together any images that featured three or more individuals."

"Ah right," Wash replied, disappointed. "Is this going to be a long job then?"

"I think so," Callum admitted, flicking through the stack. "There's a lot going on here. It'd probably take several days of the two of us going through each scrap of information."

Wash scratched his head. He'd been hoping that Callum would find something he could supplement his current theory with.

"Is Yvette in?" he asked.

"I'm not sure." Callum craned his head above the dividers. "It looks like Steve Woods is here though."

Wash chuckled.

"No thank you."

As if on cue, the main door to the newsroom opened and revealed Ms. Hamilton arriving.

"Never mind," Wash said, patting Callum on the back and walking over to rendezvous with the editor. The two of them met in the middle of the floor, Yvette smiled nervously.

"Ah, Wash. Just who I was looking for."

"Did you get my latest story?"

"I did," she said, maintaining the smile. "Let's talk about it in my office."

This was the first time Wash had been allowed entry into Yvette's working space. It was better furnished than anywhere else in the building, sporting a similar lavish floor to that of the lobby. It made a stark contrast to the fraying carpet that covered the newsroom. There was a varnished oak bookshelf behind the desk, stacked with large, important-looking volumes of some ancient text.

"You've uncovered quite the plot, haven't you Mr Parker?" Yvette said as she sat down, adjusting her blonde hair.

Wash laughed uncomfortably.

"Yes, I guess you could say I have," he replied. "What do you think? Can we publish it?"

Yvette looked into the screen of her computer, calculating the next move.

"It's risky," she said with a tip of the head. "If I was against gambling on these sorts of things, I'd pull it no question." Yvette raised an eyebrow in Wash's direction, inviting him to defend the story.

"I understand that," Wash said, taking a brief moment to consider. He was at a flashpoint here. If he could convince Yvette that publishing the story was in the best interest of the government, then she'd have no qualms. As he already suspected, she knew she was in need of impressing her superiors. What better way to do that than to alert the country to a plot against the IPCP? But given what he knew, that seemed unlikely. What seemed more plausible was the powers that be were behind all this and running the story would only expose and anger them. Not only would he be risking his own life, he would be risking Yvette's too.

"Well, if you understand, maybe we should hold fire," she said, having waited long enough for further explanation.

Wash leaned forward, waving his hands.

"That's not what I meant."

He peered down at the name plaque on the desk. It read Yvette Hamilton – Editor-in-chief and Member of Parliament. That made his mind up for him. Most of his problems at the Daily Citizen up until now had been caused by that very conflict of interest. If he could help end it by exposing Yvette, in his mind, it was worth it, in an attempting to reclaim some freedom for the press. Maybe then, he could be satisfied with his contribution to this industry. "I think we're safe to run it," he added, finally.

"And why is that?"

"Well, I trust my sources on this one. They seem to be looking out for the greater good here." He took another deep breath. "If we can tell people what's really going on behind the scenes, and let those in power know we're on to something, it will probably give us access to greater resources to bust this thing wide open."

"You think so?"

"Oh I do," Wash replied, his confidence now growing with each passing second. "Those I've spoken to indicated there's even more to this story."

Yvette started nodding her head, raising her eyebrows and gently pressing her lips.

"And you don't think we need to offer right of reply on this do you?" she asked.

"No, I don't think so," Wash replied with a frown of the eyebrows. "You do that, and they'll only do their best to stall the story. We've got to get ahead of the game while we can."

"You're right," Yvette said, sitting up straight. "We should get this story out there," she declared, typing a few minor adjustments into the keyboard. "And you're sure this won't get us in any trouble?"

"Absolutely," he lied.

"Thank you Wash, I'm sure this is going to help both of our careers." She hit publish.

The tension left Wash's body. It was done. The information was now in the public domain. While that brought new concerns of their own, at least another hurdle had been cleared.

"What's next then?" Yvette asked. "A celebration perhaps?"

"What? Oh, no not yet," Wash said, forgetting himself for a moment. "I've got some other leads to chase with Callum."

"Ah, I see," Yvette said, blushing a little. "Well, I've got a few things to clear up, and then I'm off for the day," she added, with a nod of the head towards the window, which was displaying a darkening evening.

When Wash walked back into the newsroom, the sole source of light came from garish strips in the ceiling. The hubbub was beginning to die down as advertising staff were filtering out the door. Not a single journalist had thought about home-time yet. Wash went over to Callum's desk, grateful for the drop in noise levels.

"Want to have a sit down with these pictures then, mate?"

Callum took a little time to answer, his mouth full of a cheese cracker. He tipped his head from side-to-side to indicate an answer would eventually come.

"It's alright if you've got plans tonight," Wash added. "I don't mind making a start by myself."

"No, it's alright," Callum said eventually, mouth still relatively full and spitting some crumbs out in the process. "Let's sort ourselves out with a system. I've got about an hour," he added, looking at the clock.

"Perfect," Wash said.

The two journalists moved to an empty table and spread out their papers.

"So let's start by making piles for each victim and we can worry about overlaps later."

"If we get any," Callum added, somewhat cynically.

"Well, let's hope so," Wash replied looking down at the task ahead. "Who shall we start with?"

"I guess the first victim makes sense." Callum looked down at his notepad. "Mary Scrivener. The fifty-two-year-old."

"Nice one," Wash said as he started filing through the group photos and location histories. "Wow, there's a lot of them isn't there?"

"Yeah, as the oldest victim, she's naturally the one

with the longest social media history."

"Sheesh. Let's get started then," Wash declared.

"What exactly are we looking for here?" Callum asked as he pulled up a chair. Wash remained standing.

"I want you to look out for anything that could suggest involvement in the LGBT community."

Callum's eyes grew a little wider.

"Really? You think that's what this could be about? But the story you just published..."

"Yeah I'm confident about the IPCP stuff... but that doesn't mean there's not something else going on here," Wash said. "You said yourself, there was nothing obvious linking those victims. They certainly had nothing to do with the IPCP from what I can tell."

Callum stroked his chin.

"Hmm... interesting. Uncovering that sort of information about people is not as easy as it used to be."

Coffee cups came and went. Callum's top button slipped open as he funnelled another biscuit down his neck. None of the pictures had thrown up much so far, although Wash expected more crossover later in the search. The location history was proving the most useful at this point. He'd noted down two venues that could indicate what he suspected, based on what he'd been told by Declan in the past. However, given the age of this woman, it was hard to tell if these establishments had been a hub for that sort of activity at the time.

Callum wiped his glistening forehead. Wash felt the sweat on his back too. It was a warm November night.

"This could take a while," Callum said with a sigh.

"It'll be worth it though mate, I'm sure of it," Wash

said with some gusto.

"It's refreshing to do some old fashioned investigation, I'll give you that." The older man glanced at the time. "I'll have to make a move in the next fifteen minutes, though. I hope that's alright."

Wash took a few moments to reply, head buried in the work.

"Oh yeah, sure. Family first. What you up to?"

"It's my daughter's school play tonight."

"Ah, nice. What is it?"

"Hamlet."

"Cheery."

"Indeed."

"Who's she playing?"

Wash didn't get the chance to find out. His glasses were ringing. Glancing down he saw Declan's name.

"Sorry mate, I really need to take this."

Callum understood, returning to the list of location check-ins with his pen.

"Hi Declan," Wash said, answering the call.

"Where are you right now?" His friend rushed the words out.

"At the office. Why?"

"Oh god. I'm really sorry, Wash."

"What's going on?" Wash moved into a corner by the vending machines, trying to avoid any unwanted attention.

"That story you just published..."

"What about it?"

"It was perfect. Exactly what you were supposed to find out."

"Why do I get the impression that's not an encouragement?"

Declan didn't answer. All Wash could hear was

heavy breathing.

"Dec. What the hell?"

"I'm sorry. They're on their way to the Citizen."

"Who are?"

"The IPCP and their thugs."

"Their thugs?"

"The police."

Wash started pacing, fiddling with a coin in his pocket.

"What are they going to do?"

"I don't know. At the very least they'll ransack the place in an attempt to find your information."

Wash swore.

"I trust you got hold of Mr Faversham's personal findings."

"Why are you all of a sudden happy to discuss specifics over the phone?"

"I don't have much time, Wash. And neither do you."

The call ended.

Wash dashed back to the desk where he and Callum were working.

"We need to pack this up," he said quietly.

"What? Why?" Callum looked up and saw the expression on Wash's face. His confusion turned to worry. "What is it?"

"They're coming," Wash said, losing the strength in his voice. "The IPCP and the police are coming." He left Callum scrambling to collect the papers, hoping to reach Pete in time.

"Pete."

"Yes, what?"

It was too late.

The newsroom door was kicked open.

"Everybody step away from your desks!"

A shrill woman's voice sounded from the entrance of the newsroom. Advertising ladies screamed as armed police pointed their weapons at them.

"I said everybody step away from your desks NOW!"

The woman strode towards the editorial end of the room, followed by a dozen or so officers.

"All of this will be easier if you co-operate," she added.

Pete took one look at the approaching officers, still five metres away, and desperately grabbed hold of Wash.

"Go."

Wash picked up his bag, dove behind one of the tall dividers and forced open the nearest window. Under sufficient cover, he climbed out onto the adjacent rooftop. It was a concrete space roughly five metres by two, allowing Wash to crouch just below the glass and see what was happening inside. He had made it just in time.

Pete was stood with his back to the desk, fiddling with a phone behind his back.

Wash's glasses buzzed. He answered and hit 'record call'.

"You clever man," he whispered to himself.

The woman and her troops arrived at the heart of the editorial department. Journalists were pushed away from their desks and the police officers started sifting through every piece of paperwork. Sheets swam in the air as they were tossed about by the invaders. Crackling through the speaker, Wash could hear his colleagues complaining.

"You can't do this."

"What are you doing?"

"Leave that alone."

The police officers were equally irate in their response.

"Move out of the way," one of them howled in the face of the young girl who, only days ago, had been transcribing the colonial broadcast.

Pete appeared to be one of the few who was able to keep his cool. He was now a few feet from his work station, both hands in the air, offering as much of a co-operative expression as possible. Wash's heart went out to him. The veteran reporter had been in this game long enough to see it change from one of integrity to this state-controlled circus. And he'd already seen enough of the latter to know exactly how to react in this situation. Across the dividers, Steve Woods was taking a similar approach, almost politely smiling at the assault on his office.

"Paterson, this is it," an officer near Wash's desk called out.

Wash studied the woman's appearance in earnest for the first time. In his mad rush out of the building he missed the chance to process her face. She was middle-aged, had short brown hair and a pointy nose. She matched the profile in Faversham's notes. This was the IPCP's head of recruitment and yet here she was intimidating the Citizen's journalists.

"Let me have a look," Paterson said as she stormed over to Wash's desk. She fiddled around with a few papers but couldn't find his laptop. That was stored safely in his bag. "Where is it?" she roared at Pete.

"I'm sorry?" he said, flinching a little as an officer crashed a filing cabinet to the floor two dividers away.

"You know what I'm talking about!" Paterson got

in Pete's face.

"You're going to have to be more specific I'm afraid."

Suddenly, Yvette marched into the newsroom from her office.

"What on earth is going on here?" she snapped, hands on hips.

"You," Paterson muttered, walking away from Wash's desk. "Yvette fucking Hamilton."

The editor took a step back, pale. Paterson grabbed her by the shoulder.

"Only such a pathetic shit-show such as this could happen under your watch."

"What's this about?" Yvette begged, voice trembling.

"For goodness sake," Paterson rolled her eyes as she dragged the editor towards two armoured policeman, tossing her in their general direction. "Take her."

Yvette was handcuffed and dragged off to cries of terror from the editorial and advertising staff.

Paterson rounded on Pete again.

"Right, Washington's laptop. Where is it?" she asked him.

"No idea, I'm afraid," he said calmly.

"Why not?"

"I'm not his father, even if I'm old enough to be," Pete joked. Wash had often wished that he was.

"Is this funny to you?" Paterson slammed her fist down on Wash's desk.

For the first time, Pete showed a sign of panic.

"N-no," he said quietly.

"Then why don't you know where your colleague's laptop is?"

"Because it's not my responsibility," Pete insisted, trying his best to remain confident after Paterson's violence. She changed tack.

"Ok then, do you know where *he* is?"

Pete did very well not to look out the window.

"No," he said. "Last I saw of him was when he left the office earlier."

"What time was that?"

Pete shrugged.

"Maybe half an hour ago," he said.

"You're sure about that?" Paterson circled the older man.

"Yes, I think so."

The woman broke her pattern and leaned into her shoulder, pressing a button.

"Buscema, this is Paterson. Was Washington Parker sighted leaving the building at around eighteen thirty?"

She waited a few seconds before a reply crackled through her receiver.

"That's a negative, sir," Buscema said.

Paterson frowned at Pete.

"My man downstairs says that's bollocks. Want to tell me why that is?"

Callum waddled into the conversation.

"Maybe he went out the back," he said.

Wash was confused. The Daily Citizen building didn't have a back door.

"Which one is this?" Paterson asked, turning to one of her men.

"It's the crime reporter."

"Ah yes, Callum Jamieson is it?" Paterson's eyes intensified as she locked him in her sights.

"Yeah, that's me," Callum said, slowly taking a step

back.

"Good," she replied. "You're next." The officer ushered two men in his general direction. "Make sure he doesn't disappear too," she ordered. Callum was quickly held by the arms, trapped. Paterson turned back to Pete.

"Did Washington go out the back door, then?"

"He must have done, yeah," Pete said, nodding confidently. "That's the only way he could have left the building without using the front entrance."

Wash held us breath. His colleagues were doing their best to help him out. He didn't want either of them to come to any harm over it. Paterson continued pacing in front of Pete, deep in thought. She stopped in front of the man and stared at him, for an uncomfortably long period. Then, the police officer leaned into her radio again.

"Buscema. Deploy three men to the back of the building now."

Wash let out a long breath. It looked as if they were safe for now.

Paterson left Pete behind and strolled over to where Callum was being held.

"Your turn, fatty," she said. Callum blushed.

The woman's journey away from Pete's phone meant her voice was a little quieter.

"You were the one working with Washington on the Eye Killer case, yes?"

Callum nodded.

"Right, you've got some work to do," she said to Callum, pushing him in the direction of his computer. He protested but couldn't get any real words out. Paterson and another officer dunked him in a chair.

One of the male officers unleashed a tirade of offensive words.

"I want you to give us everything Washington has been working on for this case," Paterson ordered, pointing at his machine. Wash assumed that Callum had somehow disposed of the papers they had been working, but it was probably all still on his hard drive. Thankfully most of Wash's other evidence was either in his bag or at Vicky's apartment. Either way, there wasn't much Callum could protect.

After a few moments of contemplation, Callum quietly said: "No."

"What?" cried Paterson.

"I said... I said no," Callum replied, leaning away from his machine.

"That's not an option."

"I don't have to do anything," he insisted, arms folded.

Someone screamed as the woman reached for her hip and produced a pistol.

"Alright, alright. Fucking hell," Callum blurted as he flinched away from the weapon, craning to type in his password. "Yeah fine, whatever, knock yourself out, you psychopathic bitch." Kicking his legs, the large man wheeled his chair away from the desk, allowing Paterson access. "Just be confident that this will be our top story in about an hour's time."

Paterson laughed as she kicked over Callum's draws, tossing out reams of papers and food wrappers.

"I don't think so," she said with delight, moving to the computer terminal.

"And why is that?" Callum asked indignantly.

"You'll find out in a minute."

Paterson tapped away on the keyboard for several minutes, growing increasingly frustrated. She turned back to Callum and started shouting at him again. That's when Pete's phone call ended. Somehow, Wash was cut off and he could no longer hear what was going on inside the building, although he could still see. Unfortunately, Pete hadn't noticed and, even if he had, starting a new call without being noticed would be impossible. The police officers had finished turning the office inside out now, the floor a sea of paper. They were standing guard over the journalists and sales staff.

The large number of people in the newsroom shuffled to the left, spreading out near the interior entrance. Through the dividers, Wash could not discern why it was happening. The movement permeated all along the central aisle, like a Mexican wave, until a figure emerged in the cross-section by Wash's desk.

"Oh my god," he whispered to himself.

It was Benjamin Curtis.

The prime minister looked slightly older in person than he did on the television broadcasts. He was still a tall and imposing man but was a little greyer around the edges than Wash expected. The man had enviable skin and an aquiline nose, the villainous combination of good looks and a menacing aura.

Curtis spoke with Paterson, standing over Callum as if he was a misbehaving child.

After a few moments, the journalist was hoisted out of his chair and rushed away by some other officers.

Then the prime minister found Steve and began lecturing him, leaving the head of content with a wry smile on his face. With Paterson and her men by his side, he left the newsroom a bedraggled mess.

24

"No results? What does that mean?" Zack asked.

Harper was speechless. She sighed and slouched back against the nearest tree, tossing the portable device away. It rattled as it skirted across the dirt, nothing more than a useless collection of circuitry.

"What are you doing?" he questioned.

"We don't need it anymore." Even by her usual standards, she felt particularly robotic in her explanation. "There's nobody out there."

"So James was wrong?"

"Looks that way. I guess we really will have learn to get along after all."

"What's that supposed to mean?"

"It means you get over your dead girlfriend, and I'll try not to kill you for getting me sent here on a damn prison sentence."

"Right," Zack said, watching her stand up. "That's what you're going to tell the others, is it?"

"No. I'll talk to them in the morning."

Once on her own, Harper pulled out her flask. She'd been saving the last of it for a time like this.

Unscrewing the lid she tipped it high in the air and opened her throat, still going even when it began to burn. Harper stifled a cough and threw the empty container into the undergrowth too.

★

By now Harper was used to waking up with aches and pains all over. Groaning, she pushed back her shoulders, cracked her back and got up. Every morning it got harder, and after the epiphany of the previous night, she didn't know how much longer she could do this. If she didn't get off this planet soon, she'd go mad.

Dusting off the mud from her overalls and recoiling from her own smell, Harper stepped over the nearby roots and rejoined the main group. Everyone was awake and savouring a breakfast cube except Amos. He was always the last to wake up every day because he was the last to fall asleep at night. Here we go, thought Harper.

"I've got some bad news," she said. They all stopped what they were doing. Nobody said a thing, Zoey put an arm around Shermeen and Ben folded his arms. To one side, James and Sam stared at her with blank expressions. Zack just rolled his eyes and gazed off into the distance. Now that Harper could see him in the daylight she chastised herself for not recognising him sooner. Even the red mark across his chin did little to hide the face she'd first been shown by Declan Fitzhugh.

"The search didn't come up with anything, I'm sorry." Ben let his arms drop to his side, before scratching the back of his head and looking from side to side. Shermeen's head dropped, causing Zoey to pull her in a bit closer. James' whole face crumpled.

"What do we do now?" he asked.

"I... don't know."

"You don't know?" snapped Zack. "You had all night to think about what to do next and that's the best you can come up with?"

"What's he talking about?" James asked awkwardly, looking from Harper to Zack and back again.

"The search finished last night whilst I was talking to Zack." James didn't look too satisfied with that response. "Which brings us on to something else... Last night, I realised I knew Zack from back home. Zack isn't his real name. He's called Israel Barrett and he was the leader of a racial hate group called Supremacy."

"I think I heard of them," Sam said. "They sounded really--" he looked at Zack and didn't finish the sentence, his face losing enthusiasm one it had made eye contact. The tall man looked away.

"Do we need to be worried about him?" Zoey asked from her seated position.

"Oh fuck off, lady," Zack chimed in. "I already told Harper here, I don't do that anymore."

"And how do we know that?" Ben asked, folding his arms again, his tight shirt highlighting the size of his triceps.

"*He's* still breathing ain't he?" Zack pointed at Amos.

"So we're supposed to be grateful you've not killed him yet?" said James.

"Yeah I guess so," he replied. "Although now we know there's no way off this damned planet, you'll soon be wishing he was dead."

"We're missing the point here," Harper cut in,

arms either side of her in an attempt to refocus the group. "Zack was sent here as a punishment and..." she took a deep breath before continuing, "so was I."

After a few moments of confusion, Sam asked the inevitable question.

"What did you do?"

Harper paused for a second. There was no way she would have talked about Brixton when they first arrived. It was still too raw back then. Realising Barrett had been here all along meant it was no longer in the past. Maybe she had a chance to write a different ending. She remembered the guilt she felt after the group found out about captain Case. The best way to make it up to them was to tell them about Brixton.

"Back home I was in the police's Special Forces. My unit was sent to stop Barrett – Zack -- and it didn't go according to plan. The wrong person got killed, it screwed up another operation the police were running. They wanted me out. So they sent me on this trip." Harper was amazed she'd managed to stay in control of her emotions the whole time. "The point is, we were both discarded here like dirt to be swept under a rug. As they made me part of the crew, I didn't think about it at first, but now that I know even civvies were supposed troublemakers, it makes me think nobody's looking for us."

"I didn't think I'd pissed anyone off back home," said James.

"Maybe you didn't. Obviously they were willing to take volunteers. I guess you were just one of the unlucky ones."

"I think Harper's right," Shermeen said. It was possibly the first time she had spoken since they left the beach. "Before we left, my dad worked on the

Underground. He did tunnel maintenance. He'd get called in at short notice to work a lot of nights, and one time he came back and it looked like he'd been in a fight. My mum told me he'd found something he wasn't supposed to and that he'd lost his job. Next thing I knew, we got signed up to this."

"You remember me telling you I got laid off?" Zoey asked the group.

"Yeah, I remember," Harper replied.

"Well, I played a big part in the union that fought for engineer jobs. We pissed off a lot of people. Nobody made me sign up, but when the colonisation programme came online, they targeted our group extensively." She stopped speaking for a brief moment. "Maybe they were trying to get rid of as many of us as possible," she finished.

"I'm sorry, but what does any of this mean?" Zack asked. "Surely if they wanted us gone, they'd have just taken us out to a field somewhere, shot us in the head and buried us in the mud."

"You're right, that is weird," said Ben.

"And, honestly, who gives a toss anyway? How is squealing about how we ended up on this trip going to help us now?"

"I mean, you're right, Zack." Harper admitted. "For once, you're bang on the money."

The man could only raise his eyebrows in response. Clearly he wasn't used to people agreeing with him.

"I'm sorry, but for the first time since we got here, I have nothing," Harper said. "I got nothing." She bit her lip. "No hope to offer, no plan. Nothing. Now that we know the whole point of this was to rid of most of us, it means nobody's coming. Nobody's looking for us. The people back home don't give a shit about where we are or whether we survive. They already tried to have us killed."

Harper's voice broke on the last word so she stopped, leaving an awkward silence hanging over the group. It hung in the air for an age, so prescient that it was almost tangible. She fought desperately with her eyes to contain the tears.

"We just have to keep moving," Ben said, feebly. "The longer we can avoid the creatures here, the best chance we've got."

"I'm not carrying Amos around," said Zack.

"I seem to remember you've not carried him once, anyway," Zoey interjected.

James took a considered look at the breakfast cube in his hand.

"How many of these do we have left?" he asked cautiously.

Zoey checked the bag, rustling through the wrappers.

"Looks like we've got about thirty of them," she said.

"That isn't going to last much longer," Ben confirmed. "What about water?"

Zoey leaned over to a different bag, counting under her breath.

"We've got seven left in this one," she said. "What about yours, Sam?"

"I've got four in mine."

"We need a new plan, and fast," said Ben.

"If we can find some animals and a fresh water supply, we'd be in better shape," offered James.

"And where do you propose we find either of those things?" complained Zack. "And even if we knew where to go, has everybody forgotten that we're on the run from jungle monsters and are weighed down by a dying fat guy?"

"It's back!" Amos' strained voice took everyone by surprise. They hadn't realised he was awake. Up until now, he had been leaning against the rocks, head tipped back, dozing. The man had not moved a muscle except to open his eyes. Once again, he was staring heavenward through the canopy, calling out.

"There it is again."

"Are you okay?" Shermeen asked.

"It's back!" he shouted, a little too loud for Harper's liking this time.

"What is it, Amos?" Shermeen enquired again. The young girl extracted herself from Zoey's side and rushed over to him. He was transfixed on the sky.

"It's back. The plane," he yelled, eyes wide.

All of them clustered around Amos, studying the blue expanse above them. Harper wished she could see something to give them hope. There were certainly clouds up there but there was no way knowing if they were vapour trails from an aircraft or not. Either way, there was clearly no aircraft in the sky. It didn't take long to realise that. Harper caught her head in her left hand, resting the other on her hip. She let out a sigh.

"He's getting worse," Zoey was the only one brave enough to say it aloud.

"I keep telling you," said Zack.

"You keep telling us what?" she challenged him. "That we should just kill him?"

"What choice do we have? He's slowing us down and now we know there's no medical help we can get him to." Zack argued, gesticulating angrily.

"There's no way you've changed since Earth," snapped Shermeen.

"Oh piss off, little girl. You have no idea what you're talking about," Zack said, walking away several steps.

BANG!

A localised explosion sounded from the deep recesses of the jungle. Harper nearly jumped out of her skin.

"What the hell was that?" Sam asked.

"That... sounded like a gunshot," said Harper.

"What?" replied Zoey. "Surely not."

"It sounded like gunfire to me." Ben readied his weapon.

"But, how did they get a gun?" James asked.

"Maybe it's one of ours?" suggested Sam.

"I've still got mine," Harper explained, holding hers up.

"Me too," said Ben.

"I've got the one you gave to Lucas," Zoey confirmed. She gestured towards what was hanging out of her backpack.

Harper turned to Zack, raising her eyebrows in a question.

"What are you looking at me for?" he asked, incredulous. She rolled her eyes.

"You stupid idiot," James scolded. "He must have taken it off you on the beach."

"Well I'm sorry, four-eyes," he replied. "I'll just have to try and not get smashed in the face with a machete next time."

Something fizzed through the air and a small fleck of bark flicked off a tree, close to Sam. He swore, cowering away from the shot.

Harper inspected her weapon and started moving.

"Everyone, take cover by the rocks. Zoey, you come with me. Ben you better stay here with Zack."

Already a few metres away from the group, Harper noticed a change in the terrain, as long grass begin to rustle against her knees. At pace, she jockeyed from tree-to-tree, trying to keep as low as possible.

"Hey," Zoey whispered a short distance behind. "Wait for me."

The two women ducked as another shot fizzed through the air.

It cracked into the tree Zoey was using for cover.

Harper held a finger up against her lips. She leaned cautiously around the trunk to get a better look.

Nothing.

Then it moved.

The creature was well camouflaged, spines and feathers blending into the undergrowth. But Harper had caught sight of it inspecting the weapon. Even from this distance she could see it was Zack's pistol. The wielder twisted it once more, this time some light shone through the canopy and glinted off the barrel.

Between her and the assailant was an open space of grass, roughly three metres across. Harper knew what to do. At this distance she wasn't sure she could guarantee a hit, so they needed to flush it out. She looked across to a crouching Zoey. Harper looked at the ground and found a rock. She tested it in her right hand, satisfied with the weight. Not thinking twice, she hurled it off to her left and waited for it to fall. It landed roughly five metres away, cracking against another rock.

In an instant, Harper held her weapon up and fired

two shots directly in front of her.

Hopefully she'd create the idea that the creature was caught in a pincer move. She could make out the sharp rustling of its feathers. It was clearly thinking, hesitating even.

Harper tried the plan again. Reversing it this time. She collected a smaller stone from the floor and launched it in the direction of where the shots she had fired. Once it made impact, she fired her gun to the left.

The creature began to move rapidly.

First it darted from one tree to another.

Then it made a motion for the open space.

Harper took a step to the left and broke cover.

She emerged into the opening as the creature ran past her, showing its side.

Zoey fired first, missing.

She let fly again, catching it in the leg.

The moving figure stumbled into a limp but kept on moving towards the Welsh woman.

Harper stood still.

Took aim.

Fired two rounds, rapid.

Both thudded into the creature's side.

It fell.

Still.

"We got it," said Zoey, holstering the weapon and getting to her feet.

"Wait," Harper instructed, crouching slightly and holding very still. "We don't know if it was alone." The two of them listened for what felt like an eternity. The buzz of the jungle didn't help, wind bristling through grass, branches and leaves, the chirping of insects and birds.

"Okay, I think we're safe."

"Is it dead?"

"Let's find out."

Harper edged towards the body. Getting closer, she surmised it was on its front, from the position of its feet.

"Keep your gun on it," she whispered across to Zoey, crouching over the body, covering it with her own weapon. Ready to go in even closer, she looked at her companion. Once a nod came back, she touched it, placing her hand on its back.

The plumage was rougher when clustered together. Harper couldn't feel or hear any breathing. Peering over, she noticed a deep red hole in the creature's side. Both bullets had blasted away the straw-like feathers here, leaving behind large swelling underneath.

"That looks like..." Harper muttered to herself as she prodded the flesh around the bullet hole.

Curious, she put the gun down next to her and leaned over to grasp the body by the hip, pulling it in a roll towards her.

Harper sharply retreated, breathless.

"What the hell?"

Her spine prickled.

"What is it?" Zoey asked, re-aiming her weapon, concerned.

Harper stared at the dark olive face a few moments longer.

"It's... human."

"What?" Zoey stepped out into the clearing to look for herself.

"It's a man," Harper explained.

"Bloody hell, you're right. But... I thought they

were supposed to be aliens."

"Well, maybe they are," Harper replied, not sure how to process this revelation. Maybe James was right after all. Perhaps human life on Earth did originate here. But she had never considered that Proxima B's inhabitants would be just like her and the other colonists. Instead, she focussed on what she could understand.

"First things first, we need that gun," she said, grabbing hold of it and checking how many rounds were left. "We're lucky he's the one that found us. Otherwise we might never have seen them coming."

"I don't understand," Zoey said. "What are we going to tell the others?"

"The truth," Harper shrugged. "I'm done keeping you guys in the dark. Hiding things helped nobody but myself." She tucked Zack's gun into her back pocket and started to move. "Come on let's go."

Within a few minutes they were back with the rest of the group.

James raced up to them.

"What happened?" he asked. "We heard gunshots."

"We're okay," Harper confirmed. "We got one."

"One?" said Ben.

"Yeah it was on its own. We got it."

"What did it look like?" Sam asked.

"That's the thing," Harper began, wiping her brow. "That stuff I showed you from the beach, James? I don't think it was the creature's skin. I guess it was just camouflage, possibly light armour of some kind."

"How do you know?" James asked.

"When we killed that one, those straw things fell

off. It had a human face. It was a man."

Harper could see nobody knew how to react. She could practically hear the cogs whirring in everyone's mind.

"Oh, for fuck's sake. That's it," Zack snapped, from behind her.

Harper felt a sharp push in her back. She fell to the ground.

"Okay, nobody move," he yelled, kicking her gun into the undergrowth. Looking up, she saw him holding the gun. The weapon was aimed at Amos, who sat no more than two metres away.

"Zack, no," Zoey pleaded. She'd left her weapon on a nearby log. Ben had placed his back in his pocket once Harper had returned. Nobody could stop him.

"We *have* to do something about Amos," Zack insisted through clenched teeth.

"Come on Zack," Ben said, carefully. "This is not the biggest issue right now. Did you not hear what Harper just said?"

"Too right, I did. When it was just aliens after us it was bad enough. Now we know they were human all along, they're even more dangerous," he almost sounded as if he was pleading with the group. "We need to leave now."

"Nobody said we shouldn't," said Harper. "They probably heard those shots earlier. We don't have time to fight amongst ourselves."

Zack held his weapon on Amos but looked Harper in the eye.

"And we don't have time to get him on his feet. We need to make a quick getaway, not carry on that ridiculous stretcher service."

"You sure you're not just reliving your glory days

from back home?" Ben asked.

"What's that supposed to mean?"

"You know what it means," Ben prodded some more. "You hate people like him. You've been after him since the start."

"Hey, it's not my fault that the guy holding us up is a--."

Amos suddenly woke up again, breathing heavily and muttering about the sky again.

"Look at him. He's gone," Zack insisted. "He's still rambling on about his hallucinations. You people are torturing him."

Harper couldn't bring herself to disagree. Amos' outlook certainly was bleak, especially with no way of getting him medical treatment. But she wasn't capable of letting Zack put the man down, especially knowing his past.

"You can't," Shermeen said quietly. "Please."

"I'm doing him a favour," Zack said.

He took the shot.

The bullet hit Amos just above his left eye.

It embedded itself into the thick skin, splattering blood everywhere.

Cries went up.

"No!" Harper roared. She leapt up and tackled Zack to the ground, knocking the gun away. In a mad rage, she began pounding his face with clenched fists. Soon her hands were thick with blood. In her mind, the surroundings fell silent. She could see Shermeen's face blotched with tears, her mouth wide open in anguish. Sam's hands on his head, blurting expletives. All she could hear was Paterson's voice telling her to stand down. All she could feel was the ache in her hip where Zack's hatred had cost her a life on earth. Harper's arms kept going. And going. Then one of them was caught. Shermeen's wailing came slowly back into focus, almost piercing Harper's ear drum.

She looked straight up into James' eyes. He held her hand.

"You won't forgive yourself."

Harper was drawn to the mess she had left below. The cut on Zack's jawline was now hidden under a mask of blood and bruises. The man was still breathing but on his right cheek was now a large purple swelling below the eye. She fell back and wiped her hands in the mud.

"We need to go," said Ben.

James agreed.

Harper didn't say anything. She got to her feet and grabbed her bag, stuffing Zack's weapon inside of it. Around her, Zoey and Sam gathered their things and looked to her for direction. She took a deep breath and wiped tears of anger off her cheeks.

"We're leaving him here," Harper said pointing at Zack, adjusting the straps on her bag and moving away from him. The others followed suit.

"We can't leave Amos here," Shermeen sniffled.

"There's nothing we can do for him," Zoey said, pulling her along. "Come on, let's go."

Zack slowly clawed his way into a seated position. He groaned though swollen facial wounds.

"You can't leave me here to die," he shouted. Harper ignored him. "You hypocrites! I just saved your lives and this is how you repay me?"

"Don't listen to him," Harper ordered as they moved further away. "Let's keep going."

They had been on their feet two minutes when

Harper heard running behind her. She drew her weapon and turned, aiming it at Zack.

"Don't move," she directed. He stopped in his tracks, arms either side of his head.

"You can't leave me behind," he begged.

"Yes we can. We're doing that now," Harper insisted. "Everyone, start walking. If you try to follow us one more time, Zack, I will fill you with bullets."

The man started to cry.

"I... I don't want to die." The group started to move off once again.

"Nobody does," Harper replied. "Amos probably didn't want to either."

"That was different and you know it," Zack said, shaking his head, cheeks swelling as he continued to weep.

Harper held her aim.

"Don't follow us," she said.

Beep.

An electrical noise sounded from near Zack's feet.

"What was that?" Harper asked.

"I don't know."

"Oh come on," she responded. "What are you playing at now?"

Beep.

"That's not me, I promise," Zack insisted.

Beep.

By now the rest of the group had returned.

"What's that sound?" James asked.

"Yeah I can hear it too," said Sam.

Beep.

"It's coming from over there," Harper said, realising it was emanating from the grass, roughly a metre to Zack's left. She shifted across, weapon trained on him the whole time.

Reaching the roots she saw the Concord's portable device. The one she had discarded the night before. The one that served no purpose. Or so she thought.

On the screen was a flashing message.

Incoming call.

"What the--?" Harper said aloud.

"What is it?" James asked.

"Someone's calling us."

"Well, answer it then," Sam said.

Harper clicked the 'accept call' button on the screen. She winced as a sharp static noise shot through the speakers before stabilising into a humming noise. A man's voice crackled through the interference.

"He--hello," it said. "Are you there?"

"Yes, this is Harper Mulgrew of the Concord. I'm with a group of surv-"

"Hello. Is anybody there?"

"Damn. They can't hear us," Harper complained as she fumbled with the device. The man's voice came through again.

"This is the base-ship calling Ben Cowan."

All heads swivelled to Ben. His eyes grew wider. Harper switched her gaze to the machine again, desperately hoping for a way to get through.

"This is the base-ship calling Ben Cowan. Have you completed your mission?"

"Your *mission*?" Harper asked aloud, looking back at Ben, staring straight down the barrel of his weapon.

She was now his target.

Zoey shouted Ben's name.

"What the hell is going on Ben?" Harper asked, her

hand shaking as she pointed her pistol back at him.

25

"Stangl is here," Daizen said, hanging up on the receptionist. "He's on his way up."

"Thanks, Daizen." Alida sat at her desk. Before discussing Don's latest update with Stangl, she needed to sign off some bills for the next council session. British forces had shown their hand in Choctaw and the council leader had no idea where her children were. Alida felt empty without them.

"I've also got an update from our contacts in the Navy." Daizen shuffled on his feet nervously. Alida dropped the pen and gave the young man her full attention.

"What is it?"

"Well, from what they can tell, the ANS Diamond has been missing from the yard for the last few days."

"That's his ship, right?"

"Yes, ma'am."

"For goodness sake," Alida snapped. "Why has he taken them out to sea?" Then she remembered the conversation with Tycho, the night before the kids went missing. She plunged her head downwards.

"What?" Daizen asked.

"The night before they disappeared, he was annoyed that he'd been kept out of the loop on the troop manoeuvres to Choctaw."

"What's that got to do with—"

"He told me the Navy was going to investigate."

"You think he's—"

"Yes. He's taken them with him to Choctaw." Alida was shaking with anger. "He's taken them to a god damn warzone."

Daizen was lost for words.

Alida stood up, tears teetering on her eyelashes. Voice quivering, the council leader gave some commands.

"Widen the net," she said, before taking a breath. "I want eyes on the ground in Teslapolis and New Plymouth. What's the nearest naval yard to Choctaw territory?"

Daizen moved to one of the walls, which sported an electronic map of the continent.

"Should be... yeah – Cahors. It's where the north coast meets the Choctaw Mountains. If he's heading that way, he'll have to stop there first."

"Isn't that..." Alida thought to herself for a moment, clicking her fingers. The tears were starting to dissipate, her focus returning, hatred channelled. "Cahors is where his sister lives. He'll be heading there alright. Let's get onto our men there too."

"What shall I tell them?"

"You tell them, if anyone catches a glimpse of Sean Tycho, I want him arrested immediately."

Alida stopped short as Stangl crept into the room, like a walking corpse.

"I'll do that for you, ma'am," Daizen said, edging

past the A.N. official.

"It appears we have much to discuss once more," Stangl said, helping himself into the chair opposite Alida's. She sat down too.

"Don't we always," she said. "Have you given any more thought to my request?"

"We'll get to that, Alida," he replied, putting his hands up. "That latest update from Choctaw did not sound at all good. Let's start there."

"Yes, you're right..." she admitted. "It appears the British are hostile indeed."

"Yes."

"What have you instructed your marines?" Alida asked.

"What do you think?" Stangl replied. "I've told them to do exactly what your man Stafford says. The important thing is what you've asked of him."

"I've told him to do the sensible thing. Stay alert, defend yourself if you have to but try to remain undetected. We can't afford war breaking out, even in Choctaw. Our relationship with that region is fragile at best. Politically, we're not in a position to provide support or accept their refugees, but they'll come banging on the Arkan gate, just you wait."

Stangl didn't reply, simply nodding his head. For once he was calm.

"I'm going to make you an offer, Alida," he said eventually. "Maybe you were right." She raised her eyebrows. Stangl continued: "Maybe we have been... naïve in assuming the Atlas Nations could resume a relationship with colonies in their previous form."

"I'm glad to hear you finally admit it."

"I'll be honest with you, Alida," Stangl began again. "I knew that war with the British was inevitable, but I did not think it would happen as quickly as this. Now that the Atlas Nations high council have heard about Choctaw, they want to start drawing up plans for an Earth-based conflict with the United Kingdom."

Alida wasn't at all surprised. In fact she had been banking on it to some extent. They would need more Teslanium this way.

"What will they want on Proxima?"

"Well, as things stand, I'd expect the attempted invasion here to be child's play to deal with, especially compared to the fighting on Earth. It appears as if only a limited number of assets have been sent to this world, while I'm sure the remaining bulk of British forces are still back home."

"So you don't think much will be required of Proxima forces?"

"Your military strength should be more than enough to nip this incursion in the bud, Alida."

Stangl went silent again. His eyes, usually full of fire, were practically extinguished now. His cheeks flush.

"But we will still require your help...in other areas," he said slowly. "The last decade on Earth has been a wasteful one, to say the least. In our attempts at keeping the union between nations a strong one, and we have had to be aggressive in dealing with dissenters. Going so long without fresh Teslanium means our reserves are nearly depleted."

Here we go, Alida thought to herself.

"We need our Teslanium quota, Alida, and we need it now. Without it, the high council cannot mount an offensive against the British."

Alida turned up her nose, leaning back in her chair, satisfied.

"What are you willing to pay?"

Stangl shuffled in his seat, lips moving but producing no words.

"I... we... are willing to grant Proxima independence from the Atlas Nations. And we will fund seventy-five per cent of the mining costs."

"That's a very generous offer," the council leader said, struggling to contain her surprise. She had expected Stangl to be tighter, unable to believe her luck. Picturing the ensuing press conference, she predicted that her name would go down in history after pulling off such an achievement. "You need this Teslanium badly, don't you?"

He didn't answer her question.

"Do you accept or not?" Stangl stared her down.

"Of course, I'd be stupid not to." Alida stifled a laugh. "You get this in writing from the Atlas Nations High Council by the end of the day and you can have your quota first thing in the morning."

"Thank you for being so co-operative, Alida," Stangl said, lifting his wiry frame out of the chair. He hobbled over to the door and turned back before leaving. "Oh... and I do hope you find your children."

"We're approaching Cahors now, sir," Saldana announced to the bridge. Tycho was discussing the ammunition supplies and weapon assignments with Ricketts. He acknowledged the inventory, considered which stations would be unmanned with a skeleton crew and dismissed the marine.

"Let's have a look," he said, approaching his first officer. In front of the ANS Diamond, off in the hazy distance, was the Choctaw Mountains. On their right lay the city of Cahors, raised above the conglomeration of tributaries from the river. In the beginning, it had been built on the swampy marshlands of the north coast, standing on stilts and wooden platforms. During the Choctaw War, some navy ships were based there, but not as heavily involved in the conflict as those near Pacheco and Etterslepund, around the other side of the peninsula. Cahors' population had exploded as the navy's constant presence helped boost the local economy. When the war was won, many of the sailors opted to stay and the discovery of a relatively small Teslanium mine in the mountains beyond the wetlands provided them with employment. Over the last few decades, Cahors had steadily improved from a small fishing village to a self-sustaining and profitable citadel, supported by concrete pillars drilled down into the river beds.

Even now, any Cahors merchant with a small ship and friends brave enough could sail along the western edge of Choctaw's mountain range and reach the peninsula's north coast. For that reason, the navy had maintained a strong presence to protect Choctaw's northern border beyond the mountains. Harbour walls had been constructed roughly twenty years ago to service the ships stationed and trained there. Tycho was still keen to stay undetected so was hoping to sneak into the navy base in a small craft and get the children to Kara that way.

"Everything alright?" he asked Saldana quietly.

"Stealth-mode appears to have done the trick again, sir," she replied softly. "How are you holding up?"

"Well, it's nice to spend some extra time with the

kids but I hadn't really thought out what to do with them when we get back to New Boston."

"You think there will be trouble?" Saldana asked.

"I should think so... but they'll be safe with Kara for the next few days."

"I'm sure they will. When was the last time they saw her?"

"Oh err...," Tycho thought to himself for a minute. "It's been a few years. Neither me nor Alida have been able to leave the city for some time. Must have been a Christmas or something. I better go and get the children ready."

He left the bridge and arrived in his quarters a few seconds later, dismayed at the mess of toys and books before him.

"Hey, come on kids," he complained. "What's all this?" Tycho started picking up Corinne's cars off the floor and handed them to her. "Come on, get these in your bag, you don't want to leave them behind. And Tristen, get your clothes packed please?" The young boy was relaxing on the camping bed, all his possessions strewn across the quilt. Thankfully, both children did as they were told quickly. "Come on, let's go. We need to go see Auntie Kara."

Corinne cheered and jumped up and down, bouncing her way through the corridor.

Tycho was about to open the door to the stairwell when the tannoy sounded. It was Saldana.

"Vice admiral Tycho to the bridge. I repeat, vice admiral to the bridge."

"Stay there, kids," he said, moving to a nearby panel on the wall and patching himself through to Saldana. "What is it?"

"You better come up here, Sean," she insisted. "I

don't want to play this over the ship's speakers."

Tycho's stomach dropped. He acted quickly.

"Back in my room, alright?" he said to the children.

"But dad," Corinne protested.

"I'll be as quick as I can. Then I'll come and get you. Just wait here."

Tycho ran through the ship and was shortly back on the bridge.

"What is it?" he asked, striding up to Saldana, stood over the helm.

"Listen to this. She passed Tycho a handset.

"Sean? Sean? Are you there?" It was Kara. Her voice was weak, imprecise.

"Yes, it's me," he said.

"I've been trying to reach you. There's been so much disturbance to communications the last few days. It's not safe here," she explained.

"Why not?" He looked around to see if anyone was eavesdropping.

"The police have just been here Sean," Kara continued. "They're looking for you. They said you... kidnapped the children. It's all over the news that Alida Harmon's children are missing." Tycho didn't know what to say. "Is that true?"

"I didn't... kidnap them," he replied. "I just... didn't tell Alida where we were going, that's all."

"Oh Sean, why would you be so stupid? You know how powerful she is."

"I know, I know."

The two siblings fell silent for a second.

"So are you saying it's not safe to come ashore?"

"I don't think so," Kara said. "They'll have you in cuffs the second you get spotted."

"What about—"

"You can't drop the children off, Sean," she interrupted. "If they realise I'm holding them, I'll get put away too. I can't do that, I've got a life of my own here."

"I understand," Tycho replied softly.

The bridge lurched to the left, the floor tilting.

The room was painted crimson.

Alarm klaxons rang out.

"What was that?" Sean asked Saldana.

"According to the sensors..." the first officer checked the displays in front of her. "Yes, we've taken a hit to the stern, starboard side."

"What? Have we been damaged?"

"It doesn't look like it."

"Is something wrong?" Kara asked down the phone-line.

"I've got to go, sorry Kara," Tycho said.

"Good luck."

The vice admiral ended the call.

"What attacked us?" he asked Tycho. "How can they see us right now?"

"Pulling up the stern images now," said Saldana.

"It's a police patrol boat," Tycho realised once the pictures arrived on the screen.

It was a small vessel compared to the Diamond, about the size of a luxury yacht, but armed with enough weaponry to cause them a problem, and backed up by the long arm of the law. "It must have been circling this area and spotted our tracks through the water. They've hit us with their warning shot." He wiped sweat off his forehead.

"It's hailing us, sir," Saldana announced. Tycho picked up the receiver again but didn't answer.

"Vice admiral Tycho, now that we have your attention, you are under arrest. Please stop your vessel and come with us."

Tycho kept silent as the man began repeating his instruction. He locked the handset back into its position.

"Reckon we can outrun it?"

"Honestly, I don't know sir, those things are supposed to be pretty fast."

"We can't exactly risk them following us into Choctaw," Tycho started thinking out loud. His eyes wondered, running through the different options. "We'll have to disable it."

"Are you serious?" Saldana asked, eyes wide.

"Not live rounds, but we have electro-magnetic pulse torpedoes. That will shut the boat down without taking any lives."

"It's still a risk," she countered.

"What other choice do we have?" Tycho asked. "There could be a war about to break out in Choctaw. Don Stafford could be in need our help. We can't afford to get held up here." Tycho let his steely façade down for just a moment. "I can't let them take the children away from me, okay? They're... just going to have to come with us."

Saldana took in a deep breath.

"You attack that ship, even if it's non-lethal, it's a court martial. You know that," Saldana warned, fighting to be heard over the alarm. She looked down and back to her lover. "Maybe for me too."

"You're acting under my orders," he reminded her softly.

"Yeah but, you and I—"

"They don't know about us." Tycho insisted.

"It won't take them long to work it out."

Tycho pushed that dilemma to one side. His only thought was for the children. He'd never see them again if the ship was stopped.

The ship's commanding officer waited another second and made his mind up.

"Fire the shot."

Saldana twisted a dial on the panel next to her, lining up the EMP weapon. She hit the launch button. The two officers watched the monitor. A thin piece of metal ripped through the water, hurtling towards the police vessel.

"No going back now," Saldana muttered.

Impact.

White light shone out from underneath the target. A blue wave sprung forth, engulfing it like a balloon. The police vessel shook from side to side. Then it stopped, completely immobilised.

"Let's get out of here, fast," Tycho ordered.

The Diamond picked up speed, leaving the vessel behind it. For now.

"How long before they get their engines up and running again?" Saldana asked.

"It can't be much more than half an hour," Tycho replied. "We better hurry."

Don was exhausted, muscles and joints aching alike, eyes stinging with sweat in the unforgiving sun. He had to admit that he was lost at this point, completely in the hands of the only man who knew where they were going: Orvan.

"I don't like this one bit," Gisèle said quietly to him, handing over a bottle of water. The two of them were a good few metres behind the rest.

"Me neither," he replied after a swig, standing still to drink. "I lost track of our position relative to the forest maybe six hours ago."

Don wiped his mouth. At this point in the jungle of peaks, the Choctaw prairie lands were still visible but the steep rock formations that they had passed through now obscured the Peakwood forest.

"The last place I'd want to find myself in Orvan's hands, is out in the middle of nowhere," he added.

"We must be pretty high up here," Gisèle offered up.

"You got any signal?" Don asked.

Gisèle looked up and her irises began to glow a pale blue. The woman moved her head, as if searching the sky.

"Nope," she confirmed. "What about you?"

"Same here," Don admitted.

"We're on our own for now."

"Hmm," Don replied. "Well, I'm not sure I'd want Alida's input at this stage anyway. She sounded pretty pissed yesterday."

"Isn't she always like that?" Gisèle joked. Don laughed briefly.

"Yeah, good point."

Don tested his ankle, wincing in pain. He'd lived with the metalwork for the best part of two decades but it was aching now more than ever.

"We must be getting close," Don surmised through gritted teeth.

"How can you tell?" Gisèle asked. "I thought you said you were lost."

"Well, I have no idea where we are," he replied. "But that magnetic field we discovered is playing havoc with my screws and plates."

He looked up ahead and saw Smurph had turned around. The soldier didn't say anything, he just stretched both arms out either side of him in complaint. Don responded with a thumbs up.

"Come on, we better catch up," he said, handing the water bottle back to Gisèle.

Don pushed himself to close the gap, putting a bit too much pressure on both his legs. This high up, the terrain was horribly uneven and each step felt like the shin bones were going to come off the front of his leg, like bark off an old tree.

"How much further?" Don asked between some huge breaths once he was within hearing distance of the rest of the group.

Leading from the front, Orvan turned around quickly, finger pressed against his lips.

"Keep it down," he snapped. "We're nearly there."

"Thank god," Don said, stopping in his tracks.

"That's Torsevain Rise there," Orvan explained, pointing to the highest peak, at least a hundred metres in the air, touching the sky like the steeple of a church. "Which means—"

"What's that?" Chad asked, pointing to somewhere above their current location but in the shadow of the Rise. "Look, smoke."

"Their landing site must be on the other side of that ridge," Orvan surmised.

Don followed the man's fingers which pointed to a final slope of maybe twenty metres' climb. He breathed out and swept his brow.

"Let's get going, then," he added, leading the way up the incline. The soldiers quickly overtook him, as did Orvan. Gisèle and Chad kept up the rear with

Don as he pressed down into aching joints and sockets. Soon they would know what they were in for. Don's frustration at his physical situation abated somewhat at that knowledge. Hopefully, this arduous journey would be worth it. Sally would probably be even more upset if he'd risked his life for nothing.

Half-way up, Don's left foot landed on a small stone.

It scratched against the surface.

He slipped, banging his knee.

Don stifled a yelp of pain, not wanting to give away their position.

"Are you alright?" Gisèle whispered, grabbing hold of an arm. Chad held the other one and helped the old man back to his feet. He weighed on the leg gingerly, careful not to apply too much pressure through the wounded knee.

"I... I should be okay," he replied, limping up the slope with the help of his colleagues. "Thanks, both of you."

The three of them eventually reached the top after Orvan and the troops had arrived. They were all laying on their sides at the tip of the slope. It offered some protection, enough to stay below the parapet and still get a good view.

Below was the relatively shallow incline of the other side of the mountain, which led down to the western Choctaw Sea. A wall of water dominated Don's view. The calm ocean stretched all the way out to the horizon and he could see sections of the coast off to the left, most likely the edge of Cahors territory.

Then Don peered down into the recently formed crater immediately below, between his current position and the edge of the peak. Unlike the light brown hue of the mountain rage, the ground here was soft and black, like the top of a freshly baked chocolate cake. Even several days after impact, the crater was still steaming, the air thick with some sort of chemical, It smelt like hot tar.

"What are *they*?" Gisèle asked Don, pointing to two large cylindrical objects half buried in the dirt.

"Must be the British ships," Don surmised, wincing at the growing pain in his leg.

"They don't look like any kind of ship I've ever seen."

"What do you make of them, Chad?" Don asked the young man.

"I'm sorry sir, but I'm not familiar with this design either. Whatever these British ships are, it's something new."

"It's alright. I guess we shouldn't be too surprised," Don sighed. "It's not like anyone's heard much from them in the last few decades. They were bound to come here with new tech."

"Listen," Gisèle interjected. "What's that noise?"

"What noise?" Don asked. The others' eyes flickered, ears pricked. Don quietened his breath and concentrated. After a few seconds he heard it. Down below came a distant mechanical whirring, the sound of metal clunking against metal, over and over again, muffled by the rocky surface.

"It's coming from the crater," Chad added, nodding towards the two ships.

"Yeah," Don said. "It sounds like hammering perhaps. As if they're building something underground."

He was fascinated. If the British were here to colonise, then construction, even on a large scale, would be a logical move, but why were they doing it underground?

"That must be what Honit was talking about," Gisèle said.

"I've fulfilled my end of the bargain, Donald," Orvan whispered across to him. The Choctaw man was a couple of metres to Don's right. Smurph was between the two men. "What do you propose we do now?" he added.

"We observe," Don explained. "The best way to get an accurate fix on what the British capabilities and intentions are is to remain undetected for as long as possible and move from there. I want to know what they're building under there."

"Fuck that," Smurph said.

"Excuse me?" Don whispered back. The soldier turned and looked him in the eye.

"I said... fuck that. You think they're building something underground? I doubt it's the welcome wagon. We're going in. Now."

"You'll do nothing of the sort," Don retorted. "Do you need reminding of who's in charge of this mission?"

"You've never been calling the shots old man," Smurph said as he checked his ammunition levels. "I'm here on Stangl's orders and nobody else's," he added. Gisèle slapped his shoulder.

"What do you think you're doing?" she glared.

Smurph chuckled.

"Did you really think you were the boss of me because of that night at the base? Stupid woman."

Don's stomach dropped, sickened.

"Hey, don't you dare—"

Gisèle punched Smurph's arm, to no effect.

"Come on, let's go," he said. "We're moving out." The soldiers climbed to their feet.

Don tried to lift himself and grab Smurph's leg, cursing as his knee flared in pain and dragged him down in pain.

"Get up old man, let's meet our British friends," Smurph ordered, lifting one leg over the edge of the ridge.

"You can't expect him to get down there now," Gisèle protested. "Can't you see he's hurt?"

"Fine, you two stay up here," Smurph huffed. "But you're coming with me," he added, pointing at Chad. The young man looked like a rabbit caught in headlights.

"No. He's my man. He stays with me."

"I don't think so," Smurph replied. "If he's as half an expert on these people as you claim he is, then we need him down there," he added, pulling out a small hand-weapon from his belt and aiming at the young man's head. "Come on kid," Smurph snapped. Chad panicked and immediately pulled himself up.

"It's okay, sir," he said, shaking. "I'll go…"

"We have no idea what they've got down there, Smurph," Don said, practically begging at this point, his command in tatters. "You can't do this."

"I can and I will, old man," the soldier replied without even throwing him a glance. "You coming, Orvan?" he asked.

The Choctaw chief took a moment to answer, eyes fixed on the crater. Smurph's men were already marching headlong, Chad their captive.

"You're not the boss of me, blue, I'm staying back here."

"Suit yourself." Smurph shrugged his shoulders

and followed his men down the slope.

Don, Gisèle and Orvan were left to their miserable silence.

As the soldiers' voices died down, the humming below the ground became more obvious again.

"What the hell is that noise?" Gisèle asked again, skirting around the issue. Don ignored her.

"Ah dammit," he grumbled at another shot of pain from the knee.

"You know—" Orvan tried to speak but was quickly interrupted by Gisèle.

"Just shut the hell up, alright," she scolded. The Choctaw chief raised his eyebrows and leaned back. The hardness of his face softened for just one moment.

"I was just going to say...," he began, "that I agree with you." Orvan looked down, unable to make eye contact. "I think those soldiers are making a big mistake."

"Finally, you see the light," Don said, clenching his fists. Gisèle looked over and their eyes locked. His fell away first.

"I'm sorry, Donald. I guess... I thought he'd come in handy," she explained in a whisper.

"I... don't..." Don muttered. He had long been protective of Gisèle, from the moment she first joined his unit. She was a like a daughter to him. "We... have bigger things to worry about right now."

"You're damn right, Donald," Orvan said, leaning towards the edge of the ridge. "Look."

Don and Gisèle turned around and watched as Cabbage, leading the platoon, stepped off the slope and onto the soft centre of the crater. He was too far away to make out the words, but Don could hear the soldier express surprise at the texture of the surface. The other men tested their feet against the spongy terrain, like new-born foals at water for the first time. Chad looked back up to Don, before Smurph pushed him on the shoulder, knocking him off balance a little. The soldier grabbed the collar on his overalls and ushered him forward. The group spread out, Cabbage still at the front. Diablo and Scissorhands moved off to the left to crouch over a small speck of vegetation. Flat-top and Smurph stood either side of Chad, who was moving very gingerly towards the nearest cylinder. Thrombo stood in the middle, inspecting the metallic structure embedded to his shoulder bone. The flesh of the arm was gone but the weapon had been reattached.

Cabbage was the first to reach one of the British ships, pressing his hand up against the hull. He quickly snapped it back towards him, the metal too hot to touch. At that moment, Chad jogged towards the soldier, intrigued. Smurph and Flat-top followed him, keen to keep him close.

"Shit, look," Orvan said, pointing to the tall cylinder.

Some rubble slid off as it began to shake a little. A small circular hatch, maybe five metres above ground level, opened. Smurph, Flat-top and Cabbage noticed, preparing their weapons. Their leader gave a hand signal, ushering them to wait. Weapons armed, Thrombo, Diablo and Scissorhands approached.

"What is it?" Gisèle asked.

"I don't know," Don replied.

"Well, they know we're here now," Orvan sighed, reaching for the weapon on his hip.

Something began to extend from the opening. It

was a shiny metal funnel, roughly two-metres in length, the end wider than the rest. It undulated in the air, like a snake with its tail caught under a rock, moving around as if searching for something.

"What is it? Some kind of camera?" Gisèle asked.

"No... I don't—"

The funnel locked in place. The tip flared a glowing red.

"We've got to get Chad out of there!" Don shouted through the pain.

He hauled himself to his feet and over the ridge. Unable to lift the stricken leg high enough, he tripped. His face hit the rock hard, dazing him. Don's body rolled down the slope, scraped and scratched. A few feet down, the war veteran struck out with both arms, stopping the tumble. He was flat on his front, supported by his elbows, dizzy from the fall.

The end of the funnel grew in intensity. Cabbage fired his weapon. Smurph and the others followed suit. Their shots simply bounced off the ship.

Chad saw a chance to run away.

With a roar, fire leapt from man to man.

First Cabbage, then Thrombo. Both soldiers engulfed in flames. Don's blood curdled as the two of them screamed in agony, the flesh melting off their huge frames. It dripped off like hot fudge. Metallic skeletons fell to the ground like collapsed scaffolding.

The funnel flickered and fired another burst of heat. It missed, billowing up a pillar of fire from the ground. Smurph, Flat-top, Diablo and Scissorhands pressed themselves tight up against the ship. Too close to the hull for the funnel to find them.

Chad was half-way between the invaders and the edge of the crater.

"Keep going kid!" Don shouted, slowly getting to his feet.

He heard a crunch behind him. It was Gisèle coming down after him. Don ushered her back up the slope.

Chad kept running. His eyes wide, breathing heavy. The funnel gave up on the troops below and began searching the crater. It snapped into position again. Chad was in its sights. Don stepped onto surface of the crater, surprised by the bounce. He moved slowly towards the young man. The young man was just a few metres away now.

The weapon fired.

There was a cracking noise. A spark.

In an instant, Chad was transformed into a pillar of fire.

His movement suddenly stopped.

Outstretched arms lost their life.

The body stood still, ablaze.

It toppled over, an inanimate object.

A young man, hopes, dreams, aspirations. All gone. Snuffed out in no time at all.

Don collapsed onto his knees, eyes transfixed on the burning corpse.

Something grabbed his shoulders and pulled him over.

"It's too late Donald. It's too late." Gisèle's voice was quiet in Don's head. He felt faint.

Something grazed his leg, waking him briefly. Gisèle was dragging him back up the slope. He blacked out again. A flash of searing heat burned against his side. Don was woken up by an explosion a few metres to his left.

All his senses returned.

He stood up. Gisèle put her arm round him.
Another crackle.
Another spark.
A bush ignited.
Gisèle and Don leapt forwards.

26

Wash slammed back his into the air condition-ing unit in hiding. He whispered a sharp swear word. The young journalist struggled to control his breathing, frantically running hands through wet hair. All this time, he had known the Daily Citizen was in Curtis' back pocket, but he still couldn't believe what had just happened. Not only did the prime min-ister lead a government raid on a media outlet, but the IPCP were there as his hound dogs. This ran even deeper than he or even his conspiracy theorist father could ever had imagined.

Wash kicked the ground in frustration, tears forming. They had taken Yvette and Callum because of him. All because of his insistence on finding the truth. And yet Wash was still a million miles off finding out what was really going on. Searching the night sky for inspiration, he felt trapped. Where could he go? It was probable that the IPCP were still staking out the building even if they were on a wild goose chase for the non-existent back door. His home was being watched and Wash had no way of knowing what had happened to Jay either. He couldn't put Vicky's life at risk by going to her place.

He remembered her message to Pete. The warehouse in Wapping. Wash leaned forward, preparing to leave and then laughed sarcastically at his situation. The next destination was an irrelevance if he couldn't get off this roof.

Standing up, Wash combed the surface for a way down. There was nothing, not even a roof-top door. Up this high, the wind howled over his ears and blew through his shirt, still wet with sweat. Approaching the edge, Wash saw just how high up it was. At least five stories. Night had fully descended on central London, the city now illuminated only by street lamps, cars and shop windows.

As the elements continued their assault, he could hear a clattering noise coming from the next building on from this one. It was metal on metal. There was an open window. It was rattling against the frame. Wash judged the distance between the ledge and his escape route. It was flush with the front of the building he stood on and one level up. The only way to reach it was to climb. Before he could stop himself, he looked down and quickly clutched the wall for safety. The pavement was so far away, Wash found it hard to balance. He leaned across to reach the protruding ledge below the window. He looked down once more. He grabbed the wall again. Frozen.

From the perch, Wash could see back into the newsroom. His colleagues were shaking themselves down, coming to terms with the trauma. Wash allowed another thought for those who had been hurt on his quest for the truth. That could also include Jay and Declan at this point. He had no idea what Curtis had planned for those who had crossed him.

Wash held on to the wall with his left hand, testing his right foot over the edge and round to the front of the next building. He got purchase on the protrusion, balancing against the leg that remained on the rooftop. Putting all his weight into that left leg, Wash leaned up towards the open window above him, still flapping in the wind. After a sudden blast it clattered into the frame and bounced off again. He recoiled and wobbled uncomfortably, doing his best to lean into the brickwork. Even if he could get hands on the window it could slam shut on them.

Wash took a deep breath and stretched out again, tickling the base with craning fingertips. A pain slowly grew in his shoulder as he leaned upwards. The motion placed a nagging feeling on the left foot anchoring him to the rooftop. He'd have to let it go so he could swoop onto the protruding ledge and jump to wrap a hand into the window frame.

"Don't look down. Don't look down, don't look down."

He jumped.

The foot landed. The hand hooked.

Wash let out a whelp of joy. His body was in an uncomfortable stretch across the window and the ledge below, but he had full balance, enough to get the other hand in place.

The wind continued to play at the open piece of glass.

Wash started walking up the brickwork and was able to move a sufficient distance to get one hand on the side of the window panel now, allowing for a firmer grip. The wind blasted again, closing the window on Wash's hip. He threw himself forward.

The floor welcomed him with a thud. It was painful but Wash didn't care. He'd landed. Behind him, the satchel, strap still over his head and shoulder was caught on the frame. It dropped, yanking him back towards the window by his neck, knocking him to the floor and stifling his breath. Wash pulled forward but that only tightened the grip on his throat. He leaned back into the window frame, close enough to wrap an arm behind himself. Taking the weight of the bag, Wash was finally able to stand up. He collapsed in a heap on the floor, catching what breath he had left.

The room was dark, lit only by the glow of London's night life. It was an abandoned office, pitch darkness in the corridor beyond it. Once in the hallway, Wash noticed the distant gleaming of a fire exit sign. Running toward it, his footsteps echoed throughout the empty building.

He pushed down on a metal bar and opened the door to the stairwell. Minutes later he was in the lobby. The front wall was exclusively made of glass, with a revolving door. He crept closer to the windows to allow a better view up and down the road. Nothing. It looked safe to move, finally. Wash prayed there would be a way out of here. He pushed the handle bars on the revolving door only to find it motionless.

"Damn it."

Wash backed away from the doors and clattered his feet into the reception desk. A sticker on the wall behind explained that the building was protected by Wardale Alarms. Returning to the front, he pressed his face up against the glass to get a clear view of the concrete that arched over the entrance. Sure enough, he could see a plastic unit emblazoned with the word 'Wardale'. None of the lights were flashing.

"Here we go then," Wash muttered to himself. Taking a deep breath, he strode back to the reception with confidence. Opening a rickety tool cabinet behind the desk, he found a hammer with the perfect claw on the back.

Testing the tool in his hand, Wash eyed up the glass.

He swung.

It smashed.

The noise was louder than Wash was expecting.

Paterson could have heard it.

He ran away from the building, aiming for an inviting alleyway on the other side of the street. Wash didn't look back. He wasn't sure if he was being followed. The sound of his breathing and footsteps on the concrete were deafening. Wash crashed through a puddle, splashing a beggar.

"Watch it mate," he said, the voice fading into the distance as the journalist continued his escape.

Soon, Wash had progressed maybe five streets away from the Daily Citizen. Further down the road, he could see a bank of taxis waiting outside a tube station. Jangling his pockets he guessed he had enough cash for the journey and paced to the front of the queue.

Wash opened the door and collapsed into the seat, keeping the hood.

"Where to, pal?"

Wash spoke in a fake east London accent, keeping his face down.

"Wappin' docks, mate."

The driver put his foot down.

"Going swimming are we?"

"Sort of."

✦

Wash recalled the first time he came to these docks. He remembered the innocence, blissfully unaware of the journey he would be sent on by Miles Faversham's dead body. For a moment, Wash was jealous of his former self, a man with considerably fewer concerns, and yearned for simpler times. Then he realised how self-inflicted this whole thing had been. Nothing would stop Washington Parker getting to the truth. Proving his father wrong... and right at the same time.

"Oh my god," Wash called out when he saw her. Vicky turned to face him, a bundle of nerves. "You're safe," he added, throwing himself into an embrace.

"What is it?" Vicky asked, pulling out to get a look at his face. "You look as if you've seen a ghost."

"How long have you been here?" Wash felt guilty and grateful in equal measure.

"Only about an hour, don't worry. The important thing is you're here now," she said, trying to calm him. "What happened?"

"They sacked my office," Wash explained. "Arrested two people."

"Who did?" Vicky countered, eyes wide.

"The police, the IPCP and... you'll never believe me," he said, scratching the back of his head. He was almost too ashamed to admit it, as if he would be dismissed.

"Who was it?"

"Benjamin Curtis."

Vicky's jaw dropped and she took a step backward.

"What? The prime minister?"

"Yeah... I know." There was a small part of Wash that enjoyed the look on Vicky's face, being the one to break it to her. It was why he had become a journalist in the first place, to make people stand up and listen to him. He never imagined it was a feeling that would be wrapped up with so much fear and guilt.

"Why did he do it? What happened?"

"I posted the story about Faversham's findings, did you read it?"

"Of course." Vicky nodded intently.

"Then about forty-five minutes later I get a call from Declan warning me that they're on their way. They turned up and I managed to get out onto the roof of the building next door in time to escape."

Vicky let out a long breath.

"Oh my god, who did they arrest? Any of your friends?"

"Yvette the editor and Callum the crime reporter," Wash clarified.

"Oh my god," Vicky said with a long breath. "That's so scary. What will they do to them?"

"That's the thing, I've got no idea. It's almost worse not having a clue. They could wind up as the next Eye Killer victims for all I know."

"And you only just got out in time?" She asked. Wash nodded.

"What did they do at the office?" she asked with a furrowed brow.

"They trashed the place and turned it inside out looking for information I had collected on the story," he replied.

"Did they find anything?"

"I don't think so," Wash said. "Nothing important

anyway," he added, tapping his bag. "I've got my laptop and papers in here. I assume the original documents from the body are--"

"Still at mine, yeah," Vicky confirmed confidently.

"Good," Wash replied. "Let's keep it that way. At this point, I think you're the last person who hasn't been connected with me by these people." He performed another sweep of the immediate area, in case anyone had followed him.

"I'm not sure how," Vicky said.

"What do you mean?"

"I don't know how they haven't connected us yet," she said again.

They stared at each other in silence. The cogs in Wash's mind were in overdrive, searching for any loose ends.

"So what's the plan now?" Vicky asked, breaking his train of thought.

"I've got no idea, to be honest," Wash replied, running both hands through his hair. "I feel like death," he added. "All this running... I'm exhausted."

"Maybe you need to come back to mine?" Vicky suggested, putting a hand on his arm. Wash quickly pulled back.

"I don't think that's a good idea. They're on the lookout for me now" he said. "I don't want anyone to link the two of us. We've been lucky so far."

Vicky shrugged her shoulders.

"I just don't want anything bad to happen to you." Wash placed both hands on soft bronzed cheeks and kissed her lips. "I need to stay on the move, to make it harder for them to find me." He paused before revealing his intentions. "I need to keep investigating this."

"What?" Vicky said, eyes wide. "Are you serious?

After everything that has happened tonight you want to carry on with this?"

"How can I not?"

"To save your life!"

"But I'm a wanted man already," Wash countered. "The only way out of this mess is to get to the bottom of it."

As if on cue, Wash's glasses rang. The sudden noise nearly gave him a heart attack. Recovering, the journalist could see it was Declan. He answered in a flash.

"Declan! Are you okay?" he asked.

"Yeah, I'm fine," his friend replied. He sounded indoors, which could only be a good thing. At least he wasn't on the run too. "I think I'm alright," Declan added. "What about you?"

"I'm safe," Wash confirmed. "I got out of the Daily Citizen building just in time... because of you. Thank you Declan." He tried to sound as heartfelt as possible. Their relationship had almost exclusively been based on wit in their university days. Wash felt a pang of guilt for their first meaningful words to come in such terrible circumstances. Vicky looked on with sympathy, arms folded to keep herself warm.

"Hey, that's what friends are for."

"What now?"

"That's why I called. I've got everything. I can blow this wide open for you."

"What do you mean? Isn't the prime minister sacking a national newspaper enough for now?"

"Nobody will ever believe his word over yours, Washington," Declan countered.

"Good point."

"Look," Declan continued. "Do you remember

those spreadsheets and calculations that were part of the original packet I sent you?"

"Yeah," Wash replied, starting to pace around the alleyway. "I couldn't work any of it out."

"I'm not surprised. Sorry about that, I didn't have the information I needed back then."

"And you do now?"

"Yes. I've managed to get hold of Doctor Logan Taylor's contributions to the project."

"The IPCP's head of science? The one who's been working out of an underground tunnel?"

"That's the one. He's the key to exposing this whole thing."

Wash allowed his impulses to run wild.

"But if I can't report what Curtis did, how can I publish this smoking gun of yours?"

"Well you can't do it with the Daily Citizen that's for sure, or any of our papers," Declan replied.

"What do you mean?"

"I'm sorry Wash, but I think your days in this country are numbered. Once you've got this final puzzle piece, you'll have to reach the continent and find somewhere in Europe to publish."

Wash laughed nervously.

"That's not going to be easy, Declan."

"I might be able to pull a few strings for you."

"If you say so," Wash replied, impressed.

"Look, I'm sorry I've had to be so cryptic this whole time," Declan added.

"It's okay, you were just trying to stay under the radar with this. What now? How do I get this smoking gun?"

"I own a second property not far from you, in Rope Walk Gardens. Number seven. Meet me there in twenty minutes."

"Will do," Wash said, hanging up.

"What now?" Vicky asked.

"He says he has the missing puzzle piece," he replied, blood fizzing. "This is it."

"Are you sure it's safe?"

Wash exhaled.

"Probably not, but someone has to do this."

"It should be me," said Vicky.

"What? No? It's too dangerous," Wash snapped.

"How is it any safer for you?" she replied.

Wash was a little lost for words. He knew she was right. If it came to a fight, he'd be no better than her. Still, there was no way he could let Vicky do this for him. He'd feel so helpless.

"It's not about that. Declan doesn't know who you are," Wash explained.

"He won't need to," Vicky insisted.

"Yes, he will. Right now, he can't trust anyone he doesn't know," Wash leaned in and grabbed her hands again. "I really appreciate the gesture, but I have to go." He kissed her.

"What do you want me to do in the mean time?"

"Get back to yours and protect those documents, I'll meet you there. I better go."

*

Wash edged past a small self-contained park opposite a row of ornate houses. The vegetation was growing through the gothic black bars like tendrils, as if it held an unthinkable secret. In the night, and with dark forces chasing after him, Wash kept his distance from the greenery. He had arrived at

Rope Walk Gardens, out of breath, having jogged the whole way. To the left was the row of tall buildings, each five stories high. The pavement was lined with white porches and pillars surrounding heavy doors, indulgently wide.

Walking surreptitiously past Declan's neighbours, Wash was jealous of the luxury he witnessed through the windows. In one house he spotted a room full of books, perhaps the abode of a learned scholar, every wall sprouting papers and documents. Next door was a whitewashed and clinical front room that contained nothing more than a pale rigid sofa and a polished grand piano.

Wash heaved his way up the deep steps of number seven. They were out of sync with his natural stride. Gaze fixed on the ground, Wash noticed the front door was ajar. There was harsh splintering around the lock. Looking up, he confirmed there were no lights on inside.

Confidence drained from his body like a pricked bladder.

But he had no choice.

Taking a deep breath, the journalist carefully pushed the door open to reveal a long corridor. Hanging on the wall to the right were a series of smart jackets, a tie strewn across the hooks. Below them was a metal rack, each slot filled with exquisitely polished shoes and a few for golf. Propped up against it was the case containing Declan's clubs.

It was not a particularly welcoming environment. The light from the street lamp illuminated only half of the porch, which meant Wash could not see where the hallway ended. As his eyes adjusted, he realised that there was the beginnings of a wooden staircase on the left. To the right was jet black nothingness, the corridor clearly extending beyond to other ground floor rooms. Not knowing the layout of the building, Wash felt as if he had stepped into more of a haunted house than a safe house. He closed the door behind him, as quietly as possible, holding and then gently releasing the latch so that it wouldn't snap into place of its own accord.

Wash whispered Declan's name as he crept further into the unknown, a floorboard creaking. In such an empty space it echoed against bare walls. Then, silence reigned supreme once more.

Above him the ceiling groaned slightly, then squeaked under the pressure of someone walking around. That must be Declan. The steps got heavier. They sounded like shuffles. There was a clunk, a flurry of steps and loud thud against the floor.

Wash swore, stopping in his tracks.

The commotion escalated. Footsteps struck the floor in staccato beat as someone tried to run. Glass smashed. Someone grunted loudly, as if they had been struck. Wash's body tensed.

"Declan!" he shouted.

The young man fumbled to his right. He knocked over the shoe rack with a crash.

"Come on," he rasped in a panic, spit flying from his mouth.

Another groan of pain upstairs. Wash cursed as he tossed shoes and trainers from side to side.

Something brushed against his arm. He jumped out of his skin. It was the golf bag. The journalist fumbled with the zip and pulled out a hefty wedge. He raced up the stairs, clutching the metal bar. Wash crashed into a closed door. It was the top of the stairs.

His own breath warmed his face as he huffed and puffed against the wood. He could hear the scuffle continuing beyond it. Wash fumbled for his glasses and held up its HUD to guide his way.

Footsteps approached and the door banged. Wash flinched. Someone had been bashed against the other side. A punch was thrown, and two sets of feet scuttled away, off into another section of the first floor.

Hands full, Wash tried the handle with his elbow. It was locked. He stepped back, defeated.

The fight continued on the other side.

Wash took a breath and crashed his foot against the door. It would not budge. He was on a mini-landing so there wasn't much space to get a run-up.

There was another distant smash.

"Damn it, Declan," Wash cried as he lurched into the door once again.

Nothing.

He put the glasses down, momentarily blinding himself but eventually illuminating the ceiling once in the right position. Never once did Wash relinquish his grip on the golf club. He set himself, holding the bannister, planting his left foot into the ground and swinging forward on the right. He drove the foot just to the left of where the locking mechanism must be. This time there was give. A small splintering line on the door formed.

Another kick.

It irritated the contour some more.

Wash heard a scream. It sounded like Declan. He was probably two or three rooms away now.

"Come. On!" Wash howled, landing another blow on the door.

The wood was starting to wrench away. Another

two well-placed kicks had the lock hanging off. One more *push*. He was through.

The lights were also off on the corridor so he picked his glasses up again. By now the house was filled by a haunting, gaunt silence. Wash took extra care moving forward, measuring each step reluctantly. He shut off the spectacles' display. At the end of the landing, a faint glow emanated from an open doorway.

Tiptoeing, Wash moved quickly along the walkway until he reached the edge of the aperture. Placing his back against the wall, he leaned a sliver of his right eye past the frame. There was Declan.

Half of the man's face was spotlighted by a television screen on the wall. He was stood bolt upright, like a soldier to attention, cheek streaked with blood. Wash began to form his friend's name in his throat but suppressed it when he saw the other figure. It looked like a shadow.

Dressed all in black with a hood over the face, it stood opposite Declan. Why wasn't either of them trying to get away? Wash could not tell which one had been the aggressor. Until now. The intruder edged slowly towards its prey, arms raised towards Declan's head. The movement was gentle, almost peaceful. Transfixed on the bizarre scene, Wash could not move. What the hell was going on? Soon the ominous figure was so close to Declan it was if they were locking faces. Gloved hands pressed down on soft cheeks. The fingers began to move gently from side to side. They shifted up in flash. The digits tensed, pressing hard into the eye sockets. At first there was no change in Declan's face, until red streaks began to form. His head started to convulse violently.

The hands held their grip. The shrill scream chilled Wash to the bone. By the time he knew what was happening it was too late.

Declan fell to the ground with a sickening bump; blood haemorrhaging from his skull. Without thinking, Wash launched himself through the door in a fit of rage. Declan's murderer turned to face Wash. His blood ran cold. Imaginary nails shot through his feet freezing him to the spot.

Those eyes. Those intense, elongated, glowing eyes were looking right at him, sizing him up like a greedy hyena.

Wash could do nothing but allow the stare of death to wash over him.

Where one would have expected to identify whites in the eyes, he saw a pulsating orange glare, bringing the jet-black iris and ivory pupil into sharp focus. The rest of the Eye Killer's face appeared as misty ink in comparison. Wash could not make out any other details. The creature's head moved, its skin glistening like wet leather in the light of the television screen.

It took a step closer.

Wash detected a faint vibration sounding from the eyes.

Another step.

The buzzing intensified.

Wash stood still. Terrified.

He could not stop staring into the abyss that were... those eyes.

He was being hypnotised but could do nothing about it. His face began to lose feeling. In just a few short seconds, numbness washed over him. The killer continued its approach. Now it was opposite Wash, warming his face with its breath. Somewhere in the void of the creature's face, he detected a lip-less mouth. It quivered and slathered as hands rose towards his cheeks. The journalist's grip on the golf club loosened. Fingertips touched his skin.

PING

A chime sounded from Wash's pocket.

The creature looked down.

The hypnosis instantly wore off.

He came to his senses.

Wash took a step back, resumed his grip around the handle and swung hard.

He felt the wedge hit the creature's head. It let out a high-pitched whine and cowered away.

Wash struck again, the club sinking into something soft.

The colour in the killer's eyes flickered and softened as it felt to the floor.

He stood over the creature, tables fully turned. He set himself for another swing.

Wash's legs were swept from underneath him. He landed uncomfortably on his shoulder.

The Eye Killer hauled itself up in a flash, took one look back at Wash for half a moment and propelled itself towards the window. It crashed through the glass and landed on the pavement. From the sound of its footsteps it raced away at speed.

Wash flopped back onto the floorboards, struggling to breathe.

27

Wash hauled himself into a sitting position with a painful groan. The Eye Killer had struck him hard on the left ankle. The bone was still feeling the impact.

Declan was just a few metres away. Still.

"Declan," Wash whimpered in vain hope. "Are you...?"

No answer.

The television screen was still the solitary source of light. Only a segment of Declan's perfectly pressed shirt was visible. A gentle breeze swept in through the smashed window, tickling the end of the navy tie. Even after the attack there was not a single crease in the cotton. *Stylish to the last*, Wash thought to himself. His friend would have appreciated that.

A wretch of guilt tore at the journalist's stomach. This death was his fault. Already tonight he'd subjected his colleagues to danger and now his friend was dead. Wash wanted nothing more than to release his sorrow through tears, but couldn't. Maybe it was the adrenaline still pumping through his veins but his eyes remained frustratingly dry.

Wash leaned forward onto his knee so he could stand up.

He recoiled.

The change in his position had brought Declan's face into view. It was a butchered mess.

Wash motioned to be sick, but just about managed to hold it in. This was not the first time he'd seen the Eye Killer's work, although it took some getting used to. Back in the warehouse the body had stewed in the muddy waters of the Thames, allowing the eye sockets to drain of body fluid. In a sickening contrast, the damage to Declan's face was fresh. The skin was coloured a dark congealed crimson, blood dripping into a vacant open mouth.

Wash cursed as the wider context came rushing back to him. He began to pace around the room, breathing heavily.

"What am I going to do?"

He was already on the run from the newspaper, the police and the prime minister, all because of the damn colonisation programme. Now the Eye Killer had been deployed, Declan was dead and Wash was lucky to be alive. How had he managed to escape such a grisly fate? He shuddered, remembering the how those haunting eyes had taken possession of him. Wash wondered what sort of technology could have that effect. It was like nothing he'd ever heard of. It felt like someone had reached out and clenched around every nerve in his body with a thousand hands.

Then Wash recalled the monstrous nature of the Eye Killer's mouth. He tried to drag up an image of it in his mind. But during the attack, his focus had been on the hypnotic optic centres the whole time.

From what his brain could piece together, he was sure there were no lips and the noise it had made was closer to an animalistic gargle than anything else. Wash was starting to question if it was even human.

Either way, it had been distracted by something. He patted himself down and realised it had been his glasses that had chimed. He pulled them out of his pocket frantically to inspect them. Holding the switch on the side, the journalist powered them up, wiped a smudge with his sleeve and pulled them on.

There was one notification. It was a file from Declan.

Wash swung round to his friend, hoping for the impossible. The government official was still lying on the floor, cast aside in his own blood.

Waiting for the document to load onto the device, Wash went in search of something to cover Declan with. He returned with a blanket.

Sitting in a chair, he let out a long sigh. He was careful to stay away from the windows and reminded himself he would have to leave soon.

The file was in, accompanied by a note from Declan. It appeared that the transfer had been prepared to automatically sync with Wash's device when he got close enough. Without realising it, the junior government servant had saved his life. He hoped that he could make Declan's sacrifice worth it.

Wash read the message aloud.

'The key to deciphering the data sheets in the original packet can be found in Doctor Taylor's laboratory. It's located in the tunnels between St Paul's and Chancery Lane stations on the Central Line. I've managed to find the entry code for the complex and the password for his personal computer (see attached file). All you need to do

is get down there and extract data from the folder entitled CON-74-PROPELLANT.'

Before he could formulate a plan of action, Wash heard the distant whine of police sirens. His spine tensed. He needed to move, and quickly. There was one last guilty look towards Declan. He wanted to do something about the body but knew he didn't have time.

Clasping at the golf club, Wash clambered through the dark corridor and felt his way down the stairs. The metal of the makeshift weapon clanged against the wall. He burst through the front door, hoping to close it again afterwards but, as he was hit by the fresh air, and spotted a gathering crowd. Wash stopped in his tracks to count five concerned local residents inspecting the glass on the pavement. They all turned to face him.

Wash looked to his right and noticed the dark fluid on the end of the club. The bystanders gargled with offence. He started running off to the right, back the way he had come.

"Hey! Come back!" An angry man shouted through the streets.

"He's getting away," cried an older woman.

Instinctively, Wash sped away from the scene. The target on his back was getting bigger by the hour.

Wash was confident that nobody had followed him to St Paul's station. He had patiently waited behind a line of bins in an alleyway opposite the entrance. The only problem facing was how to access the platform. He was reticent to use his card, as the government were almost certainly tracking its activity at this point. However, he surmised that it might take a few minutes for them to scramble anyone to stop him, while simply trying to vault the barriers would alert attention to him much quicker. After the course of the evening thus far, Wash wasn't sure if he had enough stamina another fight. He'd have to enter the premises legally.

The coast was clear. He unzipped his coat and slotted the golf club inside before stepping out onto the pavement. The barrier beeped to accept his card and Wash knew he was on the clock. He picked up the pace a little as he moved down the stairs and onto the platform. Walking out onto the concourse, he recognised Sanjay, outside his booth as per usual. The two caught eye contact for just a moment. The station worker looked away and then back again a split second later.

"Hey," he said angrily. "It's you."

Wash ignored him, walking away and along the platform.

"Stop," Sanjay continued. "Oi, dick head. Come back here!"

The journalist broke into a run.

"Hey, Kwasi, get the police on the phone, I've found him," Sanjay shouted.

Wash heard the man's footsteps intensify. He risked a look over the shoulder and suddenly slammed into someone.

"What are you *doing*?" a stern woman rasped.

"I'm sorry," Wash replied pathetically, nursing the increasing pain in the ankle.

Harsh hands grabbed viciously at his shoulders and hoisted him up.

"Got ya," Sanjay said from behind. "Who's the journalist now?"

"What?" Wash replied, trying to wriggle free. "That's not how it works."

Wash flicked the tip of the golf club beyond his left shoulder.

"Ah shit."

Wash had struck something soft.

The restraint loosened, allowing him to escape. He could hear Sanjay collapse in a heap. Passengers on the platform looked on in shock. Nobody dared stop Wash as he continued running. The police were on their way now. He had to move fast.

Slipping slightly on the glossy flooring, he was half-way down the platform. Looking back, he saw two things that sent his pulse into overdrive. Sanjay was up again and running towards him. To the right, Wash spotted a pair of light beams at the other end of the platform. They swept along the black wall of the tunnel and erupted into the sight of an underground train, hurtling along the track.

Wash started running again. Sanjay and the vehicle were bearing down on him. The whine of the train was tickling at his ear, steadily closing in, preparing to overtake and block his route. Then it was in the corner of his eye. The lights inside forced a squint.

"Get back here you dick head!" Sanjay yelled. He couldn't have been more than a few metres away.

Wash's ankle pulsated with pain, slowing him down.

The gap between the front of the train and the end of the platform continued to shrink, guarded by a metal panel.

Sanjay stretched and caught the end of the club.

It fell from Wash's hand.

He vaulted over the protective fencing.

He landed in the dark, letting out a groan as he struck the floor.

The smell of sparks and dust was thicker. Wash choked a little on the mucky air. He heard the chime of doors opening behind him, forcing him to his feet. The train had reached a stopping position just as he had made his leap of faith. The headlamps stared like the eyes of an angry animal. Wash searched the windows of the cabin to see if there was a bewildered train driver behind the controls. The cabin was empty. That meant either it was being controlled remotely or the operative was at the opposite end of the train. There was no way Sanjay could reach him but Wash knew he probably only had about thirty seconds to find this laboratory. He started moving, painfully knocking his knee on the metal rail to his right. He rasped out a foul word, pushing through the twinge.

Wash guessed no more than twenty metres now separated him from the train.

The sound of closing doors echoed through the tunnel.

His presence would not stop the running of the service.

The engines gradually whooshed into life behind him. The whirring grew louder. Lights swooped across the roof of the tunnel as it started following Wash around the corner. The headlamps filled the space, harshly. They exposed every detail in the brickwork.

There was nowhere to hide.

This was it. The end.

Wash welcomed death. It was over.

He dropped, chin and knees crunching into the hard ground.

Metal scraped on metal above him. Sparks crackled. Air blew over Wash's back, neck and head. More sparks. The constant grating.

Then it was distant.

Silence fell.

Wash lay still, hands still clasped over the back of his head for what felt like an eternity. He could not breathe, the body locked the terror of death.

There were panicked voices echoing through the chamber. Wash couldn't make out what they were saying but those on the platform must have assumed he was dead. That would probably come in handy for now.

Wash stood up and brushed a layer of dust off his torso and legs, stifling a cough as some irritated the back of his throat. Now all he had to do was find this laboratory before the next train came through. Recalling the timetable, Wash had about seven minutes before he'd have to duck again. The only thing Wash could do was continue moving. Miles Faversham's notes had said the Doctor was working two hundred metres from the westbound platform. Surely he could make that in time.

Along the brickwork at regular intervals were light strips that helped illuminate Wash's journey as he jogged through the pit underneath the track. With the train gone, his footsteps were the predominant noise stabbing and reverberating through the air.

"Come on," Wash whispered to himself. Each time

a new light strip came into view he hoped it would show the way but there was just more and more tunnel round the corner.

"Finally," he said, relieved as a section of track veered off to the left. It was obvious which one led to Chancery Lane and which one didn't. The public track was wider and better lit. Wash took the alternative route and descended further into the dark unknown. A few steps in, he could no longer see, forced to use his glasses to guide the way once again.

His foot cannoned into something in the pit. It was a step. Climbing up, Wash realised he'd reached the end, met with a small metallic door. To the right was a keypad, just as Declan had specified, easy enough to use with the provided key code.

There was a faint beep and the clunking of metal inside the door mechanism. It swung open gently towards him.

"Wow," Wash said quietly.

He stepped through and found himself in what appeared to be a dimly-lit warehouse. Looking left and right, he realised it was more of an aircraft hangar. There was an unmistakable shape of a spacecraft, similar to the pictures he had seen of the Concord on television. It was long and thin, functional in nature, no frills, just a grimy container ready for the new frontier on Proxima B. The room was dingy but sparse floodlights caused the ship to shine in places. On the side of the cylinder read the word 'Speedwell'. Below the ship were stanchions to hold it in place. They were attached to one long piece of railway rolling stock, wheels sat on the tracks beneath. The rails moved off to the right to a gigantic doorway, closed on them for now. It looked ready for transport.

430

Wash was completely baffled. Why on earth was the next colonial ship housed deep in the heart of the London Underground? At the very least it partially answered his question about the closures on the Central Line, but why did the government have to be so secretive about this? He remembered Declan's notes and began searching the open space for an office building. It was off to the left, a small booth, not unlike a foreman's working space on a building site. Wash carefully crept forward, ears pricked. He could not believe that such an important government facility would be unguarded, even this late at night. Cringing at the echoing sound of his foot catching on a wooden crate, he rushed to the small metal steps underneath the office.

Crouching, Wash listened out for any movement in the open space. Nothing. He swivelled round and climbed up to the door, which opened easily.

Orange eyes stared at him.

Wash stumbled backwards, feeling for the golf club and remembered it was gone. He crashed into the side of a desk to the right, frantically searching the small room for a weapon but could see nothing better than a stapler.

The journalist turned back and realised the Eye Killer was behind a sheet of glass on the wall opposite. It was housed inside what looked like a giant bath, bubbling with a translucent fluid. It lay there still, allowing the frothing liquid to rush over its face. Wash noticed that the eyes were considerably dimmer than they had been at Declan's house. The Eye Killer was motionless, perhaps asleep, recharging after their earlier encounter.

Wash rushed himself into the Doctor's chair. The

shorter time spent here the better. He lifted the lid
of the laptop computer and entered the password Declan had given him. The machine's database of files
opened. Wash started scrolling, looking for the pro-
pellant folder. He opened it, eager to find out what
was so important about the information there.

"What?" Wash muttered when he discovered it
was full of spreadsheets. Clicking through each file
he was faced with a sea of numbers, not dissimilar
to the original set of documents he had been handed
by Declan. Frantically, he sifted through everything
he could find, growing increasingly desperate. There
was nothing useful here. Declan had given his life for
nothing.

Wash put his head in his hands. The adrenaline
had finally wore off. Tears dropped onto the keyboard. He was tired. He wanted this to end, one way
or another. Either with an answer to the riddle or for
someone to take it away for him completely. There
was no way of knowing which of his friends were
still left alive. He wasn't sure if there was any place in
the country safe for him anymore and his only route
of escape, promised by Declan, was now gone.

Wash lifted his fist, ready to slam into the desk,
refraining, only when he remembered the Eye Killer.
He noticed a portable hard-drive and made a quick
decision. In a few moments, the contents had
been transferred. Wash then added a few additional
folders that he felt required further scrutiny.

Clunk.

Wash jumped at the noise behind him.

He watched as the Eye Killer's container started to
hiss and produce steam. The glass sheet was sliding
slowly upwards. Grabbing his things, Wash rushed

out of the office door and back into the warehouse. Realising there was no obvious escape from this complex, he stopped in the middle of the open space. Travelling back through the underground tunnel probably wasn't the best idea considering the police would be guarding the exits now.

"...place unguarded." A voice emanated from the entrance. Someone was in the tunnel.

Wash searched the base for somewhere to hide. The office was out of bounds. The corners were exposed. There was a walkway running around the upper walls but, again, no cover.

"This whole operation is a shit-storm." There were at least two people in the tunnel. They were arguing.

Wash continued his scan of the warehouse. The only place that looked viable was the Speedwell. There was a metal structure next to the spaceship, like the boarding steps for an aircraft, leading to a hatch. That was his only chance. He raced up the stairs and tried the handle. It opened. Wash jumped into the opening and pulled the door gently, leaving it ajar so he could monitor the outside.

Two people came through the entrance at the same time as the Eye Killer emerged from its abode. One of the newcomers was Benjamin Curtis, remonstrating with Paterson. Through the arch, Wash could see a host of heavily armoured officers, possibly the same ones who had sacked the Daily Citizen. They waited in the corridor.

"I knew I shouldn't have left security in the hands of a fucking alien," Curtis rasped. "There you are, you stupid lump." He stood opposite the creature. It said nothing.

"What happened?" Paterson asked, nursing a rifle

in both hands, her words laced with accusation. "Has the reporter been here?"

"You're wasting your breath," Curtis replied cynically. "It won't answer your questions. This thing does its talking on the pitch, so to speak. If Parker had been here I'd like to think we'd be staring at his butchered corpse."

"Ok, well, if he didn't get in here then he must still be in the tunnels somewhere," Paterson began pacing.

"Deal with him," Curtis ordered to his two companions. "I've got to get this ship on the move. We're already behind schedule."

As Paterson and the Eye Killer left the room, the prime minister moved to a panel on the wall and pressed some buttons. Wash felt his feet lurch to the left. In his crouched position it nearly knocked him off balance. The whole ship was now in motion, sliding away from the warehouse. He looked around to get his bearings. He was sat in the back-end of the cockpit, the windscreen up in front. Through the glass, Wash could see the Speedwell edging towards the gigantic door. He heard more flicking of switches and the giant mechanisms clunked and rattled together, opening the hatchway. On the other side was another tunnel which snaked around a corner.

Wash could not believe his luck. Curtis was single-handedly helping him out of the complex, away from danger. At least for now.

Ten minutes later, Wash could see the night's sky at the end of the tunnel. It was still red-brick either side of the train, scaling all the way up to a street above, but he was finally back outside. The track was now on a slight upward incline.

Some of the night air whispered through the still ajar door behind Wash. He moved back along the ship intending to close it.

The metal above him crumpled slightly with a thud.

Wash felt like he needed to urinate.

Then it happened again, a more muffled sound this time.

The Eye Killer. It had followed him.

Wash dashed for the door, desperate to seal himself in. It was too late. The metal hatchway was kicked open from above.

A dark figure jumped into the craft.

Wash fell back, waiting for the intensity of those eyes.

It aimed a weapon at him.

"Don't shoot," he said instinctively, hands in the air.

A second pair of legs came through the hatch, thinner, more slender.

The newcomer closed the door tightly and swivelled to face Wash.

She took off her mask.

"Vicky? What are you doing here?"

28

"You better start talking, Ben," Harper demanded, mind whirring. She looked at the weapon and into his eyes, sharply focussed on her. The man she thought she knew had been taken over by someone else entirely. Losing him as an ally was more terrifying than anything the jungle had to offer.

"Just put your gun on the ground, Harper. Kick it towards me and hand me the device."

The machine had fallen silent. Whoever was on the other end had given up the call for now.

Zoey stormed up to Ben's side.

"What the hell are you doing?"

"Don't, Zoey," he replied, fixing his gaze on Harper.

Zoey leaned towards the gun. He held her off using his shoulder.

"What are you *doing*?"

She stretched to reach his hand.

He swung an elbow. It cracked into her cheek, knocking the woman to the ground. Her face burned bright red, the top of each cheek glistening as nostrils flared. Zack careered into Ben's waist. He grabbed hold of his left leg and lifted it up. The motion pushed the man half a metre.

Harper rushed towards him.

"Grab his arms!" She yelled at Sam and James, each clasping a limb.

She punched Ben on the nose, took the gun away and tripped his right leg. The four of them fell on top of him. He scrambled to get loose, throwing an elbow. He caught Sam on the chin and swung a free arm at James. Zack caught it and held on long enough for Harper to get grab it too. Zoey stood on one of his legs and pressed down on the other.

"We got you, okay?" Harper insisted, kneeling on Ben's chest.

He continued to wriggle, eyebrows creasing, cheeks flushed. She flipped her weapon, held it by the barrel and smacked him between the eyes.

"Quick, someone tear me up some strips from his overalls."

Zoey frantically pulled at the frayed ends of Ben's trousers, ripping out enough to fashion some rudimentary restraints. Harper stood up and pointed at a nearby tree. "Let's get him up against this one. It will take all of us to hold him. Shermeen, I need you to do something."

They needed to act quickly. Before Ben woke up again.

"I need you to go back to our camp. Where…"

"Back there?" Shermeen asked, diffident.

"Yes, I'm sorry." Harper helped the others heave Ben towards the tree. "I know he's still there, but we need his stretcher. You should be able to lift it on your own."

She exhaled as they continued dragging Ben

through the dirt. Shermeen hadn't moved.

"Go now!"

☆

Shermeen turned and ran, face crumpling under the assault of tears. Her feet crunched and pounded against dirt and roots. As the young girl left the group's line of sight, she tripped over a rock and hit her chin on the ground. Lifting a finger to the bump, Shermeen found blood. She was shaking all over and couldn't lift herself up, fraught with confusion.

Ben had helped organise food and supplies on their first day here. Then he fought off Zack when he'd tried to take some for himself and had volunteered for all the dangerous journeys into the jungle. Ben had also saved their lives on the beach when those people attacked. It just didn't make any sense at all.

"Shermeen!" Harper's voice called through the trees. "Come on, kid. We need that metal."

Shermeen gritted chattering teeth and got to her feet, feeling the pressure.

There was Amos. It was hard not to stare. The bullet had drilled a dark and wet cavity between his eyes, blood oozing profusely from the wound. It dribbled down the nose, exuding into an open mouth and streaming from his chin to chest. The indentation gave the impression that the right eye had been sucked half-way into the crater. Its iris had been blasted into an unnatural position up into the top corner. Shermeen was unnerved by its lack of symmetry with the other, and yet still, she could not look away.

"The metal," Shermeen muttered to herself.

The make-shift stretcher lay discarded next to

him. She leaned in closer to reach it, long enough to see a fly land on the devastated eye and linger.

She dragged the sheet towards herself until it could be lifted up. Harper was right, it wasn't too heavy.

The girl took one last peek at Amos and within moments had returned to the group.

Ben's arms were wrapped around the back of the tree and Zoey was adjusting the material to restrain his feet. He was still dazed, head drooping into his chest.

"Ah good," Harper said as she came over to Shermeen. "You got it. Thank you."

The woman crouched over the metal, brandishing the plasma knife. She sliced through the plating as if it was butter, each side of the incision glowing.

Zoey came over to Shermeen.

"Are you okay?"

Shermeen nodded tentatively.

"Are you sure?" Did you…?"

"Yeah… I'm okay," she said, wiping another tear away. "I promise."

Zoey curled an arm over her shoulders.

Harper completed the first stage of her task, producing a strip roughly seven centimetres wide and thirty long. She passed the knife to James.

"Hold this under the metal. Like a candle."

She balanced the strip on top of the blade for a minute, watching as the middle glowed the same radiant blend of orange and white. Harper slipped it underneath Ben's ankles. As close to the skin without touching it, she twisted the metal into a curl.

She nodded at Sam, who poured out some water. The strip hissed as it locked into a reinforced restraint.

With a deep breath, Harper removed the tie from her pony-tail and pulled back the hair to readjust it.

"Right. Let's find out what's going on here."

✶

Harper slapped Ben's face. His eyes were loose at first, struggling to take in their surroundings. Eventually they cleared and he looked at her. Immediately his head dropped again.

"I'm sorry, okay," he said quietly.

"Sorry for what?" Harper folded her arms.

"It wasn't supposed to be like this."

She kicked his foot.

"Look, Ben, those natives could be on us any minute. We haven't got time for you to be cryptic. You tell us what the hell is going on and then we'll decide whether or not we leave you here to die."

"What do you want to know?"

"Who are you working for and what is your mission?"

"I'm not working for anyone," Ben replied, staring into the mud. Harper kicked him again. He didn't flinch.

"I told you," she said, starting to lose her temper. "We don't have time for this. Who are you working for?"

"I told you. Nobody. I... just want to see my family again."

"What?" Zoey chimed in. "You told me they were dead."

"I lied."

"So your wife..."

"She's dead, that's true." Ben finally lifted his head.

"I would never lie about that. But my kids, my two girls. I did this for them."

Harper crouched.

"Ben, you have to tell us what your mission is."

He started crying, looking each of them in the eye.

"To kill you. All of you."

"But, why?"

"I don't know. They just said that as soon as we landed, I had to kill everyone. I didn't even know the ship was going to crash, I promise."

"Who's they?"

"The colonial programme."

"Why did they want us all dead?" asked James.

"I didn't ask any questions," explained Ben. "I didn't have much of a choice." Harper knew what it felt like to be in that position.

"How were you going to do it?" she asked.

"Poison. They said there would be a stash among the supplies which would only open for my thumb print or something."

"So why didn't you kill any of us?" Harper asked. Zoey leaned in once more.

"You've not tried to hurt anyone since you got here," she added.

"Err. Hello?" Zack pointed at his nose. "What about me?"

Harper stood up and scowled at the man.

"Don't think we've forgotten about Amos." She tossed a gun to James. "Make sure he doesn't do anything stupid."

Zack rolled his eyes as Harper resumed her interrogation.

"Why didn't you kill any of us like you were supposed to?"

"I just couldn't go through with it... I procrastinated. And when we discovered the writing and then... those things... people. Well, I figured we'd have strength in numbers. I'd be better off keeping you alive."

Nobody said anything. Harper looked around the group. They'd taken some serious hits since arriving on Proxima B, but she'd never seen them so downcast.

"Where's the poison now?" she asked.

"In my pocket. I've held onto it this whole time."

Harper leaned in and slipped a hand into the opening he had indicated on his hip. She found a cylindrical medicinal container. The lid was heavy and metallic with small LED bulbs on the side. Harper placed it in her own pocket.

"There's just one last thing I need to ask you about," she said calmly. "Who are those people on the other end of that call?"

"I can't--"

Harper kicked again.

"Yes you can. We need to know now."

"They're my extraction team."

"Extraction? So you had a route home this entire time?"

"Yes."

"How come they didn't show up on the search?" James asked.

"I don't know. Maybe they were cloaked or something."

"Where are they meeting you?" asked Harper.

"I was told they would send a boat to somewhere five miles west from the landing site. Well, the crash site now."

"A boat? So they must have some base out to sea then. Surely there's something in orbit too." James suggested.

"What then?" Harper asked.

"They said they'd take me home," Ben explained. "To my daughters."

She stood up and paced, deep in thought.

"That's our ticket out of here," Harper said, snapping her fingers. Finally, there was something to be positive about. She picked up the device and pushed it into Ben's face.

"You're going to call these people back right now, tell them you've completed your mission and that you're ready for extraction," Harper ordered.

Ben frowned.

"If I turn up with you guys, they're going to kill you and me."

"We'll cross that bridge when we come to it," Harper replied, initiating the call. "You better not give the game away," she threatened, placing the butt of her weapon on his chin. "I won't hesitate to shoot you unless you arrange them to meet you."

Harper hated this but at least it was something she understood. Meeting an enemy face-to-face and taking it down by any means necessary. She felt responsible for not spotting the traitor.

Ben opened his mouth and immediately closed it again. He let out a sigh and nodded.

"Hello?" a voice came from the device. "Cowan is that you?" The man sounded impatient.

"Yeah... it's me." Ben had managed to muster feigned confidence.

"How the fuck did you miss a call you've been waiting on for weeks?"

Ben's eyes looked left and right, and then straight at Harper. She nudged his chin with the gun, raising her eyebrows.

"I was... taking a piss."

"You picked one hell of a time for it," came the reply. "Did you complete your mission?"

"Yeah...," Ben said. "They're all gone. It's just me left." His eyes looked round at the whole group as he lied through the receiver.

"That's good to hear. We can initiate our extraction plan. Crowley will be with you in an hour."

There was a click amongst the static as the call ended.

"Thank you," said Harper as she got to her feet, gathering some things. "Come on guys, let's get going."

"Hey, what about me?" Ben asked. "I did what you wanted."

"You're not coming with us," she said flatly.

"But--"

"You *can't* come with us. I don't trust you. *We* don't trust you. You saw how much effort we all had to put in to stop you just now. If there's a firefight on the other end of that boat, it doesn't matter how good a shot you are, I have no idea if you'll be on our side or not."

"I will, I promise," Ben insisted. "You can't leave me here. Those things! It's different now. I didn't go through with my mission!"

"Only to save your own skin," Zoey spat. "You said it yourself. You only let us live so we'd have enough people against the natives. You *still* had the poison on you, for god's sake!"

"Please," Ben cried. "You have to let me come with

you. I need to see my daughters. I came here for them!"

"No, it's not happening."

The man's face creased and he began to sob uncontrollably.

"And neither are you," said Harper as she turned to Zack. James already had him at gunpoint but she added her weapon.

"Oh come on," he moaned, rolling his eyes again. Pointing at Ben, he continued: "He's the one that was behind this whole thing."

"For goodness sake, Zack," James sparked up before Harper had the chance to. "You just fucking killed Amos and you think what's happened with Ben is going to change any of that? You're both as bad as each other."

"I'm nothing like him," Ben said softly, tailing off.

"Fuck you, Ben," Zack replied.

"Turn around Zack," Harper instructed. "Zoey pass me some more strips."

"You can't do this to me," Zack protested, edging backwards. "It's not humane." James and Harper moved towards him. "Okay, fine leave me behind, but don't tie me up. That's a death sentence!"

"I can't risk you following us." Harper was unmoved. "Not after what you did back there."

Zack swivelled and ran three steps. Sam sprung out and extended his leg, tripping him.

"Ah shit," Zack muffled into the mud. James and Harper arrived in time to pick up the pieces, grabbing his arm and dragging him towards a tree opposite Ben.

"We'll hold his arms, you tie the knots," said Harper to Zoey.

Both outcasts sat face-to-face. Harper considered what might happen if the natives found them. Arguably, leaving them behind was just as cold blooded than just giving each one a bullet. But the other survivors had seen too much, scarred enough already. For the remaining few she could trust, it was kinder not to shoot their former comrades in the head, especially for Shermeen.

Pocketing her weapons and collecting the leftover supplies, Harper adjusted a rucksack on her back.

"Come on everyone, let's move out," she announced, ignoring the desperate cries for help, to reconsider, to come back.

James led the way, red-faced. Zoey, Shermeen and Sam followed him, flinching at the panicked voices they were deserting.

Harper had never left someone to their death before. But if she was going to save what was left of the group, they had to cut their losses. Zack and Ben both posed a threat. This was the only way they could make it to safety.

Peeling her fringe off a sticky forehead and sweeping it to the sides of her head, Harper turned away and followed the others through the undergrowth.

✻

James could hear the familiar sound of waves again. The five remaining survivors had reached the jungle's edge. Through the trees he could see the sand's golden glow and brilliant blue of the ocean sparkling in the sun. According to the portable device's map, this should be the rendezvous location.

"We're here," he called back to Harper. She approached from the rear.

"Good. Let's get into the positions we discussed."

James and Zoey readied their weapons and spread out five metres apart, Harper in between them. She ordered Sam and Shermeen to stand several metres inside the cover of the jungle.

"We have no idea how many of them are coming ashore," Harper explained. "The man on the phone mentioned just one name, so hopefully that's all we have to worry about."

"What if there's more?" James asked.

"Well... then I guess we're screwed." Harper's eyes were firmly aimed at the beach in front of her. She was hiding her emotions well. Clearly even Ben's betrayal could not quite pierce the hard outer-layer. It was almost as if the woman expected to be stabbed in the back.

"Cheery," said James. He paused for a moment. "Did you *want* to talk ab--"

"No," she snapped. "Let's just do our jobs."

James thought about his. He felt the weapon between his hands. All his life, he had been nothing more than a clumsy intellectual. Even his fellow survivors saw it that way until a few days ago. But in that time, he had unravelled the riddle of the Rongorongo and had proved his worth in other ways. Harper trusted him with a weapon now and, even though he'd not used it yet, he drew confidence from the faith shown in him. Focussing on that was the only way to help James process leaving behind Ben and Zack. He peered out to the sea again, looking left and right, unable to spot anything approaching the beach.

Harper holstered her gun.

"Zoey, you keep watch," she said, coming towards

James.

She stood very close.

"I'm sorry, it's just... I'm doing everything I can to shut Ben and Zack out of my brain," she said, dropping the steely façade. "It's fucking hard." Harper's eyes were weak and vulnerable, desperate for validation. James looked around to check if the others had noticed. They hadn't. Zoey was still vigilant, Sam and Shermeen under cover.

"I know," he replied, placing a hand on her shoulder.

"Do you think I did the right thing leaving them behind?"

"I think you did," James said eventually, knowing what she'd want to hear. "We couldn't trust either of them, so they had to go."

"But... I can't help but think I made a mistake."

"Why? You said yourself Zack was the leader of those racists back home."

"Yeah, but he was there when they framed me."

"Framed you?"

Harper hesitated.

"Well, sort of. I did kill that woman." James raised his eyebrows. "No, not like that. It was an accident. It was their fault. The unit that was investigating Zack. They shot me while I was trying to get him. It knocked my aim."

"But what's that got to do with leaving Zack behind? If you were ordered to kill him before, surely he's the type of person you don't try to save."

Harper shuffled on her feet, uncharacteristically indecisive.

"I'm not thinking about the greater good on this one," she began. "I'm thinking about myself for a change. Let's say we are able to hijack this extraction and get ourselves some transport off this planet, where do we go next?"

"I don't know. We agreed the other day it would be risky to go home."

Harper continued as if she had not heard him.

"The way I see it, we have three choices here. Either we head for Proxima A and risk prosecution for breaking A.N. colonisation protocol or we head to one of their countries on Earth and end up in jail too. In either case, our own government won't fight for us. So it's either that or... we go on the offensive."

"How?"

"We go back to London and blow the lid off this whole thing." Harper proclaimed with a gleam in her eye.

"Are you sure that's such a good idea?"

"I don't think we have much choice."

"If that's your move, then why do we need Zack?"

"There hasn't been a night gone by that I haven't thought about killing that woman... Zack is part of it, a piece of evidence in this whole conspiracy. And... well, look, I'm not saying we should do it for me, but... he could help me clear my name. Tell everyone what happened that night and tell them what happened here. Maybe I can get my life back somehow."

"But... he's a scumbag," James said, almost laughing. "You can't trust him."

"Yeah I know," Harper admitted, dropping her head.

"I mean he might not even co-operate once we got him back there."

"Do you think I don't know that?" she snapped. There was an awkward pause. "No matter what you make of him, he lost someone," she continued. "That was *their* fault. Maybe he'd make the right decision."

"But it should have been *him*," James reminded her. "You were sent to kill *him*. You can't trust him. And you've got to remember that to make the case against the IPCP you'd need Ben's testimony too. I'm not sure we can share a trip back to Earth with either of them."

"I know," Harper nodded. "I thought we were done for back there. It took so many of us to stop him."

"Yeah. I'm not sure we want to do that over and over again between here and Earth. We can't put Shermeen through that. You know what, we just can't put her through any of that, the offensive option. Who would we even speak to in London? The press are state-controlled. Nobody would listen to us."

Harper swept some hair away from her souring face.

"I should have seen this coming. Ben, I mean."

"There's no way you could ha--"

"No, I should. I should have known there would be someone else other than the captain to worry about."

"Harper. Seriously. Nobody saw that coming. Don't blame yourself."

"You know I will anyway."

"Just, don't…"

"What?"

"Please don't take this the wrong way," James pleaded. "But don't let that anger force you into making the wrong choice. We can't go back to London, even if we want to make them pay."

"Look," Harper said, walking away a few steps. "We don't have make a final decision on this yet. There's still the matter of getting our hands on some transport first."

"You're right," James said, fiddling with the handle of his gun, pensive. He took a deep breath. "Harper?"

"Yes?" She turned back to face him.

"Why can't we just find somewhere quiet and secluded on Proxima A? Like Choctaw or something? Or maybe we could hide in the American countryside?" He was aware of how desperate he sounded.

"What would be the point in that?" Harper scrunched her nose. James paused a moment.

"Come on, Harper. We all came here to make a fresh start, to build a new life. We've got a chance to do that now. Why can't we take it? Give Shermeen, Zoey, Sam, me... you... a chance at a better life?"

She frowned and scratched the back of her head, uncertain.

"Harper," Zoey hissed. "I can see something."

"We'll finish this conversation later," Harper replied, reaching for her weapon. "Get to your position."

James leaned his shoulder into the bark and peered out onto the beach. Streaming towards them was a small speedboat, piercing the waves and bouncing on the water, leaving behind a rigid wash.

"How many are there?" James asked.

"I can only make out one," Zoey replied.

"Same here," Harper confirmed. "That should make our job much easier."

"What's the plan?" James enquired.

"We have to be ready to use brutal force. I know this is new for you both, but chances are we're going to have you know... I know it sucks, but he's coming here to kill us."

Each of them nodded.

"When he lands, wait for him to get out of the boat. He'll be confused. He was expecting to find Ben, so he should come towards the trees. When he's close enough, you two fire off a shot each. I'll come out from the middle and finish him off. We'll be fine. He won't see us coming."

The low rattle of the boat's engine stuttered to a halt as it slid onto the beach. A tall passenger stood up, revealing a bulletproof vest and combat trousers. A pair of grenades hung from the hip. He jumped onto the sand and leaned back into his boat, pulling out a large assault rifle.

"Damn," Harper whispered.

"What do we do now?" James asked. The sight of the heavy weapon drained him, weakened his knees. He jumped as the new arrival shouted out.

"Ben! Come on mate, where on earth are you?"

The man either had no idea of the dangers here or, if he did, didn't care.

The soldier muttered something and went back to the boat, leaning on the hull.

James had been so focussed on him that he had not Harper was gone, no longer behind her tree. He heard the leaves and branches between him and the beach rustling. His stomach lurched. She was about to emerge on the sand.

James exchanged a lost look across to Zoey, who shook her head and shrugged.

Harper coughed uncontrollably as she pushed her way out of the jungle. She crawled forward and crumpled to the ground.

"Who's there?" the man asked, walking forward and pointing his rifle. "Ben is that you?"

He was standing over Harper's body.

"What the--?" He gently kicked her exposed arm and crouched over the woman.

In an instant, she sprang into action.

The other arm lurched up towards the soldier, accompanied by an orange flash. Harper ignited her blade. It pierced the man's cheek. He let out a horrid scream as he was knocked back. The knife protruded from his face. It burned red with anger. The soldier kicked Harper in the chin, knocking her down, sending her pistol flying.

He reached for his weapon.

Harper swivelled on her hips and rotated her body. She tripped both of his legs. Pushing off her left-arm, she rose to a crouching position and tried to mount the soldier like a wild horse. He stopped her with a forceful knee to the side and a punch to the face.

Harper was pinned to the floor and her attacker aimed his gun.

James burst onto the beach and fired three rounds. Two of them hit the soldier's back. A bullet-proof jacket took most of the force. It was enough to knock him to his knees.

Harper leapt up and yanked the plasma knife out of the soft tissue with her right hand. With the left, she punched him to the ground. Sitting on his chest, she plunged the blade square into his forehead with a grunt. The body went limp. Harper looked at his eyes, saw no movement and flopped on her attacker, exhaling.

"What took you so long?" she said through her exhaustion.

"I've not... you know... before," James replied.

"You... did good," Harper rasped through a hoarse

throat. She sat up and heaved herself off the soldier, removing his grenade belt.

Zoey arrived on the beach.

"What's next?"

"Let's get ready to go," Harper replied, heading towards the boat.

"All of us?" asked James.

"No, only three of us should go," Harper explained, tossing the rifle into one of the vehicle's seats. Carefully placing the grenades on another, she fiddled with the steering column. "Zoey, you stay here with Shermeen. This trip isn't safe enough for her but she's going to need protection while we investigate where this boat came from."

"Got it," Zoey said. "What about Sam?"

"He's going to have to come with us. We might need all the bodies we've got left. Can you go and get him for me?"

"Yep," Zoey returned to the jungle, granting another cursory glance at their slain foe.

Harper was now in the driver's seat, familiarising herself with the controls. James stood next to the boat, tapping his fingers on the hull. Not looking up, she broke the silence.

"What is it, James?"

"Can you please think about what I said?"

"About walking away from all this?"

"Yeah... that."

There was a pause.

"I'll think about it, I promise."

"Thank you. Both for that, and getting me... getting us this far. I thought I was toast when we landed here."

"Well, you just saved my life, so I guess we're some

way to being even." Harper smiled as she tested the propeller.

She noticed Zoey, Sam and Shermeen appear at the treeline. She jumped down and explained the plan.

"We'll come back for you, I promise," she said to Zoey and Shermeen. "Right, James and Sam, help me turn this boat around. Let's find a way off this damned planet."

29

Don flinched at the intense heat searing the back of his neck. He was sprawled against the ridge, bleeding, dizzy and sore. The invading force was still laying down blanket fire with the heat ray. Their blasts ignited the slope below, each shot spraying Don, Gisèle and Orvan with debris. Another crackling flash accompanied the weapon. Don's head ached. Every discharge made it feel as if someone was pulling his brain out through the nose.

"Now what do we do?" Orvan asked, his voice muffled underneath the roar of the British attack. Don was distracted, constantly visualising Chad's death over and over again. A living breathing man one second, a pile of ash the next.

"Can you hear me, old man?" Orvan snapped, clicking his fingers between Don's eyes. "What the fuck are we going to do now?"

"I... don't know."

"We have to warn Alida and Stangl," Gisèle shouted to make herself heard, trying to start up the communication app on her iris monitor.

Stangl's name brought Don's mind back into focus.

"No," he said, grabbing Gisèle's arm. "We don't know if we can trust him anymore."

"Why not?"

"You heard what the Marines said," Don countered. "They're under Stangl's orders not mine... and who knows what else he's asked them to do."

"That may be the case, old man," Orvan interjected. "But those marines might just be our only way out of this mess." He directed Don and Gisèle's attention back to the crater. "Look."

The three of them peered over the edge of the ridge. The British had stopped bombarding the slope and were aiming for the soldiers once again. They had emerged from their hiding place at the base of the ships, spreading out into the middle of the crater.

"They're toast," Gisèle said.

"I wouldn't be so sure," Orvan replied, lifting his head up.

Smurph led the charge away from the weapon, moving in zigzag formation. The British fired off a shot, a pillar of fire erupting a metre or so to Diablo's left. Don heard a faint voice calling over the roar of the heat ray, it was Smurph barking orders.

The weapon fired.

Another miss.

All four soldiers turned and stopped, their own guns ready to fire.

They pulled their triggers in unison. The British weapon was met with a barrage of bullets. They clanged against the funnel, battering it backwards. The force of the marines' attack had pushed the tip up, away from the crater. It fought back like a stubborn cobra.

Smurph and his men gave up. They had perhaps done some blunt force damage, but the weapon was still intact. The end grew orange once again. The soldiers turned to run, fighting through rising columns of heat. Soon, they were back on the slope, climbing upwards. One blast landed close to Flat-top, forcing him to protect his face with a forearm. He let out a howl but pressed on. In quick succession, the marines vaulted the ridge and landed in a sprawled mess near to Don, Gisèle and Orvan.

The weapon fired for a few moments more before giving up. It went deathly quiet, until the distant hum of construction resumed down below.

Don didn't wait for Smurph to get his breath back.

"Still think that was a good idea?" he snapped, voice dripping with anger.

The soldier frowned and focussed his attention on the older man.

"Of course," he said. "If you want to measure intentions of an invading force, the best way to do it is to walk right up to the front door."

"Your idiotic manoeuvre cost the lives of three men," Don countered, rising slowly towards Smurph.

"Replaceable."

"Repla--Are you joking? I thought those men were supposed to be your friends!" Don roared. Smurph just shrugged, sniffing. "Those boneheads of yours might just be two more off the production line but your stupidity down there killed my man."

Gisèle was holding him back. Don knew he couldn't take the behemoth, but by God, he would unload his rage.

"We can conduct an investigation into who is to

blame later, Stafford," Smurph replied, his voice still hauntingly calm. "For now, we've got to come up with a plan to stop these ships. Our own weapons did nothing against that death ray of theirs." The soldier lifted his right arm and clicked open a small hole on the top of his wrist. A thick cloud spurted out, covering Smurph's left arm in a cooling liquid. "We overheated out there before we even left a scratch," he explained, before locking eyes with Don. "I told you we should have been allowed to bring our Teslanium weapons. That thing is impenetrable with regular ammunition. We need something with more kick."

Don tipped his head back. Chad was dead, it was Smurph's fault, but they still had a duty to protect the people of Proxima A. The soldier was right about one thing. They needed to act fast and worry about the blame-game later.

"Let's get the Teslanium in," Don said, softer than before. "If that's alright with you, Orvan?"

"It's not like I have much say in the matter anyway," the Choctaw man replied, half-smiling. "I'm just one man, it's not like I speak for the rest of my people. Besides, we've all seen what the British are capable of. I'd be a fool if I tried to stop you doing everything you can to defeat them."

"Let's make the call, if we can," Don ordered. "Will you do the honours, Gisèle?"

"Yes, sir," she said enthusiastically. The woman's gaze went cold and blue as she tried to contact Arkan City. After a few seconds, normal colour returned.

"Nothing?" Don asked.

"No, sorry. There's too much disturbance up here," she said. "Must be that magnetic field."

"Tell me about it," Don replied, running a hand

over his left leg. It ached under the unseen pressure of the metalwork.

"We'll have to get down the mountain then," Smurph announced, leaning forward to start the descent. Some of his men began to follow suit.

The underground humming ceased

It left an eerie silence in its place.

Smurph looked back over his shoulder.

"Wait," Gisèle said. "Listen. The noise below. It's stopped."

Each remaining member of the party began to look around, ears pricked.

"They must have finished," Orvan surmised.

"Finished what?" Smurph asked.

The ground heaved and shuddered. The ridge lurched up, throwing the group off balance. Everything around them shook.

"What is it?" Orvan shouted over the din.

"Look!" Don replied, pointing to base of the unnatural bowl in the mountainside.

The soft ground at the heart of the crater was moving, gently bouncing up and down like the surface of a trampoline. It groaned and began to crackle, giving way to something large underneath, trying to break free. It sounded metal, clanging as debris began to fall away and bounce against it. A mechanical whine climb up through the growing fissure. Whatever this was, it was charging up, getting ready for something.

Don was hit by a wall of air.

His ears popped.

It fired itself through the surface.

Laying on his back, Don watch a huge black hulk of metal rising upward.

Everything went dark.

*

"I thought we were seeing Auntie Kara," Corinne lamented.

"I'm sorry, sweetheart," Tycho replied, an arm around his daughter. "Another time, maybe."

It had been hard explaining their change of plans to the children. Even with Alida's forces closing in, Tycho would rather distract himself in their innocent company than dwell on the truth. The ship itself was quiet. Too quiet. Usually, there was a background hum of chatter from the crew. With just a skeleton team in place, all Tycho could hear was the rumble of the engines.

"We are coming up on the Choctaw Mountains now, sir," Saldana announced, through the internal communications system. "There's a large area of magnetic disturbance in the target area."

Tycho placed Corinne on the bed.

"Whatever happens, please just stay here," he said on the way out of the door.

Arriving back on the bridge, Tycho's stomach was weighed down like lead. Coming all this way was one thing but to find himself here with Tristen and Corinne made him realise just how selfish he had been. Things would never go back to the way they were after this.

"Thank you," he said to his first officer. The vice admiral stared at the steep cliff edges lining the shore. A thick cloud of black dust hung over one mountain peak. A blot against the leaden sky beyond it.

"What do you think it is, sir?" Saldana asked, adjusting the helm controls. Tycho looked at the scanners, displaying the area as a dark grey smudge. They couldn't register anything up there through all the magnetic disturbance.

"I don't know," Tycho replied eventually. "I just hope to god, it's not dangerous." He lifted up his left hand to double-check and confirmed it was shaking. He reached out and touched Saldana on the arm. "I've been so stupid."

The whole deck jarred to the right.

Tycho slammed into the wall.

Pain erupted in his hip.

He lay there dazed.

He dragged himself to a standing position and he helped Saldana up too.

"What was that?" he asked, stomach sick with dread.

"I don't know, sir," Saldana replied.

A screen on the right-hand control bank flashed red.

"Oh god," Tycho said. "Radiological alarm. Whoever just hit us has nuclear capabilities." He immediately grabbed a handset, excluding his quarters: "All hands, this is the vice admiral speaking," his voice echoed around the entire ship. "All hands to battle stations, I repeat, battle stations. All hands to your positions. We are under attack from a nuclear force, please take the necessary precautions."

Tycho slammed the receiver down and watched as brave men and women scurried across the top deck. They began arming the banks of cannons on each side. Only six of them would be active. He instantly regretted bringing a skeleton crew.

"How well did our shields do against that blast?"

Tycho asked.

"They're at seventy-six percent," Saldana replied.

All of a sudden, the images at the front of the bridge flickered and went dead.

"Damn," Tycho shouted, stepping backwards. "What is it?"

"Our sensors can't see a thing," Saldana replied, frantically fiddling with any control panel that would respond. "Nope," she confirmed. "Too much fall-out."

Tycho dashed for the door.

"We need eyes on what just hit us," he shouted, grabbing a remote handset from the wall.

He raced through the corridor and swung onto the clattering metal steps. There were three flights between here and the nearest entrance to the deck.

The whole ship shook again.

The jolt pushed Tycho into the metal banister.

He instantly thought of the children, knowing they would be terrified, with no idea what was going on.

The best way to protect them was to hit back at the enemy as quickly as possible.

Tycho arrived at the correct hatch, twisted the locking mechanism and heaved it open with his shoulder.

He was hit by the breeze and the smell of sea air. All around, deck hands were picking themselves up. Tycho looked up, dwarfed by the towering bridge structure to his right and the electric blue phenomenon hanging in the sky above it. The heart of the crackling spectacle was bright white, forks of cerulean lightning fizzing out in every direction. The shields were under a lot of strain.

"I'm on deck," Tycho said into his receiver.

"Acknowledged," replied Saldana's crackled voice.

"How are the shields now?" he asked, looking up at the dissipating impact site.

"We're on fifty-seven percent now."

"Not good," Tycho muttered, running forward to get a better view.

He climbed some nearby steps onto the landing platform and spotted it instantly, roughly three hundred metres in front of the Diamond.

Lurking on the coast-line was the haunting silhouette of a huge metallic spider, a bulbous body supported on eight tall legs. The whole machine slowly rose in stature. Soon it stood at thirty metres, its head raised, surveying the scene, eyeing up its prey. On the front were two glowing oval-shaped pods, like the eyes of a demon. There were faint hissing sounds coming from the legs as they carefully moved the machine down the side of the mountain.

"Saldana," Tycho called into the handset. "I've spotted it. There's some huge contraption on the mountain side. It must be the British. Swing the ship around, present the starboard side and redistribute shield power there from the port. That should give us enough protection. Fire all weapon banks now."

"Acknowledged, sir," Saldana replied, her voice immediately sounding over the ship's tannoy system. Tycho held hands over his ears as the Teslanium cannons began to boom.

The powerful magnetic fields inside them propelled the projectile along the metal rails at frightening speed. As the weapons fired, their rounds struck instantaneously. The ANS Diamond battered the side of the mountain, chunks of rock and debris blasting into the air. They created a massive dust cloud, partially obscuring Tycho's view of the enemy.

Five smaller nuclear explosives thudded into the shields.

Tycho felt like his head was going to explode, overpowered by the pounding of the Diamond's guns and the electrical disturbances occurring overhead. One erupted close to one of the starboard guns, the disturbance shorting out the circuits inside it. Two sailors, a male and a female, jumped away from the structure as the cannons deactivated. Tycho ushered them towards him, where the landing platform provided some cover.

The handset chirped.

"What is it?" Tycho asked, pressing his ear against the speaker.

"Shields are critical, sir. Fifteen percent," Saldana announced.

"Damn it, we won't take much more of this," he shouted over the racket. "Another impact and we'll lose shields entirely."

Looking up, Tycho could see some of the smoke was clearing around the enemy machine.

It was still fully operational!

"What?" Tycho rasped through a contorted face.

How had the British machine survived the Teslanium onslaught? The power behind the Diamond's weapons should have ripped it to shreds.

It stood still for a second.

He prayed the attack was over.

The front six legs of the machine crouched slightly, taking the weight. The two at the back curled up behind, each like the tail of a Scorpion ready to puncture its victim. The tips at the end began to glow a faint green, growing in intensity. The lights pulsated sharply and propelled two beams towards the ship. They travelled with a thunderous rip.

"Get down," Tycho yelled to the two nearby sailors.

He threw himself to the floor, one of them joined him.

The woman made a mad dash for the hatchway.

The two rays fizzed across the deck.

It sliced through shield, metal and flesh as if they were paper.

Tycho lurched forward to save the crew-woman. She was torn asunder in front of him. Cauterised flesh and blood sprayed across his face like confetti, thick and sodden.

Twice more the enemy machine fired off its fearsome weapon. Tycho covered his ears each time. If he didn't they might pop. He waited for the next rounds to fire. As they dissipated, he leapt up.

Tycho ran for the hatchway.

He made it.

Escaping the din, the ship's commander contacted Saldana on the handset.

"Get us out of here," he called. "Instruct the rear gunners to aim below the machine. If we can't destroy that thing, let's trip it up."

She obeyed immediately.

Tycho felt the ship underneath him slide to one side as the ship began to move away. He dashed up the stairs heading for the commander's quarters, hoping the children were still there.

Tycho burst into the room.

Corinne screamed.

"Daddy, you scared me," the young girl said as she wrapped her arms around him tightly, sobbing into his legs. She dropped Zainab the elephant on the floor.

"What's going on out there, dad?" Tristen asked. Tycho was overcome with guilt as he noticed that even his son had tears in his eyes.

"I'm so sorry, children," he said softly, as the ship shuddered with a distant bang. "This is all my fault."

The three of them were knocked to their feet.

Books flew off the shelf.

The bathroom mirror slipped off the wall.

It smashed on the floor.

"We've got to go," Tycho announced, grabbing each child by the arm. "The bridge is the most heavily fortified section of the ship. Let's go!" A man possessed, he dragged Tristen and Corinne towards the door.

"No, daddy!" the young girl wailed, weighing him down. "Wait, daddy!"

"What is it?!"

The young girl stretched for Zainab. The soft toy was a few metres away.

"We've got to go!" he yelled, giving her another yank.

Corinne broke away.

She stumbled towards the elephant.

"What are you doing?" Tristen complained as the young girl picked it up.

"Let's go," Corinne shouted as she made it back to her father.

Tycho pulled the children into the corridor.

Both of them slipped as another blow shook the vessel.

Tycho leant down and grabbed each one by the waist.

He broke into a sprint.

The trio crashed onto the floor of the bridge, amid another barrage from the enemy shifted the ship underfoot.

"Thank god, you're okay," Saldana said when she noticed them.

"Well done kids, you did great," Tycho said, rubbing each one by the hair. You huddle under there." He pointed to an unmanned control desk towards the back of the room. Tristen and Corinne were hooked on his every word and did exactly as they were told.

"How are we looking?" Tycho asked Saldana.

"We've lost five of the starboard gun turrets and from what I can see, we've got maybe a dozen puncture holes in that side of the ship."

"How far away are we now?"

"Looks like seven hundred metres and counting," Saldana revealed, eyes glued to the navigational dials.

"Good. Any luck getting the visuals back up?"

"I was about to try again. I've just rebooted the system," Saldana explained. "Here we go," she added.

Of the six-strong bank of screens, one flickered back into life, revealing the enemy machine still on the mountainside. Below it was a thick cloud of debris.

"Looks like we've been able to chip away at its foundations," Tycho noted. "Let's concentrate our fire. We should be able to feed some co-ordinates to them now," he added.

Saldana passed the command back to the gunners via the nearest handset. The Diamond's guns sparked into life once more. The ship shook again. More of the hull was sliced open by the enemy.

The smoke around the machine continued to

grow, but the top of it was still visible. It started to wobble, shaking from side to side. Another barrage of Teslanium pounded into the rocks and it finally gave way. The giant spider lost its footing and tumbled down the slope, crashing into the beach with a tremendous boom.

Tycho let out a cheer of celebration and relief. Saldana leaned over and embraced her commander. The vice admiral went over to the children, placing a caring hand on each of their cheeks.

"We should be okay for now," he said. The control panel beeped. "What is it?"

"We've got an incoming transmission," Saldana explained.

"Point of origin?"

"Looks to be coming from the mountains, sir."

Tycho raced over to take the call.

"Vice admiral Sean Tycho, ANS Diamond," he said.

The voice on the other end was crackly but Tycho was still able to make out what they were saying. He'd recognise that voice anywhere.

"This is New Boston D.O.D. operative Donald Stafford. We require urgent assistance."

Don's team had seen the whole thing. Collecting themselves from the crater's initial blast, they watched on in disbelief as the British unleashed an attack on the approaching Atlas Nations vessel, holding its own and doing considerable damage before stumbling down into the water.

Once the machine had fallen, the pressure on Don's leg had eased a little. The magnetic field had weakened. It wasn't enough to allow Gisèle to contact New Boston, but just enough for him to make a scratchy call to the A.N. vessel.

"What did he say?" Gisèle asked him.

"Tycho said he'd scramble a short-range Y-Class shuttle up here," he answered. "But we'll have to move down the mountain pretty quick. He daren't send one in as close this," Don added, nodding towards the crater.

"How many are gonna fit in one of those?" Smurph questioned.

"That's a good point," Don replied, scratching his cheek. "Not many."

"That's fine," the soldier answered, busy tinkering with his enhancements. "I'll stay up here with Flattop and Scissorhands."

"Are you sure that's safe?" Don countered, not that he was hugely concerned for the man.

"Probably not," Smurph said. "But someone's got to keep an eye on these bastards."

"He's right, Donald," Orvan said. "We have to hold the British here, by any means necessary. Once we're closer to Peakwood, we can call in for Teslanium reinforcements and equip Smurph with what he needs."

Don raised his eyebrows and conceded.

"Diablo will go with you Stafford," Smurph added. "He'll make sure you get back to Peakwood safely. Pathfinder is there too."

"Thanks," Don replied.

Smurph turned to the red marine and exchanged a few quiet words with him. Diablo nodded and led the way back down the mountain, Don, Gisèle and Orvan doing their best to keep up. The older man needed support but only Gisèle was offering him any. The two of them slipped and slid down the slope, grit and stone creeping into their boots. Once on more stable ground, the group broke into a jog. Don was still smarting at the knee but his ankle was feeling much better the further away they found themselves from the crater.

They all jumped as something roared over them, swinging round a ledge. It was the Diamond's shuttle, a long, rectangular shape with a sleek blacked-out cockpit at the front. The craft fired its retros and slowly descended, landing with a whoosh.

The side of the shuttle lifted open, revealing two rows of seats. Don immediately crashed into the nearest chair, Gisèle next to him. Orvan and Diablo opted to remain standing, holding onto overarm handrails.

The pilot closed the door and leaned back as the ship took off.

"Welcome ladies and gentlemen," he said. "My name is Sergeant Ricketts. Where would you like me to take you?"

"Peakwood," Don announced. "The people there are in danger."

"You're the boss," Ricketts replied as he laid in the course.

Orvan turned round to face Don. He could have sworn the Choctaw man was trying to hide a smile.

"Ricketts has picked them up, sir," Saldana announced.

"Excellent," Tycho replied, sat a few feet away, a

child either side of him.

The ANS Diamond had made good progress away from the Choctaw Mountains. Its commander hoped the British ship truly was out of commission for the time-being. The fact that it stood up to Teslanium weaponry was deeply concerning.

"You know, I still can't believe that was the British," Saldana announced.

"Why's that?" Tycho asked.

"I suppose... Well, I knew they were supposed to be overstepping their mark, but I didn't expect that level of firepower."

Tycho didn't have much to add. Since he arrived on Proxima A, he'd left Earth politics behind.

"All we need to know is they're dangerous," he said, kissing the top of Corinne's head. She looked up at him, the contrast of hues in her eyes adding to her innocence. "But we're safe, for now. At least until we can call for back-up."

"How are we going to do that? Given our... situation," asked Saldana.

"We'll make it work," Tycho replied, confidence restored. "There will trouble when we get back but we're the only ones who have fought the British so far. That should count in our favour."

The scanners beeped again, bringing tension back to the bridge.

"What is it?" Tycho snapped.

"Missiles, three of them," Saldana announced. "They're coming from the British crater."

"Target?" Tycho asked, fearing the worst.

"Calculating now," the first officer replied. It felt like an eternity as she pored over the data in front of her. "It's not us," she revealed. "They're on a trajectory for that village at the foot of the mountains."

"Peakwood? What strategic advantage does that place represent?"

"What do we do?" she asked.

"What do you mean?"

"Well," Saldana stuttered. "It's a Choctaw settlement," her meaning evident.

"I'm not going to sit around and let innocent people die," Tycho replied, standing up. "Kids, wait here," he said, rubbing each of them on the shoulder.

"What's the plan?" Saldana asked.

"Start configuring the trajectory of those missiles into the port cannons. We've got to knock them out of the sky."

"Yes, sir."

✫

"Watch out people," Ricketts announced to the shuttle crew, making some adjustments to the ship's flight path. "We've got company."

He flicked a switch, revealing a viewing screen on the ceiling. Flying overheard was the unmistakable view of a missile.

"What's the target?" Don asked.

"According to the vice admiral, they're inbound for Peakwood."

"What?" Orvan asked angrily. "You better get us there in time. We need to evacuate."

"Easy now, chief," Ricketts replied. "I'm going at full speed."

The whole shuttle shuddered. Something flashed past one of the ports.

"What was that?" Don asked.

"That, Mr Stafford, was retaliation," Ricketts answered. "The ANS Diamond has fired interceptors."

"The Atlas Nations ship?" Orvan asked.

"The very same," Ricketts confirmed.

There were two explosions in the distance.

"Looks like we got them," the pilot revealed. "Oh shit," he added, veering the ship off to one side.

"What's wrong?" Orvan barked.

"We've been spotted, we've got incoming. Six more missiles on their way."

"Can you shake them off?" Gisèle asked.

"In this thing? Probably not," Ricketts replied. "This is a passenger transport. Not built for serious evasive manoeuvres."

"What was it doing on one of your combat vessels then?" Orvan asked. It was the first time Don had heard panic in his voice for years.

"I'm sorry buddy, but we've not been at war for some time. We're not exactly at full capacity over here."

"I can see that," Diablo said, making a rare appearance in conversation.

The viewing screen was filled with the forest as the shuttle emerged over a small peak.

"We're nearly there," Ricketts said. "We might have a chance if I can lose that missile in the trees."

"In the trees?!" Gisèle shouted.

"It's either that or a direct hit, lady," Ricketts announced. "All hands brace for turbulence," he added. Orvan plugged himself in next to Gisèle but Diablo retained his standing position, hooking both hands into the rails.

The shuttle swept down bringing the forest much closer.

The tips of trees started to bash against the hull underneath.

Through the view screen, Don watched as three missiles streaked ahead of the pack.

A larger one flew into the trio out of nowhere, destroying two of them. More protection from the Diamond. A patch of forest instantly burst into flames. Ricketts swerved the craft towards the inferno.

"What are you doing?" Orvan asked.

"Those things are heat-seekers. That forest fire is the only thing that will save us now," Ricketts shouted. "Hold on tight."

The ship hurtled towards the blaze.

A surviving missile careered into Peakwood.

The main street erupted.

Fire leapt from house to house.

The shuttle rattled as it sped towards the ball of fire.

Don tensed.

It crashed.

★

Don was startled by the sparking of electrical circuits. He snapped back into consciousness. The ship was on fire. But they had made it. Just.

Ricketts was keeled over in the pilot's seat. He groaned quietly, blood pouring from his head and shoulder, right arm missing.

Don grunted, his body stiff. Gisèle was still in her seat, leaning forward, breathing heavily. Orvan was face down on the floor in front of them. Diablo was gone.

An almighty crash sounded to the left. Don

flinched. He looked straight through a gaping hole in the shuttle. A doorway into the forest. The vegetation slowly tickled with flame. There was another crash as a tree toppled. The smell of burning bark travelled high up Don's nose, reviving him further.

He lifted an arm to release each seating strap and hauled himself to a standing position. Gisèle was starting to come around.

"What... happened?" she asked, eyes all over the place.

"The pilot saved our lives," Don groaned, pulling Gisèle towards him. "We've got to get out of here."

"Did the others make it?"

"I'm not sure," Don said slowly supporting the woman, whose feet were dragging. "Come on Gisèle," he huffed.

The two of them stumbled out of the shuttle. They struggled to find their footing on the hard roots.

"Careful," Don advised. "Look where you're going," he added.

Soon they could see through a gap in the trees. They were on the outskirts of Peakwood. Everything was on fire. Don heard cries of distress. Women and children were screaming. Confusion reigned supreme.

"We've got to help them," Gisèle said with increased vigour.

"Ah good, you're back," Don replied, relieved. "Can you contact that ship? We're going to need more shuttles."

"I'll try," she answered, opening a call as she and Don sped towards the main street. "No good, Donald," Gisèle said eventually. "It doesn't look like a signal problem, I think my circuits were damaged in the crash."

"I'll give my handset a go."

Don pulled out a small communicator from his pockets, rushing the buttons.

"Vice admiral Tycho," the navy man said through the speakers.

"Tycho, this is Stafford. Your man got us down the mountain but we're pretty banged up. British missiles have hit Peakwood. Can you spare more shuttles and a medical crew? We have to save these people."

"I'll send what I can," Tycho replied. "But we're pretty light on medical staff. This was a skeleton crew mission."

"Anything will do," Don replied. "Sending my coordinates to you now. Tell your pilots to be careful, Tycho. This British firepower is pretty serious," he added, ending the call.

The two of them arrived in the main street, transformed into the gates of hell.

"Watch out!" Gisèle yelled, pointing upwards.

Another missile thudded into the ground nearby. It landed near the Nyusha farm. The force of explosion knocked them both over. Screams rose from one of the houses on the main road.

"There's people still in there!" Don called out, standing up. "Come on, let's go."

They arrived on the doorstep. Don crouched to avoid the burning wood above. Just a few inches inside the doorway was a woman and child. The mother was pinned under a fallen timber. Her son toiled to set her free. Don studied their faces briefly. It was the pair who had hurled abuse just days before.

"Come here, kid," Don yelled, holding his arm out,

feeling the heat.

He wasn't sure if the boy had heard him.

Far overhead, the British missiles and Diamond interceptors were still locked in a deafening artillery war, painting the sky a brilliant flashing red.

"Not without my mother!" the child replied, with equal gusto required to make himself heard.

"We'll help you," Gisèle explained, dashing through the doorway and putting her weight under the wood.

Don pulled the child out of the gap, still protesting. The mother was free. The boy calmed down.

Emerging from the crumbling building, Don looked to the right. Already, survivors were gathering on the plain where he and the team had landed a few days ago.

A roaring noise blared above Don.

He looked up, fearing the worst.

Squinting and shielding his eyes, he was blinded by the floodlights of a trio of shuttles.

"Look!" Don called out. "We'll get you out of here," he said to the mother and child.

The foremost shuttle exploded.

All four of them were thrown to the ground. Large chunks of metal scythed through the air towards them. Don felt the heat on his back, crouching around the young boy. The ship, now a metallic husk, burning up, crashed into a house. The other two shuttles had survived the impact.

An explosive blast flew between them, curiously low to the ground.

Don had expected the attack on the shuttle to be coming from above, perhaps a rogue missile creeping through Tycho's covering fire. The veteran and Gisèle exchanged a concerned glance.

"That didn't come from the mountains," said Don. "That came from inside Peakwood!"

"Donald, look!" Gisèle said, pointing to the tree-line.

Crouched between two trees was Diablo, steely-eyed, re-loading his rocket-propelled weapon and preparing a shot for the other shuttle.

"What the hell?" cried Don, his blood like ice.

Two women and a man stumbled out of a nearby burning building out into the space in front of Diablo. The soldier pulled out his small fire-arm and shot all three of them in the head. Quick and methodical. Then he aimed another grenade at one of the shuttles, damaging it on landing.

"We've got to stop him," Don yelled as he made his move.

"Don, no! You can't!" Giselle called after him. "Path-finder must be here somewhere too!"

Don pulled out his own weapon and started firing.

Diablo reacted quickly, detaching his metallic back-pack and using it as a shield. He threw it at Don.

The older man took the full force of Diablo's swing in his chest, knocked to the ground.

The red soldier stood up and drew. Three shots fired. Don felt for the wounds. There were none.

He looked up to see Diablo inspecting with three dents in his right arm. Gisèle put out her hand.

"We do it together," she said, hauling him to his feet.

The woman picked up Diablo's back-pack and placed in front of Don.

"Here use this," she instructed. "I'll keep him moving."

Don crouched behind the bulk and peppered Diablo's legs with shots.

Gisèle ran around the soldier in a semi-circular pattern, unleashing her clip. She dove behind a tree to reload.

Diablo moved closer to Don, who pulled his protection backwards along the ground.

The soldier smashed down hard.

He just missed the top of Don's head.

Gisèle re-emerged from cover and caught the soldier in the shoulder. The bullet simply bounced off the skin. He pulled away from Don.

With his back turned, Don took his chance. All around him were sharp pieces of bark, splintered in the firefight. He picked two up. He ran at Diablo as fast as he could. Don sunk both into the soldier's side.

Diablo smacked back with his elbow.

Don fell to the ground dazed. The backpack landed on his ankle, pinning him to the floor.

Diablo bore down on him, ignoring Gisèle.

"No!" she yelled, running towards the enemy.

A large grey arm swung at her head.

It connected with a crack.

The woman was dumped on the ground unceremoniously.

She lay there still.

Pathfinder emerged from behind the nearest building and gave Diablo a nod.

Don stared the red soldier in the eye. Behind him was an array of burning trees.

"Why?" Don asked, pitifully.

"It's nothing personal, Stafford," Diablo replied. "Just following orders."

A weapon was held up to Don's face.

He glanced at Gisèle's motionless body.

The Bloodaxe of Choctaw stared down the barrel of Diablo's gun.

He thought of Sally.

One last time.

His ears were punctured by a stiff slice.

Diablo's face erupted in a pool of blood.

Don looked up at the blade protruding through one of the eyeballs.

The soldier didn't even scream.

He was dead in an instant.

The huge body fell backwards.

Orvan huffed as he caught the man and held him upright. The Choctaw chief fiddled with the back of Diablo's forearms, muttering to himself. With some fingers wriggled into the mechanism, he held it up again. Pathfinder didn't have time to react.

Orvan triggered the chain-gun setting.

The grey soldier's face and chest were peppered with bloody holes.

Both marines slumped to the ground.

"Let's get out of here, Donald," Orvan said, holding out his hand. "Looks like we've got ourselves another war."

★

"You care to explain what I've just been told?" Alida raged at Stangl. She had raced to his office the second Don had made the call. Peakwood lay in ruins, partially as a result of the British attack, but the marines sent into Choctaw by the Atlas Nations had helped finish the job.

"What's that, Alida?" Stangl replied, somewhat irritated. He was half-way through a ghastly smelling

481

egg sandwich. "I thought we were on the same page once again," Stangl added.

"Are you joking?" the council leader roared.

The wrinkled old man just shrugged his shoulders, none-the-wiser.

"Really? You want to play it that way?"

More stunned silence.

"I've just heard from Don Stafford and Gisèle Etienne. They were in Peakwood helping evacuate the locals from a British attack when two of your marines joined in the attack." Alida was in full swing now, hands and arms flailing. "They slaughtered innocent men, women and children there, Lothar. What the hell is going on?"

"What happened to the marines?"

"What happened to them? They're dead. Our team had to put them out of action."

Stangl leaned back in his chair, fiddling with his thick-rimmed spectacles.

"I was hoping you wouldn't find out this way," he said eventually, placing his glasses back onto his bony nose.

"Find out what?"

"It was a perfect plan, really," he added.

Alida was momentarily lost for words.

"To be honest, I thought you'd be on board with the idea given the problems the Choctaw have caused you down through the years."

"What in damnation is that supposed to mean?" It's two decades since conflict ended with those people. What's the point in slaughtering them?"

"Just think of how many lives will be saved this way," Stangl continued, oblivious. "Atlas Nations lives, remember. We could avoid full-scale war with the Choctaw by wiping them out quickly and blaming it on the British."

"Why do we have to wipe them out at all?!"

"They've been leeching off that land for decades. It's about time it was put to proper use. It's good land."

"The Choctaw were handed that land as recompense, remember?"

"The land is wasted on them. It is rich and fertile but their lack of technology means they can never realise its potential. Atlas Nations cities both on Earth and Proxima A are full to the brim. They need to alleviate their population problems. Where better to do that than in Choctaw?"

Alida staggered backwards, hands on her head.

She snapped back to Stangl, another thought popping into her head.

"Won't blaming this on the British cause that war you were so desperate to avoid?" she added, short of breath.

"War with the British was always inevitable, Alida," Stangl replied, voice dripping with cynicism. "This way we can strike first without appearing to be the aggressors. The Atlas Nations would have heard how the British obliterated our troops and an entire Choctaw city in one fell swoop. That would have triggered maximum response from the A.N. war council." Stangl shook his head. "It looks like your man Stafford has messed things up now."

"Isn't that such a shame?" Alida sarcastically jibed. "You haven't heard the end of this, Stangl." She paced a few more steps.

Two tall men appeared at the doorway.

"What's this about?" Stangl asked.

"You're not calling the shots here anymore, Stangl," Alida said flatly. She nodded at the two security guards. "I can't have you messing up my planet anymore. I'm placing you under arrest."

"What?" Stangl roared as he was lifted out of the chair. "You can't do this."

"I don't care anymore, Lothar."

"If you do this," Stangl paused for breath. "If you do this, the Atlas Nations will... they will consider this an act of war!"

30

"You've been following me?" Wash was baffled. "And who the hell is this?" he asked motioning towards the man pointing a gun at him.

"Put the gun down," Vicky said, moving towards its wielder. She stood too close to the man for Wash's liking. "Sebastien, put it down," she repeated herself, placing a hand on his arm.

Wash had never seen the man before. It was hard to tell in the dingy confines of the ship, but he appeared to be a similar age to Wash, with slightly darker complexion and medium-length wavy black hair. Both Vicky and Sebastien were wearing black from head to toe, some kind of stealth gear.

"How can you be sure he hasn't been compromised?" Sebastien asked, piercing eyes bearing down. The man spoke with a deep voice that housed a confused blend of a south London accent and a continental undertone. Perhaps French or Belgian.

"Believe me," Vicky replied with a short glance back at Wash. "I know."

"If you say so," Sebastien said eventually, holstering the weapon.

Wash had absolutely no idea what to say. He stood there like an idiot for a few moments longer before finding enough energy.

"What the fuck is going on?" he asked Vicky. "And who is this?"

The young woman removed her gloves and came over to Wash.

"Are you alright?" she asked.

"Yeah I'm *fine*," Wash said, backing away as Vicky tried to embrace him.

She looked down for a moment.

"I should have told you sooner, I'm sorry."

"Told me what?" Wash's lungs felt like they were going to pop.

"Sebastien and I have been investigating the IPCP for the last year."

"What?" Wash asked, eyes flickering between Vicky and the man with her. "Who for?"

"The Atlas Nations," she said. Wash took one step backwards, mind whirring backwards.

"So... does that mean? When we," Wash stopped just as he pointed at the two of them. "Did you use me?" he asked quietly.

Vicky pulled the journalist to one side, further away from Sebastien, who was muttering to himself, impatient.

"At first, yes. I'm really sorry," she said, putting her hands on him.

Wash shrunk away.

"Get off," he said quietly, eager to keep Sebastien out of this conversation.

Vicky's eyebrows curled. She tucked some hair behind her ear.

"I know it sounds stupid but I promise you I only took things to another level when..."

Wash glossed over her explanation, brimming with questions.

"Why did you choose me? And how could you possibly know I'd be the one to uncover this story?"

Vicky hesitated.

"We needed someone predisposed to digging deeper and asking the awkward questions," she explained. "I know what you're like Wash, you should be flattered by that."

"Flattered that I got to be used for some A.N. spook mission? Are you joking? And, how did you know a story about a gay vicar would get me here?"

"We had our suspicions already but your position at the paper and your connection with Declan Fitzhugh were too good to be true," said Sebastien.

"I didn't ask you," Wash snapped, throwing the man a dirty look. "How can I trust you now?" he asked, turning back to Vicky. His voice broke more than he wanted it to.

"Are you going to need a minute?" Sebastien asked, condescending.

"What do you mean, a minute?" Wash could feel his blood boil in his veins. "I've just been told my girlfriend is a spy and she's been using me to find out government secrets and you want me to take a minute?" he rasped. "Fucking hell."

"Oh for god's sake, don't be such a pussy," Sebastien countered, taking a step towards him. As more of his handsome face came into view, Wash could not help but feel intimidated by the man. He was roughly the same height but had a much more athletic build and was clearly more experienced in this arena than

Wash. "Surely you knew what sort of world you were getting into when you started on this path. Double-crossing girlfriend or not."

Wash couldn't find the words to reply.

"Thanks Sebastien," Vicky said sarcastically. "Comments like that are hardly going to help with trust are they?"

He rolled his eyes again.

"Oh come on Vick, trust has never been one of your strong suits." Wash didn't like how familiar the two were with each other.

"Oh shut up, Sebastien," Vicky snapped, embarrassed. "We have work to do."

"Finally, someone is talking some sense," he replied. "We need everything you found tonight."

"Who's we?" Wash replied, still on the defensive.

"I told you," Vicky answered. "The Atlas Nations."

"How do I know that's who you're working for?"

"Oh don't be stupid," Sebastien chimed in. "Do you think if Vicky was with the British government you'd have made it this far?" Wash tried to avoid eye contact. "You've spent enough time here to know you can trust this woman," he pressed home.

Wash didn't know where to look. There was a time when he would have done anything to be involved in something like this. Now that he had got what he wanted, he regretted ever pushing against those in power. This was shit. Worse than the guilt and shame his father used to make him feel. Wash would take that over the current situation every time. Declan was dead, he had no way of knowing whether Jay had met the same fate, his colleagues had been taken and now he'd been duped by his closest ally.

"Take it easy," Vicky said. "I'll handle this." She

leaned in and put her hand on Wash's face. "You can trust me, okay?" The woman leaned in and kissed him on the lips. It was hard not to reciprocate.

Wash caught a glance of Sebastien rolling his eyes and backing off to one of the side terminals.

"Look, we need to talk about our present situation," he said, addressing the room. "We know the government are moving this ship into position but we don't know where it's going to be launching from, what its destination is or when we're going to have company."

Vicky turned to Wash, eyes wide, serious.

"We really need whatever you found back there," she said.

"Did you bring the original paperwork?" Wash asked. Vicky nodded. "Good, because I think that's the only way we're going to decipher what I found."

"What do you mean?" Sebastien asked, concerned.

"Well, the information Declan led me to was just more numbers." He paused. "I'm sorry but I don't understand any of it."

"Let me have a look at it," Sebastien said, sounding more confident this time.

"What makes you so sure you'll have more luck?" Wash asked, still on the guarding against this inconvenient new acquaintance.

"I don't need to prove myself to you, kid. Just hand it over."

Wash looked to Vicky for reassurance, she nodded. He pulled the memory stick from his pocket.

Sebastien produced a small laptop and placed it on one of the work stations. Plugging it into the machine he began working.

Wash and Vicky stood next to each other in silence, neither one sure how to break the ice. He was sure they were both relieved once Sebastien began speaking.

"I knew it," he said, half under his breath.

Wash and Vicky moved towards him.

"What is it?" she asked.

"I was right," he repeated himself, still looking down. After a few moments' pause, he stood up, bringing the piece of paper with him.

"These numbers confirm it," he said pointing to some of the paperwork.

"I'll take your word for it," Wash replied, half laughing.

"Confirm what?" Vicky asked, more focussed.

"You remember when I was talking about the fuel?"

"Yes," she said. Wash wondered when the two of them had been speaking about that. He kept quiet.

"I thought they couldn't have had enough for a journey to the Proxima system," Sebastien explained. "Not even close." After another pause, he continued, locking eyes with Wash: "Do you have anything else?" The man was in his element and the journalist felt dwarfed by him. He'd done all the legwork on this from the start and Sebastien was finishing it off.

"Well... yeah," he fumbled, pointing at the device. "I put some other information in another folder. But I don't know what any of it means."

"Did you manage to find transponder information?"

"Honestly, I don't know."

Sebastien sat down again in a huff and started sifting through the files on the device, frantically clicking away.

Wash finally brought himself to look at Vicky. His perception of the woman had been completely turned on its head in the last few minutes. She offered a smile. It didn't help as much as he thought it would.

"Ah, here we go," Sebastien announced triumphantly. "Now all I need to do is input the code into the..." his voice trailed off into indiscernible murmurings. Then he stopped to stare at the screen for a few seconds. The man's eyes grew wide as his mouth slowly opened. He ran both hands along the sides of his hair. "Oh my god."

"What is it?" Vicky leaned over his shoulder. Sebastien responded by twizzling the screen around so that both of them could see.

"Watch this," he said, pointing at the screen. "This is the Concord's every location for the last four weeks."

On the display was a red circle pulsating somewhere on the south west coast of England. Then it started moving. Wash and Vicky watched the flightpath of the ship, depicted as a constantly extending red line. It propelled away from the Earth and performed one loop of the planet before shooting off in the direction of the Moon. Once the Concord had reached the natural satellite, it wound around the dark side before leaving orbit.

"What the hell?" Wash could not believe his eyes.

The line was now returning in the direction it had first travelled, back towards the Earth. After re-entry, it stopped dead somewhere in the Pacific Ocean. A message in red flashed across the screen.

[DATA STREAM ENDED]

"I don't get it," said Wash, looking to Sebastien for

answers.

"Don't you see? The colonial ship never made it to Proxima B. Oh my god. They haven't even left our solar system. Look, they're still on Earth!"

★

Harper, James and Sam had been on the boat for nearly an hour, practically deafened by the roar of the engine chopping through the waves. It was a small price to pay for the heavenly breeze that swept over the vehicle's passengers. After such a long time cooped up in a hot and sticky environment it was a welcome change.

The evening had been dazzling bright when they left but as the beach grew increasingly smaller behind them, the sky had given way to a beautiful orange and plum sunset.

Visibility was dropping by the minute and James had voiced his concerns to Harper more than once. They had followed the soldier's route away from land but had found nothing. Even the portable device Harper brought with them was showing nothing on its screen.

"What do we do?" James asked.

"Yeah we can't stay out here much longer, Harper," Sam added. "If we don't know how to get back to the beach we could get stuck out here."

Harper, sat at the wheel, turned off the engine and adjusted her legs as the boat lost its speed and sank lower into the water. She inspected the device between her legs one last time, uncertain what to do next.

"It's not like we can call for directions either," she lamented.

"Does this vehicle have some kind of distress signal we can send?" James wondered. "Something anonymous? They can't know it's us and not Ben."

Sam moved to the back of the boat and started fiddling through some small boxes.

"I can't see anything on the control panel," Harper explained.

"Does it have a radar?" James asked.

"Doesn't look like it..." Harper said, having another look through what was in front of her.

"Hey, I've found something," Sam revealed. By now, Harper could barely see him. She turned up the screen brightness on her device, illuminating the three faces. Sam held out a flare gun.

"That might do, you know," Harper said, scratching her face. She checked the chamber had a round in it. "The man on the phone said it'd take nearly an hour for their man to reach the beach. We can't be far away now. Surely if we fire this, they'll see it, realise we need directions and send up one of their own."

"I haven't got any better ideas." James shrugged his shoulders.

"Yeah go for it," said Sam.

"Let's just remember," Harper warned, "that when we fire this thing, they'll know where we are. I'm sure they won't be welcoming when they realise what's happened."

Neither man said anything for a second, until James spoke up.

"After everything we've gone through, we can't back out now," he said.

Harper took a few steps away from James and Sam, pointing the gun upward. She pulled the trigger, releasing a flashing and fizzing trail of light into the sky. It listed lazily to the right and petered out in a matter of seconds.

"Now we wait," Harper said.

"What if they didn't see it?" Sam asked.

"Then we'll just have to hope we have enough juice left in this thing to get back to dry land," she replied.

"Where a horde of natives are trying to kill us."

"Yeah…" Harper replied. "There…"

It had been nearly a minute now and there was no form of reply. Harper allowed herself to give into the chill coursing through her veins. She realised how lonely the three of them were on the wide expanse. The fact that they could barely see any of their surroundings added to the eerie atmosphere. The sea water licked gently at the hull of the boat.

Harper sighed and looked down, disappointed but not surprised.

Something in the distance bathed the boat in an apricot glow.

"Harper!" James called. "Up there!"

She looked up and saw off in the distance a flare in response.

"Yes!" she shouted. "There they are!"

Harper stifled her smile, remembering the sobering task that faced them up ahead.

James leaned in and put his arm around her. She greeted him with a kiss on the cheek.

"Let's go get them," he said.

Pulling away, Harper returned to the steering column and punched the boat back into motion.

"You guys ready?" Harper yelled over the roar of the resumed propellers.

The two of them nodded their heads. James was in possession of his pistol and Sam now wielded Ben's.

Next to Harper was Crowley's assault rifle and pair of grenades.

"Remember, we've got the element of surprise here. We need to make the most of it. I'll use the grenade to distract them, then you litter them with shots when they're looking the other way."

A few minutes later, Harper saw some bright lights on the horizon. As far as she could tell, they were still roughly thirty metres away. All Harper could make out was a metal structure of some kind, but was uncertain as to whether it was another boat or a small landing station.

"Sam, you take the wheel," she ordered. "We're going to make a sweeping pass. I'll throw the first gren--"

Harper's plan was cut short as a huge clanking sound accompanied the dousing of the lights.

She cursed.

"What do we do now?" James asked. "We can't do a passing run if we can't see them."

"We'll just have to pretend we're Ben," she replied, cutting the motors.

"What?" Sam whispered. "You mean we're going right in?"

"We'll have to," Harper explained. "Look, don't worry. If we can't see them, they can't see us either. We've still got the jump on them once we're close enough."

The engine completed its wind down, dribbling through the water as the boat drifted slowly towards the target. Harper had given off the air of confidence to her comrades but, unable to see, she was terrified. Her body clenched around the steering column and throttle ready to pounce if things went south.

The weight of James and Sam's lives weighed heavy on her conscience. The seconds ticked by as they got closer and closer. All three passengers held their breath. Harper could make out the sound of footsteps on metal and a feint murmuring of voices. One of them laughed, another chided. Now they were near enough to hear what the tail-end of what they were saying.

"...the motor should be just fine. I'm sure he just got lost in the dark," one said.

"What an idiot," came a reply.

"Hey, I think they're just coming in now, look."

"Okay," Harper whispered from her crouched position. "Wait until the grenade has gone off and then open fire, okay?" She heard the two of them acknowledge her whispered command.

"Crowley is that you?" a man's voice asked. Harper couldn't see him but he sounded no more than a few metres away and a short distance above her. "Crowley? Are you there?" it called out again.

"Hold on a minute, there's three of them," someone else shouted.

Harper swore.

In an instant she was blinded by a harsh accusing light, shining over the boat and its immediate area. There was nowhere to hide inside the small vehicle. Harper's eyes adjusted. She lowered her arm and made out the silhouettes of four tall figures spaced out at six foot intervals from each other.

They were carrying rifles.

They started shooting.

The boat rattled and rocked from the bullets.

The water fizzed under the onslaught.

Harper got off two bursts of the rifle, both of

which hit the closest attacker in the leg. He hit the water.

A bullet smashed into the plastic of the steering column, sheering off a fleck. It caught Harper in the cheek.

"We have to go!" Sam shouted.

Harper fired off two more shots and punched the throttle. The vehicle moved towards the landing station and Harper began steering to the right. The speed of their acceleration lurched under Sam's feet and he crashed into the water behind it.

"Harper!" James called her name. "Sam fell in." He leaned to the back of the boat as they approached the underside of the metal walkway.

"No James, get down!"

Turning round to react to Harper's call, their eyes met for a split second, gunfire still rattling through the air.

James' head jerked sideways with a crack and a splash of red.

His limp body slid into the water.

Harper howled, tearing at the back of her throat.

Wash's jaw was still on the floor. He looked back and forth from Sebastien and Vicky. With all this new information landing on him in such quick succession he worried that this was some elaborate joke. But he couldn't argue with the data.

"They never left Earth?"

"But why?" Vicky asked.

"That's what we've got to find out," Sebastien announced.

"Hold on a second," Wash interjected, the cogs of

his brain whirring. "Can you get data on the other British ships?"

"What do you mean the other ships?" Sebastien replied. He searched the information on the drive. "It says here there was only ever one ship."

Wash remembered that Declan had implied there had only ever been one craft.

"But that can't be true," he muttered. "A British colonial ship was supposed to have crashed with a New Boston satellite in the Proxima system. How could it have done that if it never left Earth?"

"What are you talking about?" Sebastien asked.

"He's right Seb, that's been the chatter from Phil in Berlin," Vicky replied. "There's been an A.N. team investigating the Choctaw region on Proxima A after an orbital attack."

"How do you know so much about all this?" Wash asked.

"Now is not the time, Wash," she said. "We could have an even bigger problem now. If the British IPCP never went to the Proxima system... then someone else breached the New Boston defences."

*

Smurph, Flat-top and Scissorhands, lowered their hands, their ears no longer needing protection. The barrage of British missiles had finally stopped. The three marines had watched as retaliatory fire from the Atlas Nations warship had cut off most of their onslaught.

From their position, Smurph could not see the forest or Peakwood, so had no way of knowing how successful the mission had been. He had lost contact with both Diablo and Pathfinder, but wasn't worried at this stage. They had plenty of work to do down there.

"Boss, what's our next move?" Scissorhands asked quietly.

"We wait until we have confirmation that Peak-wood has been destroyed."

"How long do we wait?" Flat-top enquired.

"As long as it takes," Smurph snapped. "I'm sure they're fine. It's not like they would have had much resistance down there is it? That old man Stafford is weeks away from a wheelchair."

His two colleagues chuckled along with him.

"Yeah you're right," Flat-top said with a smile.

"Besides," began Smurph, "his feelings for the woman and hatred for that Orvan fella have clouded his judgement this far. I'm sure he was too busy with them to put up much of a fight."

"What if our guys got hit by British fire?"

"I doubt that we need to worry about that," Smurph huffed. "You saw that light-show over the mountains. Most of the British artillery didn't get through. Diablo and Pathfinder would have had free reign to burn Peakwood to a crisp."

"What do we do when we hear from Diablo?" Scissorhands asked.

"Then we follow Stangl's orders. We wait for the Teslanium weapons to arrive, blast that base down there to hell and back, take whatever we find and re-program their missile launcher."

"What are the targets?" Flat-top asked.

"Well, first we've got to take out that massive insect thing," Smurph replied, half laughing. "After that, we programme in every major city in Choctaw. Pave the way for some Atlas Nations expansion."

"And if that navy ship comes back?"

"It won't," Smurph said dismissively. "Looks like that machine did enough damage for it to need repairs. But if it does, we'll blow it out of the water and blame it on the British too."

The three soldiers sat in silence for a few minutes more. With each passing moment, Smurph grew more concerned, wondering why neither of his men had got in touch from Peakwood. Without contact from them, he would be unable to arrange for the Teslanium weapons drop. The longer he was left up here exposed, so close to the enemy camp, the more danger he was in.

A heavy metallic clunk sounded from the two cylinders down below. During the attack they had slipped into a new configuration. The tips were now perched on the slope between the crater and Smurph's position.

"What the fuck was that?" Scissorhands asked, breathing heavily.

"Calm down," Smurph shot back. "Let's have a look."

He leaned over the ridge focussed his attention.

The soldier heard a faint metallic scratching sound. A rectangular segment of the ship was slowly pushing away from the hull.

"Weapons ready," Smurph said, standing up. A series of clicks cycled round the three-man squad as they all took up position and aimed at the ship.

The metallic slab projected out by nearly two metres. With a heavy clank, it fell to the ground.

A body slowly rose from the hole in the hull.

It was huge, almost as big as Smurph himself.

Its skin was dark, glistening like wet leather.

Another creature joined its companion. And then another.

Smurph could not make out any of the details on their faces.

The nose, mouth and cheeks, if there were any, were hidden under a black shroud.

All the soldier could look at were three pairs of glowing orange eyes.

They stared the marine down, each eye-ball wide and ovular, twice the size of a human's.

Intense fizzing vibrations emanated from the optic centres.

Each creature increased the bright glow in their eyes, holding Smurph and his colleagues in a trance.

*

Don struggled to stay awake. He wanted nothing more than to sink into a deep sleep for a whole week, weighed down by his pain and fatigue. Orvan had helped him and Gisèle onto the last shuttle from Peakwood and he had not moved an inch since they left. The old man felt as if he had been interred into the padded seat. Gisèle, still unconscious, was beside, propped up against Don's shoulder.

All around was a mass of wounded and injured bodies. Women and children weeping and huddled together, their loved ones slaughtered, homes destroyed, livelihoods gone forever. Don was saturated with guilt. These people were so downtrodden because of what the Atlas Nations had done to them in the past, leaving them poorly equipped for another major conflict. Because he had let his guard down, Stangl and his men had abused them once again.

Don looked up and found himself locking eyes

with Jokubas. He feared another confrontation, but the steel and grit had left the man's hard face, smeared with blood and tears. The man held a blank expression for a moment, nodding as soon as he registered Don in front of him.

"What you did," said Jokubas vacantly. "Thank you…"

The floor shook as it touched down on the deck of the ANS Diamond. With a metallic whine, the door slid open, two crew members stretching out their arms to help the refugees off the shuttle.

With all the commotion, Gisèle finally woke from her stupor.

"Where am I?" she slurred with a wince and caress of her head.

"You're on the ANS Diamond," Don explained as he heaved her out of the seat. "Help me, will you Orvan?"

Rather uncharacteristically, the Choctaw chief did as he was told immediately and dipped his shoulder under Gisèle's. Together, the three of them carefully dropped down onto the deck as Peakwood refugees spilled out of the craft.

"Can you get her to the sickbay?" Don asked.

"Where are you going?" Orvan sounded a little irritated.

"I've got to speak to the vice admiral."

Orvan understood and started demanding nearby sailors show him the way.

Don reached the hatch before anyone else, confronted by a relatively young marine who was guarding it.

"I can't let you in there, I'm afraid," he said.

Don sighed.

"Come on, son," he replied. "I might look like a

mess, but I still outrank you by more than you know."

The crew member mumbled something, looking Don up and down.

"I'm the secretary to the minister of defence and I've just come back from a mission up there," he explained, pointing up at the Choctaw mountains, now a backdrop in the distance.

"Of course," the young man said apologetically, busying himself with unscrewing the huge door.

Don glared at him as he marched through. Time was of the essence.

A few short minutes later, he was outside the bridge and noticed this hatchway was guarded too.

"Any chance you don't know who I am either?" He said sarcastically.

"The vice admiral is expecting you," the woman snapped, opening the door obligingly.

"That's more like it."

Don stepped onto the bridge, immediately taken aback by two small children cowering in the corner. One of them, a young girl, waved innocently in his direction, eyes each a different colour. He took a moment and eventually returned the favour with an awkward motioning of the hand and half a smile.

"Mr Stafford," Tycho said, thrusting his hand into a shake. "I'm so glad you're safe. It's an honour to have you on board."

"Thank you, Tycho," Don replied. "We wouldn't have made it out of there if it wasn't for you. It's a good job you were in the area."

"Yes," said the naval commander, with a smile. "You could say that."

"Are you looking after the younger refugees in

here?" Don asked, nodding in the direction of the children.

"Oh no," Tycho explained awkwardly. "They're mine."

Don opened his mouth but no words came out.

"It's a long story," Tycho added with a timid tilt of the head. Don nodded tentatively.

"I really need to speak to my people back in New Boston," he said.

Tycho turned to speak to his first officer.

"Saldana can we reach the south coast yet?" He asked.

"Not really, sir," she explained, fiddling with a number of controls. "There's still some intermittent disturbance."

Don looked at the bank of screens showing the view of all four sides of the ship. Out in front was the open sea, the same view from the starboard. The port displayed the Cahors coast and behind them was the Choctaw Mountains, one of the peaks still displaying a cloud of debris from the crater.

"Is it coming from that machine?" Tycho asked.

"I think so," Saldana replied, still lost in her work.

One of the screens started flashing.

"Oh, looks like it's clearing," Tycho announced. "We've got an incoming call," he added, accepting the request.

A high-pitched wail filled the speakers, sending a chill along Don's spine. Everybody else on the bridge covered their ears.

The image was grained and crackly, constantly chopping between a dancing bright orange object and static.

Tycho shot across to calm his children whose

faces had turned pale.

Don felt sick as he realised the horrendous noise was a man screaming. Something was scratching against the caller's microphone.

"What is it?" Saldana asked, wincing.

"I'm not sure," Don said, edging closer. "Can you tell me where this is coming from?"

The first-officer investigated on a side-panel.

"Says it's coming from that British base in the mountains."

"Smurph," Don said under his breath.

The image held some quality for a few moments.

Don was disgusted by what he saw.

The screen was filled with the visage of some unearthly being. It had a giant black head glistening as if it were caked in oil. Dominating the face was a pair of emotionless orange eyes, staring into the camera with intense black pupils.

"Help!" Smurph cried through his eyecam. "Anyone. Tycho, Stafford--"

The soldier was interrupted by a yowl of pain. "My men. Dead. You've got to—"

Smurph was unable to finish.

Something dark covered the image. There was a sharp crack and the splinter of glass. An aperture broke across the image. It cut out. Static.

Silence reigned supreme on the bridge.

Tycho returned to the control panels.

"What the hell was that thing?" he asked.

"It must have been the British," Saldana said.

"That... *thing*... didn't look very British to me," Don said.

"What do you mean?" Tycho asked.

"Well... it didn't look very human at all, did it?"

Tycho and Saldana gave each other a frightened look before looking to Don for reassurance.

A distant rumble tickled the floor.

"What is it?" Tycho asked his first officer.

The faint bang sounded again, like approaching thunder. Don had to stabilise himself against a nearby work station.

"I'm picking up multiple magnetic disturbances," Saldana announced, an adjacent screen producing flashing contacts.

"Where are they coming from?" Don snapped.

"From the Choctaw Mountains," she replied.

"Do we still have visual at this range?" Tycho asked.

"Yes, sir," Saldana said, fiddling with her controls.

The rear feed zoomed in on the mountaintop.

"Look," Don shouted, pointing to a cluster of black dots launching themselves in the air, counting each one aloud. "I make that seven."

"Seven what?" Tycho asked, voice trembling.

"Looks like an entire squadron of those fighting machines," he surmised.

"Damn it," Tycho replied. "We barely stood up to *one* of them."

The vice admiral folded his arms and stood in silence for a few moments before Don broke it.

"Whoever these invaders are, they're preparing for full-scale war."

*

At a safe distance, Harper stopped the boat and collapsed on the steering column. She roared with anger and battered the wheel like a wild animal mauling its prey.

"You idiot," she yelled at herself, not processing the blunt pain of bruised hands and forearms.

Harper felt so stupid. Her plan had failed miserably and James had paid for it with his life. Sam could be dead too for all she knew. There was no way to conduct a search and rescue right under their noses. They would rip her to shreds. She still had no idea who these men were either. It seemed likely that they were working for the colonisation programme but there was a woeful lack of intelligence for to act upon.

After her tirade had died down, she placed her head on the hull, wondering what to do next. Her eyes scanned the water, ears pricked, hoping to hear the splashing or calling of Sam. There was nothing.

Then Harper looked to the sky, gently lit but the slim curved moon. She longed to be back home. She had once been resigned to her fate when they arrived on this planet but it was the hope of leaving that tasted so sour in her mouth. To come so close to finally escaping only to fall so short and lose James in the process. She could feel another swell of tears building up from behind her eyes.

"Focus," she whispered. "Focus."

There had to be something she could do. Running the possibilities over in her head, Harper realised that she had no choice but to go back in for another run. Now that these soldiers knew something was wrong, they would send more men to the island, where Zoey and Shermeen were waiting for some good news. Throw the hostile natives into the equation and there wasn't much hope that the two of them would survive both threats on their own.

Harper had to end this now.

She briefly considered another full-speed attack run but decided against it. Harper was already outnumbered and, with James and Sam taken out of the fight, it would be a suicide mission. No, the next approach would have to be clandestine in nature.

Harper removed her boots. She emptied the rounds from the pistol into a nearby metal container and dropped a few replacement magazines in before sealing it tightly shut and stuffing it in her pocket. Collecting the two remaining grenades and her knife, she strapped them to her belt, alongside the Concord's portable drive. With half an eye on the assault rifle, Harper opted against bringing it, noticing the bullet holes running along the chamber.

She jumped over the edge and slowly slid into the water, keen to avoid a splash. It was colder than she expected, although it wasn't enough to sap any of her strength. Not yet anyway. Leaning forward, she began cutting through the waves as gently as possible. A few lights on the platform were still illuminated, helping judge the distance. It was no more than a hundred metres away. Harper sped on towards her goal, head above the water line the whole time, considerably calmer than the last time she had ventured out to sea in search of the missing Tarp, but no less anxious. On this occasion, she had to stay alert enough to avoid becoming target practice.

Under 10 metres away, Harper could hear angry voices coming from above. A thin beam of light flickered over the surface. They were looking for her.

"They went that way!"

"I know, but I think they've stopped. The engine went out."

Harper could just about make out a ladder roughly

five metres to her right but was sure it would be guarded. She needed a distraction. Swimming closer to the structure, she could see four legs supporting it, probably coming up from the sea bed. Pushing on quietly, she found herself underneath the whole thing. For now, the search had been avoided.

Clinging to the nearest pylon, Harper rested, her body starting to feel the strain. After a few moments getting some breath back, she started making some calculations. The ladder was no more than two metres to her left and the edge of the platform was under ten metres away out in front. She would have to time it just right.

Harper fiddled with her belt and pulled out one of the grenades. She put all her energy into the left arm which kept her above the water level. She weighed the object in her right and eyed up the space in front of her.

Harper removed the pin with her teeth.

Wait a second or two. The last thing she wanted was for it to explode beneath the surface.

Harper swung her arm from right to left, releasing the grenade underarm. It flew in the air and hit the surface of the water.

"Damn it," she said, fearing the worst. She didn't want to waste the last grenade on trying again.

A small column of water and spray fizzed up from the sea.

It must have been close enough to the surface after all.

A crescendo of voices sounded from the top of the platform, the clanging of feet reverberating down through the metal to Harper's pylon.

The industrial lights on the far side slammed on,

gunshots peppering the water.

Harper made her move, ears battered by the commotion.

Loosening her grip, she gently moved towards the ladder and began to climb. In just a few short moments, the top was within her reach. Nobody has noticed her yet. Harper opened the metal container and plugged a magazine into the pistol as quietly as possible.

Despite the slight click, Harper remained undiscovered. She began climbing with increased pace.

Gun raised, Harper pulled her head above the parapet, ready to fire.

All clear.

She hoisted the rest of her body and pressed her back up against the nearest wall. Poking her head around it, she could see roughly six men all focussed on the other side. Hopefully that would be all of them. They were close together too. Sitting targets. The space between was open, no obstacles.

This was her chance.

Harper pulled the pin on the second grenade and bowled it along the metal walkway.

One man heard the rattle and turned around.

"Grenade!" He howled. It was too late for him.

The device exploded, ripping through three of the soldiers and tossing them away. The nearest two were obliterated in the blast, one pushed over the edge, catching his leg caught on the fencing, causing him to spin en route to the water.

The survivors did not act fast enough. They were so shocked by the surprise attack that Harper downed each them with a single shot.

They hit the deck with a clang.

It felt good.

Harper let out an exasperated breath, listening out for any further movement.

Nothing.

Only the ripple of the waves remained.

"Sam!" She yelled out.

Still silence.

"Sam! It's Harper! Are you there?"

Nothing.

Harper gave the railing a sharp push and cursed, eyes weak again.

The portable device started chirping. Someone was trying to contact it.

Harper swore quietly, fiddling with it, pressing her hands over the speakers, concerned there might still be someone alive on the platform.

Vision blurred by some rogue tears, Harper accidentally answered the call.

"Hello?" A voice said through the speakers.

Harper dare not answer, in case someone else on the platform was trying to track her down. She continued to scrabble around the options to shut the thing off.

"Hello, this is Sébastien Quina," the man explained. He sounded like he might be French. "I'm an Atlas Nations operative. Is there anyone there?"

Harper stopped what she was doing. The Atlas Nations were surely after her. One of the British invaders in the Proxima system.

"Hello. Is there anybody there?" Sebastien asked again. "We're here to help."

Harper took a gentle breath and quietly responded. She could do with all the help available right now.

"Yes," she said, keeping an ear out for any movement on the platform. "I'm here."

There was a short pause.

"Who am I speaking with?" Sebastien asked.

"My name is Harper Mulgrew," she replied.

"Who?"

Before Harper had a chance to answer, there was a muffled scratch through the speakers.

"—ve me that," came an indignant second voice.

Harper frowned, unsure what to make of this development.

"Harper, is that really you?" This one was clearly English.

"Yes," she replied, awkwardly.

"I can't believe it! You're alive," the next man announced

"Who is this?"

"Oh yeah, sorry. My name is Washington Parker and I'm a reporter for the Daily Citizen. I've been investigating the IPCP and the plot to kill you."

"What?"

"I've got hard evidence of kill orders for yourself and a... oh yeah that's it, Lisa Houghton. Did she make it too?"

"No, I'm afraid not," Harper explained, recalling the horrific dismemberment.

"Oh, I'm sorry about that," Wash replied. "But I'm confident she did not die in vain."

"Why's that?" Harper asked.

"I think we can work together. I've got pages and pages of proof of sabotage at the highest level of the colonisation program."

Harper's mouth fell open. She let out another sigh of relief. Her luck was finally turning.

"I can probably help you with that," she replied,

thinking of captain Case's decision to crash the ship, Ben's betrayal and this legion of soldiers sent to finish the job.

"That's incredible," Washington said. "How many of you survived? Is there anyone else who can corroborate?"

Harper's stomach wrenched with guilt once more as she thought of James.

"Not many. Including me, we're down to three or four," she explained, conscious that Ben and Zack might still be alive. "Where are you calling from? Is there any chance you can pick us up? We could really do with some reinforcements right now."

"Reinforcements?" Washington asked.

"It's a long story," she replied. "Can you reach us or not?"

The radio went silent for a moment before Harper noticed voices in the background. Whoever was there were clearly having some kind of heated discussion.

"We'll do our best," Washington said, eventually. "But we can't guarantee anything."

"Where are you calling me from?" Harper asked.

"We're in London."

"In London?" Harper frowned. "How are we able to have this conversation over that distance? You're not even in the same star system."

The line went silent once again.

"Hello?" Harper said. "Washington. Are you still there?"

"Well, here's the thing," he eventually replied. "You're not actually on Proxima B."

"What? What are you talking about?"

"You never left Earth," said Washington.

Harper's breath caught in her throat, stomach lurching.

"You're on an island in the Pacific Ocean."

Harper didn't say a word. Her brain hurt, breath stopped in her throat. She played the first days of the colonial mission over in her head. The crash had been so disorientating that she hadn't even considered to question the most basic assumption of all: that they were on Proxima B.

Then something clicked in her mind. It all made sense.

The writing. James had said it was called Rongorongo, a Pacific language he had last seen... on Earth. Then there was the native population who, when their disguises were removed, had proven to be nothing more than simple humanoid creatures. They weren't the ancestors of travellers to Earth at all, they were just regular humans. Their culture began here on Earth and never left. All they had done since Harper and her colleagues arrived was protect their territory from what they saw as an invading force. In his death throes, Amos claimed to have seen planes in the sky. Maybe he was right. Maybe those aircrafts had been there all along, commercial flights going about their business.

"Are you still there, Harper? Are you okay?" Wash asked. "I know it's a lot to take in."

"I'll be fine," Harper said, realising she had been silent for so long, her whole world turned upside down.

"Just try and stay alive before we get there," Washington added. "We will need your testimony to expose this whole thing."

Harper mustered half a laugh.

"I'll do my best, Washington," she said.

"Thanks, Harper. You can call me Wash," he added. "Between the two of us, we might be able to bring down Curtis and his government once and for all."

The call cut out.

Harper looked up at the stars. The Earth's stars. Her stars.

For a moment, she allowed herself a brief moment of hope.

There could be more soldiers nearby. James was gone. Sam was missing. Zoey and Shermeen were trapped on the island with hostile natives closing in. But for the first time in years Harper finally had a chance to make those bastards back home pay for what they had done.

ACKNOWLEDGE-MENTS

My wife Emily deserves massive praise for running our family home and balancing two spirited young daughters with her own business while I have been working on *WRITING IN THE SAND*. She is also responsible for the fantastic artwork. A big thank you should also go to my committed fellow writers Stephen Finch, Harry Baldock and Andrew Sarjudeen for helping me through every step of the process. Thanks to my parents for making me the person I am today. Charlie Lockwood, Dan Bryce, David Price, Eddie Summers: thank you for your input along the way.

Printed in Great Britain
by Amazon